IN THE BEGINNING

IN THE BEGINNING

The Story of An Incorporated Family

A Novel
By

THOMAS P. STRANGE

iUniverse, Inc.
Bloomington

In the Beginning
The Story of An Incorporated Family

This is a work of fiction. All of the characters, names, incidents, organizations, and dialogue in this novel are either the products of the author's imagination or are used fictitiously.

iUniverse books may be ordered through booksellers or by contacting:

iUniverse
1663 Liberty Drive
Bloomington, IN 47403
www.iuniverse.com
1-800-Authors (1-800-288-4677)

Because of the dynamic nature of the Internet, any web addresses or links contained in this book may have changed since publication and may no longer be valid. The views expressed in this work are solely those of the author and do not necessarily reflect the views of the publisher, and the publisher hereby disclaims any responsibility for them.

Any people depicted in stock imagery provided by Thinkstock are models, and such images are being used for illustrative purposes only.
Certain stock imagery © Thinkstock.

ISBN: 978-1-4759-7678-6 (sc)
ISBN: 978-1-4759-7679-3 (ebk)

Library of Congress Control Number: 2013902811

Printed in the United States of America

iUniverse rev. date: 03/09/2013

Contents

Prologue

The crash of thunder, like a cannon blast, shook Sam from his day dreaming. Who would have thought that the end result of an agreement between eleven people would change the rules of society in the 'civilized' world?

The six o'clock news broadcast across the country, the unanimous vote of the Congress of the United States to legalize polygamy, in the form of incorporated families. Twenty years to reach this point and it feels like a weight has been lifted.

His family is gathered in front of the television to witness the vote on C-Span. The Senator from South Carolina stood and prefaced his Yea vote with a reading of the names of their corporate union and a recounting of the deeds and accomplishments that have been achieved by the family.

Sam looks to his partners and his children, their smiles radiate with a glow of self satisfaction. They are legal in all ways, now.

"Well, Sam, Honey. It's official; we can now legally be married to one another. Are you ready to be married nine more times?" Ann asks as she squeezes his hand.

"You all know that we never needed the approval of that bunch in Washington to live as a family. I couldn't have loved anyone more with this law than I did before, but I would like to put us in line with the law, just in case." Everyone crowds around for hugs and kisses and he thanks God for this life and these wonderful people.

Chapter 1

HOW IT STARTS

He and Ann had just moved to Sumter with the Air Force. They met in Thailand, at Korat Air Base, where Ann is a local hire who worked for the Air Force, in Maintenance Data Processing. She is not a typical local national. Ann is taller and her figure is fuller than the average Thai. She has the same raven hair and light brown eyes, full lips and long, tapered legs. Her work with the U.S. military began as a house girl, but she wanted more and took advanced education so that she could get a better job. Sam is a Tech Sergeant in a Special Ops group. He is taller than Ann and is well muscled from years of covert operations around the world. He has most of the military schools under his belt, in languages, martial arts and international affairs.

They have been married for just four years and didn't have children yet, so are pretty free to live a little. Ann opens her own salon. Sam decides to get out of the Air Force and pursue a different line of work. They have put away enough to sustain them for a couple of years, while he lets the GI bill send him through college.

Sam, at 27, becomes a freshman at the University of South Carolina. He does well and with credits for his service and several DANTES exams, he earns his Business Management degree in just short of eighteen months.

1

"Mr. Elliott, I am amazed at your accomplishment. I've never had the pleasure of graduating anyone in so short a time." The Dean of the Business College says.

"Sir, I had something that I needed to do. I've found that when you have something to do; just do it. I find that many young people, taking the courses, spend too much time daydreaming."

Sam accepts his diploma and walks out to find a place to use his new degree. Everyone in Sumter that has a position for a manager also has a nephew, cousin, or children that they're holding the jobs for. Not that they're holding the job until their relative achieves a degree or on the job knowledge, just until they get old enough and arrogant enough to think they deserve it, without putting in the time.

Sam does find a job. Ann hires him to manage her salon. He sets up the files and hires an accountant to block all the government butt heads who try to intimidate new businesses into paying for nothing. It works. Sam fields several calls and letters with threats to audit the salon. He tells them that he would welcome an audit, but they must call his accountant to set up an appointment because he keeps no records at the salon.

"Mr. Lauder, I had a call from the SC Division for Taxation two days ago and referred them to you. Anything I should do?"

"Mr. Elliott, they won't call. They're just trying to spook you because you're a new business. Just keep referring them to me. They'll stop in a bit."

"It sounds like they're wasting taxpayer money with their games."

"They are, but it's best to just let them peter out." That's how their early days worked out.

Ann is working six days a week from 8 AM to 8 PM most of the time. The money is good and they end up raising prices to keep some people away, but it is beginning to wear on Ann. The help she has, from new cosmetologists, just isn't keeping up with the work. Sam finally tells her to close the shop on Sunday and Monday and only work half a day on Saturday. They then have some time for themselves.

They like to drive to Charleston to look around and shop. Ann is enthralled with the stories of Fort Sumter and the ghost tour of King Street and the College of Charleston, where several Civil War movies have been filmed. Sam is always happy to see the happiness on her face. It is his greatest pleasure.

Cherokee, North Carolina is an often visited place. Here Ann is treated to stories of the Cherokee Nation and the <u>Trail of Tears museum</u>. The outdoor pageant is very well done and educational. Ann loves to shop the Native American shops for handcrafted jewelry and they also pick up a couple of blankets. Authentic Indian blankets, made in Japan, must be those Japanese Indians.

Sam and Ann also spend time dining out where ever they went. At home they frequent Red Lobster, Ruby Tuesday, Appleby's and the Backyard Barbecue. Life is being good to them and they are enjoying all that they can.

Ann's salon is doing very well, but keeping qualified, dedicated operators is a real problem. She pays well, compared to most of the salons in town, but her employees, barely adult sized, are ill prepared to work the time required to build a clientele. They expect to earn in their first weeks, the same money that it took Ann and others months to achieve. Then her first real break comes following the abrupt departure of her latest two operators.

God must have been smiling on her, for on that day, through the door walks, Jessica Lea Wells and Rebecca Sue McGee, looking for work and a place for their modest clientele.

"Hi, I'm Jessica Wells, Jessie. Do you need any operators? Rebecca and I, Oh, this is Rebecca McGee. We've worked together and find ourselves in need of a job at the same time."

"Hi. Jessie is right about that. I'm Becca, I hope you can use one or both of us. We have a modest following and need a place to build our futures."

Ann is overwhelmed with joy and the thought that God had a hand in this; she hugs each of them in turn.

"Yes, yes to both of you. When can you start? I'm sorry for being so forward, but I was about to give up. Everyone who has worked here, so far, has been under twenty and without a work ethic. I was at my wits end, then yesterday, Missy and Courtney quit after three weeks. Now here you are and the first thing you say is you want to build a future. I think I love you." Ann almost sobs the last.

"Wow! I've never been welcomed so openly before. I hope we can start soon. We're not going anywhere else. Becca and I fell in love with the location almost immediately. Becca and I are both 25 and like she said, we do have a modest following. Let us know the rules and if there are days we're not allowed to work and we'll be here with bells on." Jessie says.

"Yes, thank you. When can we start? We're ready." Becca confirms.

"You can start today if you want. I'll get Sam to get you some papers for the accountant. I'm a little overcome. It's like God provided before I asked."

"Well, we have our carts and stuff in our cars and I can have a couple of my clients in this afternoon." Jessie offers.

"I have a perm for today and thought I would have to cancel, but I'll call and give her the address." Becca says.

"I love it. You're both hired." Ann smiles and gets two handbooks from the appointment desk for them and gets hugs from both of them again. This is going to be one huggy group.

"These have the pay scale, hours and some of the state requirements. I start you at 50%. We move upward from there. It's all in the book. I expect that you haven't prepared for lunch, so I'll call Sam and have him bring lunch for all of us."

Jessie is 25 and freckled all over. She is as tall as Ann, but has full tapered legs and a high, rounded bootie. She presents the appearance of a 'country' girl. Her hair is dirty blond with a slight wave that gives it body and movement. Her eyes are a kind of brown that look deep blue in certain light. Her breasts are full and she has a tattoo over the right breast, of a unicorn, with the word, 'Amazing' beneath it.

Rebecca is also 25, with olive skin and almond eyes. She is half Korean and has shoulder length raven hair. Her lips are full, pouty and overall her physical make up is rounder and softer than Jessie's, or Ann's. Ann calls her a China Doll.

Jessie and Becca acknowledge with smiles and thanks then get their roller carts from their cars and are set up quickly. Becca calls her client and immediately begins wiping down hers then Jessie's station and mirror. Jessie follows with sweeping and damp mopping around both stations. Ann is receiving her next client, but takes a moment to introduce her new operators.

"Ms. Anderson, this is Jessica and this is Rebecca. Ladies this is Ms. Anderson. She has been a standing client since I opened two years ago. Ms. Anderson, can you believe I have two people who like to clean as much as I do?"

Ms. Anderson greets and receives greetings from each of them.

"You will be Ann's friend if you like to clean. She's a little crazy with cleaning." They both smile at the comment.

The morning proceeds with an air of professional craziness. Ann is in heaven and the three together are already working like a team. Sam is there promptly, as Ann asked, at twelve. He brings lunch for the whole group and himself.

"Hello everyone. To those who don't know me, I'm Sam and I come bearing lunch. Hope everyone likes rib eye steaks, rice, gravy and baby carrots. For drinks there's, Coke, Pepsi, Sprite, and Mountain Dew. Dessert—spice cake." Sam smiles at the two new members of Ann's salon and takes the food to the break room.

"Sam, don't get everyone fat to fast okay?" Ann chides.

"Ha ha! Don't see that happening. You got some cute ones, this time."

Jessie and Becca smile at his comment and throw out a cheery, "Hi!"

Jessie and Ann come to the back first for lunch. Becca is still with her client.

"Hi. I'm Sam. I guess I'm the business manager, but Ann's the boss. I cook and take care of books and payroll."

"Hi Sam, I'm Jessie. Thank you for lunch. This is really unexpected and much appreciated. Is this an exception or ..."

"I bring lunch every day. Eventually, I'll know your tastes and at least not gross you out. Today, I figured rib eye would be good. Women don't get enough protein in their diets. Where you from Jessie?" Sam asks as Jessie and Ann seat themselves with a plate of food.

"Originally from Fayetteville, Tennessee, but haven't been there in about five years. I was in the Air Force. Truck driver at seventeen and got out three years ago and went to beauty school. I've been at this for a little over two years. Becca and I have worked together at a couple of places, not that we shop hop, but the first was a chain shop, started by a friend of the beauty school owner. He worked us like slaves, but we never got over 37 percent. The next was run by a gay guy, who hogged every client and kept booking our clients for himself. So, here we are."

"I don't do that, I promise." Ann vows. "I start at 50% for the first six months, then to 55%. I provide all the supplies and the malpractice insurance. I do the withholding and pay the employer's share of social security, but I hope that we will work so well together that eventually we divide the shop between us. Sam has his degree in Business Management and says the best companies are employee owned."

"Ann, you're not serious, that's terrific. Becca will not believe it!" Jessie exclaims as she throws her arms around Ann and hugs her. "I knew we'd found a place to stay forever!"

Rebecca comes back at the sound of Jessie's exclamation.

"Hey, what's going on? Am I missing something? Oh God, that steak smells good."

"Becca, Ann says that if we work well together that we may partner with her. She says employee owned businesses become the best companies. I don't believe it." Jessie bubbles.

"You are kidding."

Ann and Jessie both shake their heads.

Rebecca turns to Ann and hugs her.

"Jessie and I have talked about something like this happening when we first got out of beauty school, but didn't think it would happen. Every place we've been, the people are so greedy. Now, the dream is in our sight. Thank you Ann, Sam. I didn't know there were people who could be this good." Becca says with a welling of tears. The three stand up and group hug.

Jessie looks at Sam and says, "Sam, you to. Today is the start of a really great group and you have to be a part of it. Besides, I like your lunch." The last she says with a smile and a once over with her eyes.

He stands and joins the hug. Sam feels a little overwhelmed, but happy. He sees Ann's happiness and the happiness in the eyes of these two women, whom he has just met. They are so outgoing and affectionate; it would take him some time getting used to it.

"Okay, ladies, the food's getting cold."

This is the first of many lunches and many hugs. It seems Ann has found sisters instead of employees. The three can be found shopping together on their days off and many times dining together, with Sam, at local restaurants. Sam enjoys the looks that come his way when he is surrounded by the three.

Chapter 2

FRIENDS N MORE

Jessie and Becca both have boyfriends, who are less than either woman should have to endure.

Jessie's friend, Joe, is a clinging, needy guy, who has to know where she is all the time. His constant calls to the salon prompts Ann to ask him to stop, much to Jessie's relief.

"Ann, I'm so sorry about Joe. Lately, he seems more like a nuisance than a partner."

"I understand Jessie. Sam has talked with me about Joe and Becca's David. Sam is pretty good at spotting less than admirable guys. I don't know what he did in the Air force, but he was in charge of a section and knows people. He doesn't have many male friends. He's just that picky. Sam says that Joe needs a Momma because he hasn't grown up yet." Ann explains.

"I know. I've seen it to. I thought I'd hate to be alone, but now with you, Sam and Becca, I feel like I have a satisfying relationship. I think it may be time to let Joe go and find a guy like your Sam."

"You know that we'll be here for you. We already spend more time with one another than with . . . outsiders."

Jessie smiles and she and Ann hug and sigh with a kind of relief.

Ann has a special affinity with Rebecca. Ann is Asian and Rebecca is half Asian. Her mother is Korean and has passed on some of her own ethics. Rebecca is dating a guy named David, who, as Becca explains, is a slob. She thinks he is that way, just to anger her Mom, who already doesn't like him.

"I'm not dating your Mom." He tells her.

Becca also worries about the friends that David hangs around with and thinks that they might be into drugs. When she hears about Jessie' and Ann's talk concerning Joe, she asks them to help her decide.

"I am so glad I talked with you guys. Jessie you're right. Who needs that hassle? I have all the relationship I need with you, Ann and Sam. So, Good bye David. I hope I don't offend you, Ann, but I really need a guy like your man."

"I already told Ann that she is so lucky to have Sam. I only hope I can find someone like that."

"Yes she did. Sam is a mystery to me still. He is so filled with love for everyone." Ann says.

"How full do you think? I have been kinda jealous of you two since we started. Do you think he has enough to go around?" Becca says, with a mischievous grin.

"Becca! Really." Jessie snorts.

"I don't mind Jessie. I know I'm lucky. He's a one in a million. Becca . . . . I'll think about it."

The two look at Ann with questioning twists in their eyebrows and lips then smile and both circle Ann with their arms and hug her tight.

The Ann's Salon four, have become a group of close friends.

They spend more and more time together and the salon is booming. The three are working ten and eleven hours a day, five days a week. Sam insists that they not work on Sunday or Monday and close early on Thursday and Saturday. Well, not later than five o'clock anyway.

The fourth chair in the salon has never been filled. It seems like a waste to have it there and the four of them talk about selling it. Today, that is about to change.

"Hi! How may I help you?" Ann asks the young lady, in front of the desk.

"Hi. I'm Molly Johnson. I'm looking for a job. I have my license and six months experience. I would like to find a place that will let me work and learn my craft."

"Honey, I think you have come to the right place. We were just talking about selling that fourth chair. I guess we may have been premature. When can you start?" Ann smiles and extends her hand.

Molly shakes her hand and is startled as Jessie and Becca approach and group hug her and Ann.

"Welcome Molly, I'm Jessie, this is Becca and Ann is the boss. Where did you work before?"

"I was at Bright Cuts, right out of beauty school. The guy worked . . . ."

Jessie interrupts, "We know. That's where Becca and I started. Like slaves and got nothing for it. You're going to love it here."

"Thank you so much. I'm a little overcome, but I feel so welcome already. I have my things in my car. I quit there, before looking for some place else to work. I just couldn't do it anymore. My mom said I should have found a place before quitting, but it looks like I got lucky."

"Yes Ma'am, you surely did. Ann, it looks like one more for lunch." Becca says.

"Oh, I didn't bring any cash for lunch. I'll have to . . . ."

Before she could finish, Ann says, "Sam brings lunch for everyone. It's one of the perks."

"We said you'd love it here and Sam cooks like a chef." Jessie and Becca chorus.

Molly retrieves her tools from her car and sets up her station at chair four. She starts by wiping down her mirror, station, sink and chair, to the smiles of her two new co-workers and her new boss.

"Am I doing something wrong? Let me know okay?"

"Honey, you just captured my heart." Ann chimes.

"Yes Molly, you fit right in. The three of us are clean freaks." says Jessie.

"The salon always has perfect scores on inspections. It's something we can brag about, even though Ann got the scores. We can keep them up." Becca adds.

The relief on Molly's face prompts another group hug as the three rush to her. Three ladies under the hair dryers, lift the hoods to find out what is going on.

"Ladies this is Molly. She is starting with us today and we love her already. I hope you will get to love her to." Ann tells them.

It didn't take long for Molly to become part of the salon group and be just as affectionate with her new sisters and brother.

Molly is 22 and not in the market for a boyfriend, much to the relief of the rest. She is from Georgetown, on the coast. Cute as a bug with long legs and petite waist, a button nose and high cheekbones. She has the palest skin any of them has ever seen. Her eyes are deep blue and sparkle. She has an impish smile that radiates joy when she lets loose. Her whole persona is bubbly youth, with sense of purpose.

During Molly's fourth week, a mile stone in the salon, Jessie and Becca fill Molly in on all that has happened since they started four months ago.

"Wow Molly, you should have seen the mess we arrived with. I had a Momma's boy and Becca had a potential druggie, slob. Ann is the only one who looks like she made out." Jessie expounds.

"I like Sam. He seems very understanding and he cooks way to good for a guy and he doesn't hit on you like most guys I've met. I won't even talk about how sexy he is." Molly sighs.

"Ooh Girl! Let me tell you. He was in some kind of special operations group, in the Air Force and is put together real fine. He had to change a shirt here one time. Honey, I'd have some of that and he's a good guy to. Ann is lucky. He does notice you though and appreciates you from a distance, but he'll also let you know that you are highly thought of." Jessie tells her.

"What do you mean?"

"Well, he'll say to Ann, so that we can hear, 'the four of you are gonna make me rich' or 'you should see the envious looks I get when the guys next door sees me with ya'll'. He'll even say it directly, "I don't know how a guy could be so dumb as to treat you badly, you are so good to be around" and things like that. Only he doesn't get in your personal space and say it."

"Yeah. Like the guy who says it and rubs your back at the same time. I get it. He says some of the same things, but as an observation, not as a pick up line."

"You got it." Becca confirms.

"Also, he will ask one of us, about the other. He knows the word will get around and you will know that he is concerned and thinking about you. He asked me just yesterday if I knew of any problems you are having. Sam will help you solve your problems and help you make good decisions.

When Becca and I started here. We are each spending money on the same things, like rent, electricity and when he heard it, he said we should live together and split the costs. Something we should have thought of, but were too absorbed in our private lives. When we each dumped the boyfriends, the move was smooth and we have more money for ourselves."

"Sounds great. Do you have room for one more?"

Jessie and Becca look at one another and grin.

"I knew there was a reason . . . Yes, we do have room. When we told Sam we are moving in together, what, two months ago, he said, why don't you get a three bedroom apartment? The rent is only $75 more a month over a two bedroom and you'll have a guest room. I wonder if he really thought it through to here or just a coincidence."

Sam came around the corner to the break room just then.

"Ha! Ha, you'll never know. So Molly, you're moving in with these two gorgeous ladies. Whoo Hoo! Three beauties in the same apartment. The guys will be lining up."

"Yes. I guess. This Sunday, if it's alright. That's when my rent runs out."

"Sure, we'll get everyone to help." Jessie says.

Molly is overcome with emotion. "You guys are great. I really do appreciate this."

Chapter 3

A CHANGE IN THE WORKS

The salon prospers and true to her word, Ann has the three of them over to the house one evening for dinner and presents them with papers that make the four of them equal partners in the salon. Jessie and Becca have only been there seven months and Molly, who is really surprised, because she started three months after Jessie and Becca.

"You all know that this means that pay days will be unstable. Not in a bad way, but each week, we will budget for the expenses and what is left will be divided between the four of us. Since we have all been together, Sam and I have put the surplus from payroll and expenses into an account that we have now split between the four of us and here are checks for $1200.00 each. Tax paid." Ann grins at the expressions she sees.

Sam brings out a magnum of champagne and little crackers with a strawberry flavored Gruyere cheese and Pate`. The mood is festive and all at once four ladies who are co-workers are now co-owners in a highly successful salon.

Becca, Jessie and Molly surround Ann and hug her, with kisses on the cheeks and forehead.

"I'm about to cry Ann. I'm a business owner. My folks will die." Jessie sobs.

"My mom already loves you guys and now she'll have even more to love." Becca says.

"Me to Ann. I'm so tickled to be a part of such a great group of people and Sumter's best salon."

"Well, don't think it was all me. Sam was the first to show me how well it would work."

The three mob Sam with hugs and kisses that cover his forehead, cheeks and a few stray lip locks, much to his surprise and delight.

"Thank you ladies. It gives me the most pleasure to see the happiness on your faces. Your booties are good to look at to." Sam laughs out loud.

"So partners, anyone up for a night out?" Ann says.

"Sam to please." Becca pleads.

"Sam to. You up for a night out with four babes?" Jessie asks.

"Always."

This was the first of many nights. Saturday nights finds the group out for dinner and a movie. Sam, of course, accompanies them. He glows with the attention they get. They spend many holidays together and shopping trips are fun. Like very close sisters. They do get the curious look now and again, because they are beginning to dress and act alike. Most of the time Sam chauffeurs, because he likes being surrounded by pretty women and the closeness gets more and more familiar.

Rachael Rogers is Jessie's friend. They met when Jessie got out of the Air Force and was looking for a new career. Rachael was doing the same. She looked into beauty school with Jessie, but went for nursing school, while Jessie went to beauty school. They remained friends. One day, Jessie brings her to the salon for a haircut and to introduce her to the rest of the 'family'.

"I'm happy to meet all of you. Jessie has told me so much about her 'new sisters' but someone is missing . . ."

"Sam usually comes in with lunch at twelve. Stay and have lunch with us and you can meet him as well." Jessie says. "Ann already called him to bring extra. You'll love it."

Rachael is a year older than Jessie and Becca and a year younger than Sam and Ann. She has piercing blue eyes and blond hair. She is as tall as the rest and adds to the idea of siblings. Her legs are long and strong from walking the ward at the hospital and her skin is pale white. Rach's lips are full, her nose is narrow with a slight tip up at the end and she is country. It helps when dealing with a broad spectrum of patients at the hospital.

"Well, who do we have here? Did I make a wrong turn and end up at Hefner's Playboy mansion?" Sam quips on entering the break area with lunch.

"Sam this is my friend Rachael; Rach, this is Sam." Jessie introduces them.

"Good to meet you Rachael. Hope you're hungry. I'm trying to fatten up these gorgeous ladies and I'd love to add another."

"It's good to meet you Sam. Jessie talks about you a lot whenever I get to see her. She is almost non-stop about all of you. I'm kind of jealous. Ya'll seem real close."

"Honey, you are welcome to join us any time you like. Jessie can keep you up to date. Mostly we hang out on Saturday with dinner and movie, or bowling and other times, when we girls are free, we shop." Ann offers.

"I would really love to be a part of ya'll's activities. I've only heard about it from Jessie but I feel it. Family."

"Ann also wrangled them into joining our church. We do present a sight on Sunday mornings when we arrive. If you're dyed in the wool for Baptist, Presbyterian or something else, these ladies are pretty persuasive." Sam warns her.

This is how the group came together as a surrogate family. The year passes quickly and includes Rachael. Jessie, Becca and Molly move again during the year, into a four bedroom apartment and move Rachael into the fourth room.

The four share expenses and become closer than sisters. Rachael listens raptly as one or another tells about their day at the salon.

"Sam brought chicken livers for lunch today, with spicy rice and vegetables. I balked at first and then tried one. That guy is something else. I knew it was liver, but you couldn't tell by the taste. He seasoned it so that it was really good." Jessie begins.

"Yeah. I never like liver. Sam said we needed something to add iron to our diet. He said beef works but, liver delivers better iron with the same cholesterol." Molly added.

"I wish I could have been there. I really like Sam. I think I'm jealous a bit myself, that Ann has him to herself." Rach says.

"I said almost the same thing. Ann said she'd think about sharing him." Becca relates.

"Seriously. You asked her to share?" Rach asks incredulously.

"Not exactly, but a couple of months ago we were talking and Ann said that Sam was so full of love. So, I said, how full and did she think he had enough to go around. She said she'd think about it."

The four are quiet for a while, just meeting Rach's eyes as she looks from one to another.

"Mention it again to her, tomorrow and let her know that I would be interested to."

"Wow! Would Sam be surprised to find out, we all want him?" Molly exclaims.

"He's a guy. He'd probably like it." Jessie says.

"I don't know. Even though I said it, I think he's very devoted to Ann and their relationship. We'll bring it up to Ann after lunch tomorrow and see what reaction we get." Becca says.

"Oh God. Do any of you think we maybe couldn't live together in that kind of relationship? Maybe he wouldn't want us. That would be a bummer. Maybe we'd be jealous of each other. Not me. I think it would be great if my sisters loved my man . . . well, Ann's man . . . I don't know what I mean. I just know that I'd want a good man like Sam." Rach moans.

"Amen" is chorused.

The next day, at the salon, Becca is sitting with Molly and Ann in the back, while Jessie is finishing her client.

"Ann, the three of us and Rachael were talking the other day about you and Sam."

"Me and Sam, Becca?"

"Yeah. Remember a few months ago . . . this is a little awkward, but I have to ask. You said you'd think about sharing your good fortune."

Jessie comes back and catches the gist of the conversation.

"We do share, partners, remember."

"Yeah. I don't mean the business. It's great, but you have one thing that is better than the business and . . . Ann, have you thought about sharing Sam. We all love him. Rachael to. She said to tell you she would like to be included. When they made Sam, they broke the mold. There just aren't any guys out there like him."

"Oh! Yeah, I did say I'd think about it. You're serious, huh?"

"Not if it will upset you, but you have to know, we all are kinda in love with you and Sam."

"Becca, Jessie, Molly, from my heart, I love all of you and if I can convince Sam; I'd love for us to share our lives in every way."

The three crowd Ann with hugs and kisses.

"Ann, I'd love to share Sam, but you have to be crazy to even consider it. Sam is truly a one in a million. He always thinks of us before himself. It's so rare."

"Don't talk her out of it Jessie. I want a baby and I know we could make pretty babies."

"Molly you are too young to be thinking about making babies, but I know that Asian and European mixed babies are the cutest." Becca says.

"We're getting ahead of ourselves. What if Sam doesn't want us?" Jessie asks.

"Let me bring it up to him and see what he says. If he's against it, I don't want to mess us up."

"You're right Ann. We'll go with whatever you two decide."

"Thanks Jessie. It has me a little excited now, just thinking about it though. We'd be really closer than we have been this last year and a half. Let Rachael know that you told me."

They nod their acknowledgement and move together in another group hug and lots of back rubs.

Chapter 4

NEW IDEA IN LIVING
IS EXPLORED

The world looks bright. The salon is making money hand over fist. The four working the salon share, after expenses and withholding taxes, more than seven hundred fifty dollars each a week. Sam is an expense and is paid five hundred a week, after tax withholding, for his services. Sam and Ann together are making a much better living than when he was in the service.

Sam likes being the manager and full time house husband. It gave him plenty of time to enjoy life. Then just when a guy thinks that things can't get any better, Ann tells him about what the ladies have been talking about.

"What do you mean? We're one big happy family now. How do you propose to change it?" Sam asks.

"Sam, think about it. What is the one thing that is missing from their lives that a healthy woman needs? We've already talked about it among ourselves and we are a little excited about the idea. They couldn't believe that I was proposing it." Ann explains.

"Ann, I can't marry four more women. That's bigamy and it's against the law. I know, guys always fantasize about more than one woman, but . . . what did they actually say when you talked about your idea?"

"Well, first, they all tell me that they love you, then Molly was the first to say anything and it was something like, 'I bet we can make pretty babies.' Then Jessie said something like, 'Ann you're crazy. You would share him with me; with us?' Becca was next with, 'Oh yeah, Asian/European babies are cute.' Rachael is curious about whether you would want them. I know it's a big change, but I know you will look into all the pros and cons. There's no hurry. We girls have already said that we would make it work. I love you Sam and I love each of them. I hope you will to."

"I love you Ann. I'll give it a lot of thought. Just now, I'm a little excited and scared about the idea to. I don't want this to change our relationship. I love you so much."

Ann hugs him tight and kisses him. "I know."

Sam is astonished with the idea and over whelmed that Ann proposed it. The next two weeks, Sam reads everything he can find on multiple marriages, polygamy, bigamy, demographics, marriage, divorce and his head swims with things he just never considered before and hasn't anyone else seen this information in this way. He finds that for decades, as far back as statistics have been compiled, there have always been more females than males on the planet. It makes sense. Humans are just another species of herd animals. Bull and heifers, stallion and mares, ram and ewes, every mammal is paired with one male to several females. Sam thinks, Man, if cattle were monogamous, we'd have to give up eating meat.

His study turns to divorce and case studies of cause and outcomes. Overwhelmingly, the cause is infidelity and economics and it is usually the male who succumbs to the attention of another female. Probably one of the others that doesn't get attached and a guy is always susceptible to any woman who shows him attention. Men are such shallow, insecure creatures. The economics of a divorced female are less than desirable since society will discriminate in housing and credit extended to a divorced woman.

Sam also studies the history of the Mormons, who have had polygamous relationships. With all of the information available, he is able to compile a wealth of data and every night, he spends time with Ann running the information past her. They put together a kind of list of things that both believe are required for such a relationship to work.

One—All the women must like each other and above all be honest with one another in all things.

Two—All of the women must accept the idea of sharing a husband. There can be no jealousy and the husband must confirm this with each of them.

Three—Sam must accept the idea of having five wives and the responsibilities of keeping each of them happy. Like this would be a problem.

Four—Responsibilities for the household, finances and relationships between them must be understood. Sam suggests that any intimacy between him and any of them, must be the women's decision. He adds that, not all of them can have headaches at the same time, for which Ann punches him.

Five—A suitable home for them to live together, must be procured.

"Honey. These things are good. We should meet and have everyone provide an input. I am really getting excited now. Do you have any misgivings about any of this?" Ann asks.

"I love you Ann and I thought that it would only be the two of us when we got married, but now, I feel like I am on the doorstep of something that is bigger than all of us. I love you and yet, I am feeling a love for each of them that is growing in me without my willing it or me being able to stop it. Misgivings, only as far as society may want to stick their noses into our lives, but if you are for it—then me to. Look at all the money they will save. One house, one electric bill . . . aw, I'm just trying to convince myself. The facts speak for themselves. It is a good idea. I like it."

"I'll talk to them again and we can set a time to meet and put it all on the table. We will probably need a lawyer and include the accountant, we can figure it out when we meet." Ann says.

It's hard to believe that only two weeks have gone by since Ann gave Sam her idea. She and the others have, of course, talked about it at the salon, but not when Sam is there. They had already agreed on a meeting and on some of the same things that Sam put on his list. He will be surprised at how quickly everyone agrees.

It's Wednesday and the salon is buzzing. Sam is taking the day to talk to the accountant and a lawyer about how to make what they planned, legal. On his way home, he stops for a coke at the Young's market and put two dollars on a Power Ball ticket. The note in the window said the Jackpot is at 329 million. 'What the heck' he thinks, may as well give it a shot. Besides, he felt pretty good.

The lawyer suggested that they incorporate and make their names part of the corporate documents and include responsibilities in the papers. "That will make your arrangement legal. The corporation will be the entity and each of you will only be like the tools of the corporation, so no one of you can be held responsible for what the corporation does."

Sam tells them of the meeting, when he brings them lunch, then heads home. "I'm a little tired. The lawyer wanted to say everything two or three times. It was almost like a drama queen, retelling and embellishing a story."

Ann got home after seven. Sam has dinner on the stove, staying warm.

"Didja make a bundle today?"

"Yes and we decided to meet on Sunday, after church. We'll get some Church's chicken and biscuits and Jessie and the rest will stop at Wal-Mart and get potato salad and drinks and dessert. We'll eat here and then clear the table and have our meeting."

"Sounds like a winner, sweetie, Sunday it is then. I have some stir fry chicken and bean sprouts for you and rice. I put together some fish sauce and crushed chili peppers and toasted garlic. Do you want me to get you a plate of food while you relax a little?" Sam offers.

"You are a darling. Please. Just a small plate."

After dinner, they sit on the couch watching TV and doze off. Sam wakes up just before the eleven o'clock news and the Power Ball drawing. He had almost forgotten about the ticket.

"Oh! Oh! Ann, hand me the pencil. I have a ticket for this drawing."

He writes on a scrap of paper the information as the drawing is taking place . . . .

"$332 million jackpot tonight.

The multiplier is 4, if you bought the power play option and the first white ball is 34, followed by 22, the next ball is 15 and a 47 and the last white ball is the number 52. Now for the Power Ball and it's the number 27. Good luck and have a wonderful evening, from Power Ball in Orlando, Florida." The petite lady announcer shouts out to the TV audience.

"Let me get my ticket and see." Sam says as he steps around the coffee table and goes into the kitchen.

He retrieves his ticket and sits at the kitchen table to compare his numbers.

"Hmm! 15 and 22 and 34 and 47 and 52, Oh my God, Power Ball 27. Oh my God, Oh my God, Ann, Ann come here, quick. Oh my God."

"What is it? Did you win something?"

"Oh my God. Look at this for me. 15, 22, 34, 47, 52 and the Power Ball is 27. Ann, I won, I won, Oh my God, $332 million, Oh my God."

Ann almost misses the chair as her legs go all mushy under her.

"Oh my God, Sam we're rich. Oh my God, the girls are gonna die. Sam, you know what this is? It is a message from God. Has to be. What are you going to do now?"

"First, I'm gonna have a cup of coffee and let my heart stop racing and then get the form off the internet to get the money. Then tomorrow, I'll see the accountant again and the lawyer to get the money and pay the taxes and whatever. Ann, what if I apply for the money as a group of the six of us. That way the taxes they take will apply to all of us and we won't have to pay personal taxes again on what we divide between us."

"Okay. I guess. How much do you think it will be for each?"

"Probably around 22 or 23 million each. You and me included. Don't tell them anything about the money yet. Save it for the meeting on Sunday. K?"

"K, oh I love you man."

"Ditto"

Chapter 5

THE CHANGE IS HAPPENING

Thursday is a riot, the lawyer and accountant are ecstatic. Sam's idea about splitting the pot is right. The lawyer acting as Sam's agent retrieves the money and deposits it in Sam's account. The accountant has the tax paperwork and gives Sam W-2s for each of the recipients. Sam is amazed at how fast everything is happening. He never expected to have any of the money for a week, but he started with the lawyer at eight o'clock and by eleven thirty he is heading for the bank.

The manager of the bank greets Sam with a big smile. His association with them began when he and Ann arrived in Sumter. He had his house mortgage with them and his personal checking account.

Ms. Monroe ushers him into her office.

"Mr. Elliott, I am honored that you are allowing us to handle your new found wealth. Mr. Louder has already sent the tax documents and your attorney Mr. Wade has placed the lottery check in an escrow account for you. You can direct the dispersal of the funds any way you need and I will assist you."

"Thank you Ms. Monroe. You have the names of six of us, who are to share the $210 million?" Sam asks.

"Yes. All the information needed has been provided. There are you and your wife, a Ms. Rogers; Ms. Wells; Ms. McGee; Ms. Johnson and the J M A R2 S corporation. How do you want to proceed?"

"I would like to open six accounts with 11 million in each account, one in each of our names. I would like to place 47 million in a thirty year account to draw interest for deposit into our corporate checking account. I would also like to place another 47 million in a thirty year account to draw interest to deposit into a household checking account, with all our names on it, for daily needs. We'll also need six debit cards on the household account. I need a building/real estate account for 14 million and the remaining 36 million in a 25 year education account. I think that covers it. How soon can I have check books and/or debit cards for each account?"

"It should only take a few hours. Can you come back after lunch, at about 2:30?"

"Yes, that's pretty fast. Thank you Ms. Monroe."

"Thank you, Mr. Elliott. We'll see you at 2:30 then. Good bye."

Sam bids farewell and goes to get lunch for the salon. He is smiling so hard, that his face hurt. He'll have to stop, or give away the surprise.

Later that evening when Ann comes home, Sam tells her about his visit to the bank and gives her, her account papers, debit card and checkbook.

"I don't believe it yet. These are their debit cards, checkbooks and papers?"

"Yes. Maybe we should move the meeting up to Saturday, in case someone wants to go shopping on Sunday." Sam chuckles.

"Good idea. I'll tell them tomorrow. I think the day ends around 3:00 on Saturday. I'll make sure no one books any more. What should I tell them is the reason for moving the meeting up?"

"Blame me. Tell them I'm getting anxious. I'm a guy after all with a prospect of a harem."

"Ha, ha, you're right, they'll believe that. You may have to organize the food for us."

"Can do Darlin'." Sam squeezes his love and kisses her on the neck.

Saturday is busy. Ann calls from the salon and says that everyone will wait to eat later and don't want lunch. Jessie calls Rachael and tells her about the change and everyone is anxious.

Sam has arranged the food on the table when he hears the car doors outside and the garage door going up. Soon the laughter of young women comes through the back door.

"Hey mister, we're here and starving." Jessie calls out as she enters the kitchen. Rach, Becca, Ann and Molly are right behind her laughing and looking excited and happy.

"Okay you gorgeous ladies get washed up, food's on the table."

Sam is taken by surprise when each of them, as they pass, hug him and kiss him, 'smack dab on the mouth' as he would remember the day.

"Wow, thank you ladies. I see Ann has already been talking."

Dinner proceeds with different looks on all of their faces. Sam notes that the formerly friendly faces are now filled with loving, tender looks.

Dishes are cleared and wine, in fine crystal, for everyone, Sam pulls out several 5x8 spiral notebooks and passes them around, along with pens. He takes out the folder with the points that he and Ann have previously discussed. The blue folder, from the attorney, is also there, with the incorporation papers.

"Sam." Rachael said. "We've already done all of that among ourselves, as you suggested it should be. We love each other and now that it isn't against the rules, we can say that, well, I love you." Each of them reaches for his hand and voices their own, "I love you."

Sam, with tears in his eyes, tells each of them, "I love you, Rach. I love you Jessie. I love you Becca. I love you Molly. I love you Ann. I love you all so much, my heart is bursting with the love I feel. Thank you, one and all for accepting me." The last is followed by each woman coming to him and kissing and hugging the man who is going to be a part of their life.

"I only have one other thing to bring up." Sam pauses, "On Wednesday, I went to the attorney about the incorporation and on the way home, I stopped at Young's and bought a Quick Pick ticket. I won." The words didn't sink in. Each woman looks like they didn't know what he has said.

"Here are your account papers, your debit cards and checkbooks . . . ." Before he can finish, the words have hit home and he is mobbed, again. Sam continues.

"There's more. You are each, a multi-millionaire and part of a multi-million dollar corporation." His face is wet with kisses and the tears of his new loves. Everyone eventually sits down again and Sam goes over all the deposits and accounts.

"I deposited 47 million into a thirty year account. You get a higher rate when they know they can keep it for a long time. It will provide a little more than $13 thousand dollars a day into a checking account for whatever comes up. I named it the household account and the debit cards are for that account, just keep it under $13K a day.

I envisioned it paying salaries for people we may hire to help us. Maid, gardeners, cooks, whatever and some for property taxes on cars, boats and whatever gets taxed. Another 47 million is in a thirty year account to earn interest to finance the corporation. The profits will be divided each quarter among the stock holders, the six of us. Later the money may be used to finance any enterprises we may want to start. I have an open building/real estate account and we need to start thinking big, very big about an estate to accommodate the six of us and more . . . ."

"Oooh, he's already thinking about expanding the family." Becca chuckles.

"Yeah, hey Sam, how many more do you think we need to provide for?" Jessie asks, tongue in cheek, her eyes looking up to the ceiling.

"Oh, at least one from me please." Molly pleads.

"Okay, ha, ha, it's better to be prepared and yes. You think you can surround me with highly desirable young women and I don't think along those lines. We can afford it. Seriously, we have to do some planning. I know it's difficult to think, now that we are all richer than anyone could have imagined."

The mood is bubbly, happy and now charged with sexual overtones. Sam is feeling all bubbly in his chest as well. Then Ann suggests, "Let's take the table out of the way. We can throw the big pillows and cushions from the bed, onto the carpet, in the bedroom and sit on the floor. I for one am changing into something more comfortable. I have a lot of really comfortable pajamas, if anyone's interested."

"I'll pass. I have my own comfortable pjs." Sam jokes.

Rachael, Jessie, Becca and Molly accept Ann's offer and all head for the bedroom.

"Don't forget your notebooks. I'm serious about getting started on a home for all of us."

"Yes Daddy." They chorus.

Ann has a dozen of those Thai pillows that are extra firm and triangular. There are several large round, furniture fabric pillows and square pillows. Sam puts two of the thick Korean quilts on the carpet. He likes the way it feels on his calves and feet. Molly and Jessie strip and change without any inhibitions, to Sam's appreciative looks.

"Oooh my goodness. I'm pretty sure that I'm gonna die young, from a heart attack. You all know that this comfortable interaction between us is making me feel very light headed. I can hardly believe that this is really happening and that you all have accepted it. I hope you know I love you all more than my own life."

Jessie pushes him back on the quilts and lies across his chest and kisses him on the mouth with passion.

"Hey, my turn Jessie." Then Becca lays on him and kisses him, then Molly, then Rachael, then Ann.

"Okay. Let me up. We really do have work to do. I don't know about this sitting on the floor idea, Ann?" Sam pretends to be put out, but can't stop smiling.

"I think it works." Ann says

"Yes, it is a good idea. I like it. We can have our first real intimate encounter." Jessie observes.

Sam looks from face to face and feels a joy well up inside.

"You're right, it is a good idea. Sweet ladies can we think about a home for us?" He says, raising his eyebrows.

"Right down to business, eh, Sam? You have been busy already I see. Girls, I think we got real lucky. Tell us more darling." Rachael observes.

"Okay then." Sam says and continues with the description of their home, as he has seen it, in his mind. When he finishes and turns his drawing pad around for all to see, he fields questions.

"My God Sam that is big! How many children's rooms?" Becca asks.

"That's only the one side and I think six children's rooms to start, for the youngest. As they get older, rooms upstairs and as they get to sixteen, a bungalow in the back. Let them learn to live on their own without the dangers." Sam explains his thoughts.

"Sam, you thought all this out in the last two weeks? I am amazed." Becca exclaims.

"Yeah, well I have always dreamed of a big house and how to best bring up children to live in the real world. Being a Dad is the most exciting thing I can think of for a man to aspire to. Any guy can be a father, that's just lust. A Dad has to bring up a child to be an honorable, substantial citizen."

The women are all smiling and have tears in their eyes. All of them comment on how wonderful they think it is for a man to love children.

Sam is interrupted when he describes the kitchen.

"What's a butler sink?" Molly asks.

"It's smaller than the kitchen sink, but deeper, with the spigot arching high above the top of the sink." Sam explains.

"Oh, so that's what it's called. Thank you."

"Okay, anyone want to stop me and insert anything? We all have to live here." Sam asks, his eyebrows raised in question.

"You're doing great. We'll tweak everything later, when we see all of it on paper." Ann says. A chorus of 'Yeas' accompany her statement. "I'm just a little curious about, how you know about butler's pantry and butler's sink."

Sam smiles and explains, "My mother's family was part of the German aristocracy. If Hitler hadn't come to power, her family would be in the royal succession. Her Aunt, Tante Soffie, was a Countess and she gave a lot of instruction on position and station in life to her nieces' son . . . me."

"So, you would be a German aristocrat, if the war hadn't happened?" Jessie ventured.

"No. My Dad met my Mom because of the war. I have a family tree somewhere and you are all welcome to see where I come from. My Dad's family were the Sheriffs of Norwich, England, but I'll tell you more later. We have a lot to go over just now."

The ladies acquiesced and nod their understanding.

He continues with detailed descriptions of the family room, with a wet bar and fountain. Sam looks around, but everyone looks like they are ready to go to sleep. He smiles and closes his notepad and the drawing pad and puts them back under the bed.

"Time to call it a night, huh?" Jessie asks.

Sam just nods and pushes his pillow up to lay back on it. His eyes are heavy and he is drifting off fast, but not before feeling Jessie snuggle up on his left and Molly snuggle up on his right. Ann backs Molly and Becca snuggles up behind Jessie. Rachael curls her bootie up to Sam's feet. They are all asleep in minutes.

Morning arrives and Sam wakes up, but remains still and enjoys the view before him. During the night, all of them come to varying states of undress. Becca lay spread eagle and pjs completely off. Jessie's leg crosses his left leg and her left breast is out and presses his left arm, her hand is under the leg that crosses his left leg. Molly is similarly covering his right side. He turns his head to find Rach, who is no longer at his feet, then feels a breast pressing his head.

"Good morning Sam." Rach says, pressing her breast tighter against his head.

"Good morning Sam. Mmm! you feel good." Jessie says, sliding her leg up his leg.

"Good morning. Everyone awake yet. I love the scenery, by the way." Sam comments with a wide smile.

They are all a little slow at getting up, snuggling and touching, then Becca crawls on hands and knees up and over him and lays down on him full length, naked and kisses him hard on the mouth.

"I had the most wonderful dream about you and me together. Sorry sisters, but I've had the first full blown climax that I have ever had and it is just from thinking about this man." Becca blurts and kisses him again.

They all mob Becca with hugs.

"He does that to me all the time." Ann adds.

"Oh my God. Becca you have to share. Me next please." Molly pleads.

Molly and Becca change places and Sam gets to enjoy another passionate kiss and the heat of another woman pressing him into the quilt. Each of them take turns with him and while they are playing, lose all of their pajamas.

"Oh my loves, I hope you have different arrangements for our lives together. I'm sure that all of you at once will very likely kill me. I mean it's a great way to go . . . arriving."

"Silly man. Of course we do, only this is very spontaneous. You like it, don't you?" Rachael asks.

"Yes Ma'am."

"Sam, I know that I come with a lot of baggage. My Mom and Dad have been enemies since I was sixteen. All we ever heard from Mom, was, "don't let a man rule your life. You're better off not having kids" and things like that. I got to where I believed her. Then you guys took me in. I felt the love from all of you and I fell in love with Sam. Ann, you understand. I have to get pregnant, I have to have someone that I can call my own and to love and who will love me. To prove my folks are wrong." Molly cries.

"We understand Molly. We love you and you do have someone and if Sam isn't worn out, I think we should continue with this spontaneous show of—Love!" Ann states with a smile and a nod.

"Ladies, we're moving really fast. I do love the idea of being a father, but you all have to remember, I'm only one man."

"Ann is right though. I think that, since the barrier has been broken, you will have to share at least one or two more . . . encounters." Jessie snickers.

The two who are staying, sandwiched him between them. The rest went to shower and start breakfast. Sam begins to think that he would just be a sex object for them, then he thinks, Good!

Molly, then Jessie collapse on their man. Sam groans, "I'd like to be cremated if this is the end. Do I still have any nads?" The two women laugh.

Sam sits up, then pulls his pj shorts on and is on his feet. He helps each of them up and hugs each of them warmly.

"Jessie, Molly, can you tell me what makes you women want me. I'm fit, but not movie star type."

"We love you, Sam, because you had to ask." Jessie says, holding him.

"Yes Sam, you don't believe it is a right and you accept us as we are. That's what makes us love you." Molly adds.

"I'm happy that you do. It's just a bit overwhelming. I never dreamed of anything like this happening."

Jess and Molly hug him and pull him toward the bathroom. They proceed with a shower and breakfast. Before breakfast is through, Rach, Jessie, Becca and Ann have each hugged Molly and a kiss on the cheek to let her know it's okay.

"Okay guys, church this morning, or should we continue with the house plans?" Ann asks.

They decide to continue with the planning. They are all a little amazed that Sam has thought through most of the estate. By lunch, they have agreed to a plan that Sam would get a contractor to put together.

"I'll have to find a suitable property to build on. North of 378 is like tornado alley. South of Sumter is like zombie land. That leaves East or West. I am leaning to West, but open to all ideas. It has to be at least twenty acres, more is better."

"Sam, what about 378 toward I-95? Remember, we see big land sales there all the time." Ann reminds him.

"You're right. There's also that farm land on 15 near Summerton. I guess I'll have to get a realtor to help out with picking a place. It has to be able to, at least grow trees, fruit trees and room for a swamp and a clean pond."

The four are ready to go back to their apartment to change and go shopping. They're rich after all. Becca opts to stay a while and help Ann and Sam get the house in order.

"I'll be there in about an hour. I'll help Ann clean up and plan a dinner for us, for when we get back from shopping, then maybe we can sit around and plan again tonight." She says with a grin.

"Oh Becca you're bad. I love it though." Jessie says.

The others agree and hugs are shared before departing. At their apartment, Rachael plies Molly and Jessie about their time with Sam.

"Rach. I wasn't a virgin, but Sam made me feel like the first time. I can hardly believe that Ann even considered sharing. I'm so glad she did. I love that man."

"Oh man, I never even dreamed that making love was this good. Jessie is right. I would have tried to steal him, if Ann hadn't offered."

"I can hardly wait to get together again. The anticipation is wonderful." Rachael shivers thinking about what Jessie and Molly told her.

Sam drives and the six of them head for Columbia at 10:30. They stop at the Ponderosa restaurant for lunch, then to Columbia Place for shopping.

The girls are laughing and in such happy spirits as they move from shop to shop. Sam poops out around the sixth or seventh store and volunteers to sit in the Food Court with their bags and boxes of dresses, shoes and accessories and a large Coke.

About an hour after sitting, he sees his darlings coming along the mall to his left. Ann and Jessie cross over and head for Sam. Just as they get to him and deposit some more bags, a disturbance catches their attention.

A guy is confronting Becca, Rach and Molly. His voice is angry and Sam is on his feet, heading for his girls.

"Watch the bags Ann, Jessie." He calls over his shoulder.

When he gets to Becca, she looks frightened, but visibly relaxes a little when she sees Sam approach.

"Hey Buddy. You wanna get your hands off my fiancé?" Sam challenges.

"What! Who the hell are you?" The bully blurts.

"Sam, this is David. He's crazy." Becca says.

"Ah, David. I've heard about you. Hold on a minute, let me get a cop. I'll bet you don't want to explain this to the law." Sam says.

David steps away from Becca and turns to face Sam. Sam sees David's hand curl into a fist. As David swings his right in a wide haymaker, Sam blocks with his right and pushes David's punch around, spinning David around, giving Sam a target of the back of David's knee. Sam kicks at the bend and catches David around the neck, in a choke hold from behind, as David falls backward toward Sam.

"David, calm down. If I put pressure on this hold, for ten seconds, you will have even more brain damage and in two weeks will drop dead from a brain hemorrhage. Do you really want to go that way Pumpkin?"

David becomes very contrite and tries to shake his head, 'no'.

Sam lets him up and steps back and sets himself for any more dumb moves.

David looks at Sam, then at Becca and around at the people who have gathered to watch. He hangs his head, turns and trots away.

"Are you alright, Becca?" Sam asks taking her in his arms.

"Yeah. I was just a little startled at first, I only got scared when he grabbed me and I saw the look in his eyes."

Sam hugs her and feels her relax. Rach and Molly hug her and all head for Ann, standing guard over their treasures.

"Are you okay Becca? Sam, I've never seen you like that. You can handle yourself." Ann exclaims.

"Yeah Sam, you were great. I do feel safer knowing you can handle yourself." Jessie says.

They all crowd him and voice the same feelings. Sam feels a new kind of love for these women, his women, his loves. A few people who are witness to the encounter also smile, applaud and nod their approval.

"I guess I'll have to open another of JoHarri's windows and let you know the real Sam. I'm sorry that I didn't open up to you Ann. That was a part of my life that was painful, but for now, what's next ladies, more shopping? How about the Fashion Mall? I can look around the Barnes and Nobel Book Store."

They agree and are off. Sam is in awe of the relationship the five women share. They are all about the same age, from 23 to 28 and each is different but complimentary. Each has a trait that is shared and a presence that Sam is totally in love with.

Chapter 6

THEIR MAN OPENS
A WINDOW

Sam and all arrive home at seven fifteen. Then, while dinner is warming in the oven, they sit in the family room and Sam tells them a piece of his past.

"You have all looked over the family tree stuff. The coat of arms for the Elliotts is taken from the British Book of Heraldry. The German documents were passed to me by my mother. These things are now part of your history and the history of our children.

As to the dark side, I was brought up on John Wayne and Clark Gable, rough and tough. Then I joined the Air Force, because my Dad is retired from the Air Force and told me to stay away from the Army. After basic, I was trained as a radar operator, but just after that training, I was pulled into a special unit that trained me for covert operations. My Dad was upset. He said it was just as bad as Army or Marine Special Forces. I was kind of excited about it. I received training in martial arts, the killing kind, weapons of all types and languages. I speak, read and write seven languages besides English."

"What languages do you speak?" Jessie asks.

"Spanish, German, French, Russian, Farsi-Arabic, Chinese-Mandarin and Thai. The last, Thai, because of

Ann. I have a smattering of Korean, Hindi and Swahili. I can understand it, but don't have a working vocabulary to write it. So, there is one window open."

"Wait. What did you do in the special unit? He is still a mystery to me and I've been married to him for more than four years." Ann asks, wide eyed about the man she married, but hardly knew.

"Sorry Baby, I tried to shield you from it all. I would be back and go straight into the rehab therapy floor, of the hospital, to get my head on straight. It pains me to remember some of it. I would be sent in, under cover, to plant marker electronic devices, sometimes to quietly dispatch a small group of sleeping terrorists. Plant remotely detonated bombs that would draw the most fear out of those witnessing them. Laser target enemy assets for the smart bombs. I would be dressed like a civilian, thereby making myself a spy and not eligible for POW status. If they caught me, I get shot. My orders are mostly against hard military targets, but near the time I quit, they are less transparent. I even think I caused the death of an entire family. It haunts me, so I quit. I didn't reenlist. Of course the big bucks stopped when I told them I was getting out."

"Will you teach us Karate, Aikido or something to defend ourselves? It's good to have someone who knows how, better if we all do." Jessie says.

"Big bucks?" Becca asks.

"Oh yeah. I would get my regular military pay for a Master Sergeant, with housing, rations, overseas pay et cetera and a quiet automatic payment of $2k into my savings account, each month. It never showed up on a W-2 nor was it ever taxed. I was always amazed that Ann never questioned the fact that we were able to afford all the things we had, on a Master Sergeant's pay. So, there you have it. If I tell you anymore, I have to kill you. Just kidding.

Jessie, yes, I will start everyone on some basics soon. I haven't because I was and am still haunted by that life. Now is anyone hungry? I'm starving now. Remembering takes a toll on your soul." He says as he slumps on the couch.

They gather around him from both sides and on his lap and pet and kiss their strong, sensitive man, then true to the plan, they have dinner and again retire to the bedroom for more planning, but not before hours of a fashion parade, as each tries on their purchases and parades them in front of him.

The rest of the night is much like last night, except that the ladies agreed beforehand to share even more than the cuddling they had done previously. By the time sleep overtakes him, he is exhausted, but so happy he can't stop smiling. It's all pretty kinky. While each share their most intimate moment, the rest watch and add kisses and touches.

Monday morning, during the shower time, it is decided that there will be an extra large garden tub in the new house and an extra large European shower, so that they could share this moment, comfortably. They also prepare to see the attorney and sign the incorporation documents, then they will see a realtor and find a property. Today will be busy. Sam visits the contractor that everyone says is the best.

"Mr. Elliott, the house and estate that you are suggesting will be quite a job. We have an architect on staff that I'd like you to sit down with and see if he can put together a plan. I am looking forward to this job, but I need you to be very sure and our architect will save you a whole bunch of heart ache later." Mr. Hawkins tells him.

"I appreciate that. When is a good time for me to get together with him. My mind is reeling with images of what I want. My wife is with a realtor today to find suitable acreage to build on. When that part is firmed up, I need a landscaper and a pool company. Can you assist in those areas?"

"Indeed. I work with a landscaper, who is very good at planting trees and shrubbery that look like they have been there forever. I'm going to suggest my pool man talk with you. He's good and up to date on new pool technology. I'll have our architect call you today, but I'm sure that he is free this week."

"Thank you. I'm free as well."

Sam spends the next three days with the architect, but when they are through, they have a plan for a 9000 square foot house with detached garages and boathouse and an indoor pool with a string of bungalows. The whole living space is enclosed by a brick fence with controlled gates. He also convinces Sam to have a security specialist talk with him.

Ann and the ladies find three suitable pieces of real estate. Sam really likes the pasture land with the low hills to the West of Sumter and they all agree with him. It looks like it is about to happen for them. Sam makes an appointment with both the realtor and with Mr. Hawkins. Closing on the property is two days away and Mr. Hawkins says he can begin with laying out the estate on Monday. The whole job would take more than six months, so that the corporate union will have time to order furniture and all those small items that make a house a home. They move into a large five bedroom house near the Deerfield subdivision, while they wait for their home to be built. It isn't what they would like, but it is more comfortable than the 1700 sq ft. house

Sam and Ann had. Sometimes, they would rent a suite at one of the hotels and spend a few days relaxing. It also gave them the feeling of taking a vacation. The salon is still going strong, only as a distraction now that they didn't need the income. They decided to hire a manager to run the shop and subsequently hired some new people.

The next five and a half months are spent in deciding on furniture and seeing the contractor to choose equipment to be installed. The walk-in freezer is like adding a room to the house. The storm shelter in the cellar is to be outfitted with beds, table and chairs, an emergency generator, a small refrigerator, microwave oven and hot plates. The architect said it would withstand a force five tornado.

Sam also takes this time to begin the self-defense lessons. He worried that it would interfere with the pregnancies, but it begins to look like he has surrounded himself with a pride of lionesses. They take to Karate, Aikido, Judo and Tae Kwon Do like they have been brought up on it. He thinks about introducing them to small arms as well.

"You are all amazing. You don't need me for defense and I really like the idea of you being able to back me up, if the need should arise. Kinda like 'Charlie's Angels". Now, I'd like to propose a small arms range on our new estate and you all learn hand guns and rifles. Any thoughts?" He asks.

"I've got rifles covered. Remember, I'm from the hills . . . I hunt and I think Sam's Angels is more appropriate." Jessie says.

"It's a good idea. Besides, it will give us one more thing to be trained in and something we can do together. Yeah, Sam's Angels." Becca offers.

The rest agree, in one way or another, with a flag from Ann.

"I definitely want to learn to shoot for home defense. The world isn't getting any kinder, but when the children start and we will have children," vigorous nods from the group, makes Sam smile, "we will need to be very careful not to be careless about leaving anything accessible." Ann continues.

"Training for the children will help, but even as they get older, we'll have to stress the finality of a bullet. I'll definitely make sure we have gun safes and trigger locks for all the weapons. An unloaded gun is useless, but if you have a trigger lock and the key around your neck, you will be ready to use it. Funny, I never had to think about safety before, but I do know about gun safety. Must have been subliminal training." Sam injects.

Along with deciding furniture, estate planning, they have to field the scrutiny of each of the ladies parents. Sam's parents don't find anything wrong with the idea. Sam's Dad even goes as far as to tell the women, "I know I raised that boy right," which they all appreciate.

However, the first dissent is from Rachael's mother. She lives in Sumter, therefore, has the greatest need to voice her displeasure. More so since, Rachael has told her that she is pregnant.

Mrs. Rogers comes to the house one evening and sits with the six and talks about how she feels and that she thinks her daughter is making a mistake.

Sam keeps quiet and lets the girls explain all the ramifications of their relationship. Above all, they demonstrate that it is totally legal. There isn't a suggestion of bigamy, since there are no marriages. They also emphasize, that the largest part of the relationship is the sisterhood they share. By the time she leaves, she isn't as opposed and is beginning to look forward to being a grandmother.

Jessie, Becca and Molly's parents follow along later, since they all live out of town, but are less opposed as they begin to understand the value of having a stable relationship controlled by the female part of the group. Ann, Molly, Becca and Jessie are also pregnant at this time. The confinements are spread out over a month and a half, attesting to the control the women have.

Jessie's Mom and Dad arrive from Tennessee on a Saturday morning and come to the salon, just as Sam brings lunch.

"Mom, Dad, this is Sam. Sam, my Mom and Dad." Jessie introduces them.

"Hi. Just bringing the gang lunch. Good to meet you, Mr. and Mrs. Wells."

"I'm afraid I just don't understand any of this." Mr. Wells says.

"It takes a bit of explaining, I'm afraid. It started when my wife hired Jessie, then Becca and then Molly. We all became close friends and I found myself in the role of mentor and was called on to mediate problems they were having personally. Then we became closer. Ann and the ladies saw it first and I guess I was old fashioned and didn't recognize their leaning to me. They talked about all of it, at the shop, when I wasn't around and then Ann presented it to me. I was taken aback initially, but it explained the change in attitude that I saw, but failed to recognize. My emotions were stretched in every direction, because I now realized that the emotion that was foremost and totally contrary to everything I knew to be right, was that I am in love with each of them. Then Ann suggested bringing us all together and asked me to research information on such an arrangement. The economics were the most obvious. One rent, instead of five, one electric payment instead of two or five. Of course, the 1967 proposition on the California ballot proposing Corporate Unions for economics is part of my findings. I also found statistics for the last 100 years that showed females consistently outnumber males. I know it's a hard thing to understand. It's probably even harder to believe that I could love each of them equally. The biggest thing is that, they all love each other and protect each other. In the end, I defer to the women to make the decisions regarding our relationship." Sam explains.

"What was the main thing about the relationships that influenced your conclusions?" Mrs. Wells asks.

"Love. Love was the overriding influence. I also found that economically sharing of expenses and responsibilities is a positive factor. I also found that divorce is fed by two main things, infidelity and economics. Abusive relationships were also looked at and my conclusion is that a guy would be hard pressed to abuse a relationship with five women to keep him straight and as a plus for the male partner, not all five can have a headache at the same time." Sam notes a stifled chuckle from Mr. Wells.

They talk most of the lunch time and into the afternoon. Each of the ladies participates with comments and positive views. After the salon closes, Jessie takes her Mom and Dad to Columbia to shop and some private time with them. Sam and the rest go to dinner at Outback. The conversation is filled with worried thoughts of Jessie being pulled away.

"Oh, Sam. I do hope everything works out for her. I don't know how her folks felt by the time they left. Even after Dad got his haircut and Mom got her hair styled, they still seemed aloof to the rest of us." Becca says.

"I know; I felt it to. It won't be the same without her." Ann injects.

"Okay ladies, less negative. Jessie is well over 21 and will make up her own mind." Sam reassures.

"I'm worried to." Molly adds.

"Ya'll were worried when my Mom came to check us out. She didn't have near the same education as the Wells' and she understood and accepted. They may just be unable to show how they feel." Rachael says on a positive note.

The meal is overshadowed by the fears they face. They pass on a movie and go back to the house to await news.

Jessie comes in at ten o'clock. Her folks stayed in a hotel so they could leave for home early.

"They finally said right out loud that they are happy that I was happy. Since I was just as rich as the rest of you, they trusted that I could take care of myself. They are also happy about becoming grand parents. They are impressed by my martial arts training. Dad summed it up when he took me aside and said that he thought Sam is a good, strong and responsible man, who would be good to me." She says, taking Sam in her arms and kissing him. "Thank you, Sam, for being you."

"I'm just relieved that it worked out for you. When we move into the new house, there will be room for visitors. Make sure they know that they are always welcome. All of you, remember to stroke the parents, they do love you." Ann, Molly, Becca and Rach mob them with a group hug and excited squeals of relief.

Becca's Mom is into the idea and accepts it immediately. Multiple wives is not unheard of in the Korean culture. Her comment makes everyone laugh. "You just give me grand babies and you be good to my baby and you be my best son, Sam."

"Yes Ma'am. I love your daughter and I know we can make pretty babies."

Molly's parents are in the middle of a nasty divorce and Molly is ignored by both of them.

"I told them about our relationship and that I was having Sam's baby, but I could have been telling them about washing the car. If it finally sinks in and they want to object, I'll just ignore them the same way." Molly's voice is filled with sadness. Sam and the rest caress and hug her.

"Ever since you told us about your folks and how they've been for so long, I figured that they must love you and your brother and sister very much. They stayed together so none of you would have to say that you came from a broken home. Maybe if you consider it from that point of view, it will be easier for you. You only get one mother and father. They're only people just like the rest of us. They probably still love one another; they just forgot. It had to have been a great love, look at the wonderful woman they produced." Sam offers.

Molly visibly relaxes and a tear runs down her cheek as Sam's words sink in. She puts her arms around him.

"You're right Sam. It's not like I don't love them, it's just frustrating."

Chapter 7

MOVING DAY APPROACHES

"We're almost home ladies. It's been five and a half months and I got the call this morning that we can move in next week. Two weeks earlier than expected. That gives us seven days." Sam announces. "I wish it could have been sooner. I think it would have made our explanations to parents a little more palatable."

"Honey, it's all good. I can hardly believe that we will be in our own home. I love you." Jessie said.

"Me to Darling. It will be so good to go to sleep and wake up in the place we call home. I love you." Rachael adds.

"Oh Darling I didn't know I could be this happy. I love you." Becca says.

"I can hardly wait either. Even though we have all lived together in the same house, the five of us have been too crowded to get used to the idea of living together." Ann tells them.

"Next week. I didn't think it would get here. Does anyone mind if I quit doing hair. I think I want to cook and bake and do wife stuff. I like to can fruits and make jams. I know I haven't worked that long, but I'm rich to." Molly pleads.

"I think we should all think about how we are going to live from now on. I'd like to look at those green houses that Sam had put up and set up something for plants." Jessie observes.

"Yes, I think that's right. If we want a salon, we could open one that we only oversee. Like a Vidal Sassoon salon. I'd like to spend time with my exotic plants to." Ann says.

"You and Jessie have that Master Gardner certificate. I think, if you love it, do it. You can do things you love as easily as doing things that you don't like doing. The salon idea is good to. You can hire the best and pay good then send them to the best educational seminars at the salon's expense. People will clamor to the salon. Make it part of the corporation's enterprises." Sam acknowledges.

"Nursing is great and I love it, but I'm getting to where I'd like to try a little more laid back life. I'm anxious to be a Momma to." Rachael tells them. "I don't have a Master Gardner certificate, but I know about vegetable crops, that I learned from my Grandparents. I know animals and chickens and how to make them work."

"I've been thinking the same thing. I really don't want to do hair any more. Do we have room for a pottery shed or something like that? I've been having dreams about making vases and ceramic art." Becca asks. "I'd like to be free to be a mother when our baby comes."

"You all make me cry with talk about my babies. All of you. I've wanted to be a father forever. Now, you all are making it happen. I love you." Sam says with happy tears in his eyes. "I guess we have a lot more to talk out and plan."

"Monday, we go and look at the house. Call the furniture places and arrange for the delivery of the furniture we ordered. Does anyone know if the decorator you talked to has a crew that can place furniture?" Rach asks.

"Yes, she does. Since Shelly planned out the décor and we had her order the big pieces, she will have her set up crew place everything, hang pictures and all the rest. We only have to call her and she will get it all delivered." Ann offers.

"It looks like you've got everything going. How about groceries?" Sam asks.

"Hey yeah, we can go grocery shopping. How much will it take to fill that walk-in freezer?" Jessie asks.

"Don't even talk about the pantry." Becca says.

"I pretty much know about your tastes in a broad spectrum. How about you each look for your favorite things. I'll get the bulk stuff. We can also go to SAM's for wine and cheese and a lot of the bulk spices and canned things. How about the liquor store at Shaw AFB? I still have two years on my ID card as a ready reservist. I can get a wide variety just to see what we might like."

"Sam, it's a good plan. Since it's Monday and we aren't working any way, let's get started. Good idea, not working Sunday and Monday." Ann says. "Let's start with wine at SAM's and case stuff that doesn't require refrigeration."

"Ladies. If everyone is finished with breakfast. What D'ya say we get the show on the road." Sam directs.

The group scatters to freshen up and do last minute things before leaving. Sam marvels at the controlled excitement that they all exhibit. How much better it is going to be in the new house. They have all been very warm and affectionate and didn't all mob him at once, like the first days following their meeting and acceptance. The women get together and he is surprised each day with the company of one or another of them, for the night. He isn't at all surprised that they are all in various terms of pregnancy. That to, is their doing, so they're not overwhelmed with newborns. Molly's will be first. She is almost six months, then Ann at five months and Becca at a little less than five months. Rachael and Jessie are a tie at four and a half months. The place will be swimming with babies. The thought makes Sam shiver. He isn't just going to be a father; he is going to be a father, five at a time.

The trip to SAM's is filled with girl talk and girl planning. Sam bought a twelve passenger van soon after they came to their agreement. It is decked out in some high end accessories and looks like aristocracy. It is proving itself useful today. They have five captains' seats in the back, so the last row is removed and leaves a cargo area for their shopping treasures.

"Darlings. I just had a thought. Before we get too pregnant and after we are settled into the new house, how about some travel? I thought United Kingdom, Germany, Italy, Thailand, Korea, first class all the way, for at least a month or six weeks. It's probably what we should have been doing while the house was being built. Ah well!" Sam ventures.

Their excited babble rises to a higher decibel level.

Comments like, 'I don't believe it', 'How wonderful' and 'Why didn't we think of that', abound. Sam smiles to himself. They are too easy. Then the talk turns to travel outfits and shoes and what kind of things they could buy in all those places.

"I guess it's an idea then? I'll check on it. Get your passports and clothes together." Sam calls back to his family. He didn't suspect, at the time, that it would take nearly sixteen years before they actually did any traveling, out of the country.

The afternoon is filled with shopping. SAM's provided several cases of burgundy, white wine, merlot and Sam's favorite—Mogen David. Later they would look into a better quality of wine. Whole Salamis, Chicken Roll, Ham and German Bologna are placed in the cart. They bought whole wheels of cheese. Swiss, Neuchâtel, Brie and Asiago, are high on the list, along with wedges of Smoked Gouda and wedges of Parmesan, Romano and Nacho cheese. A commercial slicing machine had to be added. Sam also picked up several three packs of Ragu, Garden chunky spaghetti sauce, grated Parmesan, powdered onion, garlic, seafood spices, spaghetti spices. He fills two carts, just in the spice aisle, along with Splenda by the case, Extra Virgin Olive Oil, bulk cases of Tuna, Vienna Sausage, Deviled Ham, Chicken and several jars each of Chicken and Beef instant gravy and bullion cubes. Cases of Tomato soup, Cream of Chicken soup, Cream of Mushroom soup, Cream of Celery soup, Clam Chowder, several bulk cans of cheese sauce—Cheddar—Nacho—Pimento, and boxes of Deli crackers are also stacked up on a dolly. Everyone added their favorite drinks to the dolly and finally in the candy section . . . chocolate took a beating. Sam reminded them that extra chocolate meant extra exercises later. Molly and Becca also added bulk baking ingredients, flour, baking powder, flavorings, chocolate chips, slivered almonds, pecans, pie filling. Sam could feel his arteries hardening. He also loaded up several five pound jars of cashews, pecans, peanuts, and pistachios, but wished they had walnuts to. Walnuts have a better level of Omega 3 fatty acids.

It took the clerk almost forty minutes just to check them out. The lady, checking receipts, at the door almost fainted. She looked at it, then at the five loads, then at the six of them, shook her head and marked it off.

"We'll be back in a week or so. We need some TV's and stereos." Sam smiles and thanks her.

The load just did fit in the cargo area with some spill over into the passenger part. It looks like shopping is over for today. They decide to get an early dinner and head for home. They stop at Fire Mountain to eat. It is past four o'clock and the restaurant is close to empty. They serve buffet style and everyone soon has their favorite meal.

"That is so awesome. I love bulk shopping. Did you notice how everyone looked at us and had such odd smiles? I want to do this again." Molly bubbles.

"I know and just think, that isn't even all that we will have to store away. There's no freezer stuff, meats, frozen veggies, pizzas or very much canned stuff, or boxes of pasta. The parts that make a dish whole. No French fried onions, Roi Tel, Velveeta cheese, canned mushrooms, tomato sauce, paste, stewed tomatoes. There will be a lot more shopping, just to fill the pantry and freezer." Ann adds.

Smiles around the table indicated that everyone is thinking about what needed to be bought to fill the larder. Sam asks that they list the items that they store for him to enter into the computer for an inventory.

The week passes pretty quickly, with a few short excursions to find something that they might need, or that they wanted. Sam complains of a headache on Sunday as he sends his ladies off to church. Then comes Monday. The girls put out the word that the manager and the new operators will operate the salon this week, so that they can move into their new home.

When they pull through the gate, Sam gives quick instructions on how to punch in the combination, everyone's mouth drops open, in awe. Not much can be seen from the road, but once on the driveway, lined with Oaks along a lawn of lush blue/green grass, the mansion, can be seen. The landscaping around the house is filled with an explosion of color, as red and white roses line the front walk. The driveway circles in front of the main entrance around a raised bed that is fully twenty-five feet across of roses in various colors. The women's screams of delight is thrilling for Sam as he sets the brake and they pile out and rush the front door. "Someone needs a key, maybe." Sam calls out. Ann hurries back and grabs the key. By the time Sam gets to the door, they are inside and gasps of disbelief hit him.

"Sam, is this the right house? There's furniture in this place already." Rachael exclaims.

"Yes. Where did the furniture come from? Oh, I recognize this. This is the formal living room that we picked out." Ann says.

"It is. I recognize the Queen Anne side tables that we loved. What happened? How did it happen?" Jessie asks.

Sam is smiling and chuckling.

"I hope you all like it. Yesterday, when I was too sick to go to church with you. I called Shelly and came here to unlock the house and she had her crews move everything in. It took nearly all day. Then last night, when I went out to get the 'Rocky Road' ice cream, Shelly called and said it was done and I could lock up. She also said that they would be available to change anything you're not happy with. So, instead of busting a hump today moving things in, you can explore and enjoy your new home." He smiles like a kid that got away with something.

The chorus of squeals and groans of pleasure as they hug and kiss their man, is music to his heart. Then the explorations start.

The bedrooms for the Mommas are furnished with a Queen bed in the Rice post style. Matching night stands on each side of the bed. The mattresses are the space foam that fit the contours of your body. Each room has a 10 x 12 walk-in closet with a built in shoe rack and revolving hanger bar. There is a large dresser and vanity. A cloth covered recliner and reading lamp in a corner with a side table and a desk and chair with a computer. A 37" LED TV is also in each room. The bathroom has a shower and tub combination with an enclosed toilet and a marble sink. There is also a linen closet that opens from the bath, or the closet.

They explore the children's rooms with full beds and double closets with folding, louvered doors. The door next to the closet opens into a bathroom. One for each two rooms. The bathroom has double sinks and two enclosed toilets and a tub/shower combination. The rooms are all 10 x 12 and have a desk in one corner and a bookcase in front of the desk.

The sitting room is just the way the ladies planned it and looks very elegant. They pass into the dining room and are in awe. The table is twelve feet long with leaves to extend it to sixteen feet, in reddish Mahogany with 18 chairs around the table and none have arms. The china hutch is empty, as is the buffet, but both are gorgeous. The serving tables are against the wall and are also, without accessories. Several packing cases are in one corner of the room. Next to the pocket doors into the kitchen is the access to the wine cooler that also opens into the family room's bar.

The kitchen is Sam's baby. The pantry is huge and the door faces the twenty-five foot counter. The counter is marble and solid the entire length. The double sink is grown into the marble and has no seams. The butler sink is the same. All the sinks have large windows in front of them.

The upper cabinets are fitted with leaded glass panes, in the four inch diamond pattern, so you can see what is inside. The bottom cabinets are smooth faced. There is a set of oven over ovens to the right and a pizza oven next to them and the commercial, glass door refrigerator is at the right end of the kitchen, in front of the pantry.

The island is the Jenn-Aire range with six burners and a griddle with the down draft venting. The cabinets around the range, hold nothing—yet. Behind the range and to the left of the dining room pocket door, is a nook and a desk, where the LED TV and computer will be placed.

The far left of the kitchen, the counter right angled and provides a separation from the breakfast nook. Nook is wrong, because the table is another twelve foot table. The cabinet above this counter will hold the breakfast dishes, glasses, cups and whatever and opens from both sides. The counter itself will be the place where the moveable griddle will be and the toaster and blender or whatever.

The bay window looks out on the rose garden and the front gates.

Next to the computer nook is the door to the family room. It has a wide pocket door and inside the room to the left is a ten foot wet bar. The room is very large. Thirty feet wide and forty-five feet long. The far wall has an area set up for a very large LED TV. There is a large sectional sofa with several ottomans, two recliners built into it and long couch tables behind each section. The sofa is near the TV, along with two chaise lounges and two more recliners. Media storage space is built into the wall to the right.

A section set up for a stereo is between the sectional and the bar. This area is filled with overstuffed chairs and an overstuffed couch with heavy end tables and coffee table. Here also, is a built in media storage cabinet.

On the left side, at the far end, is a set of French doors leading to the upper patio.

On the right wall, at the same end, is the door to the gym and pool.

"Okay. No one is saying anything. How badly did I screw up?" Sam asks.

"Oh Honey, it's beautiful, breathtaking . . . ." Ann begins.

"Yes that's the word. Breathtaking . . . Sam I love it." Rachael says.

"I can't believe it. I'm in love with the whole thing already . . ." Becca adds.

"Oh Sam, yes, it's wonderful!" Jessie exclaims.

Molly is smiling and nodding at each comment.

"Good. Then we can keep going. You see that there are minimal accessories. China, vases, pictures and such. You've still got a lot to do. Many of those things are packed in the packing boxes that are strewn around." Sam observes.

Next to the family room door, is the hallway to the laundry and further down, the Master suite. The laundry room is wide and is equipped with three large capacity commercial washers and four large capacity commercial dryers down the right wall. A commercial steam press, a steam closet and counters and hanger bars.

To the left is a water closet with a toilet and sink, under a stairway that leads to the finished upstairs, with the game room and bunk rooms. At the bottom of the stairs is the door to the detached garages. The walk between the house and the garage is enclosed, with a half wall and windows. Just outside the door on the right is the freezer, like a room added on to the house. Near the house door, is another door into the Master Suite's sitting room.

Down the hall from the laundry is the Master Suite. There is an oversized King bed and a chest on chest dresser with a mirror dresser and a sitting room to the right. A large walk-in closet is at the far wall and just past that is a large bath. The tub is an oversized garden tub with Jacuzzi nozzles and to the right of the tub is a European style shower. It is as large as a walk in closet and sports shower heads above, below and at the sides. The walls are glass blocks and there is a marble bench on two sides. On either side of the bathroom door are marble sinks and to the left of the tub is the enclosed toilet. A door at this end of the bathroom leads to the gym and pool. The whole effect is of a Roman bath, without the steam.

The gym is another large area, with various pieces of equipment. The Nordic Track, tread mills, three Bow Flex units, a Chuck Norris Ab Rocket and a large Swedish sauna. A four by eight window looks out on the pool. Through the door to the left of the window, they enter the pool area.

A fifteen foot wide deck surrounds the pool. The pool itself is 30' x 60' and at the deepest only six feet. When Sam contracted the pool, he said he wanted to be able to water walk and swim. Diving is not necessary. The sixty foot interior wall has two doors, one to the showers and dressing area, the other to the state of the art filtration system that uses ionic plates to filter all non-H2O debris from the water at a rate of the entire 60000 gallons every four hours. The exterior, sixty foot wall, is double pane, safety glass and has two large double doors that opens onto the lower patio. The short wall at the far end is covered in bamboo and in that same rear corner, walled containers for plants. This feature didn't go unnoticed, as Sam first thought, when both Master Gardeners exclaimed.

"Ahhh! Orchids. Jessie, what do you think?" Ann exclaims.

"Yes, yes and bromeliads and euphorbia and liriope and elephant ears. It will make the whole place like a lagoon. Sam, what made you think of doing the planting space?" Jessie asks.

"It was the landscaper. He was looking at the pool and made the suggestion. You two are known to landscapers around here. When he heard your names, he told me that you two would love it. He also suggested the layout and placement of the greenhouses. Frankly ladies, I think it will be a long time before we are settled here. There are tons of projects and things to do. Lets go out this way and see the greenhouses and the orchard." Sam said.

"Orchard. Fruits. I'm thinking preserves already." Molly blurts with a grin.

They look with mouths agape at the row of bungalows that line the back of the patio. There are six, styled on the LaQuinta hotel rooms. The gate at the pool end of the patio, leads to the greenhouses and orchard. To the left a half finished project is underway.

"Oh, what's that going to be over there? I thought everything was done." Ann asks.

"A few days ago, someone mentioned a pottery shed. They got this far and are waiting for the ovens to arrive, before they finish."

Becca's eyes widen and she throws her arms around Sam's neck.

"For me Sam. I love you." She has to stop as tears of joy flood her face. "I'm so happy . . . . how could life get better. A man and people I love, a baby and someone who loves me and listens. I didn't think it would happen." Tears overtake her again.

Sam and all surround her.

"When you mentioned a pottery shed, I thought that it might be something we all would like. A shed sounded small and I thought if we really wanted to do ceramics and pottery, a barn would be better. With an abundance of free time, our creative juices should spill over. I even see myself at a wheel." Sam says.

They move on to the green houses and also the orchard. Ann and Jessie are excited about the greenhouses. Rachael is taken with an idea to use part of each house to plant organic vegetables for the family.

"Rach that's a great idea. Fresh tomatoes in the winter. What a great idea." Jessie tells them.

"Oh yeah and hey what do you guys think about a hen house. Chickens for eggs. I've read about chicken houses. I'd like to give something like that a try. With baking and stuff, the eggs would be really handy. I also read that you can collect chicken poop and extract methane. Methane would be cheap heating gas for the greenhouses and the hen house in the winter." Molly is starting to bubble.

"I know about chickens and grading eggs. We could also do a few turkeys and some geese. Geese are great weed eaters and could keep the weeds down in the orchard and provide goose for the table." Rachael says.

"You are all incredible. Molly, Rach those are great ideas. I'll get some plans from the contractor and get that started. Fresh veggies all winter, is great. Did I hear someone say something about canning? We have fruit trees that should start producing next spring." Sam expounds.

"Me, me. I love to can and make jams and preserves." Molly bubbles.

"Sign me up to. Ann will tell you how I love to bake, and ya'll know I cook." Sam says.

"Hey, me to. I like to bake fruity cookies and fruit cakes and stuff. Might make a business of Christmas fruit cakes." Becca adds.

"Mmmm! What about a place just for baking and canning. We have the room to build a bakery and canning house.

We haven't even seen it all yet and already ideas are pouring out of us. Thank you Ann for suggesting this union and ladies for accepting the idea. I do believe that we will make many more social and economic discoveries. Shall we get to work and set up some of our house? I'm getting anxious to move in." Sam says.

They all agree and head back to the house. Inside, Sam gives each of them their own keys and remotes for the gate and to set the security.

"We have most of the things we need to stay here tonight. The cases in the foyer and kitchen and all over the place are filled with linens, towels, pots and pans, china, serving pieces, LED TVs and Blu-Ray and DVD players. I have a professional crew that will install the TVs. There's a descent stereo in there somewhere and CD's and a couple of cases of Blu-Ray discs and DVDs. Once we get started, I'll make a trip to pick up our food and wine and get the meat packer to deliver our meat order. The linens probably need to be put through the washer to get packing chemicals rinsed out. Blankets and pillows through the steamer to freshen . . ."

"Steamer. Which one is that? I wouldn't have thought of having a steamer." Jessie says.

"Yes Ma'am, it's the tall cabinet to the right of the steam press." Sam tells them.

"I'm ready to get started. With all the washers and dryers, it shouldn't take long and if we team up, we can have all the beds made fast. Do we have detergent and dryer sheets?" Ann asks.

It took another half hour to get fully organized and moving. The sheets are washing and pots, pans, baking dishes, china, servers, tableware, silverware and a ton of daily use tools and accessories are cleaned and placed. Sam is pleased and surprised at how similar the five women are and how well he understands the way they are thinking. He takes a call from the electronics store that is going to bring the huge LED TV. Sam tells them that he is going out for an hour, but would be ready at 3 p.m.

"Ladies, I'm going for the groceries. I'll be back by noon, and I'll bring some carry-out."

"Do you need any help?" Becca asks.

"Yeah, Becca, why don't you go with Sam and we'll get everything finished here. Maybe some Chinese and burgers and fries." Ann suggests.

"Okay. We'll be back soon." Becca says.

Sam and Becca drive to the 'old' house and pick up the cases from SAM's club. He had forgotten how big a load it is. Then they stop at the meat packer and ask them to deliver their order. They head for the 'China Buffet'.

"Sam, I am so happy right now."

"I'm happy that you're happy. I do love you, ya know."

"I do. I feel it, even when we are all together; you make each of us feel loved. It is so wonderful to feel loved each day. Having very close girl friends, all the time, is wonderful."

Sam reaches out and touches her arm and squeezes her leg.

At the restaurant, Becca orders the carry-out and they leave for 'Hardees' for burgers and fries. It is almost noon and they head back to their new home.

They arrive at the gate just as the freezer truck pulls up and Sam opens the gate. While the ladies eat lunch, Sam helps the guys from the meat packers unload and store the order. The drivers are curious and crane their necks to see all that they can.

"Guys. They're friends and used to work together before winning the lottery. I get to live in and manage stuff. Kind of a dream job for me."

"Yes sir. How does someone get into a set up like that?"

"Lucky I guess. I managed their salon and they cut me in for some of the money. It's the least I could do."

They both laugh and comment on what a 'lucky SOB' Sam is.

The electronics people arrive at three o'clock and install the 90" LED in the family room and hook up the ones in the bed rooms and kitchen. The game room upstairs, is set up with game consoles and LED TV s. All the wiring was installed when the house was being built, including the intercom, stereo speaker system and telephones.

Nearly every day they find that there is something else they need. The next month is busy getting everything the way they want. It didn't take them long to figure out the pantry and freezer. Meals are usually prepared by Sam and/or Molly and/or Becca and sometimes everyone would crowd the kitchen.

The greenhouse crowd is bubbly with excitement. They set up one with exotic plants. They talk County Fair, State Fair and how they will enter their best and get a reputation and then sell plants. A new enterprise is born. Three houses are set up to grow vegetables, organically and in a forth, an experimental hydroponics garden is producing tender red lettuce. Other vegetables include, spinach, Swiss chard, broccoli, squash, cucumbers, tomatoes, peas, cauliflower, carrots, celery and spring onions. There are shelves of herb pots with parsley, rosemary, thyme, holy basil, chili peppers, garlic and those skinny green things that taste like onion—chives. Sam is in awe of their work and tells them so.

Rachael adds three smaller poultry coups, along with the very large hen house and large fenced in areas. One for turkey, one for geese and one for Cornish hens.

"These are the things my grandparents taught me."

Molly has the hen house up and running. Everyone is a little amazed at the skill of their youngest member in keeping poultry healthy and producing an abundance of fresh eggs.

"Thank you guys. I lived several summers with my grandparents on their chicken farm. Ha, ha, you could say I have chicken poop in my blood."

She and Becca have brainstormed with Sam on how to collect the methane and make use of it. They Googled the topic and are amazed at the number of sites with excellent ideas and plans. Molly is a dynamo in getting it together. Sam has to slow her down. She is 7 months along and didn't need the strain, but it seems the more she takes on, the stronger she is. Becca is just as hard working, but is spending a lot of time in the pottery shed. She is working on a project to provide the greenhouse with containers for potting the off-spring of the exotic plants.

"I thought that a small, decorative pot for the small exotics that you want to sell would enhance their marketability." She explains.

She is right. A 4" clay pot with relief art in the clay made the plants even more exotic.

The family is together every evening, as Sam suggested, for relaxing and sharing the days events. Sam records everything in a journal to chronicle their journey.

Chapter 8

THE FAMILY GROWS

The pregnancies are progressing and all the Mommas are in good health as are their babies. Sam is also glowing and as excited as the Mommas are, picking out baby furniture and clothes.

It's April and the first confinement is going to be on or about April 26th, then May 2nd, and 10th and then two, three weeks before Sam's Birthday in June. The excitement is mounting and lots of sitting together and raging hormones that made faces wet with happy and sad tears at the same time. Sam has heard about and reads everything about the moods of pregnant women and is eating it all up. It is good to be knowledgeable and able to provide the right words and comfort to his loving, moody women. The travel that they all were excited about a few months ago is put on a back burner while they readied their home.

Then just like a good clock, the hour struck. Sam remembers the day starting out like any other day. Jessie is with Sam this night. They cuddled and petted and loved one another without sex. They are naked, in bed and share their body heat. It is completely satisfying. It wouldn't be long before her time would come. Her belly is full of the love they shared nine months ago.

"The alarm is going to go off soon and the rest will be piling in." Sam says as he kisses her at the hollow of her throat.

"Yeah, I know. I just love lying here with you and feeling your body pressed to me. I never dreamed that this would be so satisfying."

Jessie's voice is dreamy as her hand rubs across his chest and down to his belly.

"One more big hug and kiss before we have to go."

Jessie presses herself close and puts her leg across his. He puts his arm around her and pulls her tightly to him. She turns her face up and their lips connect.

A soft knock at the door says the day is about to start.

"Sam, I'm going to the shower and get it ready for all of us."

"Okay Darling." He runs his hand over her thigh and calls out, "Come in."

The door opens and Ann, Becca and Rachael waddle in.

"We didn't interrupt, did we?" Ann asks and hugs Jessie. Then Rach and Becca give Jessie a hug. He can see the affection they have for one another.

The three got on the bed and Jessie heads for the shower. He loves it. His girls rarely wear anything when they come to the Master Bedroom. Now with their babies imminent, Sam marvels at their 'Earth Mother' figures. There's nothing more beautiful than a pregnant woman, he thinks to himself.

"You know there's no such thing. If we had been occupied, you all would have been welcome to join in." He smiles and kisses each of them.

Ann snuggles up on his left and Rach on his right and Becca lies down between his legs with her head on his chest. 'There is nothing like girl flesh pressed against you.' He thinks.

"Mmmm! This is nice. What are the plans for today?" Sam asks.

"We thought a little grocery shopping. Rach and I thought ribs would be nice for a day in the pool with ribs on the pit." Ann said.

They each have turned on their side and are running hands all over his chest, his stomach and lower, while Becca is kissing his chest.

"Sounds good. Now be cool, don't get me worked up. Jessie has the shower going. Has anyone seen Molly this morning?"

"Yes, she said she wanted to be last this morning. Ann, Rach and I are just taking the edge off. Molly looks like she's ready to pop." Becca says.

"Hey Sam. Sorry I'm late. Did I miss anything?" Molly asks, as she enters the bedroom.

Ann, Becca and Rach move away to give Molly room and go to the showers. Molly is very close to full term. She is sure to deliver very soon.

"Hi Baby Girl. You're just on time. A quick squeeze and we'll get to the showers."

Molly scoots closer and Sam puts his arm under her arm and across her back. She puts her arm around his neck and hugs him hard. Her belly pressed against him and he feels a little movement. They lie together for a while. He kisses her tenderly. When she leans back, he sees tears in her eyes.

"What is it Baby Girl?"

"I'm so fat and my girl place is all puffy. I just know you don't want me any more." She sobs.

"Oh my God. Sweet heart. You couldn't be more beautiful than you are now, with my baby inside of you." He pets her and strokes her back. She sits up suddenly, her eyes wide and he hears the sound of gurgling water.

"Oh! oh! Sam, my water just broke."

"Ann, Jessie, Becca, Rach come quick." He calls out.

His angels appear with towels wrapped around glistening, wet bodies and their faces alight with bright smiles.

"Molly, it's time." They chorus. Ann takes charge immediately.

"Come on Molly. We'll shower and I'll get you dressed and get your bag. Rach, would you get us a light breakfast? Toast, Jam, Tea . . . your choice. Becca will you help Rach? Jessie, will you start the van and cool it down." Ann directs, taking the role of mother hen.

"What about me?" Sam asks.

"Oh, Sam, uh—boil some water. Just kidding. Check Molly's bag and make sure she has a new toothbrush and stuff like that."

"Okay."

Ann, Molly and Sam go to the shower, all smiles, except for Molly who looks a little scared. Ann pets and reassures her.

Sam finishes quickly and retrieves Molly's bag and toiletries. When they are all dressed and ready, Sam looks at his girls with love in his eyes.

"You are all so beautiful. I called the hospital and alerted them and had them notify her doctor. I've got your bag Baby Girl, with a new toothbrush."

The drive to Tuomey Hospital is calmer than anticipated. Molly has two contractions in route, but she has plenty of support with her. Rach tells Sam which door to drive to and they are soon loading Molly into a wheel chair. Sam parks and is only minutes behind his family.

"A large group of women, all very pregnant, just came in?" Sam blurts to the nurse behind the desk.

"Yes, Mr. Elliott. Right through the doors on the right. Ah Mr. Elliott, the lady is a Ms. Elliott, your sister?"

"We're all Elliotts. Corporate family you know. Molly is having my baby."

"Oh! Right. You can go through those doors. Thank you Mr. Elliott."

Sam rushes through the doors and a nurse is coming toward him with a gown. He sees others rolling the bed, with Molly, down the hall behind a nurse.

"Hurry Mr. Elliott, she is about to deliver." The nurse says.

"The others?"

"Already on their way. Nurse Rachael is there pushing the bed with the other three."

Sam dons the gown as he hurries down the hall, after the retreating bed. He enters the delivery room and Molly is already in stirrups and looking scared and happy at the same time. Sam takes her hand and squeezes.

"You are the best Baby Girl. You have never been more beautiful."

The pain that crosses her face is almost more than he can bear. The labor isn't prolonged and she delivers after just two more contractions. Molly is a real baby maker, the doctor and nurses are amazed as are her momma/sisters Ann, Rach, Becca and Jessie.

"You did it Molly. You're a Momma. He's beautiful. Just the right mix of you and Sam. We love you Darling." Ann says through tears of joy.

"This is my first delivery as a nurse. I hope mine will be as quick. How do you feel?" Rach asks in her nurse mode.

"Better; thank you Rach. I love you all so much."

The pain crosses her face again and Rach calls to the doctor. He again lifts the sheet and his eyes open wide.

"Well, well what do we have here? It looks like . . . ." He starts.

Then Molly pushes hard and . . . . groans. Sam looks ashen, but holds her hand tight.

"You have a baby girl. Twins. Just as I expected." The doctor continues.

Everyone crowds closer to see the additional baby.

The nurse quickly ushers them out of the delivery room so that they can clean up and help the placenta evacuate. The nurse, who brought Sam the gown, leads them to the recovery room. Everyone is smiling and crying and hugging and kissing and group hugging.

"I love all of you. I don't know how life could be better and that doctor kept twins a secret this whole time."

"I can hardly wait to give you this baby." Jessie almost sobs.

"You all are going to make me the father of a big, wonderful family. I love you all." Sam cocks his head, "I hear a bed coming down the hall."

Just then the nurse rolls the bed, with Molly, into the room. Molly is dozing, but opens her eyes at the clucking of the mother hens in the room.

"I saw our babies. They are so beautiful. Both have hazel eyes and your floppy ear."

"Thank you Baby Girl. Look at the smiles around you. We are all so happy. You done good Darling."

"Yes you did. They're beautiful. You have to share, you know?" Ann kisses Molly on the cheek and squeezes her shoulders.

"You know that Ann and I will be next. I hope I am as brave as you Honey." Becca says.

The love and excitement of the rest, of the 'soon to be mothers', is contagious. Sam looks around and sees that the nurses to, are smiling and dabbing at tears.

The scene repeats itself four more times in the next two months, with Rach and Jessie delivering before the mid-year.

Sam is an unbelievable Dad. Each of his babies gets a couple of hours each day, sleeping on his stomach and seeing his face when they wake up. Dirty diapers don't faze him and he is up with each feeding. They all praise him for his dedication, but he says that he gets up, "To see those beautiful titties doing their other job."

July arrives with much noise as the family has put together their own 4th of July fireworks display. The next week, Sam comes to dinner with a black briefcase and sets it on a chair next to him.

"Does anyone know what today is?" He asks, raising his eyebrows.

"What no clues? Come on ladies, think, July 12th. What happened on July 12th?" Sam cajoles.

"Oh! I know. One year ago, we became family. We signed the papers to make us a corporate union. It's our anniversary, right?" Molly exclaims.

"That's it baby girl. Ladies, it's our anniversary." Sam confirms.

He opens his briefcase and takes out five small jewelry boxes.

"I thought about it some time ago, but didn't know how I would go about it. I took this tool, it's a jeweler's ring sizing tool and went into each of your rooms and found a ring that I knew fit you well and got your ring size. The jeweler at Galloway Moseley helped me pick out five engagement rings which I believe you each deserve and five wedding bands."

The five women crowd around Sam excited as he passes a box to each.

"Oh my God. Sam it's beautiful. I love it and the wedding band . . . it's" the tears take over as Becca tries to look at the rings adorning her finger.

"Sam I love you. This is the best present I could have wished for and I didn't even think about this." Jessie sobs.

"You are more thoughtful and loving than anyone I have ever even heard of. I love you Sam, with all my heart." Rach sobs as well.

"Sam. I don't know what to say. This makes me feel really married. I love you." Molly says.

"Honey, do you mind if I wear these rings instead of my original ones? I love you." Ann asks.

"Yes Darling, it's okay. Wives, lovers, Mothers to my children. I'm only sorry that I didn't think of it sooner. I know now that it must have been difficult for you to explain our relationship. Now you just show them the rings." Sam smiles and holds his arms open as they press to him, he kisses each and gives each an affectionate squeeze.

Independence Day also has Tommy and Carly, at just three and a half months, rolling over and trying to get up on their hands and knees, much too soon for their age. The house will soon be filled with crawling babies.

They are all baptized in the Lutheran church. Baptisms, while a rich experience for parents, generally cause screaming babies and a handful for the pastor. The six Elliott babies are the exception. Sam's family is old German Lutheran and part of their tradition is in the baptism gown and blanket. Sam's folks sent them to him for the baptisms, with the provision that he follow the tradition of sewing a strand of hair from the mother into the gown's hem. Six strands are there from his Mom for him and his brothers and sisters;

five more are for his nieces and nephews. When each child is dressed in the gown and wrapped in the blanket, they are positively angelic. As the pastor administers the sacrament with the words of institution and the sprinkling of the water, each child coos and spreads their arms wide as if to hug the whole church. The ooo's and aaaah's of the congregation are a reward that is appreciated by the family. Digital videos are being made by the church's media expert for the archives and for the family.

Sam recounts that his parents told him that this is the way he and his siblings reacted to their baptism.

The family counts the serenity of these baptisms as yet another indication of divine approval of their life together. The congregation has accepted their relationship, when each of Sam's ladies joined the church with Sam and Ann. There are questions and curiosity, but no one made strong objections. The pastor talked to them at length and found that they are within the bounds of the Bible and followed tenets set forth in the Old Testament and Judeo/Christian law. They are under scrutiny by other churches, probably because those churches didn't have the same access to the family.

It starts with a visit from a pair of Southern Baptist ministers. Sam is polite and the two ministers weren't immediately judgmental.

"Gentlemen, to what do I owe this visit? We are Lutheran, by baptism, I was born Lutheran and so are my children." Sam says as he ushers them into the parlor.

"Mr. Elliott, I'm Mathew Smith, pastor of North Side Baptist church and this is Pastor Isaac Baywater, from East Connor Baptist church." They shake hands and Pastor Smith continues. "There have been questions from some prominent people in our congregation that is causing a rift in their beliefs and turning some from the faith. We only wish to set the record straight, as it were, to mend the fences and quell the rampant rumor mongering." The elder of the two ministers said with a little frustration in his voice, like he really didn't want to be here, but is forced to come because of outside pressure.

"Ask away, we have nothing to hide and other than being a totally happy group of God's children, we serve his will as often as He has given us strength to do. We have come to understand that there would be curiosity outside of our church family and please call me Sam."

"Thank you Mr. Elli . . . Sam. First, may I say that I have no opinion either way about the questions I ask? I'm not just ordained by my church, I am educated in Theology and am currently completing my doctorate."

Sam nods his understanding. Reverend Smith really looks uncomfortable. Just then, Jessie comes into the parlor with a tray of iced tea.

"I hope iced tea is alright with everyone. I also have some butter cookies. They're Sam's favorite."

She leans over and gives Sam a kiss on the cheek. Everyone expresses their thanks to Jessie.

"Gentlemen, this is Jessica. She is one of the ladies who lives with us here with our children and is also one of the women who shares my heart."

"Hi y'all. I'm just going to start lunch with Molly. Nice meeting you."

Sam pours tea into the three glasses and settles back into his chair.

"Sorry about the interruption. You are about to ask some questions."

"The first and possibly the hardest question; do you live in sin with these five women?"

"Explain your understanding of 'living in sin.'" Sam asks.

"Do you share marital rights without benefit of marriage?"

"Only as far as man's law forbids multiple marriages, but in God's eyes we are married to one another."

Sam thinks he sees a small sliver of a smile from the elder.

"Thank you Sam. I believe I understand you. How would you justify that explanation, if asked?"

"I don't believe that I need to justify anything. We break no state or local laws and according to the Bible, many of the Old Testament people had more than one wife, ergo, in God's eyes."

The younger minister looks relieved, as if the burden he carried is off his shoulders.

"Are the children brought up with the word of God?"

"Reverend Smith, all that we are and all that we have, we owe to God's grace and love. Our children will come to understand that, when they are older and we also have Bible study several times a week. On Sunday, we go to St James for services. The congregation accepts our family and our pastor researched everything and found us within religious law. There have been inquiries from some of our brothers and sisters in the church about how to start similar unions. We lecture occasionally with the blessing of the Synod and the Bishop."

The elder stands, "Sam. I find nothing that my flock should fear from you or your family and I will report the same to them. Personally, I find your lifestyle refreshing and your thinking sound."

They shake hands and Sam escorts them to the door. The elder minister turns and looks at him. "Sam, I have the distinct impression of Old Testament about you. Are you a religious person?"

"Only as far as trying to do God's will and having my family do the same. We do attend worship, but find that private worship and meditation are more fulfilling."

They both nod in understanding and shake hands again, and then they are gone. Sam doesn't think more about it. He learns, later that Dr. Smith published a paper on, *The Biblical Right of Polygamy in Modern Society*, as part of his doctoral thesis.

When he walks into the kitchen, Jessie and Molly are there preparing lunch for the family. Both women wore aprons that cover the top and hung to mid thigh in front and nothing else.

"I'm sure happy that you didn't wear this outfit when you delivered the tea and cookies. It would have changed their religion." Sam says as he hugs Jessie from behind and kisses her neck. She turns and their lips met in a fiery kiss and Sam's hands find two hands full of bootie.

He turns to Molly and holds his arms open. She steps into them and presses her body to him and kisses him full on the mouth. Sam hugs her and also finds two hands full of firm bootie.

"The two of you could kill me now and I'd be satisfied that I had already been in heaven. You both are 'bootieful'. Let me help with the lunch, okay?"

"No sir. We've got it. Everyone is in the pool. You get changed and join them and we'll be there in a little while." Jessie admonishes.

Sam goes to his room and takes off his clothes and grabs a pair of swim trunks and heads for the pool. When he comes down the steps into the pool area, there are three naked ladies and six toddlers frolicking in the shallow end of the pool.

"Hey man, no trunks." They chorus.

"Okay. I should have known. Jessie and Molly are tempting fate around the stove, without clothes." Sam banters back.

Sam goes to his family. The children all squeal and splash in their excitement. Like water nymphs with water wings and sitting in floatation rings. The oldest is only just eight months old. Each of his darlings got a hug and kiss and full body contact. Ann held on a little longer and looked at him with love in her eyes.

"I'm so happy Sam. You've made this family work. I love the little girl you gave me. Cathy has your ear and grin. I love you." Ann hugs him tighter, before Cathy demands her time.

Sam picks her up and tickles her belly and nuzzles her neck, to her giggles and hands her to Ann. None of his babies have the least fear of the water.

He moves on to Becca and hugs her with the same full body contact. Becca is the most huggable. She is soft and rounder in the shoulders and hips. Her kiss is fulfilling and she makes little moaning sounds as she is hugged and receives Sam's caress. Raina is a miniature copy of her mother and also sports Sam's ear. Sam picks her up and receives her pucker up kiss and tickles her under her chin, before handing her to Becca.

Rach has her hands full with her Mattie and Jessie's Ryan and Molly's Tommy and Carly floating in the rings, but Ann and Becca step closer to help, as Sam hugs and kisses her and plays with each of the young'uns.

"Well, ladies. The inquisition has come and gone. I believe that we passed their inspection. If not, their loss. Our love is strong and our life is full."

Lunch arrives and everyone crowds the patio tables. Sam's pulse races, as he looks lovingly and with appreciation at these wonderful women and the children that they gave him. Looking at their nude bodies, one would have difficulty in believing that they had babies just six and eight months ago. The karate training and their morning workouts in the gym gave them back their girlish figures.

Time moves on and in the next several months, the greenhouses begin to produce in large quantities. Molly and Rach take much of the excess and freeze the fresh vegetables and carry baskets full to the local orphanage and to the Salvation Army. The exotic plants are beginning to crowd their space in the plant section.

"You could sell your overstock. Check if a store would handle it, or we could get a place and sell them yourself. Enterprise, ladies." Sam suggests.

"That's a wonderful idea Sam. Jessie, what do you think? There's more plants here than most places that sell plants have on display and these are locally grown." Ann offers.

"Hey, yeah. I knew this Master Gardener thing was gonna be good for something." Jessie says. They agree to talk about it later at the family's evening talk.

The family evening talks are Sam's suggestion to keep everyone involved with everyone else in the family. It works and offers each an opportunity to help one another.

The egg and chicken house is booming as well. The family had to hire a couple of guys to handle parts of the operation. No one in the family wanted to actually kill chickens, but it is necessary every couple of months to replace layers when they stopped laying eggs. Molly, with Rach, set up a supply line to a couple of local restaurants for her excess eggs and chicken that wasn't frozen and also sold to local users. Their product is all organic, but sells at or below the price of the hormone grown hens, since they don't have to pay stock holders.

"Molly, you have a great enterprise going. I'm very proud of you. Do you remember how you felt when your folks farmed you out to your Grandma's farm? Now look at you." Sam praises his youngest love.

"I know. I couldn't have done it by myself. Rach helps and Becca also helps with the vegetable freezing and chickens. We've started making jams and preserves from the fruit orchard with Becca's help. She knows a lot about everything. You figured out how to get the methane and store it. We all just work well together. It doesn't hurt that we all love one another so much." Molly says.

"Speaking of methane. How does everyone like the gas lights? It came to me when I was laying pipe to the greenhouses for the heating elements."

"I love them. It's so romantic to walk out there at night and have the old fashioned lamp lighting." Molly says. She, like Sam, is a real romantic.

Rebecca's pottery barn receives attention from everyone from time to time. Ceramics seems to catch the interest of each of the ladies and Sam. Becca has begun to make high quality figurines and bone china.

Sam asks Becca to show him some of her work and they walk out to the ceramics barn. She is quite talented at decorating and glazing her product. She has full sets of dinnerware stacked up on her storage space. Her figurines are in a style similar to Lladro and Hummel.

"Becca, these are beautiful. This is similar to the set we use in the house, no?" Sam asks.

"Yes. I didn't think you noticed. I made them about my third try and made it a service for twenty, so they would all look the same, instead of trying to copy them later. I also put a second complete set away for later so that replacements will also match."

"That was a good idea. I did notice, my love. Have you thought about what you will do with your extras? They are a higher quality than any commercial product. You could sell them as special orders, or retail ourselves. Open a gift shop and feature your china and figurines." Sam offers.

Becca hugs Sam and whispers, "I love you Sam. You always think about our happiness. I would love to open a gift shop. We all need an outlet to feel useful." They share a kiss and walk arm in arm, out to the orchard and the reflecting pond.

Life is very relaxed and fulfilling. The children are all within two months of Tommy and Carly, who just turned one year old. Spring is here and the birthday party is exciting for the birthday babies and the rest are all tickled. May brings another two birthdays and finally Jessie's and Rachael's. Mattie and Ryan, have their birthday parties on the 8th of June. Sam moves his up to the same time, so that it wouldn't be confusing. The family celebrates everything. Birthdays for each of them is primary. Valentine's Day, Easter, Fourth of July, Labor Day, Veteran's Day, and what ever is on the calendar. Then there are the family visits. One or another of the Moms and Dads would spend a week with them. They'd have a barbecue and go all out. The parents like the bungalows. They beat the hotels or motels for comfort and they are always amazed at the accomplishments of their daughters. Molly's parents cancelled their divorce, like they had an epiphany and are frequent visitors. Molly has never been happier.

It didn't take much for the Elliotts to decide to have a barbecue, or cake and ice cream, or to load up in the family van and head out for the beach, or mountains. The children love the beach and kept Sam and the ladies on their toes, all the while accepting the curious looks from other beach nuts. Several times, Sam sees strange women approach his ladies and smile and talk and point. Later, Sam would hear about the encounter.

"She just wondered why the five of us and the children are together with you and why you attended to us so well." Ann tells him.

"Yes, one lady asked me if any of us are married. I told her we are all married, but didn't elaborate, to let her wonder." Rachael says.

"The woman that was talking to me, made the connection. She saw that all the babies had your good looks and said it out loud. 'You all live together don't you? I've heard about it, corporate union; right?' So I confirmed it and then she wanted to know more. How did it work, are we happy, is anyone jealous of the others, stuff like that. I told her and she asked how she could learn more." Jessie elaborates.

"Well, I'm glad at least one is on a positive note."

"Oh Sam, I talked to several and they all are really positive. They each said they could see the love we had for one another and we looked like we are successful. A few also made the connection about the benefits for women who struggle with society for basic needs. How a group would keep relationships healthy. She asked if we ever countered a decision that Tom made. I told her he left almost everything up to us and only added when we are unsure. She is impressed with that and wished she could find out more." Becca adds.

"Baby that is what I heard as well. One asked if it is hard on me being younger. I told her that it is the greatest. I never had the heartbreak of a bad relationship and having a husband a little older and co-wives a little older always shielded me from looking foolish." Molly tells him.

Not all their outings are as dramatic, but the curiosity that seeing them together causes, led them to another turning point. While sitting in their family meeting one evening, they decide to write articles for the newspaper and whoever would publish to explain the idea of their corporate union. Maybe that lady who wanted to know more would have an avenue.

Their hobbies are beginning to gain popularity through their various shops. Ann and Jessie, with Rachael ran an exotic plant and flower shop.

Molly, Becca and Sam kept a bakery/gift shop going then after the first year, Sam suggests they get some commercial property and do a shopping center type of strip mall with a hair salon and spa, a gift shop, a bakery and a flower shop.

Six months after they agree to expanding their enterprises, the Crystal Palace is opened. The commercial property, the building with all the shelving and equipment and parking lot came to just under three million.

The four cosmetologists take turns in the salon and their hobby enterprise. They hired help for each place. There was already an experienced manager for the salon and spa.

Rachael and Sam take turns at each shop. They have an interconnected back hall to all the shops and a nursery is set up for their children. Sam's idea. He spends a lion's portion of each day there with his babies. The children in their terrible twos stage and are all talking now and not baby talk. That is one of Sam's rules, 'no baby talk', it only confuses them. Now they all greet their parents with a proper, "Good morning, Momma/Poppa," and greet each other the same way. The grandmas and grandpas are surprised with, "Grandma Donna, Grandpa Jim." None of that Me Maw and Pa Paw either. They are smart to. Sam bought each of them a 'Teach Me Reader' with extra books. He tells them that is how his baby sister learned to read. Their eyes are riveted as Sam touches a word on the book and they can hear it.

The children are all 22, 23, and 24 months old and well adjusted good 'kids'. They all love their Poppa. He plays with them and can make animal sounds. People ask how he remembers their names.

"Well, it does get hard at times, but they all gave me babies, I try really hard to remember their names." Then he laughs out loud at the comical expressions he gets from the questioners then everyone is laughing. Should've been a comic. Ah, could've, should've, and would've ...

Molly and Becca's bakery is doing a great business and the gift shop, with the ceramic and china wares, is also doing a good business. There is even interest, from an art museum, for Becca's figurines and for Ann's, Jessie's, Molly's and Rachael's forays into ceramics. Sam's chess sets don't last long and there have been requests for sets not yet made.

The exotic plants are selling at an unexpected high because of the Master Gardener status held by Ann and Jessie. Their booklets and pamphlets with their insights into plant health are also selling well.

People who ask why they work when they already have all that they need, Sam tells them, "We need to keep busy. It's not work, it's just living interrupted by hobbies."

Sam starts writing as well. While it is still fresh, he is journaling the life and times of a corporate union and the relationships involved. He laughs when he remembers that it is because a lady, at the beach, asked Jessie how she could learn more. It didn't take him long to chronicle the 34 months of their relationship, from the first meeting, to the incorporation, to the building of their house and the births of their children, to the enabling of their enterprises. He wrote it from love. After just a short time together, he is the happiest man alive and wondered why this lifestyle had not been explored in more depth before their experiment. It only took him five weeks to write the 97,250 words of their story. An author who is a moderator at a writing workshop Sam attended, is also an editor and looks his work over with a critical eye. She suggests some modifications and makes a few corrections and pronounces it ready to send to a publisher. Sam hires an agent, not an easy task, as the genre is not established. Three months later, Sam is at the front door to Waldenbooks, signing copies of, "The Chronicles of A Corporate Union." Jessie and Molly accompany him on his book signing and field questions from curious ladies. Sam is doubly thrilled, because at the table at the other side of the entrance is, Ally McIntire, Sam's teacher from the writing class. She is signing her own book and they exchange signed copies of their books. Sam has inscribed, "To Ally, You sparked my creative desire to write. You done good toots. Samuel "Sam" Elliott."

The store runs out of their 1000 copies in a little under five hours. Sam's hand is numb and his butt is sore from sitting there the whole time. He's glad that he didn't have to sign all of the copies. It seems the same thing is happening at all the Waldenbooks stores. A week after the signing day, Sam receives a call from the publisher asking him if he would accept a speaking engagement.

"I know it would be great, but I have so many responsibilities. You do know I have five ladies and six children I'm responsible for. Three of my ladies are pregnant now and I suspect the other two will announce their pregnancy very shortly. Let me talk to them and I'll get back to you." Sam explains.

Later that evening, he tells the women about the call and asks for their input.

"It's great Sam; do it. Maybe we could come along." Ann says.

"Yeah Honey, an opportunity like this doesn't happen often." Rachael adds.

"We don't have to worry about the shops. The people we have working with us can handle it and it would be nice to have the whole family in front of an audience." Jessie points out.

"Let's do it Sam. My folks will hear about it or see it on the news and go nuts." Molly adds.

"We love you Sam. This is your shot at being famous." Becca says.

"Okay my Darlings. We'll all go, even the children. If they say no, then none of us will go. It was interesting to hear that all fifty thousand copies of the book sold on the first day. We'll probably have to do more book signings." Sam says.

Sam calls the publisher the next day and agrees to the trip, if his wives and children could accompany him. The publisher agrees and the date is set. It didn't matter, but an advance of $250k and a tour fee of $250k is thrown into the deal. They sold a lot of books and plan to sell a lot more, Sam thinks to himself. If they hadn't been rich, it would have been a boon. They decide to donate the whole sum to the City County Fire and Police welfare fund.

The publisher sends a stretch limo to pick them up and transport them to the airport where a private Lear Jet is waiting for them. They fly to New York and another Limo picks them up and takes them to an upscale hotel overlooking Central Park. They have a suite of rooms and six child beds are in the four bedrooms for the women. The Master bedroom has a King bed and a large bath tub in the private bath.

The first day, they dine in the hotel restaurant to the delight of the children and also to several of the other guests who are amazed at the vocabulary and politeness of the children. After dinner, many of the other diners brought chairs to their table and engaged in conversation with Sam, the women and with the children. This is a little unsettling and a careful eye is kept on the children.

Later Sam would explain, "Hell, I didn't know any of them, when they came so close, I figured it may have been a ploy to kidnap our babies."

The conversations are pointed and very intelligent. Sam notices that some in the second and third rows are recording and writing as others question and the family responds. Finally Sam asks outright, what is going on.

One gentleman, who looks more like a doctor than a casual diner says, "I'm sorry to be so intrusive. I'm Doctor Weiss. Your publisher contacted me and some of my colleagues to catch you au natural, so to speak. We wanted to get your honest answers without making you feel like you are on display. I have to tell you that, for myself, I am amazed and pleased. I have been writing about the troubles monogamy creates. Your family has proved my points so well that I will begin a closer study. We may contact you from time to time."

"Seriously, we thought you were trying to kidnap our children. This talk tomorrow then isn't for you?" Sam queries.

"Oh indeed. For us and for many more of our associates. We also want to gain enough knowledge to be able to teach ways to make this type of relationship work and prosper."

"I understand. We get that all the time. Particularly from women who are interested in how the relationship works. I always make the analogy of herd mammals. In nature there are more females than males and that's how they interact, a bull and several heifers, a stallion and several mares. If we are animals in every other way, why not that way and eliminate the waste of good DNA." Sam tells them.

The talk and questions go on a little while longer. Ann, Rachael and Becca take the children up to the room to bathe and get them in bed. Sam stays with Jessie and Molly for another hour to field questions. Molly is just too cute for them.

"I was surprised when Ann, Jessie and Becca invited me to join their group. It was only a group then. Sam brought lunch to us every day at the salon and would sit and talk with us during lunch. It wasn't long before I fell in love with him, but I knew he was married to Ann. Then Ann surprises us all when she suggests that we all become one family with Sam as the husband. By then, I knew what a good man is all about. He really cared for us without expecting anything in return, like most guys, who take you to McDonald's and a movie, then expect you to sleep with them. Jessie and Becca pointed it out to me and I understood. He solved our problems, well, he suggested solutions. He never said, 'do it this way, or don't do that', he just said how he thought it would work and let us decide. Then he is always there to back up our decision. Who could ask for a better husband and his own wife is suggesting she share him with us. That stuff about there being more women than men made sense, when she explained it and I could see how desperate women could make marriage and divorce happen in a bad way. I love Sam and I love my sisters and I love the babies Sam gave me and the life we have. So there!"

There are chuckles all around them at the last statement. Molly has won them over. It was 9 o'clock when the three go upstairs. Sam is beat. The day just seemed so long. When they get to the room, the children are asleep and Ann, Rachael and Becca are in robes and have the tub filling for a nice long soak. The three disrobe and the six go into the bath. It is heaven and each of them say so. The tub is a little smaller than their tub, but the crowding is delicious. They all sleep together in the King bed and wake in the morning, ready for the day, rested and fresh. Breakfast is delivered by room service and after Sam and his ladies eat and feed their brood, the concierge calls to say the limo is ready.

The theater where they are presenting the seminar is packed. There must be two thousand people crowded into the theater. In the family, everyone is a little nervous, but the publisher has prompters prepared to guide their presentation. The only ones who seem oblivious to the crowd are the children.

When the introductions are made and the family take seats on the stage, Sam comes to the podium and accepts the publishers' handshake. He then lowers the microphone and calls his babies to introduce themselves.

"Hello. I'm Tommy. I'm a twin and I am twenty eight months old."

"Hello. I'm Carly. I'm Tommy's twin sister and I am twenty eight months old."

"Hello. I am Cathy. Ann is my mother. I am twenty seven months old."

"Yo Say Yo. That's Korean for Hello. I'm Raina. My mother is Becca. I am twenty seven months old."

Just then, Tommy and Carly rush up and lean toward the microphone and together say, "Our mother is Molly." Then bow and rush back to their seats. The laughter from the crowd of two thousand is like a warm wave that wipes away the fears the adults have.

"Hello. I'm Mattie. Rachael is my mother. I am twenty six months old."

"Hello. My name is Ryan. Jessie is my mother. I am twenty six months old."

The applause of approval and the friendly shouted comments are like warm oil that pours over the family. The applause goes on for what seems like ten minutes, until Sam holds up his hands in an East Asian prayer salute. Sam begins with his thanks for the warm welcome and the graciousness of their host.

"We are often asked about the precociousness of the children. The only thing I can say is you give me a child until he is five and I will show you the man. One of them old Greeks said it first."

When the laughter subsides, Sam talks for an hour straight. He remembers that the mind only absorbs as much as the butt can endure and stops.

"Wow. I didn't know I knew that many words. Can I get everyone to stand up? Don't go away; just stand up and flex your knees. Put your hands together like you are in church and praying and touch the tip of your fingers to your nose, like this. Then to the person on either side or behind you, say, 'I'm pleased to see you. My world is greater with you in it'. Now a deep cleansing breath. I'm sorry to have kept you in your seats so long. I didn't know that there is so much material. It only took me five weeks to write it all down. I'm only 31 years old and self employed, I have a full life, absolutely no family strife and I have the time to bring up my children. Oh, and it happened in less than four years. You may sit, or stand until the feeling returns to your back sides. I have a note on the prompter that says I'm almost there, just three more pages."

The applause flashes from the audience as everyone takes their seats. Sam finishes in ten minutes and calls for questions. His ladies field most of the questions, since most concern how they are dealing with the relationship. When all the questions have been exhausted, they stand and wave a farewell to the crowd, who are also on their feet in a standing ovation. The feeling this gives Sam and his family is so joyous, the emotion spills over in tears of gratitude.

"Thank you. Thank you all. You are wonderful. We have truly been blessed to be in the same world with you. Good Bye." Sam waves and follows his family off stage.

On the way back to the hotel, Sam tells them that the publisher has one more speaking engagement on for tomorrow, then they would go home.

"I told him that he'd better plan on keeping us one more day and show us New York. I for one want to see Ellis Island. My mother came through there in '58 from Germany."

When they got to their suite, after the second seminar, tables of food are set up in the living area. On the couches, are boxes, with new digital cameras and video cameras. A stack of little sweaters with, 'I (heart) NY' on them, and adult sweaters with, 'We are Family n We (heart) NY' on them. There are strollers for the children and also several stuffed bears, tigers, rabbits and stuffed animal pillows that snap closed for a toy and unsnap to use as a pillow. The publisher is going all out to make them happy. Sam wonders at the enormous interest their lives have engendered. Seems the world is getting tired of the way things are.

The limo arrives at 9 a.m. on the third day, as the family is just getting up from breakfast. When the family comes through the doors of the hotel to get in the limo, they are surprised by flashing bulbs and a plethora of garbled questions. Several of the doormen, make a barrier to keep the reporters back, but the crowd quiets when Sam holds up his hands in the East Asian prayer hands.

"Friends. I hope that I am addressing friends. The outpouring of love and the genuine curiosity that we have felt since our arrival is beyond gratitude. Our most humble hope is that what we have can be emulated among the population in a modest way." (A shouted question—tell us the secret) "Secret, I don't think it's a secret. You have to love one another and throw out jealousy and selfishness. Hey, who will mistreat a person that loves them? Love begets love. It's not a secret. Jesus told his followers, "Love one another as I have loved you". Thank you. We're off to see your city." Sam gives them another of the prayer hands in farewell.

Carmine, the driver and Luis, their guide, tell them immediately that you can't see it all in one day and that they have picked enough of the well known sites to fill up their cameras. Their first stop is Ellis Island, where Sam sees the hand written name of his mother on the register. Then to the Statue of Liberty, Grand Central Station, Site of the Twin Towers and several of the theaters and halls. Radio City, Broad way, Rockefeller Center, Time Square, the Bowery, and a trip to Manhattan. Everywhere the family goes, they take pictures with the children and themselves in every shot. Everywhere the family take their pictures; several people take pictures of them. They are celebrities already.

It is after 7 o'clock when they get back to the hotel. Sam tries to tip Carmine and Luis, but is told that they already have been taken care of by the publishing house. Sam thanks them and invites them and their families to visit South Carolina and Sam's family. He gives them his card with their address and phone numbers. The three exchange warm handshakes and man hugs.

The family orders room service. The children are worn out and ready to sleep. After eating and getting the children to bed, the adults, again soak in the large tub, together and talk about their day and how anxious they are to get back home.

"Traveling and seeing things is nice, but I like our home." Ann says.

"Yeah. I miss just putting a rack of ceramics in the oven to cook." Becca observes.

"I miss sitting all together in the family room and feeling the warmth and love from everyone. This place is too distracting." Molly sighs.

"Distracting, Oooh Molly is growing up. I know just what you mean sweetie." Jessie says.

"Oh well. Tomorrow afternoon, we'll be back where we belong. I know what we miss. It's having a place that needs us each day, like in our shops or in the bakery or pottery barn or greenhouse and in the routines that are familiar." Sam acknowledges.

"Well ya'll, I'll tell you what I miss. The third time. My period. I'm pregnant." Rachael blurts to the squeals and delight of all the rest.

"Rach, are you sure? That's four. Oh my. We are going to be a very large family!" Sam exclaims.

"Maybe even bigger. I wanted to be sure, but I've missed mine twice." Jessie bubbles.

Try to imagine five naked females in a tub of hot soapy water and one deliriously happy man; then you'd be close to realizing the joy that abounded in this revelation. The hugging and petting went on for a long time. Sam then suggests, "I think tonight, it would be appropriate to pull a couple of the queen mattresses off the beds and clear a space in the living area and pile pillows and blankets on them and spend this last night in New York together."

The ladies all bubble their agreement and exit with robes and towels in hand. Sam lays back and soaks a while longer. He is just putting on his robe, when the knock at the door alerts him to the arrival of his room service order.

"Mr. Elliott, your order is ready. The hotel manager said to tell you it is with his compliments."

Sam folds up three one hundred dollar bills and hands them to Michael, the delivery man.

"Aw, thank you Mike. How generous, please tell him we appreciate that. He and the staff have been more than wonderful. The tip, however, is for you Michael. You have made us feel really welcome."

"Thank you Mr. Elliott. Have a great evening." He says, noting the mattresses in the middle of the floor.

Sam rolls the cart into the room. There are three bottles of champagne and a bowl of Russian caviar and for Sam's pedestrian taste, Pate`, various deli crackers and a variety of fruits.

Just like a girl's sleep over they drink champagne and eat caviar and pate` on captain's wafers, getting crumbs all over. They talk and recount the last three days events until Jessie asks them for a favor.

"I think I'm pregnant, but would anyone mind if I . . . if we—ah . . . made sure? I mean if it's alright with all of you and Sam of course."

"Sure. You first. Sam, sorry honey, but all of us have gotten just too horney these last three days. Jessie needs a confirmation and the rest of us need a good screwing." Ann laughs.

"Yeah. All the talk about no family strife and let us go three days without." Molly says as she lunges for Sam's partially exposed package.

"Hold on Molly. Jessie first. I know, you're oversexed, but you are also the most pregnant." Becca laughs.

"Aw, you're right. Sorry Jessie." Molly is contrite.

The ladies, all take off their robes and pull Sam up and take off his robe. Their hands explore him. Jessie, on hands and knees, like a tigress positions herself over him. Sam reaches up and strokes her back and buttocks as she leans down and their lips lock in a hot, wet, passionate kiss.

Their love making is slow and sensuous and when climax happens, Sam feels her shudder beneath him. They lay there together for a few minutes until Sam slips out, spent. He rolls off and feels a warm, wet caress and realizes that someone is washing him with a warm, wet towel. Jessie smiles, kisses him then moves away.

The act repeats four more times before Sam literally passes out when he climaxes with Molly, who stays close to him for the night.

The morning arrives leisurely. When Sam wakes, he is covered in girl flesh. Everyone is stretching and touching and squeezing as sleep leaves them, like a pile of kittens untangling themselves.

"Oh ladies. If I could die now, I will have lived the best life of anyone on earth. Thank you for loving me."

"We love you mister. Don't think about dieing for at least another sixty or eighty years." Becca says. The rest add their confessions of love for him.

"Okay," He laughs, "but just now we need to get back home. I really miss the familiarity of our home."

"Yes. Me to. Bathe and dress before the children wake up." Jessie says.

They all soak for only a short time in the large tub. More to wake up than get clean. Soon, everyone is dressed and the children are rounded up and cleaned and dressed as well. The suitcases are packed and Sam calls the desk for assistance and room service for breakfast.

The limo arrives, to take them to the airport, at 9:30 and the farewells to the hotel staff are filled with a little emotion. A few of the staff have been especially kind and close to the family. Sam talks with the manager alone and gives him five crisp c notes and envelopes for the maids, the servers in the dining room and the behind the scenes people.

"You know Mr. Todd, this has been the best experience that I have ever had and you are primarily responsible for the whole thing. I thank you sincerely for it. The envelopes for the maids and the others are tokens for their kindness. Please pass my thanks on to them."

"Mr. Elliott, it has been our extreme pleasure to serve you and your family. I've bought your book. I'm 26 now and my wife has been reading about you. She and I are looking for an avenue to follow. Thank you Mr. Elliott for your courage and efforts."

Sam hugs him as he shakes his hand.

Carmine is at the wheel and makes good time to the private airfield.

"Carmine, I want to thank you for your kindness to us these last three days. Remember the invitation is open. You have our address; we will be happy to have you and your family visit any time. There are a couple of bungalows at Myrtle Beach that are always available. Summer vacations are a blast at the beach."

"Thank you Mr. Elli . . . Sam. You have a wonderful family, eh oh eh. I know my wife and kids would love to visit. We don't get away much." He says.

The ladies all add their thanks and goodbyes as they board the Lear Jet that is waiting for them.

The flight is shorter than he remembers and he appreciates it. The limo, at the Sumter Airport, is waiting for them. There is also a crowd of people with posters and signs that read, "Welcome Home Elliotts" and "We've Missed You" and "Sumter Loves You". The family is all smiles and waves to the people surrounding them.

"Mr. Elliott, Mrs. Ah, Ladies. The news has been filled with your trip to New York and your lecture to the assembled heads of so many Ivy League Universities. The praises and respect that those universities have placed on you, have also come to our city, for creating an atmosphere conducive to your successful life style. On behalf of the City/County council we welcome you home and wish to convey upon you the thanks of the citizens of Sumter." The mayor says, pumping Sam's hand and grinning for the photographers.

"Thank you Mr. Mayor, folks. We are definitely happy to be home. It is the one thing we talked about on our last night in the hotel. How good it will be to get home to Sumter. Mr. Mayor, friends, we're really anxious to get home. Thank you again for this wonderful, warm welcome. Good bye!" Sam tells them.

Sam ushers his family into the limo and turns one last time and waves to the crowd, gets in and closes the door.

"Do you believe it? A welcome from the whole town!" Sam exclaims.

"I am overwhelmed. I didn't expect it." Ann says.

"I know. It was frightening at first. I thought they were there to protest us, and then I read the signs." Rach adds.

"Do you think this could mean that we will be accepted by everyone and not get those looks?" Molly asks.

"I thought it's nice that they received us like that, to feel welcome in our own town." Becca adds.

"Me to. It was really nice. I hope all the rest is true as well and that we will be treated like people." Jessie offers.

The children squeal with delight when they see that they are home.

"We're home Poppa." is repeated by the children as they pile out of the limo and run to the door.

The family didn't take long to settle back into their lives. The first evening back, they decide to take a few more days to relax and unwind at home. Dinners with the family are animated. The children are talking more. The constant contact with adults is maturing them faster. Parenting isn't a part-time job and doing the job full-time is paying off in well developed young people. Tommy is always making observations.

"We had fun in New York, but I like home better." Tommy states confidently.

Molly is delighted at the precociousness of her first born. "Yes sir, we did have fun. I like home better to."

"Mom, I'm not sir, I'm Tommy!"

The following week, the family gets back to work. People are counting on them to be there. The salon is running smoothly. The woman that Ann and Jessie hired to manage is a treasure. Sherry 'Buffy' Conner is close to their age, but has been doing hair for a few more years than either of them.

Molly's and Becca's gift shop and bakery are doing even better since their trip to New York. People are coming, in response to the publicity their trip has given them.

The flower shop is also doing a brisk business. Rachael with either Ann or Jessie, are selling out of many of the exotic plants and answering questions from curious ladies.

Sam keeps the nursery, in the back of the center, active for his brood of children. The Moms come back frequently during the day to visit with their children and with their children's Dad. Sam is also thinking about the expansion that will be needed in a few months. Five infants are anticipated, six, if Molly has twins again. Life is good.

October is approaching and it is beginning to look like the month would corner the market on births. This time it is Becca, Rachael, Jessie and Ann who deliver on successive weeks during the first three weeks. October 18th, delivers Rachael and Ann as the last two for the month. Jessie has a girl on October 3rd and Becca a boy on October 8th. Molly's confinement comes at eleven o'clock, on November 11th. Armistice Day and she did it again. A boy and a girl. Peter and Elisabeth are just as perfect as all of Sam's children, that now numbered 12 and in just over four years of marriage . . .

The Baptisms are once more met with awe. Sam can't understand why, neither can anyone else, why his children accept the sacrament with so much joy that they coo and gurgle with delight and to the delight of the congregation.

"Mr. Elliott, my wife and I feel like God is really among us whenever you have children baptized. They sound as if they are with angels during the sacrament. Thank you." Mr. Osgood says. He is one of the elders of the church.

"We don't know what it is. They are usually quiet. Kind of unusual for infants. We have monitors with them that wake us for feedings, because they just coo and gurgle when they wake in the night. I guess God is giving us a break." Sam explains. "They do get to talking when they get older. My first two have already talked to a group of professors during the recent speaking tour we did."

This is a common occurrence for them. People are always a little awed by them and their children. Their enterprises are also gaining popularity and attention.

Molly and Becca produce jams and preserves that they sell in their gift shop and through several small grocers. Their brand is, 'Molly and Becca' Jams and Preserves. They are inspected by DHEC and passed as pure and organic.

Ann, Jessie and Rachael are producing a quality, organic crop of vegetables in their greenhouses, along with the exotic plants and annuals that they sell in their flower shop, vegetable market.

The pottery, ceramics and figurines are also being produced in a quality that make them highly desirable. Becca created a web site and began filling orders on-line. Even with everyone's help in producing standard pieces, orders are beginning to creep ahead of production. Becca asks to interview additional help with the pottery.

Egg and chicken production is exceeding expectations and orders are being taken for fresh eggs and fresh chicken for local consumption. Special orders for turkey and goose is rising. The fact that the product is certified as organic, but without the higher prices, didn't hurt the orders. Molly is beginning to spread herself thin. So is Rachael and Sam is putting in more hours than he would like. Hiring of additional help is becoming a priority.

The orchard is a job by itself and production wasn't able to support the canning, jam and preserves needs. Soon they realized that they would have to organize better and hire much more help Contracts for fruits, from other orchards, is going to be necessary as well. Expanding the orchards would mean more acreage. More greenhouses and another chicken house is in the works, but hiring people to handle all aspects of production, distribution and sales is their highest priority. This is the topic of their family meeting this evening, following dinner.

"Ladies, I believe it has come to the point that each of us will be the president of a segment of our operations and only oversee the enterprise. One, we have an orchard and also contract for fruit for the jam and preserves. Two, we have poultry houses for eggs and fresh chicken, turkey and geese, to serve our bakery, our use and for sale to local orders. Three, we have greenhouses for organic vegetables, for our use and for sale. Exotic plants and annual plants for sale in our flower shop. Four, we have a pottery barn, for our joy and for artistic works for sale in our gift shop and for sale on the internet. Now, let's hear some suggestions."

"Wow, I guess we've really got a job on our hands. I thought we were rich and didn't have to work. I guess it should be organized so that we are able to spend time with our children and one another. I vote Sam as President of the corporation and we take Vice President positions." Ann suggests.

"Good. Yes, I can see that." Jessie says. "I recommend Ann for VP in exotic plants and bedding plant sales and I will monitor and be VP for organic vegetables. I guess that we, each, will be responsible for organizing our section and hiring management and labor in our area."

"Someone writing this down?" Ann asks.

"I've got it honey. I don't know where I will fit in, so, I'll take recorder for now." Rachael states.

"I vote Rachael, part-time secretary and office manager with me. She will also oversee the poultry area, with Molly as backup. We will have family in charge of key positions." Sam offers.

"Molly in bakery, Becca in pottery and all of us back each other up. Oh and Becca and Molly in jams and preserves. That's taking off as well. The $26,000.00 a day from investments doesn't mean a thing." Sam adds.

They continue for a couple of hours and agree on many expansions, product lines and hiring of people. The best idea came from the youngest member.

"I think that if we hire people to do the hard work in each area that we pay them better than any other company in the business. High wages, benefits and a reasonable retirement plan will not only attract good people, but will also keep them working and loyal to their jobs. It's just a thought."

"Molly, that's great and reasonable. Where have you been hiding that mind? You think good girl." Ann praises her.

"Yes Ma'am, it does make good business sense. Remember our beginnings. 'Happy workers' and all that, become happy partners. I'm for it and with that many workers, word will get out about how well paid people work better and maybe other businesses will follow suit." Sam confirms.

"It doesn't make sense that a few have all the money, while the people who do all the work and bleeding, get barely a living wage. Put me down as for it as well." Ann injects.

"Me to," from Becca, Jessie and Rach.

"It's unanimous then. We hire and pay the best. One more thing. After ten years, they become owners of the company. We rotate someone from the workforce to the office, to oversee the operation and eventually they all own, work and run the operation. We'll get the lawyer, Mr. Wade to get it legal. I'll talk to Mr. Lauder about setting up payroll accounts and whatever we need in that area. Who will check out a group health plan?"

"I'll get that. I know a few people who I trust in that area." Rachael offers.

The corporation is growing and gaining a reputation for fairness and quality in product and employee strength and loyalty. The end of their fifth year boasts the expansion of production, acreage, employees and sales. Twenty acres are bought to the west of the estate and twenty-four acres to the east of the estate. Warehouses and production plants are built.

The canning plant employs twenty five people in producing the jams and preserves and other canned fruits. The product is packaged and shipped in the corporation's trucks to local stores and around the state.

The fresh and frozen vegetables are cleaned and packaged or frozen and also shipped to local stores. There are twenty vegetable greenhouses and the entire product is organic. The fresh/frozen plant employs another twenty-five people. An orchard crew, of six, keeps the orchard clean and free from disease and harvests the fresh fruits. The manager, also contracts with other orchards for certified organic fruits.

The bakery took on a new look in a modern plant. It produces breads, rolls, sweet breads, cakes, cookies, and specialty products for Christmas. Molly's management of the plant brings many compliments and praises for her loving treatment of the sixty people involved.

The ceramics operation is split into two areas, mostly for safety. The artistic floor, produces the green-ware and unglazed figurines. Becca has eight workers—no, not workers, artists on the artistic floor. The firing floor is in a separate area and has eight people running fifteen ovens in a five oven a day rotation. The kilns produce pots for their exotic plants and for their use and decorative pots for sale. Figurines in various styles, both glazed and unglazed are sold through the gift shop, on-line and in specialty shops in Columbia, Florence and Charleston. Sam's chess sets are hot sellers, much to his surprise.

The extra poultry houses require additional people and produces, not only eggs, but fresh chicken, turkey, goose and Cornish hens. Twenty workers and a manager keeps everything running smoothly. DHEC passes the production plant with flying colors, to the credit of Rachael, who has set her own sanitation criteria and inspection.

One innovation is the associate's cafeteria. Sam hired a chef and five souse chefs to cook, breakfast, lunch and a dinner, plus provide healthy snacks. An associate can eat a meal and get snacks at no charge. Sam gives the chef and his crew a venue on the local economy to ply their craft in a gourmet restaurant. Sam contracts with the chef for him to own it in five years. The chef, Raymond adds a codicil to the contract that promises that the cafeteria will always have the best chefs, after he opens his restaurant.

The thinking behind the family's cafeteria idea is innovative in itself. They had so much money from investments they didn't need to get any richer from their enterprises, so they put it back in the worker's welfare and customer good will. Feeding workers healthier also has a side benefit of a healthy worker.

The salon is booming with six operators and the manager. The gift shop has four employees and a manager, the flower shop and exotic plant store have four employees and Ann, or Jessie rotated in to answer questions and manage. They also enrolled the four workers in the Master Gardener course with Clemson extension. The shop paid the tuition. Rachael helps out with the four workers in the vegetable market. The bakery store has six people to keep the store open from 8 am to 8 pm.

The family is strong and the love between them is apparent to everyone they meet. Their children are all walking and talking. The eldest, Tommy, and Carly are seven and the youngest, Jessie's Wyatt and Rach's William, are five—almost. December will bring four birthdays along with Christmas.

Sam is happier than anyone had a right to be. Thirty-six years old, with five women who love him and whom he loves. Twelve children, who thought their dad is the greatest and more money than he could spend in a hundred years. President of a highly successful corporation with over two hundred and seventy people working at high pay and benefits and he would be embarrassed to say it—who respect him.

Sam's ladies are also held in high esteem by everyone in the corporation and by customers who frequent all of their retail stores and by the workers and families. The women plan and organize four annual company gatherings. Two in the summer as company picnics, one at Christmas and one the week before school starts. During the events, bonuses are paid to all employees. The bonus for one summer picnic was the new 42" LED 3-D televisions to each worker and a check for $500. Before school starts, everyone got a check for school clothes and supplies. The family also donates a ton of supplies to the local schools.

Sam is getting a gift this year as well. Molly reported that she is pregnant again. Three months later, Becca tells the family that she is having another baby. Sam starts thinking about expanding the estate to accommodate his growing family. Then Jessie, Rachael and Ann announce their coming events.

The next six children are spread out over seven months, with the first two, yes, from Molly on June 27, Sam's birthday. Then September 2 for Becca, November 30, brought Jessie and Rachael, and Ann delivers on January 12.

Michael and Sybil are Molly's third set of twins. Jamie is Becca's little girl. Wyatt and Edward are Jessie and Rachael's. Carrie is delivered by Ann. That brought the number of children to 18, and the family to 24.

The corporation's business is being handled by managers and only two mornings a week are set aside for Sam and the ladies to meet around a board table and make plans, with the help and input of the managers. Sam's minute manager tactic works and gets the job done and lets the people take all the credit. This to, made for content workers. Though, now after seven years of operation, they are getting to be more like friends. The businesses are doing so well, that there is always a very large surplus of cash, even after bonuses. The cash is placed into another investment account and would soon be producing more cash.

The success is attributed to the manner in which the corporate family treats the people doing the work. The demand for the corporations product is attributed to the pure, no additives guarantee demanded by the family.

In their eighth year, the company goes public and gets their symbol on the big board at the NY stock exchange. The IP is only $10. on opening, by the end of the day it had gone to $110.00 and would probably have gone up more if the market had stayed open a while longer. The next morning, it opens at $145.00 and the family begin to sell their holdings, to the workers first. They are close to $900 million and still own more than 51% of the corporation.

"My darlings, I don't know how to get out of this. We have more money than we will ever need. I would like us to be free of all the responsibility and build an estate for us that is secluded and will allow us the freedom to live fully. Our own lake, forest and all the amenities. We should be able to spend time planning trips around the world and see something before we get old. I suggest that the remainder of the stock be divided among the workers and managers—free and clear. This is what I would like, but it's your lives and our children's lives to, so let's have a discussion. Maybe ya'll want something different."

They are almost as one in their protest.

"Sam, Darling, we'd like to have more family time to. Just spend our time with one another and with our children!" Ann exclaims.

"Yes, Darling. It is like a dream that we have had for ever." Jessie says.

"I love the idea. I don't know how we got so wrapped up in business." Becca observes.

"Yeah, Sam. We can spend more time making more babies. I'm for that!" Molly exclaims. Everyone is amused by her remark.

"Honey, Molly said it all. We have a lot of work to do now. Planning a new estate . . . . Any ideas?" Rachael asks.

It takes nearly a year and they finally are free of the business. After taxes, they share nearly a billion dollars. The new estate is a hundred acres in the southern part of South Carolina. They have everything that would make life good, including full-time maids, nannies, cooks, yard help and a secretary to keep them up on appointments and dates. They pay very good wages and benefits and the most modern equipment. It is a little different with only twelve people working for them, after the plants and the over three hundred people and families.

The estate has a twenty acre spring fed lake, surrounded on two sides with Maple and Oaks and close to the water, Paper Birch. Tall poplars surrounds two tennis courts near the mansion. Attached to the house is an Olympic pool, almost like their previous home. A well equipped gym, that is the top leg of the pool building, is attached to the house. A very large greenhouse is set up to produce flowers and some vegetables for the house. They agree early, not to expand these endeavors. A studio surrounded by glass, is set up to do ceramics and for painting and other arts. For the joy of the art. They have a large library and a music room. No one played any instruments, but decided that they would learn. The sleeping arrangements are similar to their previous home, only larger and many more rooms.

They all sleep together more than they did before. Sam loves it. He says that he is beginning to feel the pressure of age already at 38 and wants to enjoy the love before he gets too old.

The ladies get together and with a little, tongue in cheek, decide to try to give him more than he can imagine.

"Honey, would you make love to me early tonight? It's not my turn, but I really need some love before your regular night lover." Jessie asks.

"If it's alright with everyone." Sam replies, "I'm up for it, ha, ha."

It's eight o'clock and Jessie takes Sam by the hand and pulls him up.

"I'm ready Darling." Jessie purrs.

Sam follows her to the Master bedroom. This never gets old, he thinks, as he watches her seductive moves.

"Whew! Jessie you are so sexy."

She turns and begins by pulling his shirt over his head, but stops when his arms are up and only his lips and his chin show. She kisses him, pressing herself to him.

"Mmm!" he moans and she pulls the shirt off. He reaches her blouse and unbuttons it, exposing a braless pair of gorgeous breasts. He bends his head and suckles each nipple until they become erect.

"I love you so much. You make sex so natural and satisfying. I wish I could kiss you and love you all over, all at once." Sam tells her.

"I love you. I cheated. I was only supposed to get one, ha, ha. Becca will be here tonight. We've set it up to give you two a night, until you tell us to stop. What do you think?"

"My Darling, my love, if I ever get tired of sex with the five of you, promise that you'll close the lid on the coffin, because I'll be dead. I could do this five times a day, every day, until I die. You all are so soul-satisfying and you've made me immortal with the most beautiful children a man could want." Sam says with a tear running down his cheek.

Jessie holds his face in her hands and kisses his lips and forehead and the tear on his cheek.

"You must know how much we all love you. Now, let's soak in the hot water a while, until Becca gets here."

Jessie fills the tub and they cuddle and soak up the heat. It is ten o'clock and Becca comes into the bedroom.

"Okay Jessie, my turn. I hope you haven't used him up."

"We're in the tub, come on in and we'll change places." Jessie calls back.

Sam enjoys another wonderful round of sex with his half Korean darling. He really loves her full lips and rounded hips and thighs.

Becca was the first to orally stimulate him and it was unexpected and appreciated. He suspected that the ladies got together and talked, because they each included it often as a warm up.

True to what Jessie had told him, every night, he is having sex with two, over the course of four to five hours. No, he wasn't getting tired of it and it became a regular happening.

Then one evening, as the six of them gathered, in the family room, the talk turned to bringing new blood into the family.

"Sam, we've talked among ourselves about bringing some new sisters into our family. We've agreed that we can accept another two sisters, if you think you can accept it. We are only thinking that your private area may like more attention." Ann says with the nods from the rest.

"Private area! My god woman, if I get any more traffic there, I'm gonna have to open a Star Bucks."

They burst out in laughter. Molly rolls on the floor, with tears in her eyes and Jessie curls up on the couch with both hands covering her mouth. Ann, Rachael and Becca are also overcome with laughter.

"Any way, I'm not young any more. There probably aren't many, if any, women out there that are still searching for a mate. Particularly ones that haven't had failed relationships and bring their baggage to the family and any that are there, are probably under 25. I can't see anyone that young wanting to be with a guy who is thirteen years older. I don't know." Sam explains, shaking his head. "I mean, I'm really comfortable with our life as it is. You all aren't disappointed, are you?"

"Darling, we couldn't be happier. We are just thinking that you might want something new. You are all we will ever need or want." Jessie says.

"My loves, my Darlings, I am so happy and fulfilled that I am constantly surprised that I don't explode with all the love I have built up inside of me."

This is the first and only time that additions in the form of more adults is ever brought up. Their love is tangible. It is something they could hold on to and cherish.

Chapter 9

LET'S ENJOY LIFE

Life moves on at a leisurely pace for the next five years. They all are proficient in martial arts. Sam found an Aikido master in Charleston, who was the brother of Sam's Air Force roommate fifteen years earlier in California. Master Suinaka commended Sam on the training he has given his ladies.

Sam learns the piano and saxophone; Ann learns to play the clarinet and piccolo. Rachael plays the flute; Jessie plays the sax; Becca plays the cello and Molly plays the harp and flute. The children are each learning instruments and will be part of the family's orchestra. The music room turned out to be another good idea.

The children are old enough to take a little more responsibility for their selves. The parents are training them to be fully functioning people. Tommy and Carly are going on fourteen and accepted their role as the eldest brother and sister. Cathy, Raina, Matt and Ryan looked up to them, even though they are within a month or two of one another. Sam is so proud, but understands the value of close parenting. At 42, he is beginning to worry about being there, to guide his progeny, to and through college. He brought up his thought at an evening family gathering.

"I was thinking—well, not just today, but for some time. My eldest child is 14 and my youngest is 8. When I'm 46, they will be 18 and 12. I hope I will be here when the eldest are in or through college. I'll be 54 or 55 when the youngest finish college. I'm getting old, my loves."

"We all are, but for me, I don't feel it at all. I'm 35, yeah, the youngest, but I still feel like 25. We'll be here a long, long time. I am happy and I love you more and more every day. I love my sisters so much and I believe that our love will keep us feeling young. Don't worry Darling." Molly says.

"Sam, I think we need to take some big vacations and see some of this world. I hate to be the one to say it, but I'm glad we all decided to stop at three pregnancies. I trust Sarah and Annie with the children and Mary, Brenda and Sue will help and take care of the house. We need to get away and let the world know how much we love one another." Rachael states as a matter of fact.

"I agree. We have people that are very good and we need close time with each other and away from the safety of our home. I believe it will strengthen us." Ann offers.

"It's been, what, fifteen, sixteen years. It's time. I'd like to take us all to Korea and Thailand. I know that having multiple wives is an accepted thing there and we should feel at home, plus the scenery is great." Becca explains.

"I'm ready to travel. I'm a country girl and never traveled much growing up. Just thinking about traveling with ya'll gives me goose bumps. I love everyone so much and seeing us in a foreign country, gets me all misty." Jessie tells them.

"It's a go then. We'll check our passports and I'll call a travel agent to set up a real vacation, first class all the way. We've got luggage shopping to do and easy care clothes, comfortable clothes and shoes. Get our cell phones tuned for overseas and to be able to call home and talk with the kids. We've got a few things to do. Someone has to talk to the staff. Don't want to leave them in the dark. It's after 9. I'm kinda ready for bed." Sam expounds.

"How about we all get to your bed tonight? I'm for a hot soak in the tub, with lots of touchy, feely and lots of snuggling." Ann offers.

"Yeah, include me." Molly exclaims.

Becca, Rach and Jessie also chime in.

It's kinda difficult for six lovers to hug together and walk, but they all head for the Master bedroom and the hot bath.

Sleep overtakes them after midnight, satisfied and happy. Sam's smile lasts through falling asleep, sandwiched between warm female bodies.

The flight is very long, but comfortable—first class all the way. The stop over at Narita, in Tokyo is overly long, but their arrival in Seoul is a welcome stop.

They are met by the Tour Company and a limo takes them to the Ritz-Carlton hotel, in the Gangnam-gu section of Seoul. Becca is all smiles. She has been to Korea a few times with her mother before she went to beauty school and it is a prime topic for her, along with photos. Everyone is anxious to see all that can be seen.

The hotel manager and staff greet them with open affection and warmth. The family's arrangement is pleasing to the Korean people. Sam receives many handshakes and a profusion of bows.

They are led to their suite and are surprised and pleased to see a large sitting room and a single large bedroom with a bed that is over ten feet across, with ten or more big fluffy pillows and piles of those thick Korean quilts.

"Oh my, this is wonderful Sam. We'll spend all our time together here." Becca says.

"I know, did anyone see the bath?" Jessie asks.

They crowd the bathroom and are again amazed. There is a bath that is almost a small pond, with Jacuzzi jets all around and a separate shower enclosure with multiple shower heads.

Sam tips the people that brought their luggage and the ladies from room service, who brought baskets of fruits, drinks and a cart with several covered trays.

"Who ordered room service already?" Sam calls out.

"Sir, this is gift from manager and staff to welcome—family." The young lady tells him.

"Oh my; thank you. Please tell the manager that we very much appreciate his kindness and the staffs'. Thank you."

The young lady bows and turns to leave. Two young men are at the doors and close them as they back out.

"Is anyone hungry? I'm sweaty and tired. I'm glad we got here near night time."

"Honey, I have the bath running and Becca, Ann, Molly and Rach are unpacking. We'll eat a little, then bathe and get some sleep. I feel real dreamy tired myself." Jessie tells him.

Soon, all are lounging in the sitting room and nibbling on some of the delicacies, then they soak in the tub, with the Jacuzzi jets massaging them, for forty or fifty minutes. They all dry one another and flop on the big bed, covering themselves with the big quilts. Soon, after much petting and kissing and caressing one another, they sleep.

The next morning, after a fruit filled breakfast, in the room, they decide to see the Changdeokgung palace. It is originally built in 1405 as a secondary palace, but when the Gyeongbokgung palace, Seoul's principle palace is destroyed by the Japanese in the 1590s, it became the primary palace. All the Joseon palaces have mountains behind them and a stream in front, like good pungsu or feng shui. You can feel the way it must have been, a bustling beehive buzzing around the king. Gossip, intrigue and whisperings can still be heard and behind the palace, to the right, a dense woodland. Suddenly you come across a serene glade, this is the highlight. Biwon (Huwon), the Secret Garden. Pavilions at the edge of a square lily pond and a two storey library, where Joseon kings relaxed, studied and wrote poems.

Becca is happy showing her family the sights of her mother's country.

"My mom took me here several years ago. The guided tour is a lot longer, but you have to listen to the broken English script. I'm just showing the most interesting parts. We can go to lunch at the Bonjuk. They have the best ginseng chicken and rice porridge."

"That sounds good. I love it. Everyone is giving us such a warm welcome, even the people who are tourists." Rachael remarks.

"They can see that we are together and it is an accepted lifestyle here." Becca explains. "After lunch, how does everyone feel about going to the Theater? There is a show starting at 2 o'clock at the Kayagum Theatre. It is traditional Korean music and dance and a Western/Asian cabaret revue."

Everyone agrees that they would love to see some real Korean theater.

"I can hardly wait to show everyone Bangkok and my home." Ann says.

They tour several museums and art centers in and around Seoul and take a river trip on the Han River ferry. The tour begins at the Yeouido pier and includes a BBQ buffet and live music.

On the fifth day, the ladies get a break and go to the Spa Lei, for women only. The spa is a luxurious, immaculate place with saunas and saltwater pools, ginseng, mineral and rose baths. There is a restaurant and café patio. Their staff are all accustomed to handling foreign visitors.

"Sam, you wouldn't believe it. There were a hundred women, mostly naked, bathing and soaking in mineral baths and the food at the café is really great." Molly bubbles.

"I'm glad you all had a good day. You are all beautiful and fresh. I went to the sauna in the hotel and relaxed in a eucalyptus steam bath. What shall we do our last evening here? The plane leaves at 9 A.M."

"Can we just have room service and the way we did in New York and just pile together in the bed?" Rachael suggests.

"Good for me, Darling." Sam concurs.

Everyone agrees that lounging together on their last night is just what they all need.

After eating, they soak in the tub for a while and then sit on the mattresses in their thick robes and talk about their week.

"I'm happy that we got to go to that Chongdong Theater. The Gayageum performers are outstanding and the Pansori soloist and the fan dancers really entertained. The Nanta Theater was a real treat. Circus and magic and the kitchen comedy was unbelievable." Sam offers.

"Sounds like you enjoyed yourself. What did you think of the Namdaemun Market? You bought a bunch of things." Becca asks.

"Yes. It was great. I found a coin place and got some really good buys. The brass candle holders are something I'd been looking for, for a long time. The swords and daggers are well made and will look good as wall decorations around our bar. That Namsangol Hanok Village was very educational as well. I'm glad we had the cameras and video stuff with us. The kids will go nuts, when they see them. Some of those buildings are in some American Kung Fu films."

While they exchange their individual experiences of the last week, Molly stacks pillows behind Sam. Then she sits down behind him and leans back against the pillows, putting her arms around him, she pulls him back to lean against her.

"Well, what's this? A woman pillow for the old man." Sam laughs.

"Hey girl, whatja doin'? No fair." Jessie says.

"I thought of it and I just felt a little lonely. We can share, huh, Sam. You like it, don't you?" Molly asks.

"Hmmm! It's nice. I'm game for some closeness from you and from everyone."

"It's okay Molly. I'm just a little jealous that you thought of it first. No doubt about your love for the man." Ann says.

Sam feels a flush of love for this woman. Molly isn't afraid to voice her love all the time. Rach, Jessie, Becca and Ann are all, so very dear to him and just now, their love is like a warm flow that engulfs him.

They enjoy the evening in quiet love making and warm, tender kisses. Soon, each of them drifts off to sleep. Morning comes with a wake up call at six thirty. They have to be at the airport by seven thirty, only one hour away.

Luckily, they had packed earlier last night and had their travel clothes laid out. They are in the lobby at seven and the limo has just pulled up to take them to the airport.

The manager and several of the staff that have cared for them, lined up and bowed their respect for the family. Sam, of course, presents the manager with envelopes for the staff and special thanks for his service.

"Mr. Han. Thanks to you and your staff. Our stay will be remembered for a long time. Please convey our thanks to your people."

"You are most gracious Sir. It is hoped that you will return for a visit again."

The ride to the airport is uneventful. Becca got a little misty, since none of her mother's relatives are able to be there, because of their harvests up north. Still, the excitement is building for Ann, who had been on the phone earlier, alerting her cousins of their expected arrival in Bangkok.

The Bangkok airport is enormous. They built this new facility a few miles from the old airport, as Sam remembers. They are met by two of Ann's cousins, who brought their 12 passenger van.

"Sawahdee krup. Sabai dee mai? (Good day 'respectful' greeting). Are you well?" Ann and Sam greet them and Ann introduces Rachael, Becca, Jessie and Molly.

The smiles are bright and sincere. Sam is fluent in Thai and understands that they thought Ann has a very good arrangement.

The trip to Nakhorn Prathom took over an hour. Sam remembered when it didn't take that long. The whole area is built up and the traffic that once had been two lanes is four lanes in each direction and the breakdown lane and shoulder are also used, in both directions.

Ann's mother is beside herself. She goes around Thai custom and hugs Sam and kisses him on his cheek. Sam knows that she is happy that Ann is going to bring the babies next time. She acknowledges each of the women with sincere affection. Sam knows, 'Gaulie', is Thai for 'Korean' and that she is referring to Becca. She hugs her longer and when she steps back, Becca puts her hands together and touches the tip of her nose, in a highly respectful Thai greeting. Mother is almost in tears in appreciation.

Ann visits with her mother, after sending her cousins to the store, a Circle K, that is a lot like Wal-Mart. Sam and Jessie go with them and Becca, Rachael and Molly keep Ann company.

Sam and Jessie pick up tons of meat, crackers, cheeses, fruits and all the things that would make a good family reunion. They also get several cases of wine, champagne and some real American Whiskey and Vodka. It is quite a load when they load it into the van. At the checkout, Sam thinks about soft drinks and ice. Lucky, because mother's fridge only has a very small amount of ice. He had to get a couple of coolers to.

Ann is ecstatic when they return and start unloading. The amount and quality of the treats testified to Ann's wealth and is a large source of pride for her mother. The women went to work and start preparing mouthwatering treats for the expected crowd of family that would be here at sundown.

Sam took the opportunity to take a nap. It is only, just past 3, but he is worn out.

"Anyone object to me crashing for a couple hours?" Sam asks.

Mother's eyes widened and she smiles ear to ear as the women go to Sam and hug and kiss him and offer that he should get a rest.

Sam wakes at 5:30 to laughter the tinkling of glasses and the unmistakable sound of Thai music. He stretches and feels great. The bathroom is typical Thai design and he scoops a bowl of water from the large clay crock and pours it over his head. He dries himself and changes into a male sarong, white shirt and sandals. When he comes out into the living area, there is a bustle of activity. His ladies are doing traditional Thai dancing with Ann and some of her female cousins, who have come early to help. From the talk that he hears, all of his ladies are picking up words and phrases in Thai. Mother is beaming, as she sits in a place of honor and claps as she keeps time to the music. She motions Sam to come and sit with her. He smiles and begins to sing in Thai and do a parody of the dancing that the ladies are doing, to her great amusement.

Ann and Molly leave the dancers to tell him that all the food is prepared and they expect people to arrive soon. The three sit with Ann's mother to enjoy the dancing. Jessie, Becca and Rachael aren't out of place with Ann's cousins. The young women move through intricate movements with fingers curled back as thumb and first finger touch.

People start arriving in fives and sixes and soon the area is packed. There are introductions and Ann has name tags in English on each of her cousins and in Thai on Sam and the four ladies. Ann does a lot of translating back and forth, but soon, Sam notices that Molly and Becca have started talking with some of the young women, without an interpreter. Jessie and Rachael are also making themselves understood and there is much laughter.

Challat, a male cousin, and 'Joe', stayed close to Sam. Each of them spoke a little English and with Sam's Thai, they got on well. Sam wasn't surprised that he remembers it so well, even to reading the labels and signs. The whiskey and vodka is appreciated by the men. The ladies sip champagne and eat little crackers with expensive caviar.

The food is outstanding. Soon there is a karaoke machine going and there is singing and dancing until nearly

3 AM. The crowd grew and diminished often during the festivities, as cousins and neighbors came and went.

Sam crashed after Joe and Challat bid their farewell. He didn't even notice the crowd of bodies around him, until almost noon. His ladies have all pulled mattresses and blankets off of beds and placed them around his mattress and curled up near him.

"Oh man, I slept good. Anyone awake yet?" He asks as he stretches and reaches a hand out to pet a nearby bootie.

"Mmmm! Yes, barely. Oh goodness I feel wonderful. Hey, girls! It's time to get up and I'm hungry." Jessie says.

"Ohhh! Me to. Sam are you awake?" Molly asks.

"Not so loud. I must have had too much champagne. My head is about to explode." Becca groans.

"So my darlings what's on for today? Sight seeing, or lounge around a bit." Sam offers.

"Lounge around!" Is the chorused reply.

"Ann. How about you?"

"Sam, I'm with my sisters. Lets just lounge around today and plan for tomorrow."

"Okay. I'm for sleeping in to. Becca, take a drink of water and a drink of champagne. It'll get rid of the headache faster than aspirin." Sam tells her.

"I'm going to get some of the finger foods and soft drinks for us to nibble on. Come on Becca, I'll help you with the headache." Molly offers.

They do just that, all morning long. Doze, pet their man, receive his touch and nibble on the leftovers. Ann's mom is sleeping in as well and around two o'clock, Ann takes her some food and hot tea.

Ann, Jessie, Becca, Rach and Molly pull Sam into the bath room and they pour water over one another, from the large, clay, water pots. The water is especially cold, due to the evaporation of the sweat on the outside of the pots. The air temperature is around 88 degrees F, but the water is around 65 degrees and it feels good.

The squeals and laughter from the women is a joyful caress to Sam's ears and warms his heart. These five women, that fate put together with him are building a new way of life, or reviving an ancient way of life that is set forth in the Old Testament writings. It said, "Marry and multiply". No where does it say marry one and multiply and why would God put more women than men in the world, if he only wanted you to pair with one? This question has been on Sam's mind a long time and at every turn, it looks like God is saying okay, you've figured it out, go with it and Sam is going with it. They have written about their life, given lectures and met with some real highbrows about their corporate union. Now, it is flooding his mind again. Did he miss something? Sam's reverie is interrupted.

"Sam, hold me, I'm cold." Molly says. Sam puts his arms around her and hugs her tight.

Then, like a ballroom dance, Jessie taps Molly on the shoulder and 'cuts in'. Thus it goes as each take their turn hugging and being hugged by the man they all love.

Fresh and dressed in light, summer clothes, they lounge around and wait on Ann's mom. Sam doesn't know how they did it, but all of them are becoming fluent in Thai and hold conversations with Ann's mom. Yai, as the women begin calling her, is almost bubbling with happiness. Sam can see it in her face and eyes. She's no longer the hobbling 74 year old lady with painful arthritis and dim outlook. She looks at Sam often with a warm loving gaze that he understands is her thank you for giving her daughter a good life.

"Ladies, I had a thought. Let's hire a limo and go shopping in the morning. Looking around, I think we could upgrade this place a bit and make Mom more comfortable and ourselves as well."

"That's a great idea Sam. Ann, ask your mom if she would like to go shopping with us and ask her if there is something that she would really like to have." Jessie says.

Ann talked with her mom and came out with a broad grin.

"She said that the only thing she really wanted is for us to stay here a couple of years, with her grandchildren."

"Oh my goodness. She's such a cutie, Ann. We ought to try to get her to come with us for a while. It's not like money is a problem." Rachael offers.

"That would be great. It would surely eliminate Ann's worrying about her." Sam says.

Ann is on the phone and gives them the news.

"The limo will be here at nine in the morning and we can have it all day for less than a thousand baht. Well, 900 baht exactly, or $45.00."

"Wow, that's good. Does Mom want to go?" Sam asks.

"No, she said she would like to sleep in and then enjoy the gifts that we brought." Ann tells them.

The next morning, everyone is ready early and eager to shop. Even Sam is anxious to see what treasures he can find to add some comfort to the home.

The limo arrives and Sam and the ladies pile in. Ann tells the driver where to go for their shopping trip. Rachael asks if there are reasonable places to purchase air conditioning. Everyone agrees that a few window units would be welcome. They talk up a storm, all the way there and come up with a number of things that would make life more palatable.

Beds and mattresses are high on the list. New sheets and pillows and some of those 9' x 12' area rugs to put by the beds and throw rugs for the bath. Molly suggests canned foods and an electric can opener. Sam offers that the canned foods should be from European, American or Australian sources, where canning is regulated by health departments.

"Good idea Molly. Mom doesn't eat right most of the time because fresh food is hard to keep. Canned food should offer her better nutrition." Rachael said. Her nurses training showing.

"Thank you Rachael, Molly. You're both right. I don't know why I never thought of it before. She could have had a much healthier life if . . ." Ann says.

"Don't, if only, my love. I didn't think of it either. Besides, there's no proof that she would have eaten better. She's happy and healthy now, we just have to make sure she stays with it." Sam consoles her. "When we get back home, we should also think about all of our parents and do whatever we can to make their lives better."

"Sam, I'm feeling really stupid, just now. I'm a nurse and I never even thought about how my mother lives, until just now. I see it all clearly now. My God, you saw it as something we all should have seen. I love you mister." Rachael said.

"Me to. I never thought about it, and my mom is Asian and probably thinks the same way as Yai!" Becca exclaims.

"Okay my darlings. We will pay closer attention, when we get back. How about for now, we try to enjoy the shopping and we can also be thinking about some of the same things that are missing from our parents lives. I love all of you and I certainly love the people responsible for the wonderful women you are. Just a little more upbeat for the rest of the day."

"Sam always sees through the BS and gets us back on track. There's the first store I thought we could shop." Ann observes.

The store is an Australian company. They have everything. Sam remembers a place in Charlotte, North Carolina that had acres of merchandise of all kinds. Furniture, linens, towels, pots, pans, vacuums, sewing machines, TVs, dinnerware, glasses, appliances and so much more. This one is similar, and includes another 40,000 square feet of hot tubs and above ground pools. When they started out, Sam thought it would be several stores, but this store had everything they were looking for and then some. They bought bed frames and mattresses, five Queens, the space foam kind, three 28,000 BTU window air conditioners, sheets, pillows, rugs, new pots and pans and a 52" LCD TV. The last item they looked at, is a joint agreement, from all of them . . . a 35' oblong, above ground pool, with an automatic awning and a 35' x 12' deck. All their big purchases would be delivered the next day along with a crew to install the pool and deck and an electrician to put in the window Air Conditioners. Sam is surprised that the whole thing only comes to a little over $7,400.00. He thought that, back home this would have cost over 12 thousand.

"Sam, my Mom is going to go crazy when she sees all the stuff we bought. She won't use the air conditioners. She'll say the electricity is too much. I'll tell her that we will pay the electricity a few years ahead and hope. The pool will be used by everyone in the family. I'll have to tell my cousin to keep the water clean. I hope he knows about pool chemicals. That Australian salesman saved us some heartache."

"Yeah. I would have never of thought of where to get the water for the pool. I just assumed we would fill it from the house." Sam said.

"It would have taken weeks to fill that pool from the house water pipes. I'm glad he handled the whole thing. His crew will be out in the morning to set up the pool and deck, then the tanker will come with the water. We should be able to baptize it by the weekend. Ohhh! Tomorrow is going to be busy."

The limo deposits them at Yai's gate and they unload the soft goods that they purchased and the groceries. Sam unloads the LCD set. He remembers when a TV half this size weighed 80 to 100 pounds. This monster set, only weighs about 20 pounds.

Mother's eyes are all wide open as the women and Sam carry the bags and boxes into the house. Ann and her are talking a mile a minute with sudden bursts of, 'Dhai Ankuan, Ta mai?' Ankuan is Ann's Thai name. Mom is definitely happy with the treasures.

"Ann, did you tell her about the pool?" Sam asks.

"Not yet. I'll slip it in later, when she calms down a little. Becca, Molly, will you help me with dinner? Dinner at 7, okay?"

Sam, Jessie, Rach all agree and set to unpacking their treasures. Dinner is wonderful and enjoyed by all. They got lucky and didn't have a mob of family visiting tonight. Sam set up the TV and a DVD hook up and they lounged around watching a Thai movie with English subtitles. His women are really picking up on the language and it has only been three and a half days.

The delivery truck is at Mom's gate at 6:30 AM. The electrician made short work of adding power lines to the windows that would get the AC units. The pool and deck crew is great and get right to setting up the pool and deck. They finish as the tanker truck pulls in. After the pool is filled, the crew sets up the pump and filters. It is almost lunch time and Sam hands out several 'red notes' 100 baht notes to each of the people in each crew and the tanker guys. Yai saw Sam handing out the money and her smile is ear to ear. Ann tells him that she is proud that her daughter and husband are rich enough to pay very well.

The pool is ready the next morning and Sam and the women decide to go for a water walk and splash a bit before breakfast. The automatic shade rolls over the pool quickly and quietly and blocks the harshest of the Thai summer sun. Summer is earlier here since it is closer to the equator. They have been in the pool for only a few minutes and Yai comes out, dressed in a 1920's bathing suit.

"Oh wow! Hey Ann, think we should look for an up to date suit, for Mom?" Rach asks.

"Good idea Rach." Ann says. She talks with her mom a bit and there are smiles.

"She says she hasn't been swimming in fifty years. She loves the pool."

They splash and play for an hour or so and then Sam and his ladies go to wash and dress. Ann and her mom are taking them to Ayutthaya, the ancient capitol city.

The drive to the ruins is filled with wonder and ooohs and aaaahs!

Ayutthaya was the political and trade capitol of Siam between the 14th and 18th centuries and maintained warm diplomatic ties with the French court as well as Portuguese, Spanish, Dutch, Persians and East Asian countries. Their influence is reflected in the architectural style at the Bang Pa-In Palace as well as temples located inside the city moat.

The ruins maintain a revered feel, as you try to imagine what might have been the original, before the Burmese ransacked and burned the city to the ground.

They tour the Wat Maha That. The temple is over 600 years old and was the heart and soul of Ayutthaya people, before the Burmese burned and totally destroyed it. The Wat na Phra Mane remains in perfect condition, as it was used as the Burmese military headquarters.

Ann and Yai do a running commentary of the sights that they are seeing, almost like a tour guide. Later they have lunch at an outdoor buffet that is set up for European tastes.

After lunch, they went to Wat Lokayasutharam, whose origins are lost in time. The temple surrounds a large reclining Buddha image, in the style of the early Ayutthaya period.

A short river cruise and they return to their limo for the ride home. Everyone is worn out, but happy and ready for some family time in the evening.

When they pulled up in front of Yai's gate, Sam pays the driver, double his rate and thanks him for his service. The women go through the gate and are standing, like deer caught in headlights, mouths open.

Tables are set up with bowls and platters and steaming pots of Thai foods. Sangob, Chunjai, and Praiyom, three of Ann's cousins have prepared the meal for them. Yai gives and receives the traditional 'wai', a formal greeting done with hands together like prayer hands and the tip of the index fingers touching the tip of their noses.

"How wonderful. Ann please tell them how much we appreciate this, and ask if they can join us with their husbands. We can have a smaller family gathering tonight." Jessie says.

"Sorry, Jessie. It is a gift to us. I will tell them how much we appreciate their kindness. They will do the 'wai' to you also. Respect would be for you to do the same to them. They will cherish that, for years, in their memories."

The cousins did as Ann said they would and Sam and the ladies did their formal goodbye and added variations of, Khup Khun Mahk Kah. Which is Thai for Thank You Much Ma'am, but a man would say Krup instead of Kah, so the word is more like a formal acknowledgement of the person rather than Sir or Ma'am.

Jessie, Rach, Becca and Molly enjoy the new tastes and textures of authentic Thai food. Sam is kind of used to the tastes. He particularly likes the Panang Curry. It is something he likes to make at home, with extra coconut milk added at the end of cooking to sweeten the spicy Panang curry paste.

"We should throw a family gathering again. Maybe a pool party. Ann, you could get Challat to agree to keeping the pool up. I'll spring it on him to." Sam suggests.

"Darling that would be great." Ann agrees.

"I'm starting to get the hang of the language and I like Sangob, Chun and Prai. Just like an extension of our sisterhood." Rachael says.

"I like it. We should get some extra swimwear tomorrow morning, as gifts for them and those robes like we have . . . oh did we bring enough? Anyway, what do you think, shopping in the morning?" Molly offers.

"Good idea Molly. We should have thought of it when we are out before." Jessie says.

"I'm for it. Sam, do you want to go?" Ann asks.

"You'll be okay together. I'd like to think some things through, if you all wouldn't mind. You should think about pool toys, maybe ribs and we can use that big hibachi to barbecue and . . . oh man. We better make a list. Really, what about an American barbecue with ribs, potato salad and corn. Maybe some melons? I'm a little excited now. Beer. Is there enough left?"

"Sam, we'll handle it. Sisters, lets get a list. I'll call the guy with the limo for 9 AM. Okay?" Ann says.

"I'm down for that honey." Becca offers.

"Me to." Molly confirms.

Sam sighs. "Thank you my darlings. You have it all together. I feel so good and dreamy. I'm gonna lay down a bit."

Sam gets up and each of his ladies comes to him for a kiss and hug.

"Thank you my loves. That mattress is just so good and I'm just a little tired lately."

"Sam, do you want some company?"

"Hey Molly, what's going on with that? Is it your turn already?" Jessie chides.

"I think it is her turn. I've been trying to keep us honest on this trip." Rachel offers.

"Yea! My turn Sam." Molly exclaims.

"Okay, you two have the King bed." Ann says.

"My darlings, Good night."

Sam and Molly head for the King bed with the admonishment to be careful about noise, there isn't any real privacy.

"We, may join you two, later, it's just too early right now." Ann tells them.

Sam and Molly cuddle for a while, until sleep overtakes Sam. Molly falls asleep right after. It is almost midnight when Jessie and Ann pile on the bed and Rachael and Becca slip in with them. Kisses and tender touches are exchanged through sleepy eyes and dreamy heads.

The morning arrives, bright and surprisingly cooler. They stretch and yawn and slide legs up and down one another's legs and Sam feels more than a few gropes that are not unpleasant.

"Mmmm! I do feel wonderful. There's nothing like waking up to nekked women. Good morning my loves."

There are several and varied Good mornings from the women. Sam thought that it really did feel wonderful having these warm bodies pressed to him on all sides.

They slowly untangle themselves and head for the bath. The water is especially cold this morning, but feels wonderful. They pour bowls of water over one another and soap their bodies. Sam is afforded the lion's share of rubbing soap on naked females. He is in his own heaven and each lady expresses their love of this caring man.

Yai meets them when they come from the bath. They are in their robes and with towels on their heads. Yai tells them that she has tea and breakfast for them. The women all understand and do a respectful wai and say thank you in Thai. She smiles and does that clucking thing that first endeared Ann to Sam when they met.

They are soon dressed and head for the kitchen/dining area. The tea is welcome. A kind of Chamomile and mint. Very soothing. Breakfast is a mix of rice, egg, pork and finely chopped chili peppers, with spring onions and some tender vegetables in small pieces.

"Yai, this is very good. Thank you." Sam says in Thai.

Yai smiles and accepts his compliment.

The limo arrives a few minutes to 9 and the women head for the gate. Yai is going with them. When they open the gate, Jessie whispers something to her sisters and they reach out to her and pat her. Jessie steps back and waves to them, closes the gate and turns to Sam, who is still on the veranda.

"I get to stay home today. Are you okay with that honey?"

"Yeah. I thought I'd just float in the pool all morning. Maybe, we can take a look around the property, or something."

"Yeah. What happened to our morning water walk. Once and then . . . ." Jessie begins.

"Yeah. Well, you want to water walk for a while? Then walk that wide path around the rice patty, lunch and nap. I wonder how long it will take them to get everything."

Jessie and Sam enjoy the morning quietly in the pool and walking around the property. Sam notes that there is a place for a pond to seed with fish for Yai. His head is spinning through thoughts of how to make life better here, for Yai and the rest.

It is noon and they put lunch together. After lunch, Sam cleans out the hibachi and finds the charcoal bin. It is a little low and he calls Ann on the cell phone to tell her to get more charcoal.

"Hi Ann. How you guys doing? No, nothing wrong, just checked the charcoal and it's a bit low. Maybe you could get some while you all are out. Good. Yes, we just finished lunch and I checked the hibachi. How much longer do you think you'll be? Okay, you'll be back around 4:30 or 5. That should give us enough time to get things ready. I'll fire up the hibachi around 4:30 so we can get ribs on as soon as you get here. Love you to. Bye."

"So Sam, nap time yet? I'm a little sleepy. I guess it could be the heat."

"Sure Jess, I feel a little sleepy myself."

They strip to their shorts and spoon, then got a little excited and a little more, then loved one another warmly and passionately. Then they fell asleep.

Lucky that Sam had set his alarm on his cell phone for 4. They ran through the bathing and dressed to await the return of their family. Sam wondered if anyone could imagine their life together. They are happy and instead of a husband and wife vying for power and taking offense over misunderstood words, there are five women, who work well together and sincerely like one another and one man who loves them all and takes care of them all and cares for their emotional and physical health. The women have control over the interactions between themselves and the man. They set the limits so that the man will never need to look elsewhere for affection. It doesn't hurt that they have money and each can go if they want to. That must be freedom.

He remembers something his Dad told him, when he first went to the Air Force. "You marry because you want and need the person you are marrying. If you do not feel comfortable with being able to say 'no' at the alter, then it wasn't meant to be. You have to feel free to say 'no.'"

"Maybe, I'll write it."

"I'm sorry honey, I didn't hear you." Jessie queries.

"Sorry, I didn't think I said it out loud. I was thinking about our lives together and wondered if anyone could imagine how happy our arrangement is and I guess I said it out loud that maybe I'll write it. It's been ten, eleven or so years since our first writing and speaking tour. Something to bring everyone up to date on how well we are doing, still."

"That would be great. If you do, we could all contribute our own points of view and make it a family story."

"It bears thinking about . . . I hear a car stopping. They're home."

"Hey. You made it. Did you get everything?" Jessie asks.

"Everything and then some. Sam can you get the bags of charcoal from the trunk?" Ann asks.

The limo is unloaded in short order. Everyone pitches in. The soft goods went to the bedroom. The ribs went to the large hibachi along with the three bags of charcoal. They bought some boneless chicken breasts as well and Molly is mixing up a marinade for them.

"Wow, what's this? You got baking potatoes! Great and sour cream. This is fantastic." Sam exclaims.

"That Aussie store had them and they weren't that much. I think it worked out to about $3.00 for a ten pound bag." Rachael said.

"This is going to be great and I see little watermelons and cantaloupe and honey dew. This will definitely be an American barbecue. I'm rubbing down the ribs and the fire is ready." Sam tells them.

"I'll wrap the potatoes in foil. How many should I do. Will everyone want them?" Rachael asks.

"I'm sure they will all try everything we make. Sam did you see the 2 gallon tubs of ice cream?" Ann asks.

"Oh, you're kidding. Real ice cream?"

"Yes sir and not the Thai stuff. This is from New Zealand, full cream and I got strawberry, vanilla and chocolate." Ann smiles and gives Sam a squeeze on his behind.

"Wow lady, not while I'm cooking. I'm not looking for a wienie roast."

All the women laugh and continue with their preparations for the night's festivities. Ann's Mom laughs to. She is picking up on the language as well.

Family begin arriving at 5 and Ann passes out swim suits. When her cousins look at the suits, they step around and look outside and see the pool. The excitement really starts then. Their seemingly excited babble is more grateful appreciation for having a pool that they would be able to use. Yai will not have to worry about having people around now.

The changing is quick and soon everyone is laughing and splashing in the pool. The pool toys are being put to good use. Sam is beside himself with the joy he is seeing in these new friends of his. Ann takes his arm and squeezes.

"This is a very good idea honey. Challat has one copy of the maintenance booklet and he said he understands how to keep the pool fresh. Mom will always have people around now. She's . . . oh Sam look."

Sam looks where Ann is pointing. Yai is in a one piece bathing suit and grinning ear to ear as she walks across the deck and down the steps into the pool.

"Ann that's wonderful. She looks like she's twenty years younger already. I'm glad you guys got her that suit and talked her into wearing it."

Yai is cavorting in the pool right along with her younger nieces and nephews. Jessie and Molly are in the pool and drawing appreciative looks from Ann's cousins. Rachael and Becca are in suits and robes and still setting out the food and paper plates, something Sam didn't think they used much over here. He was sure the ladies will appreciate that they don't have to wash them and just throw them away.

The aroma of the ribs and other barbecued meat and potatoes is filling the area with belly rumblings. Soon people are leaving the pool and are surprised and appreciative of the robes that both dried them and offered a modest covering.

As Sam had guessed, they are both amazed and appreciative of the paper plates. Becca bought the heavier ones so there would be no accidents that would dissuade them from using them.

Joe is the first to comment to Sam on the festivities.

"Sam this is very good together for family. (I am paraphrasing and in English) I like very much the ribs. This is what you call?"

"This is an American barbecue and pool party. I'm happy that you like this. The ribs . . ." Sam waves a rib. "are first steamed in Coca Cola, then on the charcoal with onion, garlic, Thai pepper and tomato paste with beer."

"Oh ha! Yes, beer. I taste, make very . . . how you say, soft to eat."

"Tender." Joe nods his understanding. "Enjoy my friend." Sam says and pats Joe on the back. Challat and Yim are listening intently and Sam turns to Challat.

"Challat, Ann said you can keep the pool clean." Challat nods. He can't talk through the mouthful of ribs. "I want to leave you some money so that you can buy chemicals for the pool and for more ribs and beer. If you don't mind. I hope that Yai will keep active with more family gatherings. Ann and I and the rest of my family, will be back more often and probably bring others with us."

"Sam, is good idea for pool and for family. Would like very much to meet more people. Like very much you come back with family many times."

"Thank you Challat. Yim, are you enjoying everything? It is you and your wife and two other wives that gave Ann the idea of adding to our family. I have to thank you for that."

"You are very happy with five?"

"Yes. Each is different and each is the same. They love each other and that is important."

They continue their talk and Sam is grateful that the Air Force had trained him in the language. Joe and Challat are good men and he liked them. Yim is okay, but is overly cautious and not very outgoing. Sam expects that he will come around as he becomes comfortable with him.

Later, Ann tells him that Yim is a little jealous that his relationship with his family is not as happy as ours and that made him withhold any openness.

"Ann, maybe you could talk with his wife and mistresses and tell them how insecure he feels and it's up to them to give him some loving help in fulfilling his position."

"You're right. Is that how you feel? Our love pushes you."

"That's it Darling. I try very hard to provide a loving atmosphere and keep evil away from our door."

Ann throws her arms around her man and hugs him tightly. Her kiss is filled with love and Sam feels it deep in his heart.

"Uh hum! What's going on you two?" Jessie interrupts.

"Just a little booster for the old man." Sam chuckles.

"Sam is asking me to talk to Yim's people about helping Yim with their love. He said that it's what keeps him going. So, I gave him a love booster."

"Me to. Sir, may I give you a booster?"

Jessie puts her arms around his neck and locks her lips to his and puts all of her love behind the kiss. They to are interrupted by Molly and Becca and Rachael. Then all are expressing the love they feel for one another. The spontaneity of their love is not lost on the onlookers.

Ann and Sam explain their actions to appreciative applause.

"Some times our love for each other is so strong that we have to come together to share the warmth and the good feelings." Ann explains.

Then the music starts. Sam and Ann start out in an approximation of a traditional Thai dance and get laughter from her relatives. Everyone joins in and Sam weaves around his ladies. Yim and his wives dance together along with Challat, Joe and their wives. Ann's girl cousins dance with their husbands and Yai is swaying to the music. Her smile is contagious and soon everyone is smiling and the mood again becomes festive.

The American barbecue is a success and their example also inspired Yim and his relationship, much to the delight of Yai and Yim's ladies.

Sam and family spend another week of traveling around Ann's country with Yai and a couple of times with one or another of the cousins. It is all too soon coming close to time for them to move on.

"Sam, I told my mom that we'd be back with all our babies and with some other people. Is that okay?" Ann pleads.

"Of course. I told Challat and Joe that we'd probably come back often and bring others with us. I'm thinking that we may want to acquire some property and build a bigger house here and maybe one near Seoul."

"I heard that honey and that would be so wonderful." Becca says.

"Sam that sounds really good. I'll tell mom. She'll be so happy."

"I like it to, Baby. My folks would love to travel and meet Ann's family and Becca's." Rachael said.

Molly and Jessie voice similar approval.

"I guess the next visit, we contract for a bigger house here and one in Korea."

The end of the week is also the end of their visit. They decide, with Yai's invitation, to build onto this house, expanding and improving on the existing structure. They are able to contract with a New Zealand company that is building in Thailand. The people there know just what they are looking for and a plan is drawn. Sam puts down a sizeable down payment and Ann puts money in her Thai

Bank account for Yai to draw on to pay for the completed home. Sam also solicits Challat to look in on the project and advise Yai on when to make a payment. Everything is in place for them to leave and not worry.

"I'm glad we got that house contract done this time. I'd have probably worried about it the whole time we're gone."

The trip home is long, even in first class, but it is good to be able to sleep on the way. The plane change at Narita in Tokyo is long and drawn out. They spend the time in the VIP lounge and look through the upscale gift store that is attached. When they re-board for the flight to IAD, that's Washington D.C.'s Dulles airport, they are treated to sharing their first class section with Alyssa Milano, from the, 'Who's the Boss' sitcom and from 'Charmed'. The ladies bubble around her and the talk is animated. Alyssa is very interested in their arrangement and asks tons of questions. Sam has his eyes closed, feigning sleep and listens.

"So none of you are jealous of the others?" She asks.

All of the women shake their heads, 'no' and smile and pat one another.

"I have to admit that you don't look like the polygamous families that we've seen on the news or that Sister Wives show. You don't get home and change into long gray dresses with aprons and bonnets?"

"Just the way we are now. Oh, we do dress down, to work in our pottery barn, and our bakery. I wear coveralls and gloves in the greenhouse, but the things we do are just hobbies that have also provided revenue. Molly, among other things, is our expert in poultry and dresses appropriately, but we are just one big family and love one another and our man. I would like him to talk with you, but he's pretending to be asleep and listening." Ann explains.

"How close in age are all of you? Is . . . Sam the oldest and everyone very much younger?"

"Well, Sam is the oldest, then I am a few months younger. Rachael is a year younger than Sam and me. Jessie and Becca are two years younger and our baby is Molly, who is, what . . . five years younger. So, no there is no cradle robbing." Ann tells her.

Ann goes on to tell the story of how they came together in the salon with Jessie and Becca. Then Molly came to work and the three moved in together to share expenses. Jessie's friend Rachael joins the group, but is a nurse instead of a hairdresser. She told about Sam's bringing lunch to them each day and the times that they spent at dinners and movies, just like they are family already.

When she reaches the point of their current trip, with nearly grown children at home, Alyssa is enthralled.

"Wow. That is some story. Has anyone written it down yet?"

"Sam did write, from his journal and we did a speaking tour in New York for the publisher."

"Why haven't I seen it in the stores? What is the title?"

"The Chronicles of A Corporate Union" Ann tells her.

"I can see this as a motion picture, or at least a Hallmark TV movie. May I have your contact information?"

"Yes. I always carry some bios, in case I'm asked."

Ann pulls out a bio sheet from her purse. Sam asked her about it once and she said that you never know when someone wants to know.

"This is great. If I can drum up some interest, I'll be in touch."

The rest of the trip to IAD is animated for the six women. Sam enjoys listening to them share stories and recount adventures. Alyssa is big in the Japanese music industry and has just completed a tour of Japan, Korea and her first foray into Beijing.

Sam joins the conversations during dinner, over Montana or Minnesota. He is a fan of the TV shows and she has questions for him as well.

"So, how do you keep them in line?"

"There's no keeping anyone in line. We love one another and that's the long and short of it. We can do what ever we find makes us happy and we've found that when you offer that same freedom to others, they get to be happy. As you are reading our story, you'll see that we run things with love as the bottom line, not money. The result is enough money to free everyone from fear."

"Fear?"

"Sure, that's what holds people back. Fear of failing, fear of not having enough to eat, fear of looking bad, and fear of not having descent clothes. When that is taken away, the imagination soars. We have people working with us . . . oh, and I never say, working for us, because that is servitude and it diminishes the individual. If you are working with someone for yourself and your family, you are in control of your destiny. No one is pulling your strings. You work better with brighter goals. No one in the corporation needs to worry that their children will not be financially able to go to college. College is a guarantee for every person working in the corporation."

"Whoa! Sam, you're getting on your soap box." Jessie admonishes.

"Yeah. Thanks. Sorry, I am a little passionate about our corporation and the way people work in it. But, I don't control these women, we share and the only control and that's not the right word, is in our intimate relationships. They decide when and where and with whom. It's never dull. There is never any need or desire to go outside these wonderful people for relationships and it is one thing that I believe is a factor in divorce among monogamous unions. It gets dull, the interest fades and one or both seek fulfillment outside the marriage. Can't happen here."

"What about when they want a change?"

"Ms. Alyssa. I know that being a woman . . ."

Sam is interrupted by Becca.

"Sam, I'll do this one. Women and I'm sure you'll see it when I say it, don't need sweating, grunting sex every time. We want tenderness, cuddling and romance. None of that requires sex. Well, a little, but a man that can be tender and loving without having to ravage you for his own needs, is a treasure that you will not want to lose. A change happens every time. One time romance, one time cuddling and tenderness and the next time sex. It's a win, win deal. He never gets a dull day and neither do we."

"I do see. Why hasn't anyone seen this before?"

"They have, but the nuances of such a relationship are hard to define. We found that we are friends first. Then the friendship got closer and then we became partners and friends. It is a logical next step to form a working, loving and close unit. The corporate family union." Jessie elaborates.

"At this point I usually tell the statistics. Steadily over the last two thousand years, females have outnumbered males. Ten years ago, there are 3 females to each male on the planet. Today that number is no different. Nearly all other mammals know this instinctively and form groups that reflect the ratios. There is a bull and many heifers. There is a stallion and many mares. The same for sheep, deer, antelope, buffalo and so on. If bovines had decided to be monogamous, we wouldn't be eating steaks or burgers. Crude, but that's the picture. How much valuable, creative and genius DNA is lost by keeping others from sharing?" Sam explains.

"I am definitely reading your book and you know that I am really intrigued by your lifestyle. You are wonderful to be around and I do love the positive feelings that I get from all of you. Sam, you are a remarkable man and Ann, Jessie, Becca, Rachael and Molly, you ladies are people I am grateful to have met. I know a screen writer, a friend. I bet he would love to tell your story for the screen."

"Sounds great Alyssa, here is a copy of our book for you." Ann said.

The rest of the flight is quiet. Alyssa got off in Chicago for her connection to her home. The family went on to Dulles in Washington D.C. for the connection to Columbia and home.

They arrive at Sumter airport in the middle of the afternoon. Their car is in the security area and they pile in, like they are in some kind of hurry. Tom drives slowly, well the speed limit, to their home.

He parks in the garage and they go in quietly, through the laundry door and through the kitchen. They stop at the family room doors and look in. Sarah sees them first and she taps Michael and Sybil and points to the door.

"Momma, Poppa, Momma Poppa. Ahhh!" The two shout and run to them, followed by Carrie, Jamie, Wyatt and Edward.

While the mommas hug and kiss little faces, Tom greets his first born. Tommy and Carly are smiles and hugs for Dad. Raina, Cathy, hug their Dad and Mattie and Ryan shake hands and hug and step back for the second set of six, Alex, Brian, Delia, Peter and Elizabeth, and Richard.

"I missed you guys. How is it? Anything I need to do for you?"

"Yeah Dad. Get out the pictures. We've been aching to see the places Mom told us about on the phone." Tommy says. "We missed all of you to."

"Well, surprise. We set a plan in motion while we were there and everyone is going on the next trip. We'll probably spend the whole summer, this year."

My twelve, sixteen, fifteen and ten year olds all flushed with excitement and talk excitedly back and forth. It draws the attention of the Mommas.

"Told them about going back this summer, huh?" Ann asks.

"You guessed. How could I keep it from my team. They're gonna help getting the 24 of us on target for this summer. Well, Thai winter, I guess."

The Moms fall on their older children with hugs and kisses and to field tons of questions. Sam sits on the floor with the youngest to pet and kiss on them a little. Mike and Sybil hug his neck, Carrie and Jamie sit on his lap and Eddy and Wyatt hold his arms and sit close beside him.

The family sit together for more than an hour. Hugging and petting the babies and one another. Sam is misty and proud of his family. Tommy, Carly, Mattie, Ryan, Raina and Cathy help the Moms with the youngest.

Mary, our cook announces that there are refreshments in the breakfast area and dinner will be at seven.

They troop into the breakfast area and sit at the table. Jessie and Molly retrieve the camera memory cards and plug them into the computer that's hooked to the 32" LCD, so the children could see the pictures while they snack and listen to one or another of the Mommas narrate. The excitement is building as the anticipation of their upcoming trip engulfs them.

"Three months to get ready guys. Passports are first for the children. Tomorrow, a couple of us get paperwork from the county office. Children to the photographer for passport photos after school. Wow, I should be tired, but thinking about all of us going to Asia together. It's making me excited." Sam exclaims.

"Me to Dad. I can't wait to see our—what should we call her, them? Grand mothers? When are we gonna learn some Korean and Thai?" Tommy asks.

"Tommy, I will sit everyone down and teach some of the Thai words and customs and Momma Becca will teach some Korean words and customs. We'll make sure that you will feel at home. Momma Molly, Rachael and Jessie have also picked up on the language and we'll all talk together, that should help. Your Dad speaks Thai and a little Korean to, so you all will fit right in." Ann tells him.

"We can do some authentic Thai and Korean foods to get you in the spirit. We can take turns preparing them, so everyone will have a chance to cook some exotic things." Sam offers, to a sea of shining faces.

"I'm getting excited to. The pictures are great, but I want to see it myself." Carly adds.

Brian, Matt, Ryan, Delia and the rest add their excited and happy enthusiasm to the conversations.

Sam is very proud of his family. 'His' ladies are beautiful and they have just come back from a long visit and are excitedly planning a return trip in just a few months. His babies, are smiling and giggling at their Moms and older siblings.

Michael and Sybil both ask, "Poppa, are we going on a airplane?"

"Yes you are. We are all going. Are you happy to fly on an airplane?"

They both nod enthusiastically and Jamie and Carrie join in, with Eddie and Wyatt, confirming that they to have been listening.

"Honey, what if we also take Sarah and Annie to help with the children and Mary to help with cooking?" Becca asks.

"Great. We have to clear it with them and invite their other half if they agree. Passports and all will have to be acquired. You guys figure it out. We have three months, more or less."

Chapter 10

FAMILY VACATION

The next few weeks were busy getting back to the care of their children, their poultry, organic vegetable greenhouses and ceramics. The passport problem, was not such a problem. They were given the VIP treatment everywhere.

Ann talked with Sarah, Annie and Mary about making the trip with us and they were also enthusiastic about the adventure. None, of the three, are married, but have boyfriends who they assured would not miss them that much.

The three months seemed to fly by and it was nearing their time to travel. In the final weeks, Sam surprises them with an unexpected announcement.

"Family, we're going to charter an entire airplane for our travels. I've already arranged for a Luxury Boeing 737-400 that will accommodate all of us and extra luggage. There are sleeping berths, showers, a kitchen and all kinds of amenities that I didn't understand all of it."

"Wow, Sam, was it terribly expensive?" Ann asks.

"No more than First Class for twenty eight people and we get to take all the luggage we want, without paying extra. They gave us a good deal on a three month rental. We get two attendants in the deal, to help and one of them is married to the pilot, so they won't be separated the whole time. The other is engaged to the co-pilot."

Everyone is excited and happy with his news. The older children gather in a group with the younger ones and share their happiness, with the youngest.

Sam and the women do a lot of planning. Sarah, Annie and Mary are included in the planning. Rachael suggests taking an unusually large amount of medical supplies. She says it may come in handy at the house in Thailand. Anything they don't need can be donated to local clinics.

Mary asks if she should plan to bring foods and is given the go ahead to pack foil packs and Zip Lock packages of family favorites. Later, Sam is amazed at the amount of food that is packaged to go with them.

The inventories of necessities and a very large amount of gifts for the cousins and Becca's people, becomes two hundred plus pages of items. They will be taking three vehicles to the airport. One large U-Haul van with just luggage and their inventory. The planning, passports and amassing their haul is complete and ready for their trip, a week before they are scheduled to leave.

School is out and the older children are anxious about leaving their friends and special friends. They are also anticipating the adventure that they have helped to plan these three months. All of the children have a working knowledge in Thai and Korean, thanks to Ann, Becca and Sam's tutelage. Some days, one would think that the house was filled with foreigners. Even the nannies and house staff were included in the lessons and added, both Thai and Korean as a foreign language skill.

The last week seems to drag on, but finally the day arrives. They meet the Captain and crew at the airport. It was different, not going through TSA's security screening.

Captain Brewster and the co-pilot, who introduces himself as Harris are former Air Force B-52 pilots. The two attendants introduce themselves. Sandra is Captain Brewster's wife and Barbara is Harris's fiancée. The relationships make everything seem very homey and comfortable. The flight crew is fascinated by the family's relationship.

Sandra ushers everyone aboard and familiarizes them with the facilities and the amenities. Boeing does an excellent job of putting together a luxury flying machine. There are 30 captain's seats where first class would be and behind that section, an area like a big living room/dining room, then the kitchen and the back third is a sleeping area. The seats in first class lay completely flat and are wide enough to be beds as well.

It is almost an hour before all of their luggage and packages are loaded and the captain announces that we will be leaving and to take seats and buckle up.

Tom and Carly help Cathy, Matt, Ryan and Delia get the younger ones strapped in. Sam had to stop calling them the babies when Carrie, as spokesperson, came to him with Jamie, Wyatt and Edward to inform him that when they reached eight years old, they were, "Not babies any more, Dad! We are older now."

"Mr. Elliott, when we reach our cruising altitude, the Captain wants to speak with you and the family, in the living area." Sandra tells him.

"Thank you Sandra. I'll tell them. We brought a few DVD movies to distract the children after the Captain speaks." Sam responds.

The take-off was exciting for those children, who have not experienced air travel. It is only a little while, before the FASTEN SEAT BELT sign goes off. Sam and his ladies unbuckle and help the older children unbuckle the younger ones and head back to the living area. Sandra and Barbara have drinks ready. Sarah and Annie usher the youngsters to seats and help Sandra and Barbara with the drinks and snacks for them. Mary is in the kitchen—galley preparing the evening meal. Sam can hear her fussing about how she can't find anything and laughs to himself.

Everyone is settled when the Captain comes back to the family with a large portfolio type of folder.

"Mr. Elliott, ladies and gentlemen. I have the itinerary mapped out and hope that you like the bit of island hopping I have put in the plan. We make one stop in San Francisco, then to Oahu, Hawaii. The stop in Hawaii, to see Honolulu and Diamond Head and for me to file our flight plan through the Libe Islands, through Samoa, Fiji, the Solomon Islands, to Papua and on to Bangkok. It's Monsoon season and the weather changes rapidly. If we get any turbulence, I'll let everyone know to buckle up, but we've done this route before and we're pretty good at navigating through any weather. Any questions. Sandra and Barbara have put up some really nice meals, but I understand you brought your own cook?"

"Yes, Mary is with us, she loves to help and try new things. I heard her in the galley trying to figure out the arrangements. Thank you Captain Brewster, I trust you and your crew." Sam tells him.

"Bill, Mary introduced herself to me and Barb. She's a treasure and will be a big help getting things ready." Sandra confirms.

"That's it then. Enjoy the flight. Art Harris and I will be playing cards in the cockpit. This is one great airplane, flies itself." Captain Brewster chuckles.

Sam goes to the couch and sits with Ann, Jessie and Molly. The couch folds out like a large recliner and Sam is soon dozing with Ann's head on his lap. Rachael has set up the movies for the younger children and whoever wants to watch. The older children are at the back of the living area with some music and games. Becca is sitting with Jamie on her lap and Carrie in the next seat, watching the Disney movie. The scene is serene, calm and comfortable.

Over the next three hours, Becca and Rachael change places with Ann and Molly, who go to the back to see Mary in the galley. They are an hour and a half from San Francisco when Mary, Sandra and Barbara announce dinner.

Sam wakes to a mass movement to the dining tables. Sam watches as Sarah and Annie get Mike, Sybil, Jamie, Carrie, Edward and Wyatt settled. They are just working too hard for a vacation.

"Sarah, Annie. You two are doing marvelously, but don't work so hard. Have some fun to."

"Yeah, you two. They're getting big enough to do some things for themselves. Relax a little." Ann adds.

"Thank you. It's fun for us to help them get situated." Sarah responds.

"Yes and its good training, for us, when we have our own children." Annie says.

Ann asks Sandra, Barbara, Sarah, Annie, and Mary to join them for dinner.

"Sandra, maybe Bill and Art could also join us. One at a time or . . . they can't both come at the same time or—Oh wow—you know. Everyone is invited every time, okay?" Ann offers.

Sandra laughs a little and Barbara gets up and takes two plates forward. "Bill will come to dinner, Barb and Art will eat in the cockpit. Thank you for offering. We don't usually get people who don't treat us like servants. So, it is doubly appreciated Ann."

Bill joins them for dinner and the inevitable questions come up. Sam and the rest respond with their corporate union narrative. They have told it so many times that it is almost like a radio drama with everyone putting in portions of the story.

Bill, of course is interested in the polygamy parts, but also is surprised to learn how well their enterprises flourished. He likes how they involved employees to the point of giving away their industry to them and are able to begin again.

"I don't think I have ever heard of anything like it and you are all so happy and your children are . . . I don't have a word. Like, already capable individuals and children, at the same time."

"Bill's right. I almost wish we were involved in something like this. We're both in our mid thirties. Bill is 37 and I'm 34. I have several single friends, who are in the airline business, but I don't know how we would support ourselves the same way."

"I wouldn't advise you on how to live your lives, but with five incomes and only one household to support, there is a huge savings. Wise investing and most of all, love. Everyone must love one another and trust one another. I can give you our books and DVDs from our lectures. There isn't a rush. It's like whenever everything is right." Ann tells them.

"Honey, I didn't know you were thinking about . . ." Bill starts.

"Oh no Bill. It's not like that. I mean, they are so happy and the idea of having women like me around all the time to share."

"I know. Girl talk. I love you Sandy Girl."

"Ditto, Billy Boy."

Sam and his ladies can see the love between the two and their smiles shine on them. Tom and Carly and the other grown up children are also smiling. They realize the affect that their family has on others and they have accepted that they are special.

The flight to San Francisco is uneventful, aside from the dinner revelations and they are off to Honolulu. Cap Bill says it will take about three hours. We will get in late in the day, but we can sleep on the plane and see the sights in the morning.

The plane lands in Honolulu at around 9 PM and everyone is tired and ready for bed.

Morning arrives and everyone is rushing around to get ready. Then they discovered the showers on the plane.

"Sam, there's a couple of showers at the back of the plane." Jessie exclaimed.

"Some in the middle of the plane, to." Sam adds.

"Folks, there are ten shower stalls on this aircraft. Three of them can accommodate more than two people, kind of like a gym shower. There is plenty of hot water, so don't be afraid to use it up. We will refill all our fluids while in Honolulu this morning." Barbara announces.

Showering goes on for an hour or more to the squeals and laughter of the children and a few of the women. When everyone is dressed, Mary announces breakfast.

"Dad, this is way cool. I want to do a lot of traveling." Tom says.

"Me to Dad. This is great. No one will believe that I took a shower on an airplane." Raina exclaims.

"Daddy, can I shower again?" Carrie asks.

"Later baby. I think we're gonna be sweaty later. At least we'll be covered with salt water. Who's for Waikiki beach?" Sam calls out.

He is met with a roar of yeas and me, me, me . . . . The children are definitely enthusiastic.

"I would like to go to the beach to, Sam and I can watch the children with Tom, Carly and the other grown children's help." Sarah offers.

"Thank you Sarah. I appreciate that. Everyone is welcome. We can tour Makapuu Point and Pearl Harbor, then around the Iolani Palace, the Bishop Museum then on to King Kamehameha I statue and end up at the beach. Swim a little then dinner at Kapahulu or one of the Five Diamond Hawaiian Regional Cuisine restaurants. Have to make a reservation for that I bet, if we want to get all of us in. Thirty one and everyone is invited." Sam starts his plan.

"I'll do the reservations Sam." Sandra states.

"Thank you. I forgot, you are probably more familiar with this place than I am. I appreciate that Sandra."

"It sounds like you know a bit about Honolulu yourself Sam. I know Pearl Harbor, but I didn't know those other places are here." Becca says.

"I read a lot."

They enjoy breakfast and as they disembark, a tour bus is waiting for them next to the plane.

"Oh, who did this?" Rachael asks.

"Bill ordered it for you. When he heard what you wanted to do and he also says Thank you for offering dinner for all of us." Sandra relates.

Everyone boards the bus. It is a high window bus with extra comfortable seats and flow through air. They are off on their adventure. The stop at the Arizona Memorial is both somber and stirring. These young men gave their lives so that we could go on and be the nation that we are today. The tour takes most of the morning and Sam is thinking lunch. Just then, the driver pulls into what looks like a weather worn fishing warehouse, with just a handful of cars in the parking lot.

"All off for Lunch." He announces.

The family steps off the bus and follows the driver to an awning covered set of double doors. When he opens the door, they are assaulted with the most wonderful aromas of cooking and inside is a Luau set up in the center of the floor with a large stage behind it and low tables and cushions all around. They are met by several hula skirted ladies with leis and smiles.

"Ma hallo Elliott family. This way please. There is seating for everyone."

They follow the hula ladies to a section to the left of the pit that all the wonderful smells are coming from. The children are excited, especially the younger ones. The older ones are trying to look like they do this all of the time.

Sam asks one of the young ladies, "I thought you do Luaus in the evening."

"That is correct sir, but you and your family will be at the Five Diamond this evening, so we have set up a special luau in your honor, Mr. Elliott."

The family take seats on cushions around the edge of the stage and enjoy a lunch and dinner show. The children are all smiles and the youngest ones are clapping and laughing. Sam enjoys seeing his family happy. It is still his greatest pleasure.

They are treated to many wonderful and delicious traditional Hawaiian dishes and a hula and torch show, all to the delight of the ladies and the children.

It is half past one before they continue their adventure. The ladies, including Sandra, Barbara, Mary and Annie want to go to the shopping district.

While the ladies exit the bus, Sam gazes down the street that they will be shopping. The street is filled with thatch covered stalls, some with umbrellas in red, green and blue. Trays of jewelry and trinkets made from seashells and woven grass skirts, made by the local inhabitants. There is also a profusion of colorful, dried fruits and smoked octopus.

The street is crowded with geriatric tourists in big hats and flowery shirts and acres of ankle length muumuus. Sam almost wishes he could go with the ladies, but knows that it wouldn't be fair to Sarah, who is giving up her chance at shopping.

The driver continues with Sam, Sarah and the children to the beach.

Waikiki beach is something to be seen and experienced first hand. It is impossible to describe with any justice. Sam is in love, immediately. Not because of the acres of almost nude young women, but the serene vista of the gentle waves . . . . NOT. It's the babes.

The children are enthralled and very soon the family is surrounded by people with chaises, beach umbrellas and trays of drinks. Part of Sandra's doing. She had the Cabana club look out for them and provide the luxury service. They brought a tent like structure for changing, but the boys had their suits under their shorts.

"Tommy, Cathy, Carly, Raina, Matt and Ryan. Have fun, but watch out for the younger ones. Help Sarah and me keep everyone safe, but still have fun."

"You got it Dad." Tom takes the lead. The rest assure Sam that they understand.

"Let the rest know that there are drinks and snacks right here with the big blue umbrella."

"Yeah Dad, all the umbrellas in this part are blue." Cathy points out.

Sam looks around and laughs. "Okay then. Figure out something. I'll be right here."

The older children pick up some beach toys and herd the younger ones, although Carrie and Wyatt object a little about being led. They are all, soon laughing and playing in the surf.

Sam and Sarah take lounges and stretch out under the umbrella.

"Sorry you missed shopping with the girls?" Sam asks.

"Oh no. I love the beach. Waikiki. I would have never thought I'd get to be here. Thanks to you and the family, I'm getting my dream vacation."

"You are more than welcome. You have been a real treasure to us."

Sarah smiles and blushes a little.

They lounge for the afternoon, drifting in and out of sleep. Sam keeps one eye open and watches his babies playing in the surf and building sand castles. The children love it and at five o'clock they are surprised by the arrival of the shoppers.

"Back already? Run out of money or what?"

"It was fabulous Sam. How are the children?" Ann asks.

"They're having a great time. Want to get wet?" Sam asks.

The ladies all head for the changing tent, which has reappeared behind him. Soon there are nine more gorgeous, semi nude, babes on the beach. Sam marvels that they are drawing appreciative looks from others along the beach. He hadn't realized how good looking his staff is. Annie, who is closest, in age to him and his ladies, has a beautiful figure and perfectly tapered legs. Mary to, is a knockout in a bikini. Sandra and Barbara, are eight years younger than Jessie and Becca. Sam appreciates both of them. Sandra has proved to be very resourceful and she looks good to.

Molly, Ann, Jessie, Rachael and Becca run to Sam and grab his arms and pull him up and almost drag him to the water. Their playful struggle ends up in all of them tumbling in the water, to the shrieks of laughter from their children.

The whole family playing together finally gets some attention, as people begin to recognize who this army of children and women are. They are soon the center of attention and the ladies are fielding questions about their corporate union.

"I bought your book and your DVDs, but I never thought I would get to see any of you in real life. Wow. You're all one family?" The young lady asks.

"Yes, we are. We're on our first, real family vacation." Becca answers.

Several more questions and comments come from the gathered crowd. Sam, Sarah, and Annie, along with the older children are keeping a constant vigil on the younger ones. This would be a good opportunity to snatch an Elliott for ransom, although Sam thinks the 8, 9 and 10 year olds would put up a good fight. They were all belted in Karate, Aikido and Tai Chi, minor belts, but good at what they know.

The family is saved by the driver and Sandra, who has changed into her clothes and announces, "Elliott family, the bus will leave in fifteen minutes."

The ladies make their apologies and gather the children to change. Sam and the boys get a separate changing tent and are waiting when the girls and the ladies emerge.

"Thanks Sandra. It's usually a struggle to disentangle ourselves from the curious."

"You must know, Sam, your lives are interesting. Especially the fact that five women are willing to share one man and give him children."

"I guess. It has always seemed the natural thing for us. I, of course, couldn't be happier. I have always said and I believe it, being a Dad is the highest honor that a man can aspire to. I love it. I love being in a prime position to bring up happy, fully functioning people, who care and have compassion for others."

"That's beautiful Sam. You all are doing a great job. I'm happy to be allowed to get this close to all of you."

Sam blushes a little and thanks Sandra for her kindness. Everyone is on the bus and talking about the wonderful afternoon. Barbara stands in the front and announces, "We're going to the plane now, to shower and dress. We have reservations at the Five Diamond restaurant, at seven, then a show, if anyone is still awake, or back to the plane and wind down, your choice."

When everyone is off the bus and going up the steps to the plane, Sam turns to the driver, "If you are driving this evening, bring your lady and children and join us for dinner. I sincerely appreciate the job you've done getting us around Honolulu and saving us at the beach. I know I enjoyed the tour and my children will remember it for a long time."

"Thank you Sir. We would like to join your family tonight. My kids will be so tickled. My name is Ron, Ron Lau and I'll also be driving."

"Thank you Ron. Call me Sam." They shake hands and Sam rejoins the family.

The children are anxious to shower the salt and sand off of them and dress in some cooler clothes. Sarah, Annie and Mary get them started in the showers and lay out their clothes, then take turns in the shower.

Sam and his ladies squeeze into one of the large showers. They are all in withdrawal, not having any body contact for so long. Sam is enjoying the attention and returns his affections. The kissing and hugging are the most enjoyable. It's almost like cuddling. The women are all so warm and feel so good under his hands.

"My Darlings, I don't know how to say it. I love you all, so much."

Each of the women express their love in return.

"I love you Sam. I love this trip, the shopping, the children, but mostly I love you." Ann kisses him warmly.

"Me to, Sam Cat. This whole thing is great. I love it. I love you, man." Molly says.

"I don't think anyone needs to tell you how much we love you. I want to show you." Jessie says and locks her lips to his and presses herself tightly to him. The sensation is overwhelming.

Becca and Rachael repeat Jessie's display and Sam is in heaven. All five of the women are group hugging around him and exploring him with their soapy hands.

"Thank you. I am the luckiest man alive. Thank you for loving me. I will always love each and everyone of you, as often as I can . . . ." Sam laughs out loud.

The women begin bouncing up and down and pressing close. You could package the love that encompasses them.

When the Moms and Dad are dried and dressed, they wait for the rest in the family area of the plane. Bill and Art come in from the front, dressed in comfortable tropical slacks and shirts.

"Hi, you two. Don't we look like tourists?" Sam observes

"Hi Sam, ladies. Ready for dinner. I think you're gonna like it. This is only one of several Hawaiian Cuisine restaurants. There aren't any rivals."

"I'm looking forward to the evening, Bill. Art, we don't see much of you."

"I'm around. I make sure everything is good, so Bill has one less worry. Barb and I are having a good time. Tonight will be great. We thank you for letting us be ourselves. Is this the way you ran your corporation."

"More or less. We just love everyone. It's hard to disappoint someone you love. Sandra and Barbara were real treasures today. Sandra got us out of a crowd, of people, curious to know us and Barb got everyone settled on the agenda for this evening." Sam explains.

The children make their entrance with excited babble. Sarah, Annie, Mary, Sandra and Barbara are elegant in tropical silk that matches the outfits that Ann, Jessie, Becca, Rach and Molly are wearing.

"I guess this is some of the things you found shopping?"

"Do you like it? Silk and cool." Becca says.

"Yeah Dad, Mom got me this silk shirt. I think I'm gonna wear silk all the time." Tom expounds.

All the children make similar expressions over their, "cool silk shirts".

"So that's where this shirt came from. Thank you ladies. It is comfortable."

They disembark once more into the waiting bus. The driver is the same one who brought them earlier and he has his wife and two children with him, per Sam's invitation.

"Welcome Ron. Is this your bride and family?"

"Yes Sam, this is my Marie and my son Jonah and daughter Esther." He says, nodding toward the woman and children at his side.

"Pleased to meet you Sam. Thank you for inviting us. We don't get out that much." Marie says.

"Our pleasure Marie. Good to meet you Jonah and Esther. Let me introduce you to the ladies. Ann, this is Marie, Jonah and Esther would you get her and the children acquainted with everyone?"

"Of course. Welcome Marie, Jonah, Esther." Ann takes them to the middle of the bus and introduces Marie and children. Soon, they are just like part of the family. Sam thinks how lucky he is to be a part of such wonderful women.

Sam sits near Ron, the driver, as they head for the Five Diamond restaurant. The drive is only about fifteen minutes and Ron pulls into the parking lot of an elegant building, decorated in modern Polynesian. The doors are decorated with groups of five diamonds. A dozen or more hula skirted greeters, usher the family and friends to cushions in front of the stage. The younger six children sit near their Moms, the older children try their best to look like they're used to this kind of treatment. The men sit together and Sandra, Barbara, Marie, the nannies and Mary, their cook are mixed in with Ann, Jessie, Becca and Rach, and Molly.

Trays of delicacies are brought to each table and the feasting begins. The pit roasted pig is delicious and the poi is flavored with smoked calamari. Music, singing and traditional hula and torch dances entertain them throughout the meal and the after dinner drinks. Everyone is smiling and enjoying a wonderful evening.

"Sam, Art and I are going to excuse ourselves and make sure the ship is fueled and everything is ready for our departure in the morning." Bill tells him.

"Thanks Bill, Art. You guys are something. I appreciate you more than I can say."

"We thank you. Normally, we wouldn't be invited to share an evening like this. You and your family are a rare kind of good people. Besides, we want to be in shape for the flight to Samoa, then Fiji. Tomorrow, we will do two hops, then on to the Philippines, then Bangkok."

The Captain and his co-pilot depart and Sam and Ron settle back and enjoy the evening. It is after ten, when a man that Ron knows tells him that he is there to complete the drive back.

"Mr. Elli . . . Sam, this is Tony, he is going to drive your family back to the plane and me and my family back to the depot."

"Good to meet you Tony. I'll get everyone going."

Sam passes the word to the ladies and to the older children to get them ready to leave. The greeters and servers gather to bid the family goodbye as Sam stops at the desk and is informed that the whole evening has been taken care of and there is no further charge. Sam insists on leaving money for gratuities and is gratefully received.

They get to the plane and say their goodbyes to Ron and Marie. Everyone is tired and opt for sleep, morning will be here very soon.

Sandra woke everyone at eight thirty to get ready for departure. Sam and the ladies roused the children and got everyone through the shower and dressed. Mary and Barbara have breakfast ready and everyone has a hearty appetite. It was ten and all have taken seats in the forward section for take off.

"Good morning Elliotts and friends. We are in line to take off. The cruising altitude will be 30 thousand feet. Our next stop will be Upolu Island, Samoa for a half day then to Fiji. There is some weather after the Philippines, but shouldn't give us a problem as we will be flying above all the action. Settle back and keep your seatbelts fastened; we are next."

They reach their cruising altitude and everyone begins to move around to find something to do. Sam and the ladies sit together in the family area, exchanging warm hand holding and talking about their time in Honolulu and what they expect in Samoa.

"Sam, as nice as the tropics are, I'm not all that interested in anymore islands and seashells." Jessie announces.

"Yeah Sam, after Samoa, ask Bill to skip Fiji if he can." Ann adds.

"Hey, does everyone feel the same. Don't forget the children. Some of them may want to see . . . ." Sam begins.

"Sam, I have tons of videos of the islands in the South Pacific. I can run them with the children and they'll feel just like they've been there. I'm sure Bill can do a reroute at the airport in Faleolo." Sandra offers.

"That's wonderful. I think it will work. Thank you Sandra. Well, my darlings, it looks like we'll get to Bangkok a little earlier. It should surprise Yai." Sam says.

Barbara and Mary bring out drinks and snacks for Sam and the ladies. They also bring snacks for the children and themselves and they settle in with the children to watch the Travelogue that Sandra is showing. Soon sounds of delighted youth are coming to the Mommas and Poppa.

"Sam, can we all just cuddle a little? There are just too many people around to be affectionate privately." Molly asks.

"I'm sure. I do miss holding everyone."

Sam notes the smiles and nods between them as Ann moves to sit beside him on the couch and snuggles up on his left side. Molly sits on his right and snuggles up. Sam turns left and kisses Ann, then right and kisses Molly. He has an arm around each of them and both put their head on his shoulders.

"Nice, my darlings. I feel all dreamy and sleepy. If I fall asleep, just be gentle." Sam chuckles.

"Sam we just woke up. You have a job now mister." Molly says as she kisses him. The women take turns getting hugs and kisses from their man and showing him their love. Sam always loves cuddling.

"I get as much love from this as our intimate times. This just warms the heart."

The nannies, Mary, Sandra and Barb cast appreciative looks their way as they followed the Travelogue. Sam sees Tom telling Sandra something.

"Dad and the Moms really love one another. A lot. Hey, Miss Sandra, there are eighteen of us." He raised his eyebrows and grinned.

Sandra just smiles and shakes her head.

The flight takes four hours and Sandra and Mary announce lunch an hour and a half before their expected arrival.

"Good job. We won't have to waste time eating when we get there. There are some great natural wonders that we can see. Restaurants are nice, but when there is so much to see and so little time . . . . Thank you Sandra and Mary. It does look good." Ann tells them.

Sam nods agreement and smiles. "Yes Ma'am, a feller can get a might hungry romancing these fine women." Jessie pokes him and laughs. Becca and Rach laugh. Molly leans over and kisses his forehead. "I love you man."

Tom, Carly, Raina, Cathy, Matt and Ryan are holding down the fort with the rest of the children. They are very mature and dependable. The second group are paying attention and all of the children interact the way one would want their children to be. Sibling rivalry is unheard of. The only complaint Sam has heard, was the change requested by Carrie, to have the youngest, be referred to, as the youngest, not the babies.

Sam watches them eat their lunch and thanks God for those wonderful young people.

When the FASTEN SEATBELT sign comes on, everyone takes a seat in the forward section and straps in for the landing. Through the windows, all that you can see is water. Upolu must be a small island.

They land at the Faleolo International Airport landing strip and taxi to the side of the terminal, where Sam sees a funny looking bus. It reminds him of the Jeepnies that they had in the Philippines, when he was there so many years ago.

The Samoa Getaway Tour greets the family in the traditional island way and takes them away on a whirlwind tour. The first stop is at Lake Lanotoo. The family takes many pictures of the scenery and of one another in various poses then they are whisked away to Papapapai Tia Falls. Sam is thinking that as beautiful as it is, he wouldn't have flown half way around the world for an up close look at a waterfall, but the family loves it. The trip to the next stop takes a little time and Sam nods off. Molly is sitting with him and gets an extra share of cuddling. They arrive at Ole Pupu Pue National Park and the lava tube caves. Everyone is fascinated by the formations within the rocks that line the caves. The tour takes them to two sandy beaches and the children run in the surf. It is getting late in the afternoon before they return to the airport and re-board the aircraft.

Sam notices the wonderful aromas, as they enter the plane to shower and dress for the evening. He is abashed to see that Sandra, Barb and Mary had dinner ready and he hadn't realized that they were not with them on the tour.

"Oh Sam we'll see the pictures. I know the children probably took hundreds. Besides, it gave us a nice afternoon to nap and take care of other things. There is one thing I would like to ask about." Sandra says.

"Shoot."

"Yeah. I was in the baggage hold and you have several crates of weapons and ammunition. I was curious about that. It's okay, no rules broken or anything like that."

"I brought all of our hand weapons, hoping to show Ann's family that we can take care of ourselves. We may decide to live there later on. All of my wives and the children are belted in several martial arts, Karate, Aikido, Tai Kwon Do and Tai Chi. I also brought hunting rifles, some as gifts and some for us and enough ammunition for . . . well a long time. I was in the Air Force, Special Operations and I really over prepare most of the time."

"Oh that's how you speak so many languages. That's interesting. I'll have to ply the ladies for information."

"Yeah. They are fluent in a couple of languages now, as well. Well, at least Thai and Korean, the children included."

"You guys are something else. I'm really envious. Bill and I are probably too old to start something like you have. It takes time to form the bonds, I imagine."

"That might be a question for the ladies. Me, I feel like they are a part of me and it started almost from the day we agreed to the arrangement and everyone was full of touchy, feely intimacy. When the pregnancies started, well, for me that is the greatest expression of love and I was totally committed, from the top of my head to the soles of my feet."

"You do have a wonderful way of expressing yourself. I won't hold you up any more. I have to help Barb and Mary

170

and you were going for a shower. I'll see you at dinner." Sandra smiles. "Thank you!"

Molly and Jessie were the only ones not showered when Sam got back to the shower.

"We waited for you Sam. It will be a little private for a little while." Molly grins.

The shower is both refreshing and invigorating. Sam feels his adrenalin racing through his veins. He also realizes that he has been missing this intimacy and tells Molly and Jessie, "Mention to the rest that we can still do the intimate stuff in the shower, like this. Mmmm! I miss this. Hot, soapy bodies pressed close."

"Me to. Miss Honey misses Mr. Petey." Molly says in a baby girl voice. Sam laughs and kisses her cheek.

"I'll tell Ann, Becca and Rach. I don't know why we didn't think of this sooner." Jessie says.

"Darlings it's only been three days." Sam laughs.

When they emerge from the shower and get dressed, Ann and Rach look at them with smiles.

"You three took a long shower." Ann says.

Jessie takes her and Rach aside and tells them about the sharing in these close quarters. Sam sees the nods and acknowledges the smiles. Becca comes to see what is being said and grins.

Bill tells everyone at dinner that the new flight plan has been put in the system and in the morning, at nine fifteen, they will fly southwest to Sydney, then north northwest to Manila, then on to Bangkok.

Everyone applauds the news and Bill looks pleased with the appreciation the family gives him. Sandra is also beaming with pride in her man.

Dinner is great and Sam is amazed that such a meal could be put together in an airplane galley. After dinner, he snoops the galley to see the secrets.

"Ah ha! So that's it. It's not a typical galley, this is a kitchen. One more mystery out of the way." He says to no one in particular. Just then Mary steps into the galley.

"Can I help you with anything Sam?"

"No, I was just curious about how you put together such a great meal in an airplane galley. I guess it's not really a galley, but a kitchen."

"Yes, I was surprised. Airplanes usually don't have this kind of food area?"

"Usually it's just hot boxes and prepared meals are stored on trays."

"Oh, that's why Sandra let me handle most of the meal and just stepped in like a souse chef. She is used to a galley, galley."

"Must be it. Mary, I really want to thank you. You are a real treasure. Not just on this trip, but at home. Uh, I don't mean to get personal, but you are pretty and a great cook. You have a wonderful, friendly personality and your boyfriend didn't have a problem with you coming with us? For that matter, why hasn't he asked you to marry him? Sorry, that's too personal. Forget it. It's just, I over worry about people, when I'm so happy."

"You make me blush. Thank you for the compliments. I love to cook and your family is just the greatest, all the way down to the youngest. As for Kenny, I don't know. It's not like he's getting the milk, so he doesn't have to buy the cow. Maybe he just doesn't want to commit."

"Well. He doesn't know what he's missing. I hope it works out for you. You deserve a shot at a good life."

"Thank you. I'm just going to straighten up a bit. Sandra is going to help and Barb is putting together movie snacks, for later."

"Okay, I'll get out of the way. You know that we're all here, if you need to bend an ear."

Mary nods, smiles and mouths a thank you.

Sam rejoins the family, who, with the flight crew, Sarah and Annie are settled down to a movie that grabs Sam's interest, as he settles between Becca and Ann.

It was still early at nine forty five, when everyone decides to get some sleep. The youngest are asleep already. The Captain says they will depart after breakfast in the morning. Sam suddenly feels very tired and with more help than necessary, gets into his sleeping shorts. Ann and Rachael slip under the cover with him and they cuddle a little before sleep overtakes them.

"Sam, Sam. Time to get up and ready." Ann wakes him.

"Oh wow. I slept good. Today is gonna be another great day. What time is it?"

"Just after seven. Breakfast is ready. The children are up and already eating. Just you, me and Rachael left to get up and at 'em."

Sam rolls out and the three are through the intimate shower, dressed and at breakfast.

"Good morning everyone. Oh man, I slept good. Ready for another great day." Sam exclaims.

Chapter 11

FATE TAKES THEM

"Sam, I'm pushing up our departure a little. There's a storm coming down from up around the Philippines. It shouldn't affect us, but I'd like to be sure."

"You're the man, Bill. I trust your judgment in this."

The family and all take their seats early, per Bill's suggestion. The FASTEN SEATBELTS sign comes on as the plane begins its taxi out to the strip. Soon they are at their cruising altitude and everyone begins to move around the plane again.

"Dad, weren't you in Sydney once before?" Tom asks.

"It was a long time ago. I was there to meet an Aussie Special Forces guy, Harmon Rabb, for some intelligence on a mission I was involved in."

"What was Sydney like?"

"At that time it was hot. The streets were immaculate and the people were the greatest. I got a real kick out of hearing them, 'Guddai Myte'. You couldn't be a stranger there. I really liked it, but I was only there for such a short time."

"Thanks. I'm reading about it and just needed something first hand. The book says they are some of the friendliest people in Australia. Will we be there long enough to look around and talk with some people?"

"I'm guessing we'll be there at least a day and a half. Plenty of time to have a cuppa and watch your billy boil, 'ave a foite wid a roo, eh myte."

Tom laughs as he turns and returns to his seat. Sam smiles and closes his eyes. He day dreams a little about the last couple of days and the places they have seen. One or another of his ladies sit next to him for a moment and exchange loving touches. He hears the children in the next section watching and commenting on a movie they are watching. Sandra comes through with a cart of soft drinks and tells him that they are two hours from Sydney and that the weather front is moving quicker than they told Bill, but he isn't worried.

"Don't tell the others. Unnecessary worry and all that." Sam tells her.

"I won't. They are so calm and relaxed and Bill is sure that he can get around the weather."

Just then, the plane lurched up then down, spilling the cart and dumping some drinks over. Sam jumps up and helps Sandra up and to move her cart to the safety of the galley. He looks around the cabin where the children are watching the movie and sees that they are still in their seats. Rachael is crouched over, like she is just getting up.

"Rachael, are you okay?" Sam calls.

Rachael nods. Jessie, Becca, Ann and Molly are up and gathering the children to get them in their seats in the front section.

"Sam, the seat belt sign just came on." Ann calls to him.

Soon, everyone is seated and belted in, including Sarah, Annie, Mary and Barbara. Sandra comes in from the cockpit, her face is ashen.

"Sam, folks, Bill said that Flight Weather just updated the forecast and we are about to enter a Typhoon. That's a

Pacific Ocean hurricane. Bill and Art are good pilots, but this is not a usual scenario for . . ." She is interrupted by another violent drop of the aircraft. She catches the back of a seat and steadies herself, then takes a seat and belts in.

The captain comes on, "We are in a bit of a weather fix. Don't worry, we will do all that we can to avoid the major force of the storm, but we will be a little late in our arrival at Sydney. Just relax and keep your seats until you see the seat belt sign turned off. Thank you."

"Okay family. Relax. Maybe a little nap. I'm kinda sleepy." Sam says as he stretches and pretends to settle back to sleep.

"Daddy's right my darlings. We can read our books or who's for a family sing a long?" Rachael says.

The adults try their best to be reassuring for the children. Sam is starting to worry just a little. He looks at a map that he brought of the islands from Hawaii to Fiji. The area from Samoa to Sydney is like a desert in the ocean after Fiji and Tonga and west across the Tasman Sea. He thinks, God please help Bill and Art get us out of this mess.

The plane begins to bounce around violently and makes a very deep drop and buffeted left and right. Sam grips the arms of his seat and tries to look calm as he makes eye contact with his ladies. He can see fear there and it disturbs him.

An explosion rocks the airplane and Sam sees the engine out of the right side spewing flames and smoke. The captain must have initiated the fire suppressant and the flames stop, but smoke still rolls out of the engine. The plane was listing hard to the left as the flight crew tries to keep the aircraft level. Then it all begins to shake and shutter.

The children begin to cry and the mothers also are beginning to lose their composure. Sam is now very worried, as he feels the nose of the plane dipping very low in the front.

"Ladies and Gentlemen, please take positions for a rough landing. Attendants, please give everyone that doesn't have one, a pillow." The captain announces.

"Everyone tighten your seatbelt and take a pillow and put it in your lap. Lean forward and put your head on the pillow and . . . pray." Sandra instructs.

Sam looks around and sees that the youngest are sitting next to their mothers and the older children are with one another. Sam makes eye contact with his eldest son and daughter, Tom and Carly, who don't look near as frightened as the rest. Tom smiles at his Dad and Carly mouths, "I love you Dad." Sam smiles back and fights back the tears of pride that he has for his children and their courage. The captain comes on again, "Prepare for crash landing. I will ring the alarm three times just before we touch down. May God protect us."

Time seems to stand still and Sam finds himself wishing that it was over already. Then the alarm sounds . . . Brriiing! Brriing! Brriing! A heavy bump and the aircraft cried like a dieing beast that sees it's end coming. Then the sound of water rushing, then scraping and the sound of metal tearing. Sam sees the right wing fold away and is gone. The aircraft begins to turn slightly and Sam thinks that it will begin to roll, but it slides back to straight and is beginning to slow noticeably. The suddenness of the stop, feels like the seatbelt will burst their bladders, then silence.

"Is everyone alright?" Sandra calls out.

"Kids, Ann, Jessie, Becca, Rachael, Molly. Is everyone okay?" Sam unbuckles and rushes to his family.

"Sam, I think Brian has a broken arm and Mathew has a bump on the head. I can handle it. Check the others." Rachael explains, shifting into nurse mode. God, Sam thinks, I am so glad we have her.

"Dad, I checked all of us and we're good. Sarah, Annie and Mary are okay. Annie has a scrape on her leg and Sarah is taking care of it. How are you. Has anyone checked the captain?" Tom says.

A scream from the front answers the question about the captain.

"Sam, Sam, can Rachael come up. Bill is hurt badly and Art—my God Sam, Art is gone." Sandra cries.

Sam looks around for Barbara and sees her in the dining area, on the floor. He rushes in and checks her. A bump on her head has left her unconscious. Probably best to delay hearing about Art.

Rachael rushes forward to see Sandra and check Bill's injury. Brian has a balloon splint on his arm and Ann and Jessie are taking care of the bumps and scrapes. Becca goes with Rachael and Molly brings Sandra out and gives her some pills that Rachael gave her. They go to tend to Barbara and Sam sees that she has awakened. Molly gives her some of the pills and Sam surmises that they are some kind of sedative.

Sam looks out the windows on both sides and determines that they are on a beach. Far off on the horizon, the sky is black and the clouds look like they are moving off to the east, or what Sam thinks is east. On the other side, he sees sand and fifty or so yards away a forest and stands of very large bamboo trees.

It has been an hour and forty minutes and everyone is regaining their calm. Sandra has regained her professional composure and moves about the plane. She brings out hot coffee and tea and hot cocoa. Her hands tremble a little and it is apparent that she is worried about her husband.

Rachael reappears from the cockpit and announces that Bill is stable and she has stopped the bleeding.

"It will be some time before he is out of the woods, but he has a chance. He said we should stay in the plane until tomorrow morning. It's close to dark now and there is plenty of power for the lights and life support. He wants to see you Sandra. If you come along, we will get him out of there and into a bed. Rest is what he needs now."

Bill looks pale, but smiles as they carry him to a bed in the back. Sandra is holding his hand and she smiles as they pass.

The efficiency that Rachael displays is a comfort to everyone. Jessie is the first to say anything.

"Rachael, I'm sorry I said anything about the amount of supplies you wanted to bring. I guess God was telling you something and I'm glad you heard him." She gives Rach a kiss and hug.

Rachael receives several more hugs and kisses from her sisters and a huge hug from Sam.

"I hope it doesn't come to it, but if we need it, I am so happy that you had the foresight to cover us."

"You are my family. Like I said, I would rather be wrong on the side of being prepared for nothing. The plasma came in handy this time. Bill is alive because of it. Brian will have a real cast on his arm before morning and everyone will take some quinine before we go out in the morning. I also brought vitamins and supplements for a year for thirty people."

Mary comes to the front and says, "Anyone hungry? I have hot soup and a ton of sandwiches."

A relieved sigh rises from everyone, including Sam, who is up and heading for the dining area. He sits at the long table and dips soup into a soup mug and a napkin holds a ham and Swiss sandwich. Brian sits next to him and Sam dishes him some soup and Tom hands a sandwich over on a napkin.

"How's the arm Brian? Does it hurt much? You're being mighty brave." Sam says.

"It's okay Dad. Momma Rachael gave me some medicine to take the pain away. She said it was a clean break and didn't need to be set. She's gonna put a plaster cast on it a little later."

"You let me know if you need help with anything Buddy." Tom tells him.

"Good man, Tom. You're gonna be my right hand with Ryan and Matt until we get rescued. Let the two of them know and we'll sit down and do some planning tonight."

"Sure Dad, you can count on us."

Most of the apprehension that has pressed on Sam is fading away. He heaves another big sigh and feels the tension leave him. As he looks around, he sees that the children are visibly relaxed and the mommas are smiling and talking to the younger children. Then from the front, Barbara, walking like in a daze and looking furtively around.

"Art, Art, where are you? Has anyone seen Art?" Her voice is strained like someone who knows the answer, but doesn't want to admit it.

Rachael and Becca go to her. Rach has a syringe at her side and they sit Barbara on the couch and Becca holds her in a warm hug as Rachael administers the sedative.

"Get some sleep honey. It's been a long day." They tell her.

Barb slumps and her eyes close. Becca and Rach take her shoes off and loosen her skirt and blouse, to make her comfortable.

"We'll have to keep an eye on her for a while, so she doesn't wander off and hurt herself. I wish we could have done something for Art, but his neck was crushed when his head hit the windscreen. It was quick and he didn't have time to know what happened." Rachael explains.

The light begins to fade through the windows, as night falls on them. Sam and the older boys sit together and plan for the morning. The mommas and Sarah, Annie and Mary are sitting together making their plans. It's the one thing that Sam really appreciates about his family, their ability to work together as a team. Sandra is sitting close to Barbara and checks back with Bill often.

"I don't think we can count on having power for too long. We need to see how to work the radio and try to get in contact with someone."

"Dad, I can do that. I looked at their radios when we first came on board back in Columbia. Mr., er, Captain Brewster gave me a tour of the cockpit." Ryan tells them.

"Good job, Buddy. The radio is your baby. Have Richard with you and show him how to work it, oh, Brian to. Need to make him feel needed, even with a broken arm."

"Dad, I think we should unload the baggage compartment and move stuff back from the plane. If we get a lightening storm, it may set the thing on fire and we'd lose everything. I think we should be armed to. We don't know what's here." Tom reasons.

"You're right. We'll have to help the ladies to. Clothes and the boxes of supplies that Mary brought. The medicine chests for Momma Rachael. Yes. Everyone needs to be armed. Pistol belts with three days of ammo and the .44 Magnums for the older boys and girls and the .32 SW automatics for the ladies and the fourteen year old boys and girls."

"Dad, we also have a case of hunting rifles and bandoliers for them. A couple for hunting . . . God, I hope we don't have to be here that long . . . pigs, or deer, or whatever is indigenous." Tom offers.

"Better to be prepared. Unload the tool boxes. I brought axes to cut bamboo at Yai's house and saws. There is a stack of boxes with hemp rope and some nylon rope. So, first we find a place away from the plane to move our equipment and to possibly set up a shelter. We shouldn't forget the inflatable rafts that the plane has stored for their water ditching and we should also dismantle the showers and see what kind of water tank it carries. The galley equipment and salvage everything that we can from the aircraft. We're gonna be busy."

"Great for us, Dad. We'll all be working together toward a real, worthwhile goal." Mathew says.

Sandra has overheard some of their plans and offers. "There are four floor hatches, to the baggage hold, if you wanted to get some tools and begin to dismantle some of the interior this evening. It's only 6:30, we could get a lot done in the time left before sleep."

"Thank you. I wondered about access to the hold."

"As to the power, you can run all the lights and cook three meals a day for eight days on the stored power. We won't use all the lights, all the time, so that will give us a day or two more. The radio is on separate batteries in the nose and the emergency beacon is another separate power source and is running now. I hope it was just the storm, but Bill said he couldn't raise anyone as we were coming down."

"Well, at least we know. We'll prepare for the worse case scenario and hope for the best. Sandra, would you tell the ladies what you told us and let them know we are going to begin to dismantle some things and get some things up and near the doors for unloading."

"Will do. I guess you have inherited the mantle of command of the aircraft. You are gonna be our rumor control."

Sandra pointed out the hatches in the galley and the sleeping area. The boys and Sam opened the galley hatch and went below to get tools and pull arms and ammo for the morning. Extra seats are the first to be unbolted and the rafts are taken out of the ceiling storage. Sam has the boys bring up several of the suitcases. They also unload the crate of camping gear and each of them takes a canteen and fills it from the galley water supply before getting ready for sleep.

Mary brings out coffee for Sam and the women. The boys excuse themselves and go to wash up and go to sleep. The coffee is welcome and Sam appreciates the time with his ladies.

"How are you all doing? I think the boys and I have a plan that will give us a measure of security until we are rescued. The pistol belts and the .32's are for you and the 14 year old children. Sarah, Annie, Mary and Sandra are included. Just in case. What help will you need, in the morning?"

"I think we have it handled. We, also thought about moving things away from the plane. A couple of us will go with the boys and pick a place, while the rest pitch out the cases from the baggage compartment. Mary said she has supplies that will feed all of us for some time. Rachael has an extensive medical kit. These two things are the first things we will move to safety." Ann says.

"Good job my darlings. You have it all together. We should break it up into teams. I think the 9 and 10 year olds will like to help and they can move things. Have to have one of the older girls, maybe Raina or Cathy watch out for them and guide their efforts. We don't know what dangers are here, so Raina and Cathy should be armed. I would feel better, if Art's death wasn't so heavy on my mind. We will have to take care of that as well."

"Sam, Rach and I will remove him, when everyone is away from the plane and move him away as well. Later tomorrow, we can bury him." Becca says.

"Are you two sure you can handle it alone. It seems such a dreadful thing for you to have to do."

They both nod and pass a somber look around the table.

"I'll help them Sam. Art is . . . was a friend, and Barbara is like a sister." Sandra offers.

"I guess we are settled on tomorrow's activities. Anything else we should talk about?"

"Sam. If the galley will work for another eight days, I think we should leave it for another day to dismantle and move it."

"Right Mary. The boys and I looked at the hook up to the gas tanks in the hold. We can do it in one move as soon as we have a place to move it to, but yes, it can wait for a day or two. One other thing. Until we find a water source, I suggest we use the planes supply sparingly."

Nods around the table confirmed their understanding.

"Sam we can bottle several five gallon jugs that are in the hold and move them in toward the forest . . . or whatever that is . . . jungle." Sandra says.

Another round of nods and acknowledgements.

"Well, good night everyone. God please watch over us, Amen."

"Amen." is spoken by all.

The night goes by slowly. Sam wakes frequently to the sobs of one or another of his darling women. He pets and hugs to comfort them, until they fall back to sleep. Sam wasn't ready to let the events affect him, until he was sure that his people were safe.

Chapter 12

SURVIVAL

At 7:00, Sam hears Tom, Matt and Ryan moving around and untangles himself from Ann and Becca, who wake when he moves.

"What's wrong Sam?" Ann asks.

"Nothing. It's seven and Tom, Matt and Ryan are up. We're gonna get started. We need to explore a little before we get very deep into the move."

"Ummm! We'll be along in a bit. We'll help organize breakfast." Becca says.

Sam nods and moves out of the berth. He pushes a wet washcloth over his face and goes out to meet his eldest sons.

"Morning men."

"Morning Dad. What should we do first?" Tom asks.

"Explore first. We'll use the door over the wing that we still have. I looked out and it is all the way into the sand, no jumping. Get your canteen and side arms, a couple of axes and maybe a shovel or two."

"Got 'em. Cool. The canteen and shovel attach to the web belt and the axe attaches to the shoulder straps." Ryan observes.

"Real Special Forces gear Buddy." Sam ruffles Ryan's hair.

The four gather their gear and step through the emergency door onto the wing and walk to the sand. The sun is rising over the horizon and the air is moving off the ocean in a refreshing breeze. They start off toward the tree line and see that there is an expanse of large bamboo trees off to the right, about a hundred and fifty yards away. The trees in front of them look like birch or poplar with whitened trunks and the foliage between the trees is deep green. As they get closer, they can see that the ground is not all sand and is darker, suggesting soil. Ryan and Matt brought machetes and hack at the foliage to clear it from the trees. After only two or three yards into the brush, the ground is clear. Sam and Tom immediately see that there are six good size trees that are evenly spaced like the perimeter of a rectangle.

"Tree house." Tom says.

"Looks like it." Sam agrees.

Ryan and Matt smile and nod.

"Dad, the bamboo will fit in for floors and walls." Matt says.

"I think we should clear the area around these trees as a place to bring our supplies and things. While the younger children and ladies move their things here, we can go to that bamboo stand and cut some to bring here. While we are down there, we can dig a grave for Art. Momma Rach, Becca and Ms. Sandra will bring him there. It has to be done soon, before healing can take place."

"Okay Dad. Makes sense. What about a bonfire later? Kinda like Tom Hanks in that movie where he is alone." Ryan says.

"He says, 'Look what I have done. I have made fire.' It was good. We can sit around the fire and listen to the ocean and the sounds of the forest." Tom offers.

"Sure. Maybe cook something on sticks like we are camping. Okay. Good idea guys. Let's move the cut brush off to the left there. Maybe twenty yards or so. It can be the base for the bonfire."

They have only been working three hours. They have sixty or more bamboo trees that are forty and fifty feet long and seven and eight inches across. The area is clear and ready for supplies, which Sam sees, are about to be here. Jamie, Edward, Carrie and Wyatt are dragging suitcases toward them. Raina and Cathy are bringing a large case and Michael and Sybil are both bringing five gallon jugs that are each, half full.

"Right on time worker bees." Sam says to his youngest offspring. They all smile and set down their loads.

"Mom said we could combine the jugs when we get here and bring an empty one back." Mike explains.

"Ya done good guys. Raina, Cathy, keep your eyes open. We still don't know how safe it is. Love you guys. Tom wants to build a bonfire for tonight, so let's get our things here." Sam tells them. Raina and Cathy are beaming and have their hand on Mike and Sybil's shoulder.

The two youngest, are smiling broadly at their big brother. Becca is approaching with a large case, in tow, atop a piece of metal.

"Hey darling, that's a good idea. Does it make the load lighter?" Sam asks as he kisses her on the cheek.

"Yeah. Jessie and Molly took a piece of the torn wing and hooked rope from our cache to the corners and it slides good . . . Sam we've taken care of our other job. We saw the place you guys made for him. Thank you. Barb is awake and has accepted Art's death. Bill is awake, but he has a high fever. Rach is with him."

Sam accepts the news. It isn't the best, but it's what they have.

"We have a good place cut out of the woods and a large supply of bamboo. We'll start on splitting the bamboo and putting a roof up."

"Mary, Ann and Jessie are putting together lunch. It will be ready in an hour or so. Most of the stuff we want to move here is already out of the hold. We will get it all moved today, but this afternoon, we want to do a service for Art."

"Yes. That's good. We're gonna get started. Have someone call us for lunch."

Sam and the boys split bamboo and untwisted some rope to lash the pieces of bamboo together to a cross piece between the trees. Soon, they have a roof that is fifty feet facing the beach and angled down at the back for more than thirty feet. Sam has to stop and thank God for providing such a beautiful stand of bamboo. They lash bamboo to the trees around the perimeter of the rectangle and begin laying floor pieces between the front and back. Tom suggests five low walls of bamboo every five feet, from the front to support the floor in short sections.

"You're right. I'm glad you thought of it before we tried to lay out a thirty foot piece and have it sag to the ground in the middle. Wow. That would not have been good. Thanks Tom."

"You would have thought of it before we started. You have a lot on your mind." Tom says.

"Thanks Buddy. I can't afford to let it get to me yet. When you guys are safe, I'll cry."

Tom, Matt and Ryan hug him in a group hug. They continue and are almost finished with the floor and test it, when someone calls from the plane.

"Lunch!"

The four with Cathy and Raina, who delivered more boxes, return to the plane for lunch. Sam is really proud of his children. These, the eldest were almost adults. They acted like adults already.

"Where's Carly? I haven't seen her, have you Tom?"

Before Tom can answer, Cathy offers, "She's been with Momma Rachael tending to the captain and keeping an eye on Ms. Barbara and helping on the plane, between the galley and the . . . hospital area."

Sam nods his understanding.

The conversation at lunch is animated. Sam lets Tom, Matt and Ryan field the questions about the shelter. Everyone is surprised to learn that the roof and floor are up and solid.

"Dad says we'll put walls up this afternoon, after the . . . uh, the service. We could bring bedding up, or some of the unused seats. I asked for a bonfire this evening, if anyone is interested."

Tom's statement was met with pleasant acknowledgements that that was just what they needed.

"This is a great lunch. I do love soup." Sam compliments.

"Thank you. We had a lot of help. Mary also unloaded the boxes of supplies that she stowed in the hold." Ann says. "We need to guard the cases from animals, if we move them to the shelter."

"Yeah. Maybe rig a sling up in the ceiling of the shelter. Someone will think of something." Sam says, looking from face to face of his sons.

Rachael enters with Carly, Sandra is between them. It doesn't look good.

"Sam. We lost Bill." Rachael says.

Sam gets up and goes to them. Sandra nearly collapses into Sam's arms, sobbing deeply.

"Sandra, I'm so sorry. Oh my God. This is a real tragedy. I don't know enough about this kind of thing. I'm sorry, I'm so sorry." Sam was in tears.

"He didn't suffer. Rachael kept him comfortable until the end. He just sighed and was gone. We think he must have had internal injuries that we couldn't detect. I'm going to miss him, oh my God, Bill. We were going to let me stay home and have a baby. I'm all right, I'm all right. Bill would want me to be strong."

"Yes he would. He was that kind of man. You have to go on for him honey." Jessie says and hugs her. Jessie turns and hugs Sam and kisses him warmly.

Ann, Molly and Becca add their condolences with warm hugs. They each hug Sam and kiss him as well. Barbara comes into the dining area and goes to Sandra. The two embrace and cry on each others shoulder.

Everyone moves away, silently, to give them some privacy, to share their grief. The family moves to the forward area and sit together. They are soon joined by Tom, Carly, Raina, Cathy, Matt, Ryan, Richard, Delia, Alex, Peter, Elizabeth and Brian. The youngest have gone to the back and are napping.

"Family, we have to prepare another burial place. We'll rest for a while, then I . . ." Sam is interrupted.

"Dad, me, Matt, Ryan, Richard and Peter will do another . . . burial place, next to Art's place." Tom says.

"Thanks guys. Take your weapons and at least two keep watch at a time."

"Yes Sir. We'll go now and everything will be ready by the original two o'clock service time that was set before." Tom adds as the five boys stand and collect their gear.

Sam and the rest put their seats in recline and try to relax. It's difficult to keep from thinking about their predicament and rest. Sam's mind is churning. God please don't let me screw up. He thinks and worries about his ladies and children. Now he would have to worry about all the rest.

His thoughts are interrupted by Sandra, who comes into the forward section with Barbara.

"Sam, family, we need to . . . we need to take Bill and . . . bury him." Sandra chokes out the words.

The ladies all go to her and hug and pat her and Barbara. Sam hears the soothing words. Carly, Elizabeth and Alex join in the soothing words as Rachael and Becca slip away. Sam follows and helps them wrap Bill in a double sheet and tie it off with rope. The three carry Bill to the exit and off the wing onto the sled that Jessie and Molly fabricated earlier. The boys are just finishing their job as Sam, Rach and Becca arrive. Sam notices a pile of split bamboo nearby.

"What's the bamboo for Tom?"

"We quartered it and lined the bottom and sides. These are to go over them after . . . . we thought it would make Ms. Sandra and Ms. Barbara feel a little better."

"Very thoughtful Thomas." Rachael says.

"Yes Tom that is thinking with your heart. Very nice." Becca adds

"Aw, the guys did all the work, splitting and placing the bamboo. I only thought of it."

My man. Sam thinks. He is so grown up already.

"Sam, it's almost time. I'll go back and bring them here. Get this behind us and maybe we can work on a rescue or at least survive." Rachael says.

"Right. First we need to stay safe. We'll have the shelter done this afternoon and get most of the gear under cover." Sam points out.

"Dad, there are a ton of fronds, that look like that stuff they do thatched roofs with. Matt, Ryan an I walked into the jungle a little and there were berry bushes. I didn't recognize them. There is a lot of new bamboo, I remember that the shoots are edible. I think that there might also be coconuts and bananas."

"You guys be real careful. Any signs of animals?"

"Didn't see any, but we didn't go in too deep. We didn't want to be in there, lose track of time and it get to dark." Matt answers.

"We'll get an exploring party together tomorrow. Ryan tells me we have to get an antenna up higher."

"Yes Sir. It was all dead air. Everything was working, so that is the only thing I could think of that was keeping us from reaching anyone." Ryan explains.

Becca is coming back with the others for the service. Sandra and Barbara seem to be standing up straight and holding hands. Everyone's face is somber. The youngest are holding hands with their mommas.

The boys have the bodies on bamboo supports and ropes so that they can lower the bodies into the grave with a little dignity. The gesture is not lost on Sandra or Barbara, who force an upturn to their sad countenance.

"I don't have the words that can make any of this better. As we made our rapid descent, I kept thinking, well the three of us should be able to take care of our people, I never expected this. Bill Brewster and Art Harris, we will miss you both. God, we beg you to receive these two men into your loving care. They were two good men and this world will be less without them. Bring comfort to their loved ones and to all of us who knew them and were just beginning to appreciate how wonderful they were. In Jesus name. Amen." The assembly voices Amen and Sam nods to the boys, who take up the ropes. Richard takes the fourth end and lowers, first Bill, then Art into the prepared grave. Sandra drops a handful of dirt into the grave and Barbara drops a handful into Art's grave. They stand back and watch as the boys place the bamboo cover onto the bamboo uprights along the four walls. It looks almost like a vault and the sight gives a measure of comfort to those looking on.

Hugs for the two mourners continue for a while and Sam and the four boys, pick up their weapons and tools and move into the jungle to explore a little as they move toward the partially completed shelter.

Twenty yards into the jungle and they spot smaller bamboo and the berries that Tom couldn't identify. They take a sample to look at, back at the plane and a laptop with loads of information. When they are half way back, they come across an arm of a creek and decide to follow it inland a ways. They go in another quarter mile and can see the source coming out of a wall of stone that is the base of a small mountain.

"We'll have to explore this further, but for now, this can be a source of water when we need it. Do we have something to take a sample in?"

Matt produces a nearly empty bottled water container. He drinks the rest and takes a sample. "How's this Dad?"

"That'll work Matt. Let's get to the shelter. We can finish it and we'll map out our work for tomorrow."

The boys agree as they head for the shelter.

The girls and women are stacking up boxes and cases. They have a pile of deadfall and cardboard boxes for the bonfire all ready. The older girls have side arms and the women are all carrying .32 automatics. Peter and Delia are shouldering rifles and are eyeing the edge of the woods. Delia sees Sam and the boys first and calls out. "They're back."

Tom organizes the boys into two teams. Matt and Ryan are set to split the large bamboo trees into long strips. Richard, Edward and Peter are untwining nylon rope. Cathy, Raina, and Carly volunteer to untwine rope and help weave the rope and bamboo strips into walls. Tom took the job of engineer and calls for some bamboo split and tied into rectangular frames for windows and doors. Some of the women go into the jungle with Alex and Elizabeth to gather grasses and fronds. Sam follows them with a rifle, just in case.

"We'll be okay Sam. Liz and Alex have rifles and we all have our side arms." Ann says.

"I know, but I'd feel better if I am with you."

They are busy and each of them loads a large bundle on their shoulders. Jessie lashes together several long pieces of dead fall for the fire and drags them behind her.

"Mary and Sandra are getting campfire food together for the bonfire. Barbara and Annie are collecting sticks, I think it was bamboo, or willows to hold food over a fire. The kids will love it and the work is therapeutic for Sandra and Barbara." Jessie says.

"I'm amazed at how much we have done so far. I hope we don't need it, but until we can figure out how to get the antenna high enough, we need to be ready for a long term survival scenario." Sam voices his concerns.

Everyone is gathered around the shelter and admire the work that is being done. Sam is a little amazed at how fast the long walls have gone up. Cathy, Raina and Carly are working with Molly and weaving the strips of bamboo with the twine at two foot intervals that makes the walls firm and stable. The walls are then lashed to larger poles of bamboo that go from the floor to the ceiling cross beam.

"You ladies are amazing. This is really good. Strong. We need to think about some light for tomorrow night. I think it would be good to test out a night before we do a major move to the shelter."

"Right honey. I could stay with you tomorrow night." Molly grins and hugs him.

"Okay Molly. Trying to muscle in huh?" Jessie laughs.

Sam sees Mary and Sandra coming with large coolers. Becca goes to help them, with Ann close behind.

"Anyone hungry yet?" Mary calls to them.

"Anyone know what time it is?" Jessie asks.

"The sun is about two hours from setting. We must be south of the equator. The sun comes up, over there to the right and see it's gonna set off to the left. Probably about five, six o'clock. It'll get dark pretty fast when the sun dips into the ocean." Sam observes, as work stops on the construction and the boys bring out seats from the plane.

"Dad, we are bringing the spare seats first and some of the tables that we don't usually use." Tom says.

"Good idea man. I think we would like to use some of the planes comfortable spaces for a couple more days."

"Sam, I tested the water that Matt brought me. It's good. The berries are indigenous to the islands in this part of the world, and are also good." Rachael says.

"Rachael. I think I've missed you. Thank you. I knew you probably brought some kinds of test gear. How are our invalids doing?"

"Brian is good. He got his cast last night and has been helping with his right arm. Sandra and Barbara are coping. Mary's scrape is healing. I think over all we're okay."

A pop draws their attention to the burn pile. Ann, Tom, Becca, Sandra and Barbara have the fire started. The rest of the boys are milling around and Mary has a long folding table set up with trays of skewered meat, hot dogs, veggies and marsh mellows.

"Let's join the others." Jessie says.

Sam, Rachael, Molly, Sarah, Annie and the rest start toward the fire. Everyone gets comfortable and Sam takes a mental inventory of his responsibilities. Someone has set up a five gallon jug of water on a peg at the corner of the shelter. A hose from the jug is tacked to the tree and a plastic spigot sticks out from the end of the hose.

"Sam, you can wash up, if you like. Brian, Michael, Ed and Wyatt rigged up that water jug. The water is ok, it's from the creek. A branch runs off from the spot you guys found and goes east and fills a small rock basin." Becca says, there is pride in her tone for her son.

"Good for Brian. We made a good son there didn't we darling?"

Becca hugs him and he returns the hug with feeling and kisses her upturned face and lips.

Sam goes to the jug and takes some water and splashes his face and rubs his hands together. He shakes the water off his hands and Carrie is there with a hand towel for him. Sam smiles at his youngest daughter and takes the towel.

"Thank you Carrie. I forgot to bring one." Sam dries his face and hands and Carrie takes the towel and drapes it over a bamboo rod that looks like it was made for drying towels.

"Poppa, can I sit with you at the fire?"

"Yes baby girl. I would like that. You've been busy today. Would you like to wash up?"

"I did Poppa." She takes his hand and walks back to where he was sitting and takes a place next to him.

Ann comes by and brings two skewers with fire roasted steak for them.

"Thank you darling." Sam says and gives her a squeeze and his lips meet hers.

"You sitting with Daddy, Carrie?" She asks her youngest.

"Uh huh. Daddy said I could." She says smiling.

Sam hugs his baby girl. He hears the boys talking animatedly with the older girls. They are making plans for tomorrow. Sam is so proud of his children. He needs a new word. They are no longer children.

Everyone is sitting comfortably and enjoying the warmth of the fire and the seared meats and vegetables. As the sun starts to slip into the ocean, Sam found more and more of his ladies and children gathering close to him. Before it was totally dark, a new light was rising at 28 degrees to bring it's light to the night and Sam sees two boys with torches walking toward the plane. As they go, torches light up on either side of them.

"That's Tom and Matt. They made bamboo torches, like the Tiki torches for patios. He's already set it up to refuel the torches each day, so we'll have light at night, to and from the plane." Molly was also sharing her pride in her first born.

"I love you all. Just had to tell you. As bad as our situation seems, everyone has pulled together and I have every confidence that we will survive. I love you."

"Thanks Sam. It could be that you may have to do just that, if we do get stuck here." Sarah grins, "With everyone's consent, or however you all come to agreements."

"Oh Sam. I didn't even think of that." Ann says.

"Me either, but that's right. What do we do?" Becca says.

"Not to worry, sisters, we will persevere, if the time comes. We've made difficult decisions before." Rachael observes.

"Not a problem for me. I've always said, the more the merrier." Molly offers with a broad grin that makes everyone feel good.

"Yes. I love Sarah, Annie and Mary already. They have never felt like employees. We almost offered this once before. Sam said he was happy already, but we didn't tell him who we wanted to bring in then. When the time comes that we decide that we are gonna be here, Sarah, Annie, Mary, any or all of you have my vote." Jessie says almost diplomatically proposing a treaty.

"Nothing to say about it Sam?" Ann asks.

"My Darlings, you know I bend to your will and desire. I've always liked your choice in these three women. I'm sorry ladies, but I have had those thoughts. I kept my place because I knew that you were pursuing relationships, at least I knew about Kenny and Mary."

"Thank you Sam. We've always liked you. Especially the way you always treated us and your family. Respect and love was always there. If the time should come and I'm a real pessimist, I would welcome a relationship." Annie says.

Sarah and Mary nod their concurrence and elicits raised eyebrows among Sam's ladies.

"Well, I guess that says everything. We will finalize this when it becomes apparent." Ann says.

The evening continues with cheerful banter and real planning for the days ahead.

The moon is overhead when they decide to move it back to the plane. The fire is a pit of glowing embers. Tom puts several deadfall logs into the coals and pulls a large piece of metal from the wing over it.

"What're you doing Tom?" Sam looks puzzled.

"If I cover the pit, to reduce the oxygen, the logs will turn into charcoal that we can store and use later."

"Right. I remember. Yai does that to. Good job Tom. Let's get back. Thank you for a great day. You are a good man, son. Matt and Ryan were great to."

"Dad, we just wanted to make it a little easier on you and the mommas. I know how much you worry. We love you. Ryan and Peter are going to set up a cistern and divert the creek to keep water close. Cathy, Delia, Alex and Elizabeth are going to weave the fronds into mats and curtains and some for floor coverings. Raina will take some of the younger ones and collect rocks and driftwood. Matt and I are going to go to the rocks where the water comes out of and check for animal spore. We all talked and if you don't mind. You stay with the mothers and women to make them comfortable and organize the supplies in the shelter."

"How did you get to be so good? Let the kids know how much I appreciate all that you and they have done. I couldn't be more proud of anyone. Thank you."

Tom smiles and looks away, like he is embarrassed by the praise. The two men continue to the plane. Molly and Ann are at the doorway watching for them.

"You two were taking your time." Molly admonishes.

"Man talk, woman." Sam says with a broad grin that made the two woman smile.

Everyone washes up and get into clean sleeping clothes. Sam slept harder than he has in a long time. He didn't even know when he became surrounded with girl flesh, until loud talk and laughter woke him. The cabin was filled with sun light and Sam turns to roll out and is pressed up to Jessie on one side and Rachael on the other.

"Morning Sam. We needed a little pick me up from you this morning." Jessie says, locking her lips to his and pushing her pubic arch against him. Rachael was pushing herself against him on the other side. He turns his head and she locks lips with him.

"Well ladies, the men have told me that they have today organized and I am to stay with the mothers today and make you all happy."

"That sounds like a plan to me. Let me tell Ann, Becca, Molly and the rest." Rachael says.

Hunger finally drags them out. Everyone is eating breakfast already. Smiles greet them as they take plates of food and sit with all the rest. Rachael goes to Ann and Becca and whispers to them. Their smiles tells their understanding.

The day progresses into days and the days into weeks. It is beginning to look like they are going to have a permanent home on this island. The plane has really been dismantled. The seats and beds are in the, expanded shelter. The showers have been moved to an area with a dressing shelter. The water for the showers is in a large storage container that they have put up on a tower. Tom's water tower, gives all connected faucets water pressure. The kitchen has it's own shelter and attached storage, that is built extra tight to keep animals out. There are small deer like animals on the island and pigs. Some smaller mammals that haven't been identified. Quail like birds, chickens and cows. A small herd of six or eight cows and a bull were located in a grassy valley on the other side of the island. There aren't many calves and Sam wonders what happens to the extra cows. Predators, still haven't been located. Sam admonishes daily the need for being armed and for watching out for each other and not letting the younger ones out of sight.

The boys found a small bay that provides, oysters, or clams, crab and what must be Australian lobsters. Sam has only seen lobsters this size, when he was in Sydney many years ago.

Something that might have been disturbing, is explained by Sandra.

"Sam, Bill and I were really looking to get out of the air and start our family. The AK-47s and RPG launchers, with all the ammunition, was going to be our nest egg. Bill had a buyer in the Philippines, who would have removed it all while we were at dinner in Manila. The sixty automatic rifles would have been a quarter million with the RPGs selling for 5k each. The ammo would have brought us up to a million."

"We'll still store them away from the plane. God, I hope not, but good to have if we need them. I just had a bad vision of pirates, or someone who knew about the shipment and wants it for themselves." Sam says.

"I'm sorry Sam. We should have told you. I hope you can understand."

"Sure. Don't worry about it, Sandy. I would have done the same to get to retire with my loves."

Sandra puts her arms around him and hugs him and mouths her, Thank you. Barbara comes to them and says, "Me to Sam. Art and I were going to be married after this trip. The cases of antibiotics and the C-4 and detonators were our nest egg. Sorry." She concludes with a hug.

"Let's get with the others and let them know what we have. We're armed like a small army now, which could be comforting, as long as we all know everything. Anything else we should know?"

Both women shake their heads, no. Sam smiles and touches the cheek of each of them. They present the new information to the rest and it is decided to do some training in the use of these new weapons. All of the Elliotts have extensive training in small arms and martial arts. Sam, Tom, Jessie and Becca take to providing their training to

Sandra, Barbara, Sarah, Annie and Mary in pistol and rifle. Tom and Matt study the manuals for the AK-47. Sam has prior experience with both new weapons and helps the boys understand the mechanics of them.

The group of survivors are into their fifteenth week. Life is settling into one of those reality show settings, with evening campfires, except here, everyone, everyone loves one another. Sarah, Annie, Mary, Sandra and Barbara have assumed a place as part of the corporate union. The week, his ladies made it official, nearly killed Sam, who fulfilled his obligations with all of his ladies. Rachael keeps him on schedule with vitamin supplements and watches his diet. Sam has to keep it to himself, but he is more happy than he should be with the addition of the five new women.

The sixteenth week delivers their first predator. A large black cat. Panther, female, killed by Tom with one shot. The boys and Sam back track the cat. They can't afford to leave her family or pride free to avenge her. Tom spots another big cat in a tree, thirty yards ahead of them and drops it; male and in a hidden spot behind the tree he was in, three juvenile cats. Ryan and Matt take care of them quickly.

"Keep sharp men. There may be more. Good work. At least we don't have to worry about these carnivores. There must be more, to have kept that herd of cows small." Sam says.

Sam and the boys spend the whole week trekking the island, searching for more predators. They find and dispatch two more groups. One with three females and a half dozen babies—kittens. They find no other traces of carnivores during the next ten days of exploration, but do discover a banana grove and several nut trees, that look like walnut and pecan. They are beginning to feel safer and with the water and natural food available, feel like they can survive.

Ryan and Richard keep up the radio, but only try it when it is that time of day that there would be air traffic. Ryan explains that the horizon is only 25 miles away, after than it is hit or miss if there is an antenna that will receive them.

The group of survivors are into their fourth month, when Sarah, Mary and Sandra report that they are pregnant. Annie and Barbara tell the group that they to have missed two cycles. The rest of the women are ecstatic. Sam is happy, but reserved. He is worried about any complications with the deliveries. Rachael sees his concern and talks with him privately.

"Sam. I'm pretty certain that everything will be alright with their pregnancies. I'm also sure that I can handle anything that would threaten an uncomplicated birth. I brought a lot of medical supplies. I did have an idea of opening a clinic near Yai's house."

"Darling, I have every confidence in your abilities, but it's my job to worry." He kisses her warmly and she returns the kiss with her own passion.

Sam is sitting in front of the shelter when Raina, Peter and Delia come out of the forest with plastic pails filled with liquid.

"What cha got there guys?" Sam calls.

"Poppa, we tamed the cows. Mary said they would come to salt and we picked some tender grass and wet it and put salt all over it and they came over to eat. Delia touched one of them on the nose and the cow mooed and kept eating. She patted her down her side and then set the bucket under the udder and began to milk. Raina did it next with another cow and I milked one to. We have milk. Is it okay to drink?" Peter says.

"I'm pretty sure it is, but we'll have to boil it first. You know, "Pasteurized and Homogenized", like the store bought stuff!" Sam says.

"Oh yes, it will be great. I'll get a big kettle heating, but first we let it sit and let the cream come to the top. We scoop it off and clabber it for butter. You three have changed our diet in a very good way. Thank you." Mary tells them.

Their faces beam with pride. Sam is beaming as well. They are his babies.

"How is it Delia jumps on the, milk the cow thing, so fast?"

"Oh Poppa. My mom told me about milking cows when she was little."

Jessie hears them talking about the milk and comes over.

"Baby, you milked a cow? Sam, our child is a born farmer. Raina and Peter to. You three can be in charge of our family dairy." Jessie smiles and pats each of them. She turns to Sam and hugs him tight.

New discoveries and improvements take place nearly everyday. The children are extremely inventive. Sam spends most of his time looking at plans and cataloging their advances. The plane has been mostly dismantled and is a skeleton. The fuel presented a problem. Sam remembered that AVGAS boiled at very low temperatures and warned that they could be on fire and not know it. It was Peter, their chemist, who found that oil from the hydraulics could be added to the gas and make it more like kerosene or camping fuel. The family acquired 1500 gallons of useable fuel. Sam couldn't remember when his sons became so smart.

Some wall segments with the windows in tact, become walls of their expanded shelter. Nothing is wasted. Flooring and ceilings, overhead baggage compartments and of course the showers, beds and seating. The oldest kids build a dining room onto the shelter and set up all of the planes dining equipment. The beds are in a room, separate from the living area. There is no privacy, but then, none is needed, except that the children have a separate shelter with a covered bridge between them and the adults. Most nights, there are acres of female flesh surrounding Sam in the improvised bed. Several times a week, four, or five women help Sam stir up his testosterone and they get to stoke their estrogen levels. None of them ever go more than three days without passion. Sam enjoys unlimited love. It is definitely keeping them healthy. Molly pushes the envelope, but her love is sincere and Sam appreciates her enthusiasm.

The family still enjoys movie night, thanks to Tom and Richard, who find one of the planes small generators and rig a windmill to turn the dynamo and provides electricity to recharge the batteries for the DVD projector. Movies were Sam's second major shipment, after the weapons and he brought more than three thousand movies in all the genres that the family liked.

The generator also provides for the galley refrigerator, stove and microwave ovens that have been relocated to the kitchen shelter. Brian's arm healed and the cast was removed with the electric medical saw. Brian, in that same week, dismantled the planes interior lights and then strung them through out the shelters, with individual on/off switches. He says that he had a lot of time to just think. The water tower, is filled from the diverted creek with the water hoisted by containers attached to a belt that dips, then rises and dumps the water into the tank. The belt is turned most often by a small windmill and other times by two pairs of pedals that work like a stair master and is appreciated by the ladies, who still worry about their figures.

The pool that the creek fills is expanded by the boys, who build a run off down a level, into a 20 x 20 x 4 ft pool that is lined with sand and covered by the insulation plastic from the plane's cargo hold. Some of this same plastic sheeting covers shelter roofs just beneath the thatched cover. The plane's carpeting covers shelter floors; ceiling and wall panels cover the interior walls of the shelters.

At 44, Sam feels more and more like a patriarch—da God Fodder—to these young men.

"Dad. Mary has a large wire rack that she isn't using and says that I can have it. I thought we could build a kind of barbeque with the rack as the cooking surface. We looked through the stored data on the metal that is available and most of the plane's metal heats out some toxic chemicals but the rack is stainless steel. What do you say?" Brian asks.

"Sounds okay with me. Check with Tom. Your job, but I want to be sure everyone is on the same page."

"Yeah. I understand. Mom said you all had evening family meetings back home to keep everyone up to date. Can we start it here?"

"That's right, Brian. We would sit around the table and everyone would tell what they did for the day and what they planned for the next day. We would then be able to supply help where needed and prioritize our work. Good idea. You talk with Tom, Matt and the older kids and I'll bring it up with the Mommas. Good work son." Sam shakes hands with his son and pats his back. Fourteen and is more man than many I have known. Sam thinks.

Sam presents Brian's suggestion to the ladies—whew, ten women and five pregnant. They receive the idea with something akin to astonishment.

"Why did we stop doing that? It really kept all of us in the game. Brian is growing so fast. Becca, you can really be proud of that young man." Ann says.

"Any dissent to our meeting later. Maybe over a campfire and some drinks, not too late. We have youngsters still and a few expectant moms." Sam says.

All agree that they will meet at six, after dinner and let the kids do the last of the marsh mellows, until the sun goes down and the fire dies down to coals. Mary offers, "The girls killed a pig today and dressed it out. When the fire burns down, I'll put the pig in the coals and cover the whole thing with that piece of iron plate that the kitchen sat on when it was in the plane."

"Good idea. If there isn't anything pressing tomorrow, which we will find out at our meeting tonight, we can just relax on the sand and enjoy the pig roast." Sam smiles like he has thought of something.

"All in favor of . . . what Sam just said, raise your hand!" Ann exclaims. They hear cheering and loud laughter coming from the children. They were voting on the meeting as well.

The family meeting happens more like a reunion, as much love and warmth passes between mothers and children and between the children and the adults. Each person with a topic is given a chance to speak and a few great ideas emerge that will make life easier. Brian's barbecue is approved and work will start in a few days, after a formal plan is drawn and site selected.

Cathy, Raina, Carly, Elizabeth, Alex and Delia present their plan to grow some vegetables. Carrie, Jamie and Sybil want to help with the garden and it is agreed that the girls will be the farmers, but need the boys to help clear enough of the ground to give them room. Sam asks about the seeds and discovers that Cathy has packed vegetable seeds, hoping to start a garden in Thailand when they get there.

There is a short and emotional moment of thanks to God, who it seems provided the wisdom in all of them to bring the things they needed to survive. Sandra and Barbara, were also a part of the plan with the materials that they brought, not knowing that this would happen.

Sam thinks about all the seemingly unnecessary things that each brought for their trip to Yai's house. It was supposed to be a vacation, yet, Sam brought Weapons and DVDs, Rachael brought extensive medical supplies, including vitamins, antibiotics, sutures, syringes, anti venom, laxatives, antacids, blood pressure cuffs, scalpels, clamps, defibrillator, splints, stocking gauze, plaster of Paris, gels, salves and bandages and more.

Mary brought foil packed tuna, salmon, chicken, ham, canned soups, in the family size, coffee, tea, Splenda, Tang, flour, sugar, spices, condiments, instant stuff, like potatoes, grits, Ramen noodles and on and on. A separate shelter had to be built onto the kitchen to store the boxes and crates. Plus, she brought the iron skillets, witches pots—cauldrons, stainless steel pots and pans, utensils, dinnerware, plates, cups, bowls. Sam figures she wanted to move to Thailand from the amount and variety of kitchen/dining things she packed.

Tom packed extra laptops with extra batteries and several complete libraries. One in mechanics, one in chemistry, one in flora, one in fauna, one in animal husbandry, one general knowledge, one in building and several more.

Ryan packed three dozen two way radios with extra batteries, fishing gear, nets, crab traps (the ones that fold flat), extra hooks in a variety of sizes and extra heavy line.

Cathy brought seeds, Delia and Raina brought sewing things, with bolts of light weight, light colored, cotton cloth for—"blouses, Poppa, we can make our own", Elizabeth and Alex brought flutes, clarinets, piccolos and not just a few, but several of each. Sam could see his music room nude of instruments.

Richard brought tools. Sam's whole double tool chest, with the hand saws, hammers, chisels, mechanics tools, carvers tools and some power tools, saw and drill.

Clothes . . . no one would ever need clothes while they were on this island. Sarah and Annie, being in charge of the children, packed a school. Not just paper and pencils, but books in each grade, video programs, music CDs and chalk boards.

Each of the Elliott women also brought an abundance of shampoo, conditioners, creams, powders, hair spray and since at least four were cosmetologists, scissors, razors, combs, brushes, clippers, trimmers, blow dryers, table top hair dryers and perms, tints, lighteners. Much more than would have been needed for three months in Thailand.

"My Darlings, my children, my daughters and my sons! My new Darlings. I have just catalogued, in my head, the amount of supplies that we brought for our three month stay with Yai in Thailand and concluded that we brought enough for at least two years." Smiles raced from face to face as Sam continues. "We must be destined to do something here and the Almighty has provided for us to do it without being short of needed supplies. I think that, despite our seeming predicament, we must be thankful that we are alive and in good health and able to survive. I want to pray." Everyone bows their heads and folds their hands. Some of the children and mommas kneel as well.

Sam prays aloud, "Heavenly father, we are your children and we wish to do your will on earth. We thank you for delivering us from the tragedy and thank you for giving us the foresight to bring the materials we need to survive and indeed flourish. Your humble servant thanks you for these wonderful women and these wonderful young people that you have put before me. Bless them one and all and please Father, let us know your will so that we can be your instruments. In Jesus name, we pray. Amen."

In one voice, Amen is voiced by everyone.

Their idyllic life goes on with little to distract them from enjoying each day. The occasional rain and wind were a welcome cleansing of their home and beach. As peaceful as it is, there are infrequent issues that cropped up. One afternoon, Ann, Jessie, Becca and Molly approach Sam, who has just started talking with Rachael.

"What is it, my darlings? Rachael was just about to tell me something."

"Sam, it's Sandra. She is in a blue mood. I think she wants to talk to you. We've all tried to get it out of her, but she isn't talking." Ann says.

"We just came out to tell you that she is in the bedroom. I think she has something to say." Jessie says.

"Would you go in and talk to her or whatever it takes to get her turned around. We really thought Barb would be the depressed one, but surprise." Jessie asks him.

"Sure. I bet it's just hormones. With five pregnant, there should be plenty of moods." Sam says as he turns toward the shelter. "You may want to keep the youngsters away, just in case."

Sam goes in and finds Sandra sitting on the side of the big bed. He goes over and pulls up a chair facing her.

"Sandy, everyone is worried about you. Your sisters sent me in to see if I can help. Will you talk with me? You know I love you and it hurts to see you unhappy."

"Oh Sam. I feel terrible." She sobs.

"What is it baby girl. Baby blues, or . . ."

"Sam I just woke up feeling like I am cheating on Bill. I know he's gone, but I am almost ashamed that I feel this good and going to have the baby in two months, that was supposed to be his and mine. I, I'm just so sad that he isn't the father."

"Oh Darlin' I do understand. You knew Bill better than any of us. The Bill I knew would want you to have a full life, that's why he planned for it. He didn't expect to be gone, but I know in my heart that he will rest so much easier knowing that you are fulfilling his and your dream."

Sandy throws herself on Sam, who comes out of the chair to catch her. They hug fiercely and Sam turns as they lose their balance and fall on the bed, Sam first, Sandy on top. Sam can feel the life in her belly and takes her face in his hands and kisses her warmly.

When their lips part, Sam tells her, "Sandy, if this baby is a boy, we will name him William. If it is a girl, the poor thing will be Billy Sue."

"Thank you Sam. Every day I know more and more why those five women want you, because I do to."

The family looks casual, sitting around the front of the shelter on chairs and at tables with drinks when Sam and Sandy come out.

"My Darlings, may I present Sandy. She's happy again, but tender." Sam quips.

Sandra joins the rest and Sam hears her telling the women what caused her feelings. Rach, Jessie and Ann admonish her to bring those feelings to them whenever she is feeling low.

Thank God, that's the worse thing that they have had to deal with in the ten months that they have been on the island. Sam and the boys have explored the whole thing. Ryan took a radio on one excursion to see if he could reach anyone from the other side, or from atop the—mini mountain.

During one foray, they discovered a wrecked converted B-25. There were no skeletons and Sam assumed that they had jumped before it crashed. Several crates that had all but rotted contained metal gears and ball bearings. Nothing useful. Ryan found a packed parachute in a metal container in the area that would have been the radio room.

"Should I keep it Dad?"

"Sure. If it hasn't rotted and it looks good, we can use it as a sun shade for a large area."

Chapter 13

THE FAMILY GROWS AGAIN

The next two years are idyllic. As Rachael has predicted, Sandra, Barbara, Sarah, Annie and Mary deliver beautiful babies all in the same month. June has become a popular birthing month—Sam, Ryan, Mike, Sybil and five more at the end of their first year.

Sandra delivers William on the 6th of June, Barbara delivers Ashleigh on the 18th of June; Sarah delivers Marie and Annie delivers Luke on the 22nd June and Mary delivers Joan on the 26th. All the babies are healthy and very evenly tempered. The Elliotts, who have been around, miss the traditional baptism, but talk with Sandra, Barbara, Sarah, Annie and Mary agree that when they get close to a Lutheran church, they are baptizing this newest generation.

The second year finds the family in a comfortable acceptance of their fate. Sam and the elder boys and girls, who are now seventeen, refine their living conditions. The small generator is providing them with the power to at least stay in touch with civilization by keeping the laptops operating and the movies playing. Ryan and Richard make forays into the hills to try the radio a couple of times a week. The girls' garden is growing well and providing fresh to their stored supplies. Delia, Peter and Alex have taken

Jamie, Carrie and Sybil into their dairy job and are looking at making cheese, with some nice successes.

The women set some traps and caught the island's version of chickens. They are like pullets, but the eggs were good and with a little control, they multiplied and soon there was fresh chicken. Roosters mostly, but some of the older hens when they stopped laying eggs. Molly and Rachael had the most experience in poultry.

The beginning of their third year is quiet and finds Sam and his ladies spending more and more time in the pool and in the sauna that Brian, Richard and Mike built and set up as a gift for the parents. The older children are getting a little antsy. They will soon want to find mates themselves and there just wasn't anyone. It wasn't a disabling problem, yet.

The children occupied themselves with hunting, fishing, crab trapping, gardening, exploring and studying the libraries that Tom brought and Sarah's educational DVDs.

It looked like it would be another of those mild tropical days. Sam was sitting out in front of the shelter, Ann, Becca and three kids went up the beach to look for some bamboo shoots and some smaller diameter bamboo poles. The older children were cleaning rifles used in yesterday's hunt. The garden crowd were doing the gardening. Some of the ladies were cleaning the shelters and Molly and Jessie were preparing the midday meal. They have taken to eating a good breakfast and heavy lunch and light dinner.

Sam was dozing off and on and enjoying the mild breeze that was coming from the ocean. A shout came from up the beach, in the direction that Ann and Becca had gone and captures his attention.

Running toward him and waving her arms, is Carrie. When she gets closer, Sam can see her face wet with tears.

"Baby Girl, what is it. Calm down, Tell me what is going on."

As she composes herself, Tom, Matt, Ryan, Cathy, Raina and a few of the others come to see what has happened. Jessie, Molly and Sandra were right behind them and have shocked looks on their faces.

Chapter 14

PIRATES HAPPEN

"Poppa, poppa the men have Momma and Momma Becca and Wyatt and Jamie. They have guns Poppa and they were hollering. I was in the bamboo trees and ran to tell you. Oh Poppa . . ." Carrie sobs.

"You're alright baby. You did right. Can you tell me how many men there were. What kind of guns they had."

"I think there were six or eight of them. They had a motor boat and a ship. The guns were like the ones in the boxes at home. In the glass boxes."

"Sounds like M-1s or M-2s, maybe M-16s. Tom, Matt, Ryan, I'm going there to see that the Moms are alright and talk to the pirates."

"Are they pirates Dad?" Ryan asks.

"Sounds like it. Look boys, you three and Richard, Peter and Brian, get weapons and hide in this area with a clear field of fire toward the plane. Ladies, get everyone else East, at least a couple hundred yards. When we are done, we'll send someone for you."

"Sam, you be careful. They may shoot you on sight. We can't do without you." Jessie says.

"Are you kidding. Those people don't have a chance. I've got ten women, twenty three children and we love each other. Those guys are dead meat."

Jessie, Molly and Sandra tell the others and begin herding them East, explaining on the way, what is happening. Cathy and Raina stay and ask Sam if they can help.

"Ladies, Gentlemen, I didn't want to say it in front of the rest, but when and if I can get them to come back this way, I'll get our people down and you will take out the bad guys. The key is to not be seen. I will tell Ann and Becca and the kids to DROP; that is when you open up. No wounding shots, all must be kill shots. Understood?"

There is a chorus of, "Yes Sir." from his young men and women. They go and collect their weapons and Sam hears Tom positioning the shooters.

Sam moves up the beach toward the place Ann and Becca are. As he gets closer, he can hear as well as see the group of bandits. He recognizes the language as a derivative of Mandarin. Sam listens hard and knows they are up to no good. He steels himself and calls out in Chinese, a greeting as if they are here to rescue them.

"Hello. Friends. Welcome. I am so happy you found us. We have been lost for so long. Thank you. Thank you."

The apparent leader turns toward Sam at his first call and starts walking to Sam with his weapon at the ready. M-2s as Sam suspected. Sam holds his hands up and calls out to him.

"My friend. Thank you for finding us. We have been lost. Let me welcome you. I don't have a gun."

The surly bandit gets close enough, so that Sam can see that he is some kind of Chinese. The bandit shouts to Sam, "You speak Chinese well. Who are you. Who are all of you?"

"My name is Sam, I taught English in Beijing until the government got greedy and tried to cheat me out of my pay. I quit and we were flying to San Francisco through Sydney.

Our plane crashed and we've been here for almost three years. There are many good things still in the plane. The cargo was weapons and American whiskey. We don't like weapons and we only used a little of the whiskey. Come to our camp and enjoy a meal and some drink."

"What kind of weapons are in the plane?" He shouts.

"I'm not sure. I think they look like the Russian ones they have in the movies."

The pirate's eyes widen and he looks to his followers with a broad grin.

"Will you help us. We want to go home." Sam pleads the last.

"You show. We help you go home." He said, but his posture and tone suggested that he was going to be a bastard.

Sam reaches his hand to Ann and Becca, who come to him, each with a child in tow.

"Sam you don't trust him do you?" Ann asks.

"When I say DROP, hit the sand fast." Sam whispers. "We have some food ready. It is almost lunch time. I hope Molly has enough for all of us."

The pirate leader looks at Sam with suspicion. "What do you tell them?"

"Oh, I told them that lunch was almost ready, I hoped there was enough for all of you. My sisters were cooking when I came looking for these two and the children. What is your name, how do I address you?" Sam says in his best formal Mandarin.

"I am Chin Lee. I am master of the ship, "Mao Ti Mao Se."

"I greet you Master Chin Lee."

They are passing the place that they buried Bill and Art.

"What is this place?" Chin Lee asks.

218

"This is the graves of the two men who flew the plane. They died in the crash."

Chin Lee nods and grunts. He turns and tells his followers what Sam has said. They move on and they can see the shelter and the skeleton of the plane a couple hundred yards ahead. When they get within seventy five yards, Chin Lee observes, "I do not see your sisters. Call them. Tell them to come out."

"Molly, Jessie, come out. We have guests. They're probably in the kitchen, there on the back of the shelter."

As they look toward the back, two figures emerge and come to the front of the shelter and sit on the steps. Sam sees that it is Jessie and Molly and hopes that there hasn't been a misunderstanding. He doesn't see his shooters and is glad of that.

Chin Lee moves on when he sees the two women come out and sit on the steps. Sam looks to Ann and Becca and smiles and mouths, "soon". The group is now in front of the shelter, in the clear area between the fire pit and the path to the plane.

"Master Chin Lee, that's what is left of the plane. You can see that part of the cargo hold is still full of boxes. Some are whiskey, a few crates are the weapons and there are bullets, but I don't know if they fit those weapons." Sam says with a flourish of his hands.

Chin Lee steps toward the plane and tells his men that they will get the cargo. When they are a few feet from Sam and the rest, Sam shouts, "DROP" and is relieved to see all of his people hit the sand. At the same instant the explosive staccato of automatic weapons sound. The sound is sharp and short lived and Sam sees that all of the pirates are on the ground in grotesque postures. Tom, Matt, Cathy, Carly and Ryan rush to Sam and the women. Sam stands and Tom comes to him.

"I think we got them all Sir."

"Yes, you did. Give me your 45 son. I'll show you how we make sure."

Sam takes Tom's .45 cal automatic and chambers a round and walks over to Chin Lee's still form and fires into his head. Sam repeats this with each of the stricken bandits.

"A dead enemy will never come up behind you, when you least expect it, so it's good to make sure."

Sam comes back to the shelter and looks at his warriors and smiles a proud smile.

"My sons and daughters, today you have saved the lives of your father and your mothers and your younger brothers and sisters. Put aside any feelings you have about this killing. It was necessary and you did what was necessary. I am extremely proud of you and I love each of you more than anyone has ever loved anyone."

His grown children, all of them at or near nineteen years old, gather around him and they group hug, then Sam hugs each one individually.

"We have a couple of more jobs to set ourselves to. One, get rid of the trash; two, we have to see if their ship is still populated and if it is, how to get rid of the infestation and take the ship for ourselves. Any ideas?"

"Sir, if we dress down and carry some bottles. We can go as the light is fading and get close enough to see and maybe even get aboard." Tom says.

"I like the part of going as the light fades. I can sound drunk and sing something Chinese. Everyone have their weapons ready to fire, no sliding bolts or pulling hammers back, ready to lift the weapon and fire. When we get close enough, I'll call out that we have treasure to load. If there are people on board, we keep our heads down, but watchful and pull up close. If anyone pops up, they're dead and we try to get over the rail and take out any others. If not, no problems."

Nods of agreement and understanding come from his small band of warriors. The rest of the afternoon, they clean weapons and nap or talk quietly among themselves. They haven't realized it yet. If they win the ship, they have a way to get home, at last.

It's an hour before sundown and Sam and his band, with faces blackened with ash from the pit and some of the rags from the pirates swagger up to the landing boat, keeping a watchful eye on the ship. They load and head for the bigger boat about a hundred and fifty yards out. Sam begins a drinking song when they get within seventy five yards and the others mumble the peas and carrots that sounds like a group of drunks. When they are twenty five yards away, Sam calls out in Chinese that they have treasure to unload. All hands on deck!"

The launch bumps against the hull and they look up at the rail. Five heads and upper bodies lean over the rail and their lives are ended. Sam and Tom scramble up and over the rail and finish two others who are just clearing the hatch. Matt, Ryan and Cathy clear the rail and keep their eyes in both directions. Sam and Tom go below. They are there only a few minutes and Tom calls for Ryan and something to cut metal.

"Cathy, Matt. Keep a lookout. There doesn't seem to be any more of the pirates." Sam calls to them.

"What did you find Dad?" Matt asks.

Several long minutes and Tom appears at the top of the hatch. He steps aside and helps, first one, then two, then three, then four and two more young Asian women out of the hatch. Six hostages or slaves, for the sex trade.

Cathy tries Korean, then Thai. She gets a reaction with Thai and tries to comfort those who understand Thai.

Sam comes up to the deck and sees Cathy ministering to the young women. He talks with them and their eyes brighten.

"You are safe now. We have killed all of the pirates. My daughter will take you and one of the men and bring you to our house and some food and friends."

"Kup Chi Mak Kah" is the response from two of them.

Sam tries the little Tag alog, and his greeting words of Japanese with no result. Then he tries French and two more join the group in understanding.

He tells them the same things that Cathy has told the others and they are soon smiling. Sam discovers that they are from Viet Nam. The six women are in the launch with Cathy and Matt heading for the beach. It is a little dark now and Sam watches them as far as he can see and then sees the torches being lit where they left them at the mooring for the motor boat.

Sam, Tom and Ryan tie weights to the dead on the ship and toss them over the side. With buckets tied to ropes, they bring up sea water and splash the decks. There is a semblance of clean now and they begin to explore their prize. The whole thing is only seventy or eighty feet long and maybe thirty to forty feet wide at the mid ship. Everything is filthy, but the engine looks clean and surprisingly free of oil leaks. The galley will be salvageable. Their stores are limited and of questionable quality. There are limited billets and will probably have to be removed and burned.

It only seemed like a short time, but they cut their exploring short when they hear the motorboat approach and someone calling out to them.

"Dad, Tom, Ryan, we're back. Are you ready? The Moms want you back." Raina called out.

"Hi Raina. We're ready, just gonna shut down the power. Found a nice lamp with a long beam. Let's take the boat to the beach near the shelters, the lamp will light the way. Cathy stay with the women?" Sam asks.

"Yeah. Matt brought me with him."

"Oh hey Matt. I didn't see you."

"I forgot to take off the charcoal dust."

"Yeah guys, lets lose the rags and get us a shower."

They load into the launch and as Sam asked, head for the beach near the shelter. They have to beach the boat at the tail end of the plane and pull it out of the water and tie off the rope.

The whole front of the shelter and the area around the pit is all lighted up with the lights that Brian set up. Sam sees the women sitting around tables and eating. Ann and the others who speak Thai are talking with them. Rachael, who speaks French is keeping the others occupied. They have gotten through to four of the six, but two are still a mystery. One of the two puts her face in her hands and sobs.

"Does no one speak Chinese?" She says in perfect Mandarin.

Sam is beside himself. He never tried Chinese, but soon the two are smiling and showing signs of relief. Ann, knows enough Chinese to understand and be understood and helps Sam communicate.

The Elliott women gather the six to shower and get them clean clothes. The older girls, with Cathy leading, make up beds for them with some of the fold down seats and the planes pillows and blankets, although the ambient temperature is delightful without blankets.

They seem to be less fearful and even do the formal Thai wai, holding their hands together and touching the tip of their nose. They are all soon in beds and falling asleep.

Sam and his ladies gather in the bedroom and discuss the events of this day.

"I know you don't want to talk about it Sam, but how do you feel about everything that happened?" Ann asks the question they all want to know.

"Relieved. I knew it would happen eventually and now it is behind us. The boys and the older girls were great. Real warriors. I hope I impressed on them that this was my kill and they did everything right. I still don't think anyone realizes that we now have a way out. The ship is filthy, but it should make it to somewhere."

"You're right Sam I didn't think of it either. Oh my God. We can go home." Rachael says.

"The cleaning will be a real chore and the bedding is not salvageable. Tomorrow, some of you should go out to the ship and make a plan. We got rid of a lot of junk and rinsed the deck. I'm just a little sleepy now. Peter has volunteered to take first watch tonight. Delia and Alex will relieve at four hour intervals. Wyatt, Edward, and Mike will sit with each of them, to keep each other awake."

"Sam do you think we have anything to worry about?" Molly asks.

"Not really, but we don't really know these women. They may be kidnapped, or the girl friends, who are tied up in case the ship is boarded by the authorities. I'd rather not take a chance. I'll have my ears on all night as well."

"Me to Sam. Maybe each of us should stay with each of the watch teams. I'm staying with Peter. It's only four hours." Molly says.

"Yeah Sam, I'm gonna sit with Delia." Jessie says.

"Sam, I'm with Alex." Ann tells him.

"Alright my loves. Wake me for the last watch anyway. No later than sun rise." Sam relents.

Molly kisses him and he returns the kiss. She picks up her side arm and heads for the door. Sam can hear Peter and Wyatt's surprise when they hear her say she is staying through their watch.

Sam and the rest stretch out and are soon asleep. The night passes without incident and Sam feels a little sheepish that he worried about those women.

Mary and Sandra are in the kitchen when Sam comes in.

"Good Morning my Darlings." Sam says as he hugs and kisses each in turn. "Any coffee. I've got cobwebs. I woke up too early."

Sandra hands Sam a cup of coffee and leans her head on his shoulder. "Sam. I am so happy and I love you so much. William is beautiful. I never thought that I would have this chance to be a Mom. My life suddenly became wonderful." She kisses him on the lips and he returns the affection.

Mary smiles and says, "Breakfast will be in about twenty minutes. The pig bellies work wonderfully for bacon. Lots of fruit and more coffee."

"Thanks Mary. I'm going to watch the sun rise and take in the morning. I hear people moving around. We'll get started early."

Sam sits in a reclining chair, under a thatch cover. He puts his coffee on the table and surveys the area. Becca, Rachael, Barbara and Sarah come out stretching and digging their toes in the sand. They come to the table where Sam is sitting.

"Good morning ladies." Sam says accepting and giving loving kisses to each in turn.

"Mary said breakfast will be here in a few minutes. The night was uneventful."

"I know. It was nice and quiet. I started thinking about going home. The Thai, Viet Namese and Chinese women are up and taking a group shower. I think they haven't had good smelling soap in a while." Becca observes.

Tom and the five older boys come up and greet Sam and the Mommas.

"Peter. You're up early. You didn't get to sleep the whole night." Sam says.

"Dad. It's good. I want to help the guys get things done. I'm kinda anxious to get home."

The rest of the boys pat his shoulders and slap his back. My sons. Sam is so proud.

The family begins to sort through the things they need to clean the ship. Sam takes seven of them out in the launch. Ryan has activated radios for them and those remaining behind. Raina and Elizabeth take weapons and will guard the Moms as they inventory and clean the ship.

Ann, Becca, Rachael, Sarah, Sandra, Annie and Barbara form the work party on the first trip out. Sam comes back to the shelter and helps Mary, Jessie and Molly package portable foods. Water jugs are filled and stacked on the beach, with the help of Sybil, Jamie, Carrie, Wyatt, Edward and Mike.

I really can't call them the babies. They are my youngest. Sam thinks and smiles. Carrie is the youngest at 13, the rest are from 3 to 6 months older. The seventeen year olds are with the older children and are removing the foam mattresses from the unused seats and beds. They will use them to replace the infested ones on the ship. They also prepare the master bed for movement, but leave it in place for the time being.

Tom packs five of the laptops that they have downloaded their pictures onto and the written account of their last 37 months.

Delia and her helpers, milk the cows and store the milk in two of the 5 gallon containers and put them in the shaded part of the creek to keep cool. They also collect the eggs from the chickens and store them in hard plastic containers.

They have been working for a little more than three hours and Mary appears on the front of their shelter.

"Sam, will you pick up the cleaning crew. Lunch is in thirty minutes."

"Will do, my love." He says and waves to her. He pulls out his walkie talkie and calls the ship. "Hello, Raina, this is Dad."

"Hi Dad, what's up?"

"I'm on my way to pick everyone up for lunch. Let the moms know."

"Roger that."

Sam chuckled as he goes to the launch. He calls to the workers that he is going to pick up the moms for lunch. A couple of the youngest acknowledge him with a wave.

They spend the next three days getting ready to leave. On the last day, everyone takes hundreds of photos. Sandra and Barbara make their final visit to their dead loved ones. All are somber and torn between this place that they have called home for nearly three years and anxiety over going home to their luxurious lifestyle.

It takes five trips out in the launch to get everyone and the last items aboard. Matt and Tom have studied the engine and the navigation, steering systems and pronounce that they are confident that they can sail the ship somewhere.

"Dad, when do you think we should go?" Tom asks.

"Well, it's 8 o'clock already, sun's up. We head up with the sun on our right until it is overhead, then a little to the left until it goes down. Watch the compass and we'll keep it on the last setting, over night. We should run into some shipping lanes, or at least get in radio range of someone." Sam says.

Sam goes out on deck and surveys his family. Most are on deck.

"Everyone accounted for? Don't want to leave anyone behind!"

"Sam, Oh my God. Cathy! Alex! Carrie!" Ann calls and gets three giggled responses.

Each Momma inventories her own babies and Sam checks on Sandra, Barbara, Sarah, Annie and Mary. Everyone is here.

"Tom, Matt, set the course, warp factor 4—engage." Sam parodies Captain Picard from Star Trek.

Matt is at the wheel with Tom and the engine turns over several times and catches. The smooth roar of the motor sounds comforting. What ever these pirates were, they kept their engine in it's prime. The anchor is winched in by the automatic anchor retract motor. The bow begins to move forward, then out to sea.

Sam's grown sons are beaming with pride at their achievement. When they are a few miles out, everyone is looking back at the island. The skeleton of the plane is visible and the shelter looks like a tropical vacation hotel. There's a thought, Sam muses. Someone would have to get there before it is overrun by cattle, since Sam and the boys removed the predators.

The planning pays off. There are things for everyone to do and the ship has a substantial water reservoir. So they can shower when needed. It is around one o'clock and Mary calls everyone to lunch.

"You'll have to come down in groups, get a plate and then retire to somewhere else to eat. The crew area is kind of small." She says.

All morning, the older children and a few of the 13 and 14 year olds come to the bridge and get some instruction on handling the ship. By lunch a few of the older boys and girls are spelling Matt and Tom at the wheel.

Lunch is good and Sam makes sure that Mary knows how much he appreciates it, but she is only the cook by her choice, it's no longer her job.

"Sam, I know. Molly and Sandra also helped. Becca came down and made the egg rolls for snacking, later." She says and kisses him on the cheek.

Sam takes her in his arms and kisses her back, full on the mouth. "Mary, I know we haven't been in an intimate relationship for very long, but you are as much an Elliott as anyone and I love you just as much. Little Joanie is the cutest little girl. You done good lady." Sam hugs her tight.

They both go on deck and Molly is carrying a jug of iced tea around and refilling glasses. Sam takes a seat, in a reclining airplane seat, next to the rail and looks to the bow and the horizon beyond.

Seats and cushions are all along the rails and filled with his ladies and children. The rescued hostages are also interspersed with Sam's family. They are talking animatedly and smiles abound. Ann, Becca, Rachael, Jessie and Molly stand in the middle of the assembly. "Safety. Keep your eyes open and stay away from the rail. Partner up and watch out for each other. We have been so blessed in our survival and our soon to be rescue, from this adventure, I don't want any tragedies. I am speaking for all the mothers." Ann says and the other mothers nod and look from face to face.

The first day passes with a feeling of adventure and excitement. As the sun begins to set in the West, Sam goes to the bridge and checks on his sons. He is surprised that Brian and Richard are at the controls.

"Hi guys. Tom and Matt taking a break?"

"Yes Sir. We've got it. Matt and Tom are good teachers. Matt said he would come back before it got too dark and record the compass heading. This is a great ship Dad, real smooth and the engine sings." Richard says.

"Yes Sir. It's really great to learn about sailing a ship. One more thing. Dad, what should we do with the weapons? I'm almost sure that AK-47s and RPGs are illegal." Brian asks.

"I didn't think of that. In the morning, bring it up again when the women are awake."

"Will do. You gonna get some sleep?" Brian asks.

"Yeah. How are you guys rotating the bridge duty?"

"We will be on until midnight, then Tom will be back with Peter until four AM, then Matt will be back with Ryan. Everyone will get eight hours and the last two will take the 8 to midnight turn." Richard says.

"Good job men. I guess I'll get some sleep. Good night."

The boys bid their Dad good night and Sam retires to his seat by the rail. He thinks, he's lucky to have such smart children and please God hold off the rain and storms until we are rescued.

The next morning the family discusses the weapons over breakfast.

"Brian brought it up to me last night and it bears thinking about. If we keep them, we could face some kind of charges with whatever government we run into. I think we should throw them overboard and I'm glad we didn't bring all of them, we agree not to say anything about them, including how they were used to defeat the pirates. We did it all with our side arms and our hunting rifles. Anyone want to say anything, anything at all?"

"Sam, if it is going to cause a problem, I'm to blame." Sandra says.

"No, Darling. It's our problem and we are real good at solving problems." Sam tells her.

"I like the idea of throwing them overboard and everyone just carry the side arms, so that whoever we run into will, first impression that, we all use the automatics. The hunting rifles and ammo, are just the things we were taking to Thailand in the first place." Jessie says.

Several others nod their agreement. Sam nods and smiles at all.

"We are agreed then. Let's gather the contraband AK-47s and lose them. Everyone strap on a side arm."

The ten weapons are piled on the deck and four cases of ammunition and several dozen clips for them. Sam, Peter, Tom and Brian, drop them into the ocean, one at a time, as the ship continues making it's course and speed. There will be a string on the ocean floor instead of a cache.

"Okay, family. It's done. One less worry. Now we tell the story over and over of how we defeated the pirates with our hand guns and hunting rifles. Especially to ourselves so we don't accidentally say anything about those other weapons. Are we all on the same page my darling?"

There is a chorus of affirmatives from the ladies and the children.

Molly stands up and walks to the hatch, turns and smiles. "Who wants something hot to drink, coffee, tea, cocoa and some cookies? Becca and I baked them early this morning and they're still warm."

Smiles broke out everywhere and "Yeah!" from everyone, even the rescued women, who it seems are already picking up the language.

The rest of the morning is spent in relaxing and surveying the horizon. Some of the women and some of the children were on the laptops. A few were playing DVDs and two or three are watching the story, with them. Sam dozes and keeps an eye on the bridge. The boys have a handle on the operation of the craft and have a working schedule.

"Dad, we figured it out and if we're right, we've come around six hundred miles. I looked at some old charts and we should be a day or two from Australia, or New Zealand or some civilized areas. Ryan said that he did hear some chatter on the radio, but no one responded to his call." Tom tells his Dad.

"I hope you guys are right. I think I'm ready for some civilization again. You know I'm very proud of you guys. I saw you had some of the girls at the wheel to. We'll have to invest in a yacht or something when we get home."

"That would be something. Cathy, Carly, Elizabeth and Delia learned the ship really fast. We agreed yesterday that we would always have two at the wheel at all times and we did talk about maybe convincing you to invest in something when we get back." Tom chuckles.

"Great minds, eh! Think alike." Sam says.

Sam goes below and looks for a place to stretch out. He suddenly feels tired. Their big bed is about a quarter smaller to fit in the Captain's cabin. They moved everything else out and it was still almost too big for the space.

Sam goes in and is surprised and pleased to see six naked women stretched out across the bed.

"Wow. Looks like God is watching out for me." Sam says with a grin.

"Get them clothes off mister and get in here." Jessie tells him.

Sam can feel the tension leave him as he is pressed between warm female flesh.

"Easy ladies. I don't feel real clean."

"Let's shower, then love." Annie says.

The seven of them head for the shower. Soon they are all wet and soapy and Sam revels in the female flesh. It's as satisfying as sex for Sam. The shower takes some time for all the ladies to get a share of their man's love.

One by one they move off to dry and get back to the bed. The last one, is Becca. She spends a wonderful moment sliding her sex against Sam.

"Let's get to the others Darling, I'm ready for beaucoup loving." Sam sighs.

He spends the next three hours satisfying his loves. The call to dinner brings them all from dreamy to fully alert. They dress quickly and head for the deck.

The evening meal is a stove top tuna casserole, made from all packaged supplies. The last of the foil packed tuna, packaged steam and serve egg noodles and cream of mushroom soup, with a tin of cheese sauce.

The family sits together on deck, watch the stars and reminisce about what they missed back home in Sumter. The children begin to slip off to bed below. Sam notices that the stars are disappearing and tells the ladies that a storm is coming. He goes to the bridge and tells Carly and Ryan, who have the helm until midnight, that there is a storm coming up. Ryan goes to tell Tom, who tells him that he and Matt will come up when the storm hits and help them.

Sam feels better, but tells them to get him if they get too freaked out, then goes to bed. The darlings who already took advantage earlier this afternoon, let the rest snuggle next to him. The ship is rocking pretty steadily by the time his ladies are sleeping soundly. All, but Molly, who wants to continue cuddling. She can never get enough closeness and Sam loves it.

It was nearly five AM when Sam wakes suddenly. Everything was way to calm for a storm. He pulls on some shorts and sandals and goes to the bridge. Tom and Matt are there with Carly and Ryan, who are napping in the corner.

"Hi men. What happened with the storm? I fell asleep when the waves were rocking the ship slowly and was startled awake a few minutes ago."

"No worries Dad. The storm wasn't that bad. I think we lost some of the umbrellas off the deck, but even at it's worse, there was just rain and wind. We all stayed and talked most of the night." Tom tells him casually, like talking about the amount of alcohol in beer.

"People, you done real good. Thank you."

"Yes, kids, thank you. You all are amazing." Ann adds as she comes in behind Sam.

"Morning Mom." Cathy says, coming in for her shift with Ryan. Carly rubbed sleep from her eyes and turned toward the hatch. "I'm sleepy. Hi Dad. Tommy, are we done?"

"Yes Sis, Matt and I, are going to get some sleep and take it back at eight or nine." Tom says.

"Yeah, you guys get some rest. We'll wake you when breakfast is on." Ann tells them.

Chapter 15

RESCUE

This is the morning of their fourth day and it starts out nice and peaceful. Breakfast is quick, because everyone is getting anxious about finding civilization and Sam wants to get some eyes on the horizon.

Sam enlists some helpers and passes out five of the seven pairs of binoculars. The sixth, he keeps and the seventh is on the bridge.

"We're going to be lookouts today. We will scan the ocean all the way to the horizon, until we see something, or the sun goes down. Is everyone down for the job?"

There are nods and smiles from his little group.

"Dad. What should we do if we see something?" Jamie asks.

"Sing out Baby. Like, there's something out there and point."

She nods her understanding.

"Do you think we'll see anything?" Wyatt asks.

"It's the right time. We've come over three thousand miles."

"Listen to Dad kids and we'll bring lunch up. Drinks and snacks and if you need a potty break." Rachael says. Several of the youngsters laugh.

They've arranged seating in the bow, close to the rail and kick back, with the binoculars up, begin to scan the ocean in all directions.

Sam looks at each of them and thinks how glad he is that he takes the time to know them. Jamie, always a little shy and loves to read. Mike, one half of the twins is thoughtful and always thinks before he speaks. His sister, Sybil, is quiet and cautious. Carrie, who wants to be her Dad's baby, but so wants to be grown up. She is also interested in medicine like her older sister, Cathy and spends a lot of time with Rachael. Wyatt, Jessie's youngest is trying to find his niche. He spends time with Ryan, his older brother, studying radios, but also helped Delia with the cows and calves.

Today the five of them with Sam, are keeping an eye out for civilization. Then, about mid morning, Jessie, Ann, Rachael and Molly come up with drinks and umbrellas.

"We thought you could use a drink and some shade." Molly says.

"Where'd these come from?" Sam asks.

"Brian made them this morning. He brought some bamboo and we still had that parachute. He worked on this all morning. Some of us helped, when we saw what he was doing. Sam, he made a couple of big ones that we have on the deck. He's still making more. We lost some of our umbrellas in the storm. We have 15 this size and the two big ones." Molly says.

"Thank him for me and I'll add some more later."

"Poppa! Poppa! Something over there!" Carrie exclaims.

Sam brings his binoculars to bear, to the West North West, where Carrie is pointing. He strains to see what she has discovered. Then, there it is. Almost at the horizon, like a flagpole in the water. Sam stares and tries to hold steady, when the pole rises and behind it, a great square of gray metal, then to the right, a triangular piece rises. Sam knows what it is.

"A submarine. Ryan! Ryan! Get on the radio. Tom bring the bow to port 5 degrees!"

"Dad, I see it. I'm heading toward it." Tom shouts back.

"I've got 'em. I've got 'em. Dad it's the Australian Navy. They've spotted us and are coming to intercept."

The women and all the children crane their necks to see. The binoculars are passed around and the entire event looks like the crowd that greets the pope. Sam's ladies are in tears and Sam is fighting to keep his tears back.

They are within 100 yards and someone on the submarine calls out, "Heave to."

"Tom, cut the engines and drop the anchor." Sam calls out, but Tom is already shutting down the ship.

The sub launches two rubber rafts with 5 men in each. As they get closer, the leader in the first raft calls to the ship, "Prepare to be boarded."

The ladies and children crowd the rail and are waving and cheering. The officer boards first and very quickly, all of his men are on board.

"Who's in charge here?" He asks no one in particular.

"I guess that's me. Sam Elliott and this is mostly my family. We are very happy to see you."

"Sir, this vessel is the pirate ship Mao Ti Mao Se."

"Well sir, No pirates here, uh, I'm not good on Navy ranks, Lieutenant? The men who tried to rob and kill us, were not very skilled. My family and I dispatched them on the island that we have been stranded on for close to three years."

"You were shipwrecked? What ship sir. I don't recall a ship going down in these waters."

"Have a seat Lieutenant, I'll tell you all about it."

Sam recalls the events from their departure from Faleolo airstrip, Samoa to the wreck, their survival and the fate of the pirates.

"The leader was a Chinese fellow, called himself, Chin Lee. Those women there," Sam points to the rescued women, "we found, chained below. I heard him talking to his thugs about my ladies, like he planned to take them. When they accosted 2 of the ladies and children, one child, Carrie, slipped away and gave the rest of us a warning."

"And you over powered them? How many were there?" The Lieutenant sounded unbelieving.

"Well, with Chin Lee were seven others and on the ship another five . . ."

"Seven Dad. There were seven on the ship." Tom corrects him.

"Thanks Tom, that's right. Seven on the ship. Oh, Lt. this is my eldest son, Tom. He, Matt, Ryan and Richard, oh all of these wonderful young people, have kept the ship in order."

"Excuse me. The captain is calling me on my wireless."

The Lt. steps away and Sam can't make out what he is saying. When he comes back, he turns to his men and says, "Put your weapons away men." Then to Sam, "You should have said. Sir. You're that corporate family right? Half the world has been looking for you. Are all of you okay? Do you need anything? The Captain says that a rescue vessel is on the way, with a crew to take the ship into port. I'm sorry if we frightened you or your family. We know the ship, but not the crew and when we saw the weapons . . ."

"Don't trouble yourself Lieutenant. We're still very happy to see you.

"The Captain will need a complete, in depth report."

"Can do easy. We recorded almost continuously. Lieutenant, can some one mark this location and try to back track our trip, to find the island. Tom put the heading down and the speed, time and the time it changed and the new headings. We just didn't know where we started from."

"Yes sir. We can take that information and plot it backward on a valid chart."

"That's fine. We would like to find it again, some day."

It was lunch and Sandra offered lunch to the officer and his men, who accepted. The Navy guys were surprised at the quality and quantity of the lunch.

"You are very self sufficient. This is a great meal. Thank you."

"The vegetables are organic, grown in our gardens. The girls were our gardeners. The chickens we raised organically ourselves. The ladies were the chicken farmers. The cheese is a recent development. We have, er, had our own cows. The boys read about cheese making and this is one of the results. Self sufficient. Yes, but long for our own home." Sam explains.

The sailors stay with them for another couple of hours, until a much larger ship is spotted bearing in the direction of the sub. A crew from the ship boards and Tom and Matt explain what they have done and where everything is. Sam and the family say their goodbyes to the sub crew, as they head back to the sub. The Captain of the rescue vessel, boards and meets everyone, then sits with Sam and with the ladies input, tells the whole story again.

"Captain. Are we in some sort of trouble? I've told this story a few times. Is there something going on that I should know about?" Sam asks.

"Mr. Elliott . . . Sam, eventually you will have to tell the story again and in greater detail. Your son, Tom, gave my navigator the headings, times and speed and we have back tracked it on, very up to date, navigational charts and frankly Sam, there isn't an island in that area for five hundred miles in any direction. Satellite imagery for that area is blank as well."

"I don't know what else to say. It did happen. We crashed on an island, sailed away due North for eleven hours, and then came to a North, North West heading for another 15 hours and then due West, until the sub spotted us. Captain, we spent nearly three years there. It has to be there. Maybe the pirate's charts have a clue."

"We'll keep investigating, don't worry. The island won't be lost for long. Well, when we get on board and your family gets comfortable, we'll talk some more . . . . by the way, the news of your recovery has already spread. Expect some media, when we reach Sydney."

"Thanks. We are kind of used to being plied for information."

The family is on the rescue ship and Sam and his sons are sitting together in the ship's dining area.

"Well, guys. We're on our way. Anxious?"

"A little bit. Any of our friends that are still around, will seem a little childish after this. I don't know, I got kind of used to struggling day to day." Tom says.

"Yeah, Dad. It was like survival after a world disaster, like in the movies. The only thing I am anxious about, is whether I can relate to my girl friend, if she isn't already married." Ryan says.

The others laugh, but are restrained.

"I guess that's really it. We all are worried that we will be looked on as freaks and girls won't want any part of us." Matt adds.

"I understand your feelings, guys. I wouldn't worry too much about being able to attract girls. You are all chips off the old block, ha, ha. Handsome as they come. The three eldest will be off to college. We'll work something out to get your high school diplomas and some late SATs so that you can qualify. Surviving for nearly three years has got to count. I would bet that your big problem will be keeping the girls away. You've all become real men and real men are very attractive to young ladies."

"Attractive, Sam really. These men are handsome!" Molly exclaims.

"You're right Darling. I didn't want it to go to their heads."

"When you guys are ready. Showers are wonderful and dinner, we are told, will be at seven."

"Thank you. We're ready."

Sam and the boys follow Molly out of the dining area and head for their cabins. Sam and his ladies are split up among six cabins. Sam is alone in one and the women are paired, two to a cabin, in five others. The shower is like a locker room shower and Sam gets a surprise when he enters. All ten of his loves are hot and soapy.

"You to Molly, I thought you said . . ."

"Sam, I said the showers are wonderful. The way they are set up. Almost like home."

All the showers are running and Sam enjoys the love of each of his darlings. It takes more than an hour, until. Sam suspects that he will be called on for more than, hot, soapy, hugs and kisses.

"How are the kids and showers going?" Sam asks.

"There are four of these big showers on the ship. The girls took showers, while the boys held on to the two year olds, then the boys took showers. We were the last. We waited for you mister." Jessie says.

"I'm happy you all did. I really miss the intimacy and with so many more. I may have to retire from everything else, just to satisfy everyone. Oh my, the husband's work is never done." Sam laughs.

"You better stock up on carbohydrates at dinner. I believe we have something planned for you." Becca tells him, with several rises of her eyebrows.

"Help!" Sam chirps.

Sam is just putting on his shoes when the gong for dinner sounds. He steps into the passageway and is greeted by several of the ladies, who are on their way to dinner. His young men and young ladies meet them, just outside of the dining area and they enter as a family. They're applauded as they enter, by several of the crew and dining room staff.

During dinner, Sam notices that his daughters are drawing the attention of some of the younger sailors. Cathy, Raina and Carly are blushing demurely and enjoying the attention. He also sees Tom and Matt talking to a few and Sam surmises that they are telling the sailors that Elizabeth, Alex and Delia are only seventeen. Those three to, are smiling, ear to ear at the attention and the defense that Tom and Matt are providing.

The Captain corrals Sam, after dinner and brings out a bottle of Scotch and two glasses and pours three fingers into each. Neat.

"Sam. The crew that I left on the ship made a discovery, a few hours, after we departed. I know you and your family are wealthy, but you should know that there is a substantial amount of gold and jewels on that ship. Much of which, will never go to the rightful owner. The salvage on the ship alone will net two or three million. I would like to wire ahead your plan for the disposition of it all."

"Captain. I—we don't need any of it. If I can, I'd like to have it all placed in a welfare fund for the Australian Navy. You guys are rescuing us and I know that most of the jobs that a military person does, never gets proper recognition."

"Thank you Sam. From me and from all of us. Thank you."

"No worries Myte!"

The Captain laughs at Sam's mimic of Australian speech. He motions to someone behind Sam and an officer with a pad, pen and a tape recorder sits with them.

"Sam, this Commander Hogan. We're going to get as many details of your experience written down, officially. Maybe this will be the last time you will have to repeat it."

"Hi Commander. Call me Sam."

"Thank you, Sam, I'm Martin."

They question and answer for two hours, then Commander Hogan calls it a night and offers that he will meet with Sam after breakfast. Sandra is sitting at a table, behind Sam and comes to him as the Captain and Commander get up to leave.

"Sandra. Waiting for me?"

"Of course. We drew straws for who would walk you back and I got lucky. I hope you're not too tired."

"Never. I've kind of missed you lately. Maybe just getting old."

"Stop. You can't get old now. I still have some years left. Sam, do you know how much I love you?"

"I've got a pretty good idea, in the son you gave me."

"Then, you'll like this. I want to make love to you, tonight, to celebrate something."

"Celebrate something. Hmmm! What could it be . . . ."

"Sam, I'm pregnant." She looked at Sam with expectation in her eyes.

"Sandy, that's wonderful." Sam turns and locks her in his arms. His lips find hers and he kisses her with his heart. "My God. Are you sure? How far along. This is wonderful."

"Ann, Jessie and the rest told me that you loved having children. When William was born and you were so good and caring. I knew that I had to give you another baby."

"Oh Sandy. I love you. Let's get back to my cabin, don't want to upset the sailors."

She laughs and puts her head on his shoulder as they wend their way through the passages to his cabin.

"Sam, I have you for one hour. You've got a job and I am first."

Sam slowly removes her blouse and skirt. Their love making is slow, tender and warm and Sam revels in her sensuality even as the news she brought washes through him. A dad again at 48, he thinks.

Sam doesn't hurry with any of his loves. Each is so special. He finally gets to sleep at four AM, with, you guessed it, Molly.

"Molly my Darling, how is it that we end up together, for the night, so often?"

"I'm just one lucky lady. You must know how much I love having you pressed close to me all night and waking with you beside me, in the morning. I love you so much, always have, and always will."

"Ditto, Darling woman. You have always been the most spontaneous and innovative loves in my life. You've given me six of the most wonderful children. Only one thing tops all of those wonderful qualities."

"What is it. Sam tell me. What one thing is better."

"You taste wonderful."

Molly laughs deep inside, as Sam begins kissing her neck and moves lower, and lower.

Morning arrives with little fanfare. Sam and all head for breakfast, after their morning ablutions and are treated to NY strip steaks and eggs, with hash browns. Sam looks from face to face and sees a calm that has been missing for too long. Commander Hogan comes in as some of the ladies and children are leaving. He comes over and introduces himself to Ann and Rachael, who excuse themselves.

"Good Morning Sam. Ready to finish up?"

"Ready Martin. What about the six Asian women we found in the hold of the pirate ship?"

"They're fine. Our doctor has looked at them and some of our nurses with Thai, French and Chinese language skills have assisted in debriefing them. All of them repeat, how grateful they are that you and your boys freed them. They have all, talked by radio to their people. It appears that all of them are from very wealthy families, who are also grateful to you and your family."

Sam answers questions for two more hours and Commander Hogan is very pleased.

The Captain meets them as Sam navigates his way to the deck for fresh air.

"Good Morning Sam. Hope you and the family are getting rested. We should get to Sydney tomorrow morning. Did Commander Hogan tell you that all of you are heroes? The parents of the Asian women will be waiting there to thank you. The Admiral said to me this morning, that there will be a media blitz and he is calling in another company of Shore Patrol to get everyone through. He asks that you and some of the family prepare to give an impromptu press conference."

"Not a problem. We've done this before. Is there a way for me to contact my own people in South Carolina? I'd like to give them a chance to prepare and regain some composure before we arrive."

"I'm sure that the radioman can get you a hook up. I should have thought of it myself. Let me check with him and I'll send a runner to guide you back to the radio room."

"Thank you Captain. I think I'll walk the deck a little. I haven't seen my sons or daughters in a while, other than meals."

Sam begins his walk and remembers everything again. The hard parts make him shudder. The crash, Bill and Art's death, the funerals, the predators, the storms, the additions, the pirates, the shoot out, the seizing of the ship, sailing the open sea, all of it now washes over him. He held himself in check. His pride in his sons is almost something you can hold and package. They acted and performed better than many of the men that Sam has taken into battle at his side.

"Dad. Am I disturbing you? You look deep in thought." Tom says.

"Tom. Good to see you. I was just thinking about the last thirty plus months. The subdued tensions just washed over me and I was shedding them. Where is everyone? We're not a small group."

"There's a kind of ballroom, theater, auditorium. We're watching some television and news about us. Brenda and Sue were crying on the news, happy that we are coming home."

"Lead on Mac Duff. Tom, if I haven't said it often enough, Thank you for being a man sooner than you should have had to be."

Tom smiles and puts his arm over his father's shoulders. "My pleasure Dad."

Tom leads him to a really large room. Television is being projected onto a big screen. Sam sees all of his family sitting, as in a theater, rapt attention on the screen. He takes a seat near the back. The seat is overstuffed movie house seating. Sam dozes.

"Sam. Sam honey. Do you want lunch? It's time." Ann says as she gently pats his shoulder.

"Oh goodness. I slept hard. What time is it?"

"It's just half past twelve. The lunch gong sounded about five minutes ago."

"I'm ready." Sam says as he stands and puts an arm around Ann's waist. They go out and enter the dining area. Everyone is sitting around tables in mixed groups. Sam and Ann sit with Tom, Molly, Carrie and Brian. The table has several large plates and bowls with roast beef, potatoes and gravy and bowls of vegetable.

"Hello everyone. Sorry Tom. I guess I was more tired than I thought. The Captain told me that we should reach Sydney in the morning. He said the Admiral wants us to do a news conference. It seems that the Asian women are the daughters of some high powered folks and they are very grateful." Sam takes some beef roast, potatoes and gravy. "It also seems we have the salvage rights on the ship and contents. I'm sorry, I made a unilateral decision to donate the whole thing to the Australian Navy's welfare fund." He looks around the table.

"That's was good Sam. We agree." Molly said, with Ann's nod and Tom also smiled an affirmative.

"I just hope no one gets upset. There apparently was gold and other valuables stashed aboard. His crew found it as they searched the ship from one end to another for evidence. I guess they have to report the pirate ship and activities to clear their books."

Tom, Brian and Carrie finish lunch and excuse themselves. Rachael comes over with Becca, Jessie and Sarah. The steward brings cups, saucers and a big pot of coffee.

Sam tells the rest about his decision to donate the salvage to the Aussie Navy and is warmed by the agreement of the rest of his darlings.

"Sam, I have come to believe that is what the Elliotts are all about. Sharing the bounty with as many as possible." Sarah says.

"Thank you Sarah. You do know that you are an Elliott now."

Sarah blushes and smiles. "I know. Uh, is this a proper time for an announcement?"

"Good as any sweetie." Jessie says.

"I'm pregnant again." She looks at Sam.

"Oh my Darling. That is wonderful. Two now." Sam says.

"Two? Sam who?" Rachael asks.

"Sandra told me last night that she is about three months along."

"The family is growing. Sam, it is wonderful. I would never have believed it, when we first met that I would be in a family with so many wonderful people and have beautiful children and a man who has so much love." Ann says.

"I didn't do so badly either, my love. This is your doing, after all. Maybe give some credit to Sumter. If there had been a better work ethic in those girls that worked with you before, there wouldn't have been room for Jessie and Becca, or Molly. If they had worked for better people, they wouldn't have come to the shop looking for work. Does everyone see how this all was set in motion by a hand greater than ours?"

"You all wouldn't have got together, not amassed wealth and prestige to attract good people to work your enterprises, not needed help with your household. I could have also stayed there, instead of going on your vacation with you. I see it. You all were great to work with, but even better to love with. I love you all so much and I'm gonna be a mother again." Sarah says with glistening in her eyes. Sam is beside her hugging her tight. Ann, Jessie, Becca, Rachael and Molly add their love and hugs.

Across the room, Annie and Mary see the smiles and the hugs and come over to see what's happening. Barbara comes along with Sandra.

"What's going on? What did we miss?" Annie asks. The four new arrivals stand by and hear the news of Sandra and Sarah's pregnancies. Mary and Barbara put hands up and cover open mouths. Mary expresses her surprise first.

"People, I was waiting. I didn't want to be the first. Sandra, Sarah, I am so happy for you and I will make it three."

"Make that four." Barbara says.

"Five." Annie follows.

Sam's tears and smile is almost too much for everyone and the hugs and kisses go on for twenty minutes or more and attracts the attention of the stewards, who also gather around.

"The Elliott family is growing again!" Sam exclaims.

Two of the stewards approach with Champagne buckets and trays of glasses.

"Mr. Elliott. Compliments of the galley. Congratulations and thank you. The skipper told us about your support of our Navy fund. Roger and I each, have followed you and your family. Oh, sorry, this is Roger Seymour. We purchased your book and DVD lectures. Roger has three wives and I have three. All of them are in the hair business and the pool of our resources, in just three years has provided us with a sheep ranch and sugar cane plantation. Roger is the sheep man and I have the sugar fields. We're neighbors and work together on many of the same things you have. Chicken house, greenhouse and an orchard." The steward says.

"Thank you. That's wonderful. What is your name?"

"I'm Sydney, Sydney Langley Sir."

"Well Sydney, Roger, thank you for your kind words and the champagne. I really hope it works for you as well as it has for us. I wonder if it's the mix of Cosmetologists and Military men that makes it work." Sam laughs. They all grin and laugh at the comment.

The two stewards excuse themselves, "Enjoy the champagne, we'll be in the pantry if you need anything." Roger says.

Sam and the ladies relax and sip champagne and talk about the new additions that are expected and returning to their home. Jessie sits up and looks around the table.

"Hey. What about finishing our vacation? We started out to bring the children to Thailand and meet Yai, and baptize the house."

"Oh my God. I didn't think about it. Sam, sisters, I've got to call home. My mom probably saw the news. I'll be back." Ann blurts as she hurries from the room.

"Well. I have to admit, I didn't think of that either. Jessie, great idea. Should we discuss it further?" Sam asks.

"Sam, Jessie, it sounds great. Will we still stay for three months? I kinda need to see to my mom." Rachael says.

"Three months may be too long for all of us. We may have to split up the visits. Ann, Cathy, Alex and Carrie will probably stay with Yai and after two or three weeks, Becca, Raina, Brian and Jamie will go to Seoul and stay, then after

250

two or three weeks, the rest of us will fly home. Ann and Becca with their children can follow at their convenience. I just hope that Yai can handle 34 visitors at one time."

"Sam, if any of the children want to stay with Ann or Becca, do you think it will be okay?" Rachael asks.

"Should be okay. If any of you want to spend more time than two or three weeks, that should be alright to. I know Rach, you're torn between setting up a clinic and seeing your mom. You may have to pass on the clinic, since most of our supplies are lost on an island that no one can find."

"Yeah. That's right. But I was thinking about Matt and I bet Tom will want to stay for a little longer." Rachael says.

"Sam, no one needs to go to Korea. My mom is in Sumter and the kids can see it on our next trip." Becca offers.

"You're right baby. I think we may have to make a trip real soon, once we get our homestead settled again. Summer is still a few months away."

They continue for another half hour. It seems like old times, sitting around planning. Sam notices that Sandra and Barbara are holding back.

"Sandra, Barbara, my loves. This is for you to. Where will we find your families. I just assumed you are both from Illinois, because that's where we got the plane."

"That's right Sam. We're both from Peoria, but there aren't any family there. My Mom is in a home in Chicago. She has early onset Alzheimer's disease. The last time I saw her, she didn't know me. I doubt that she is still alive. I don't know where my brother is. He's older and has his own life. You guys are my family and I'll go where you go." She says with a little sadness in her voice.

"Ditto, Sam. All I have left is an older brother in the CIA. I don't know anything about him now, or if he's married or what. We weren't close. Art was going to be my family and even he had only a sister. I guess I will let her know about Art, but like Sandra, you guys are my family and I'm happier than I ever expected to be in this life."

Sam went to his two Illinois dolls and holds both of them, with kisses and love pats. Jessie, Becca and Molly are first to add their love and comfort to their newest sisters. Rachael reaches them and adds her love.

"What's happening?" Ann asks as she comes back to the dining room.

"Sandra and Barbara just told us about their families, or lack of families and let us know that we are their family now." Becca tells her.

"What's the word about your Mom?" Sam asks as Ann hugs both Sandra and Barbara.

"She cried. Happy crying. Said we have to see her soon. She thought she had lost all of us and even cried over Becca, Jessie, Rach and Molly."

"That's just what we have been talking about. We sort of decided to continue with our trip and stay with Yai a few weeks and let her see everyone. You all will have to plan on outfitting this bunch. Swim suits, robes and all the stuff we'll need there and gifts and liquor. I sure could use a drink, my mind is racing again. So much time, so little to do . . . reverse that." Sam says.

They all laugh and nod at the thought of planning.

"Sam, this evening we'll sit here and plan and write everything down. Tomorrow and probably the next couple of days, in Sydney, we will have some time to shop. Now, I'm ready for a nap and a little cuddle." Ann says.

Everyone agrees and crowd the companionway to their rooms. Sam suggests a couple of them bring their mattresses to his room and they'll make a big bed on the floor.

"Yeah. Sounds good to me." Molly says.

Sam wonders how he's gonna cuddle ten women and still have energy for dinner. It's a big job, but someone has to do it. Ha! Ha!

Surprisingly, he accomplishes the job and still has time to sleep. He wakes to movement around him and finds all the ladies with bathrobes on and towels over their arms.

"Wake up time, Sam. We decided to shower before dinner. Tom came by and said the captain has a special dinner for our last night on the ship. So, get nekked mister." Jessie chides.

"Yes Ma'am." Sam says with a wicked smile.

They head to the shower and are soon fresh and dressing in clean, semi-formal clothes. Commander Hogan stops at Sam's cabin. He has a Yeoman with him, who hands Sam a stack of yellow legal pads and a dozen pens and a dozen pencils.

"Sam, I heard from the steward that you would be planning your next couple of days in Sydney and wanted to make lists and write a plan out. Thought you could use these." Hogan says.

"Thank you Martin. Very thoughtful. I really appreciate all the courtesies that you and the Captain and crew have given us. I hope not, but if we're ever lost at sea again . . . Ha! Ha!"

"My pleasure Sam." He says and grips Sam's hand in a strong handshake. "Oh by the way. The radioman says he has a contact for you to make a call to . . . South Carolina."

"Thank you. I'd better do it before dinner."

"Yeoman Sanders will show you the way."

They exchange goodbyes and Sam follows Sanders to the radio room. The patch through to Sam's home is complicated, having to go through radios to a radio/

telephone switch, but soon he hears the phone ringing. Brenda answers the phone on the third ring.

"Elliott residence, Brenda speaking. The Elliotts are not available. May I take a message."

"Brenda, this is Sam."

"Sam who?"

"Sam Elliott. I'm calling from the rescue ship. Hello, Hello. Brenda."

"Oh Mr. Elliott, I saw it on the news. We didn't believe it. When are you coming home. Oh my goodness, is everyone okay? How is everyone?" She rambles.

"Brenda, calm down. We are all doing fine, healthy, happy and anxious to be home, but we are going on to Thailand. Ann's mother is pretty shaken up by everything. Will you call Mr. Wade, the attorney and have him get with the accountant and wire us a line of credit, to Sydney, Australia."

"That's in Australia. Sydney. Yes. I have it. I'll call Mr. Wade first thing. Oh my. Mr. Elliott I'm so happy you all are safe . . . Sue, Sue, it's Mr. Elliott. Yes they're all fine. They're coming home soon. The news was right. Oh Mr. Elliott, sorry, Sue came in to see what I was on about this early. It's almost nine in the morning here."

"That's fine Brenda. It's almost seven in the evening here. Tell Sue we missed you two. Sarah, Annie and Mary are fine, well more than, I guess. They have joined the family. Kenny still hanging around?"

"No sir. Kenny took off the same week you flew to Hawaii. Haven't seen him since."

"Good. Really didn't want to have to explain to him that Mary is an Elliott now and has a cute baby girl, well not a baby any more, almost two."

"Mary has a baby and Sarah and Annie?"

"Yeah. Sarah and Annie to. Sarah has a little girl and Annie a little boy. You spread the news, okay and get Mr. Wade and Mr. Louder on getting some money to us. Tell them to wire it to the American Embassy."

"Yes sir. The American Embassy in Sydney, Australia. Take care Sir and tell everyone Hello from all of us here."

"Good bye Brenda."

"Good bye Mr. Sam, good bye."

Sam thanks the radioman and wends his way to the dining room. When he enters, the tables have been rearranged into a banquet setting with a very long head table and two long rows of tables at right angles to the head.

The children are already at the tables, the older children looking after the youngest. The ladies are at the head table and a big space is open in the middle. Ann stands and waves him to the big space beside her. When Sam reaches the proffered space, he sees that there are two chairs there.

"Here Sam, sit here. The Captain will be next to you. Mr. Hogan is down that side, between Jessie and Rachael and the doctor is on this side, between Becca and Molly. The women we rescued are there on the right line of tables and our children are on the left. The Captain said that there would be singing and the stewards Roger and Sydney said the cooks were especially gifted tonight." Ann tells him.

"I'm ready. I talked to Brenda and asked her to have Mr. Wade and Mr. Louder wire us a cash credit to the American Embassy in Sydney. She was all tickled and Sue was there. She couldn't believe that Sarah, Annie and Mary have babies. Kenny, she says, left almost the same time that we did and hasn't been back."

"You'll have to tell everyone later, when we do our planning meeting. Oh, here comes the Captain."

Sam stood to shake hands with the Captain and the stewards are coming in a string from the kitchen. Each has a large tray, with several plates with plated food, just like a gourmet restaurant. Behind them are a line of stewards carrying wine baskets and pour glasses for the head table and for the oldest children. Sam wonders at the sommeliers on a rescue ship. The meal is outstanding. Even Sam's pedestrian pallet appreciates the texture and flavor of the food. During the dessert, the ships choir, or glee club enters and line up at seats facing the head table and just past the two lines of tables. They are very skilled and give a medley of old American rock n roll tunes and Australian folk songs. Sam and his older sons, join in when *Waltzing Matilda* is the next selection, to the delight of the ladies and the Captain.

"Sam. You are full of surprises and you sing. You sing Australian songs." The Captain laughs.

"Been around a while. I was here back when I was in the service. I came to Sydney to meet one of your agents. He brought me some information so that I could complete a mission for SEATO."

"What line of work were you in?"

"I was in Special Operations for my whole military career. My records show that I was a Weapons Controller. A WC takes fighter planes to a target and brings them home again. Not too glamorous, but was a good cover for me being gone all of the time."

"Sam, were you known as Sugar Easy Poppa?"

"How did you hear about that? That was my code name in Ops."

"Sam, my brother was the agent you met in Sydney. Harmon Rabb, Special Forces. If you knew him, it explains how you overcame the pirates."

"Of course. Rabb, Captain Rabb, sorry, I didn't make the connection. How is Harmon? Well I hope."

"Sam, Harmon is running his own ranch in the Northwest Territory. He's been very successful, for an older brother."

"That's good to hear. We were only together for three days, but I remember him well. He introduced me to Fosters. After about four, he says, "Fosters is made from only the best, purest, donkey piss." I do love that kind of humor."

"That's Harmon. If I may, I'm going to radio him and tell him I met you. He may or may not be able to meet us in Sydney."

"That's fine Captain. If he can't, tell him Hi from me."

"Will do. If you will excuse me. I'm going to retire early, so I can be up early for the maneuver to get us into port."

"Good night Captain Rabb."

Sam rejoins the ladies and oldest children. They've set up tables in a horseshoe pattern and pads, pencils and pens at every chair. With the oldest, Sam and the ladies, they have seventeen chairs. The stewards have placed glasses at each position and several pitchers of ice water on the tables.

"Family, are we ready to plan?"

"Yes Sam. Uh, what was the Captain talking about?" Jessie asks.

"I met his older brother about twenty five years ago, in Sydney."

"Dad, the Aussie Special Forces guy, you told me about?" Tom asks.

"That's right Tom. The Captain says his brother, Harmon, is a successful rancher in the Northwest Territory. He said he would try to get him to come to Sydney when we are there."

Several comments from the ladies about what a small world, then they took to the task of planning their purchases. They continue until after ten o'clock. The kids pooped out around nine. Only Tom hung on to the end. They were going to be busy shopping, news conferences and interrogations while they were in Sydney.

"Tom, ladies. I'm beat. Let's wrap it up and get some sleep."

There was unanimous agreement and the group moved away to their cabins.

The mattresses were still on Sam's cabin floor and they all decided to sleep there with Sam, but without their clothes. Sam, of course, hated the idea ... NOT. They were all asleep within fifteen minutes, despite the warmth and errant hands of the women.

Morning came with a slowing of the ship. Sam and the ladies woke up and stretched and untangled themselves. They could sense the slowing and begin to be excited.

"We're slowing down. We must be getting close to docking. We should shower and get dressed." Ann says.

"We didn't pack anything and we have clothes that need washing. Oh, Sam. Do we pack the dirty clothes?" Molly asks.

"Let's get done what we can for now. We'll worry about the rest when we're dressed and get a report at breakfast." Sam says.

When they get back from the shower, they each, find their clothes cleaned and neatly pressed or folded on their beds. The ladies sort out the clothes and pack them.

"Who did this? Sam we should find out and thank them. This was a real welcome surprise." Jessie says.

"I'll ask the steward. They're probably the ones responsible." Sam says.

They put the rooms back in order and set their bags beside the doors inside each cabin. They head for the dining room for breakfast and a briefing from the Captain or his Number one.

When they enter, Sam waves to Sydney, who comes over.

"Yes Sir. What can I get for you?"

"Sydney. When we came back from our shower, our soiled clothing had been laundered and pressed or folded. We want to thank whoever did this wonderful thing for us."

"Sir, it's part of the service. The purser's people are responsible for the cabins and passengers. The stewards also helped. We listen well and heard talk about finding a washer and an iron. The rest was our pleasure. We can't repay your generosity, but we can help to make the trip better for you and your family."

"Well Sydney. Thank you, and will you tell the guys how much we appreciate their hard work. The ladies were particularly relieved, that they didn't have to pack dirty clothes."

"Will do sir. Have a great day. We're in the final twenty miles of the dock."

Sam brings the news to his ladies who have started breakfast.

"Sam that is so nice. It really did relieve us. I am anxious to get going in some familiar places." Ann says pouring him a cup of coffee.

"Yes Sam. How long do you think the media and questioning will take. I'm anxious now, for some normal things, like shopping." Becca laughs.

"I guess I'll add my two cents. This has been a real adventure. Something to write about. Just like Ann and Jessie, I long for civilization and normalcy, even though, I wouldn't trade these last . . . nearly three years for anything. The strength of our children has multiplied ten fold." Rachael says.

"My Darlings. You probably don't realize how wonderful you all are and how much I love you. I sat with Tom a while and we punched up the whole story on a laptop. Tom got some paper from the Yeoman and printed two hundred copies. I hope that will get us through most of the media. The Captain and Commander Hogan assured me that they have the most complete report they can think of having, so not to worry about a long debriefing. The ladies we rescued also gave full accounts of their time in captivity and our rescue of them. If the people from the embassy have our money from home, we should be ready to shop by noon tomorrow."

A large sigh came from each of the women. Their relief is tangible.

The rest of the morning is spent getting the children packed and having all of their bags and the laptops and camera bags inventoried and tagged. Tom gave laptops and or cameras to each of his siblings 13 and up and charged them with their safekeeping.

"Brothers and sisters. These pieces of gear are the record of our lives these last 30 plus months. Attach them to yourselves. Protect them. Holler if someone tries to take them from you. I'm totally serious, this is probably the most important thing we have now."

"Tom's right. We have some good stuff on these cameras." Richard confirms.

"I know. The babies being born with Mom Sarah, Annie, Mary, Sandra and Barbara, is something that can't be recovered." Carly says.

There are nods from the rest.

It's almost eleven when the purser announces the ship has docked. Sydney announces lunch, but everyone is too excited to eat and offer their apologies to the stewards as they head for the deck. Their bags are already being unloaded to the Customs secure area at the dock. The Captain is at the gangway to greet the family and received messages from the port authority. He is reading a message, when Sam and family arrive to disembark.

"Sam, ladies. I just had word that you have a clear way to the port authority auditorium. You will enter from the back and avoid all the paparazzi. You will have a brief, the Admiral emphasized brief, news conference and then in a private office, four of the girls' parents will meet you and your ladies. There are some others waiting to meet with you, then off to the hotel, where a suite has been prepared for all of you."

"Thank you so much Captain. Any word from Harmon?"

"He won't be able to make it. He's in the middle of a round up, but he says, thank you for remembering him and have a couple of Fosters donkey piss for him."

Sam and the Captain both laugh and shake hands. The Captain shakes hands and hugs each of the ladies and Sam's grown children. The family walks down the gangway to a bus waiting for them.

The brief news conference turned into an hour and a half. They were ushered to the office and the four parents were there. The liaison officer introduced them to Sam. They were surprised that Sam greeted them in their own language.

Dr. Yim Songkra from Thailand and the father of Mahlee, did the respectful Thai greeting and Sam introduced him and his wife to his ladies. More surprise as all of Sam's ladies speak Thai.

General Som Limsuwan, also from Thailand, whose daughter was Suchare, shared a salute with Sam. He introduced his wife and Sam in turn introduced his ladies.

Tran Nguen Kei is the father of Lynn, the girl from Viet Nam. Sam understands Mr. Kei's daughter when she tells her father to speak French.

Ling Tao is the Chinese father of Soo Li Tao. He is alone and greets Sam like a long lost brother and speaks in English.

"Mr. Elliott, my humble thanks. Soo Li is all I have left. My wife died many years ago and my only brother died in Japan, in an earthquake some years ago. You saved my baby. All I have is yours. You have my undying gratitude."

"Mr. Tao, I couldn't be happier to have been of service. Soo Li is a lovely young lady. I accept your friendship as payment in full." Sam says then switches to Mandarin and is flooded with a big laughing smile, "and call me Sam."

"I am Ling, Sam. My friend."

Sam hugs him. Soo Li hugs both of them, then finds Matt and brings him over and introduces him to her father. More hugs and hand shakes.

"You have something for Soo Li, Matt?" Sam asks his son.

"She's cute Dad. Kinda like Momma Ann. I gave her my e-mail and phone number and she gave me hers. She is coming to the states in the fall for college and her dad is coming with her to set up an apartment and work the Chinese consulate in Charleston."

"Wow. That is some news. I guess we'll be seeing more of them from now on." Sam says, as he catches a glimpse of Tom coming his way.

"What's up Tom?"

"Dad, Dr. Songkra and his family are moving to the states later this summer. Mahlee is going to college at,

College of Charleston and Dr. Songkra is going to teach at MUSC in Charleston. Uh, you wouldn't have an objection if I were to . . . uh . . ."

Sam interrupts him, "Go for it man. She's a doll and you both speak the language. Let them know that they are welcome at our home when they get settled."

"Thanks Dad. Hey Matt, did you tell dad about Soo Li?" Tom asks.

"Yeah. We're good."

The family makes some new friends and Sam's sons maybe more. As the group begins to separate, the consulate meets Sam.

"Mr. Elliott, I'm the American Consulate here in Sydney. Tom Baker. I'm sorry, we were unable to process a money transaction for you, but I think your problem is solved."

"It's good to meet you Tom, I hope your resolution will get us on our way. The ladies haven't been shopping for almost three years."

Mr. Baker laughs and puts his hand on Sam's shoulder and turns him a half turn.

"Hi Sam!"

"Wade. Oh my God and Brenda, Sue and Louder. I guess you guys brought the money. Mr. Baker said he had a solution to my problem."

"Yes sir. We weren't sure how much you were thinking, so we also brought your credit cards, letters of credit for the banks and a hundred thousand in cash."

"That's fine. If it helps, post your transportation and any fees to the corporation. You can't know how pleased I am that you all came.

"Sam. We did book the flight with the corporation, but the President of the United States provided our transportation. That's how we got here as quickly as we did. You would be surprised how much richer you are and what action, the news of your rescue, has triggered on your behalf." Mr. Wade says.

"I don't understand."

"Well, Sir, if you can believe it. The week after you were reported lost, the stock market began to sink rapidly. It leveled out, when the enterprises continued to produce quantity and quality as always. The consensus was that your business ethic was still in tact and operating. The stock that you still hold, suddenly sky rocketed and the earnings were unbelievable. Companies and businesses across the country were clamoring for copies of your corporate manifesto. In the first year, the United States advanced in business so much that the government was able to pay off a third of the national debt. Corporate unions have sprung up across the country and enterprise is booming. When the news came through that you had been rescued, I had to put on a staff just to answer telephones."

"Yes sir. I had to put two extra accounting people on your accounts. For the time you've been gone, taxes and debts have been paid and investments documented and banked. I am glad you're back." Dale Louder says.

"Thank you. Thank you both. This news is pretty hard to believe. I hoped our lifestyle would catch on, but the rest—Wow—is hard to believe.

Brenda, Sue, so good to see you." Sam says hugging each in turn. A sound behind him catches his attention and suddenly the room is filled with Elliotts, who are talking all at once and hugging everyone. Sam, turns to Mr. Wade, the attorney and tips his head to move to the edge of the crowd.

"Mr. Wade . . . Robert, I have five new Elliotts and five new Elliott children and five on the way. When you get back, will you take care of the documents. Tom has a folder with the particulars, names and such."

"Will do Sam."

"Oh and Robert, take some of the cash and you, Dale, Brenda and Sue enjoy some vacation time."

"Will do Sam and thank you."

"I have to excuse myself. They haven't been shopping in a long time. It was the one thing they are anxious to do. I think Tom has some media and will need copies taken home."

"I'll talk with him Sam. Have a good time. When can we expect you in Sumter?"

"Ah, most of us will be there in around three or four weeks." Sam says. He looks at the credit cards in his hand and counts them. He looks at Wade and says, "There are nine with names and two without."

"We just knew that Sarah, Annie and Mary were part of the family and Brenda said that there were two flight attendants. I didn't have names, so I put Any Elliott on the two." Wade says.

"Good thinking Robert. Thank you. It will help make them feel welcome. You have some fun. I'm going shopping."

Sam joins the rest of the family at the bus. It is after three already and they order room service as soon as they get in the suite.

"Sarah, Annie, Mary, Sandra and Barbara, Mr. Wade brought cash and credit cards for all of us. These are yours. Ann, Jessie and the rest of my darlings, he brought yours to."

The women crowd to get their cards.

"Mr. Wade brought about a hundred thousand and a letter of credit that the banks will honor. What say we shop tomorrow. The adrenalin rush of the last several hours has taken all of my energy." Sam says.

"Ditto Sam. I'm bushed. Maybe take a nap after eating and dinner in the hotel later?" Molly says.

Everyone agrees with nods and smiles. Soon they have all found comfortable places to stretch out and nap. Sam had only been sleeping for an hour when a knock at the door rouses him. He forgot about room service.

"Your order sir. Apologies from the kitchen. They wanted to serve something that may not have been available to you."

"Mmmm! What have we got?"

"Hot roast been sandwiches, French fries, onion rings, green beans and pearl onions, milk shakes and for dessert, hot apple pie."

"Wow. That sounds wonderful."

Several of the ladies have come out from the bedroom, drawn by the wonderful aroma of the food.

"Mmmm! Sam hot roast beef. Suddenly, I'm starved." Jessie says.

"Me to. Oh, onion rings and milk shakes. Mmmm!" Becca says.

"I guess the kitchen knows us pretty well. Thank you, and please convey our thanks to the kitchen. Uh, our children are in the next suite . . ."

"Yes sir. They were surprised as well. Pizza, cheese burgers, chicken nuggets, tacos, fries, milk shakes, Coke, Pepsi, Root Beer, and milk." He tells Sam.

"Well, thank you. I'd like to give . . ."

"No sir. Your thanks is enough. Everyone is proud to be of service." He smiles, turns and closes the doors behind him.

"Time to eat ladies, I mean, it's time to eat, full stop, ladies." Smiles, grins and throaty laughs greet him.

"This is wonderful. I don't think I'll be hungry later. It's after four now." Sandra observes.

"Right. This is wonderful and an hour nap won't do it for me. I'm napping for two." Sarah grins and bites into another onion ring.

"If everyone concurs. I'm for lounging around in the air conditioning and maybe watch some TV and see what has been happening in the world while we were gone. Robert, says the world has changed because of us and we are richer than when we left."

"Changed, how Sam?" Rachael asks.

"He said that when news of our loss hit the news, stocks plummeted. Companies were struggling to stay afloat, then when news came out that our enterprises were still booming, well they finally realized that it was our business ethic that worked. The corporation was swamped with requests for training. Now, hundreds of companies have adopted our business style and there are also more and more corporate unions all over the country and the world. I love you all so much. You knew that love really does make the world go round."

Sam became engulfed with loving women. At 48, going on 100, he was the happiest man on earth, maybe in the universe.

The whole family spends the evening together in the parent's suite, talking, watching TV, listening to music and snacking. The children filter out from 8:45 to 9:30. Tom, Carly, Cathy and Matt take charge of the five two year olds, who are already in dreamland.

"How are we going to do the shopping tomorrow?" Sam asks.

"Sam, we've talked and will handle most of it, if you don't mind. You and the kids could sight see or hang around the pool." Ann says.

"Yeah. We could also arrange our transportation to Bangkok. I wonder what the local cinema would think of twenty four in one group. We'll be fine. You, my darlings enjoy shopping. Get our newest additions used to not having to worry about money."

"You are a darling, Sam. Thank you." Sandra says.

The suite's tub is big, but only big enough for six. Like a hot tub, but a step down into the floor.

"I guess we don't get to bathe together, huh!" Sam says.

"Not so fast mister. Five of us in the tub, five in the shower. The shower people trade. You my fine sir are in the tub for a double soaking and that other stuff." Becca says with a laugh.

"Yes sir. You don't get off that easy." Jessie adds.

"Sam. We promise not to be too rough." Barbara says.

It never gets old and Sam is always amazed that they are so uninhibited, that they can share their most intimate time with their man, in front of one another. Later they tumbled naked, onto the mattresses of four beds pushed together and slept deeply.

The next two days were a whirlwind for all. The ladies shopped and Sam and the kids toured and went to a movie. Tom met with Mr. Wade before he, Dale, Brenda and Sue left for Hawaii and gave him copies of all the media cards and DVD copies of all of their data.

Tom told Sam later that day that he also mailed a large package of the same copies, to himself, in Sumter.

"Good man, Tom. Taking no chances, that's good. There's a lot of material there that is irreplaceable."

"Yes Sir. Not that I don't trust Mr. Wade, it's just . . . well, we crashed."

Friday morning and the family was packed and ready to go to Bangkok. The hotel had breakfast sent to the rooms early and collected their extensive number of suitcases. The concierge called the room at eight and notified them that the transportation was ready to take them to the airport.

Sam stopped at the desk and was told that Mr. Wade and the Consulate had taken care of the whole bill and very generous gratuities for the staff.

On the bus, Sam told the ladies what happened at the desk, "The Consulate and Mr. Wade paid the hotel and did the gratuities for us. I feel kind of special."

The ladies concurred and suggested that Mr. Wade be given a proper thank you, when the family returns.

The plane arrives in Bangkok and Sam and family are greeted by the American Ambassador to Thailand.

"Mr. Elliott, on behalf of the American people. I welcome you to Thailand. Americans everywhere are rejoicing in your safe return. When your family is ready to return to the U.S., the President has authorized your use of Air Force One, just give us a few days notice."

"Thank you Mr. Ambassador. I'm not sure what to say, or why we are to be given this attention. I know I speak for all of us when I say that we do truly appreciate this. As to leaving, we plan to stay here at least three, maybe four weeks. Some will remain longer and the rest of us will go home."

The Ambassador turns and waves to an assistant, who steps forward with a briefcase.

"Mr. Elliot, uh, Ladies. These cell phones are for you. They will operate here and you can also call the U.S. or anywhere there are cell phones. A gift from the National Association of CEOs."

He hands them out, including chargers, to each of them and takes his leave.

"Well family, we're off to see Yai. I ordered an air conditioned bus to meet us." Sam says.

The bus is just leaving Bangkok, when they are met by an convoy of police cars and official limousines. The driver pulls over and stops on the shoulder.

Sam asks the driver, "Do you know why we are being stopped?"

"No sir. The cars carry the flag of the King."

"Family, the driver says the cars have the King's flags on them."

Several men, dressed in black suits and a younger man in an iridescent navy blue suit approach the bus. Sam asks the driver to open the door and Sam steps down.

The dignified gentleman, at the head of the entourage greets Sam. "Mr. Elliott, I apologize for this interruption. We had intended to greet you at the airport. His Royal Majesty wishes to welcome you and your family and his son, His Royal Highness is here to offer you and your family an invitation to come to the palace."

The younger man steps forward and Sam does the formal Wai, but instead of putting the tips of his fingers to his nose, he raises them to his forehead and receives pleased gasps. The gesture is a sign of respect for the royal house. The prince smiles and reaches his hand toward Sam and shakes his hand like an old friend.

"Mr. Sam, welcome to Thailand. I have followed the stories of you and your family for many years. As the chairman for our industrial councils, I have ordered the adoption of your business practices. My father asks if you would come to dinner, with your family and your Thai family as well, on Saturday of next week."

"Your Highness, it would be my distinct honor to come to dinner. Please convey to your father, the King, my humble gratitude for his kind invitation."

The prince's aid talks to the driver and gets directions to Yai's house. He talks to Ann and gets the numbers of her family and the Elliotts that will attend.

"It seems my aid has all the necessary information. I look forward to seeing you again, on Saturday."

The entourage about faces and walk back to their cars. Sam re-boards the bus and addresses the family.

"I guess you heard. The king of Thailand has invited our family to his place for dinner a week from next Saturday."

"Sam, the aid asked me to bring my mother and my aunts, uncles and cousins. I told him that it would be more than thirty people and our family. I hope the king has a big table." Ann says

The rest had a laugh at her comment.

They arrive at the house and a truck, from the Aussie store, was unloading some of the things the ladies had ordered while in Sydney.

Yai and several cousins, their husbands and Ann's aunts and uncles were at the house. When the family begins to get off the bus, Yai is really excited and runs to Ann and hugs and kisses her, completely against Thai custom. Jessie, Becca, Rachael and Molly recognize several of the cousins and greet them and to are surprised that they have abandoned custom and hugs are exchanged. When the children begin stepping off the bus, the excitement escalates. Yai is overcome with tears, when she meets, Cathy, Alex and Carrie. She is grinning hard and her eyes fly open when each of the grandchildren speak to her in fluent Thai.

"Goodness. Listen to my grandchildren speaking Thai." She exclaims.

"Aunt Jumjim, they all speak Thai. All of the women and all of the children." Ann's cousin Chun says.

Her eyes were wet with tears and she is happier than anything, when she spots Sam.

"Oy, Sam. I am so happy. My baby, my grandbabies, everyone is so beautiful." She exclaims and throws her arms around him. Sam hugs her back.

The children are being introduced to everyone and are amazing everyone with their fluency in Thai.

Challat is there and tells Sam that the pool is still going strong, but wonders how all of us will be able to get in it.

"Maybe tomorrow, we get a bigger one." Sam laughs. "Thank you for keeping it up. You must have run out of money some time ago."

"No Sam, had money from house building left to get chemicals. I made a good deal with the pool supply."

"Good. How have you been? We should have been back a couple of years ago. Now we show up with five more women and 23 children."

"Yes. You must tell the story. Everyone wants to know about your adventure."

"Yes. We will get settled in and one evening, maybe tomorrow, or the next day, we'll have a family day and tell the whole story."

Sam's five new loves are laughing and talking with Ann's cousins. Jessie, Molly and Rach have introduced them to Sangob, Chunjai and Praiyom. Sarah, Annie and Mary had studied Thai back home when the family was teaching the children. Sandra and Barbara learned from them while on the island. Sam sees that it has made them very comfortable with their new friends.

Sam sees Becca, with Ann and they are talking with Yai. Everyone looks comfortable with one another, like they've lived together forever. The children are talking with some young people, who have just arrived.

"Sam. My cousins' children are here. It looks like a day for a family reunion." Ann tells him.

"I'm down for that." Becca says.

"Great. Poll the population." Sam says.

Soon the excitement grows. With all the extra people, the delivery was put away quickly and the cooking started. Thais love to eat when visiting each other. While everyone is busy with the preparations, Sam inspects the new addition to the house, the showers, the garden tub, the bedrooms and the new beds.

"Big. Huh? I wondered where you were going. I forgot about this addition." Molly says.

"Yeah. Just needed to see if we could be family here. I'm glad you all thought about ordering the beds, bedding and stuff while in Sydney. I didn't even think about that store we shopped here, would be part of the parent store in Sydney. Thank you."

Molly puts her arms around him and leans in to kiss him. They stand there in a warm embrace for several minutes.

"Thanks Molly. This is nice."

"Mmmm! It should be quite a night."

"Quite a crowd down there. How you feeling?"

"Good. It is much better than last time. I enjoyed it then, but now that I can talk with everyone, much better. I do like Ann's three lady cousins. Chun, Prai and Sangob. Since last time we were here, they have each brought new women into their relationship with their husbands and loving it. Probably as much as we each love our sisters."

"I am happy. I hope your new sisters are enjoying this."

"They are Sam. Sandra and Barb said to me, that they were thrilled to be a part of the family. Sandy says she never would have thought that anything like this was possible and the idea of having dinner with a king is an event that will be in her memory forever."

"Oh my, I forgot about the dinner already. I bet Ann hasn't told anyone yet."

"No! There'd be a riot and we wouldn't get anything ready for our get together."

"I'll check with Ann and maybe we can make an announcement later, when everyone thinks nothing could be better. Ha! Ha! This could be a real hoot."

"I bet. Oh, I'm going to unpack my bags a bit before I come back down."

"Okay. Yeah, probably need swimwear before the night is through."

Sam gives Molly a kiss on the cheek and goes down to mingle with the rest of the family. The music has started and the aromas of cooking are filling the whole house. Yai is sitting on a lounge chair, with Ann next to her on the left. Sam takes the seat on the right side of her and tells her how nice it is to be home.

"Oy Sam. You want to make this your home now?" She says with eyes bright with expectation.

"For a while Mom. Ann will stay for some time, but I have to see to our home in Sumter, but I'll be back for a longer stay. The children want to get back to school and the older children have to make plans for college. We'll see."

In Korean, he says to Ann, "Did you tell her about the king yet? I thought I'd tell everyone after eating and everyone is settled down this evening."

Ann continues in Korean, "I haven't told her. That will be good, after everyone is feeling good."

"Ankuan, what are you saying that you don't want your mother to hear?"

"Mom. It's something very good. Sam will tell everyone later tonight. You will love it, I promise."

The food is wonderful. Sam really missed his curry. The coconut milk added at the end of cooking softens the spicy red peppers and adds a little sweetness to the curry. The eating and drinking goes on for hours. Around nine o'clock, the party starts to wind down. Sam picks this time to make his announcement.

"Family, friends! I have an announcement. Earlier today, on our way here, we were pulled over by the police and Thai official cars. The prince, his Royal Highness, greeted us and invited us and you to the palace for dinner a week from this Saturday. All of you are invited to dinner with the king."

The silence was deafening. All of the Thai family have blank faces, like they are trying to understand what was said. It continues for several seconds, then the gleeful noise erupts like the top coming off a volcano. Cheering and laughter and shouts of joy goes on and on. Yai is crying and laughing at the same time.

Cathy, Alex and Carrie are surrounding her and hugging and kissing her forehead. Ann and Becca are talking with the cousins and doing a lot of nodding, as if confirming the things Sam has told them. Challat and Joe are clapping Sam on the back and thanking him for including them. The happiness of this evening will be a part of all their lives for a long time to come.

The talking and drinking go on to nearly midnight. Tom, Carly, Cathy and the other older children have put the youngest to bed and the 13, 14 years olds have dragged themselves to bed. The cousins' children have similarly found places to sleep in the extra bedrooms. Chaises have been turned into beds. Sam is nodding off, when Molly and Jessie take him by the arms and direct him to their bedroom. Sarah, Annie and Sandra are already stretched out. Barb and Mary are in the bathroom showering. Jessie and Molly strip him and pull him to the bathroom. The three step into the shower with Barb and Mary, but the shower is just for cleaning and in very short order they are all in bed and very quickly fall asleep.

The morning didn't come until almost noon. The sounds of Tom and the older children, downstairs, cooking and feeding themselves and their siblings. Sam woke, nude, with nude and semi nude women all over him and the bed. He raises his head and looks at his wonderful loves.

He sighs and pets the flesh closest to his hands. On his right, he feels a hand slide up his thigh and take hold of his manhood. He looks and sees that it is Sarah, her head on his thigh, her warm breath sending adrenalin coursing through him. Beside him on the right is Jessie. She stirs and opens her eyes and is looking at Sam. She smiles and puts her arm across his chest.

Molly is on his right, her head on his shoulder and Becca was on his left to. She is petting his left thigh and competing with Sarah.

"Oh my goodness, my darlings. Don't kill me by accident." The two stop their eager petting. Sam sits up a little more and reaches to Becca and Sarah, who move higher and are looking him in the eyes. Jessie and Molly move back a little and Sam kisses, first Sarah, then Becca.

"Thank you Becca, Sarah. It is a great way to wake up in the morning. I love you both. Molly, Jessie you to." All of them smile and Molly and Jessie cat walk closer and exchange kisses with their man.

"Looks like everyone else is still out."

"Sam, except for Mary, the rest didn't get to bed until after three." Jessie says.

"I'm ready for a shower and some breakfast. Anyone else?"

The four slip off the bed and Sam follows them into the shower. They spend twenty minutes in soapy, sensual luxury and the four women take their pleasure with their man.

Yep, not a bad way to wake up, Sam thinks.

Downstairs, Carly and Cathy have made a big American breakfast and warmed some leftovers. Sam goes for bacon and some rice with curry. Molly takes pancakes and Jessie gets eggs and toast with butter. Sarah has a little of everything. She looks at the faces watching her.

"Guys, remember, I am eating for two now."

Everyone laughs.

Sam goes and chats with Tom, Matt, Ryan, Richard, Brian and Peter. Carly brings a larger pitcher of iced tea. Cathy and Raina bring glasses.

"Dad, is anyone else awake?" Raina asks.

"There may be a few more stirring by now."

"I'm gonna check. I think Yai and Chun want to go shopping for outfits to wear to the dinner."

"Good. You can check and wake Momma Ann and Mary and tell them about Yai."

"Thanks. Love you Dad."

"Love you Raina."

"Boys, do we need to find us some duds for this dinner?"

"Not really. We have sport coats that will fit Peter, Brian and Richard. Edward, Wyatt and Mike should fit . . . ." Tom is saying and interrupted.

"No sir. We are going to get new suits for everyone Tom. You older boys' coats may fit Peter, Brian and Richard, but theirs won't fit Mike, Ed and Wyatt. We're gonna look good when we go to see the king." Ann tells them as she comes in. "Count on it boys, you to Sam." Becca says.

"I don't believe it. Something this important . . ." Rachael begins.

"Okay, Okay, I get it ladies. New suits for the men. Better get ready guys. They'll be shuffling us out soon." Sam relents.

It is the middle of the afternoon before they get on the road to the tailors. Yai, directed the driver to a large clothing store in the middle of Bangkok. Sam's eyes got big when he saw the name, Lord and Taylor.

"Sam, you and the boys will get suits here. Ann called them and I talked to them. You will get the best suits. My daughters will go with me and to the ladies fashion store." Yai explained to him. "Call on the phone when you are ready and we will send the driver back to get you."

"Thank you mother. You are too good." Sam says and does a formal Wai. She laughs and grabs his head, pulls it down and kisses his forehead. Sam had to blush a little, then the ladies were off.

They entered the shop and were greeted by a gray haired Thai man with a tape measure around his neck.

"May I help you sir?"

"Hello. I'm Sam Elliott and I need a suit for me and my boys that will be good to wear to see the king."

"My goodness Yes sir. We have been expecting you." He says and turns to the back and calls out for his people to come out. Seven men come out with tapes and pads and pencils.

"Please sir. Be comfortable. Have sons take off shirts and belts."

The boys take off their shirts and belts and are bent and turned and measured. Soon, there is a rush of people running to the back with the pads filled with measurements. The older fellow, who first greeted them says to Sam.

"Please be comfortable. Something to drink? We will have first cut of your suit very soon." There is a bustle inside the back door and three ladies appear with trays of Coke's and Scottish shortbreads.

"Thank you. How nice. Boys. Scottish shortbread." Sam says.

It was about forty minutes and the tailors come out with almost suits on hangers. Sam doesn't know how they remember which suit goes to which boy, but soon they all have the coats on and are being marked with tailors chalk and pins. The trousers seem to be close to right at the first fitting. Sam can see that these guys know their business.

"Sir. We will make one more sewing; we must then launder and press. Is it possible to return tomorrow for finished suit?"

"Of course. We don't go until Saturday, next week." Sam tells him in Thai and gets wide eyes and a smile and a formal Wai. Sam thanks him and says again, in Thai, how professional his tailors are and how happy he is to come to this shop.

After the last fitting, everything is ready. They bring out white shirts and ties, tie tacks and matching cufflinks. They fit the Elliott men quickly, then bring out shoes and socks.

"All will be here tomorrow when you come to pick up suits." The gray haired tailor tells Sam.

"Thank you. Please, may I know your name?"

"My apologies sir. I am Sahn Li Liang, Master tailor."

"It is my extreme pleasure to meet you Mr. Liang. You have a most professional staff."

"Thank you Sir. You have very good sons."

"Thank you. We will return tomorrow to pick up our suits. May I pay now."

"It will be most appreciated Sir."

Sam gets the bill and isn't surprised. The ten suits comes to just 330,000 Baht. Sam gives him, his Master Card. When Mr. Liang hands Sam the card and receipt, Sam hands him ten crisp $100 bills.

"Many thanks for your kindness Mr. Liang. This is for you and your staff."

"Thank you Sir. You are very generous."

Sam and the boys exit and gather on the sidewalk. Tom is already talking to someone on his cell phone.

"Mom says they will be a lot longer, but will send the bus back and take us somewhere to wait on them."

"Good. Where do you think you'd like to hang out?" Sam asks.

They decide to hang out at the Klong Toi. It's a kind of outdoor, indoor Mall with a variety of shops and eating places. It has come a long way since Sam saw it years ago. Suddenly it is like boardwalk at Coney Island.

The boys and Sam go from shop to shop and see some neat things, some unusual things and some things they buy. They stop at a big American style food court and have monster burgers and real French fries with gobs of ketchup. The menu says the beef is from Australia and is certified by some Australian food and drug agency.

The Thai cooks got the fries just right and Sam and the boys had double servings, washed it all down with strawberry milk shakes and Coca Cola.

"Oh man. I didn't know I missed burgers that much and the fries; Mmmm!" Sam says through a mouthful of fries and ketchup.

Tom confirms the feeling, "Aw yeah, Dad. This is great."

The other boys are also nodding vigorously, cheeks packed with hamburger and fries. Sam loves it. He sees himself in each of them and he is so proud.

They take some relaxing time to look at some of the purchases they made. Sam picked up forty or fifty very old silver coins. The dealer was impressed that Sam passed on the very old Morgan dollars and Seated Liberty coins. Sam pointed out that they had flaws that marked them as Chinese counterfeits.

He also picked up antique looking Thai swords and daggers. Tom found Crocodile belts, billfolds and boots. Matt and Ryan also bought several belts in varying sizes and styles. Sam was impressed that they were thinking of having future belts that will fit at their grown up size.

The three young boys, Mike, Ed and Wyatt followed their big brothers and were proud of their purchases. Sam sees that they all have identical Crocodile boots and smiles. My boys, he thinks.

They decided on an arcade visit and were deep in the games when their cell phones go off. Each of the elder boys, answer.

"Dad, Mom says they are outside the market, if we're ready." Tom says.

"My Mom to Dad." Matt says.

"Ditto." Ryan adds.

"I guess that means everyone is ready. It's seven thirty already. I hope they're not hungry. Everyone is shopping, no one cooking." Sam says.

They wend their way to the exit from the market. They see the bus waiting for them and hurry aboard.

"I hope you found everything you needed. We have to come back tomorrow to pick up our suits and stuff." Sam says.

"We had a wonderful time. Even the babies have beautiful new clothes. Yai is gonna wow them." Ann says.

"What we gonna do about dinner?"

"Don't worry Sam, we ordered a catered meal from the Aussie store. They have a catering service and said it will be there by 8:30, so we have to hurry." Jessie tells them.

The week passes quickly and then it's time to visit the king. Everyone is rushing around primping and dressing. The whole family gets the treatment, since there are four cosmetologists. Everyone is ready when there is a commotion on the street. The gate is opened and there are a dozen limousines to take the family to the palace. The chauffer of the first limo comes to the gate.

"Sir. His Royal Majesty has sent your family a car."

"I would say so. Okay family, let's get this show on the road." Sam calls out.

The drive to the palace is met with awe and curiosity from people along the way. They enter the gate between guards who render smart salutes and bring their arms to port.

There are several dignitaries at the entrance to the palace and Sam recognizes the American Ambassador standing with them. The family leaves the limos like soldiers leaving a landing craft. They are an impressive sight gathered in front of the palace and walking between, impeccably dressed statesman.

His Royal Highness, the prince, greets Sam and family. When he greets Yai, she almost faints. Ann introduces her cousins, aunts and uncles and her sisters. Each of Sam's ladies introduce their children. The prince began to smile after the fourth introduction and was grinning when Molly, the youngest introduces the family's eldest son, Tom.

"Mr. Sam. Elliott family, it is a great honor for my family to meet your family. Please follow me. Dinner is being served."

The army, of family, follows the prince. In the dining area, which is massive, they are ushered to seats around the table. Sam to the King's right, Ann on the left, then Tom next to Ann and Carly next to Sam, until all seventy family members and dignitaries are seated. The prince has the opposite end of the table with his mother, the Queen on his right and Yai on his left. Yai is as proud as a mother can be.

A gong sounds and everyone rises as the King enters. He walks to his place and is seated by two liveried attendants. Before he sits, he puts his hand out to Sam and shakes his hand.

"It is my pleasure to finally meet the Elliotts. Welcome to my home."

"Your Majesty, it is indeed our pleasure and honor to be here."

The king turns to Ann and she gets pale as the king reaches his hand to her. The confusion is flashing across her face. Sam imagines her thinking, do I shake hands, do I make a formal Wai, do I say anything?

"Ankuan. Welcome to my home. Your accomplishments, as a part of the Elliott family, bring great credit and pride to your Thai people. Thank you."

"Uh, I, Uh Thank you, your Majesty." Ann stutters and shakes hands.

The king sits and almost immediately the food is served.

The evening is filled with entertainment, good food and talk. The king is very interested in the business ethic that the family incorporated into their businesses. He understands the polygamy, but is fascinated that Sam can be a husband to so many women.

The King and Sam talk for most of the evening. At ten-thirty, the prince approaches the king and tells him that some of the younger people are ready to go to bed.

"Yes, of course. My apologies Sam. Your children are getting tired. You will consider my request for your help."

"I will, your Majesty. In the mean time, Ann and Becca have said that they will stay on for several weeks. Both have an abundance of knowledge and experience in our businesses. Some of the innovations were their ideas. I will have our attorney and accountant send our seminar material and I can present a few seminars before I leave with the rest."

"That is most kind, Sam. My people will be better for this new knowledge."

"Your Majesty, I have followed you for years. You are, by far the most enlightened monarch that the world has every produced. It is my honor to serve."

The King smiles and says, "Thank you. You are kind. Good night Sam."

Sam does a proper Wai and bows from the waist and backs away. The family has already started down the passage to the entrance and Sam is behind them. Tom falls back and walks with his father.

The next three days are filled with non stop talk about their dinner with the King. Ann's Thai family is very happy with the memories of their dinner, and their new celebrity status with their neighbors.

Sam, true to his word, presents two seminars with very short notice to Thai business leaders. The first seminar is attended by more than three thousand executives and their front people. The second seminar has standing room only. Sam has the DVD's from his seminars, duplicated in mass and gives copies to all attendees.

Chapter 16

HOME AT LAST

The day arrives and Sam, Jessie, Molly, Sarah, Annie, Mary, Sandra and Barbara and their children board Air Force One for their trip home. The goodbyes are tearful. Cathy, Alex and Carrie stay with Ann and Raina, Brian and Jamie stay with Becca. Rachael's three boys choose to stay. Rach says she will only be there for three more weeks. She has been setting up the clinic ever since the dinner with the king.

Ann, Becca and Rachael are in tears and hug and kiss Sam until he is wet with their tears.

"My darlings. It's just a long flight to home. Keep your phones charged and we can talk every day. I love you and love that you are going to share our lifestyle with a whole country. I love you. All."

The hugs between sisters and children and all go on for a while. Sam admonishes Ann's, Becca's and Rach's children to take care of their mothers. Mathew is the oldest boy staying, Raina is the eldest, then Cathy by eight days.

"Dad, Rich, Ed and I will take care of them. Brian will help, he's coming along like a trooper." Matt says.

"Thanks guys. I do feel better knowing you all are here with them."

The boarding is complete and a final wave through the window as Air Force One taxies out to take off. The plane isn't nearly as comfortable as the one they started out in, but hopefully it makes an uneventful trip.

Somewhere over the West coast, Sam sees a tanker, above and to the port side, with it's boom lowering. He asks one of the attendants about it.

"Sir, Air Force One is in-flight refueling capable. This is a non-stop to Shaw Air Force Base, South Carolina."

"Good to know. I wondered how we'd get home. Sumter doesn't have anything to handle a plane this size."

"Yes sir. I understand that transportation has been arranged from the base to your home and that there will be a news conference at the aircraft."

"Yeah. We're used to news conferences."

The flight was only 16 hours. I guess they got to fly faster on the presidents' plane. Jessie, Molly, Sarah, Annie, Mary, Sandra and Barb were fresh and dressed. They had all the children ready when the door opened and they stepped out on the step to tumultuous cheering and shouts of welcome from a throng of five or six thousand people. They all wave to the crowd as they descend. Several Officers are near the raised dais where the news people were. Both of the bases Generals are there and the base commander. There are two high school bands, both playing as one, the theme to *Welcome Back Cotter*.

Sam recognized both bands, Sumter High School band, and Crestwood High School band and the Sumter High Show Choir. They had rearranged the words and the song was Welcome Back Elliotts.

Sam, Jessie and Molly step up to the microphones. The rest half circled behind them. Each of the ladies held a two year old in their arms.

"Thank you. Thank you friends, neighbors, family. Generals, thank you, Colonel thank you. I've always loved Shaw. It was my last assignment before I hung up my spurs."

The comment elicited a round of laughter from the crowd.

"We're back." Applause and cheers erupt again. "We did survive for more than 30 months on a deserted island in the South Pacific and actually flourished." More applause and cheering. Where's Ann, Becca were questions shouted from the crowd.

"Ann, Becca, Rachael and nine of the children stayed behind in Thailand. Rachael is setting up a clinic in Ann's town. Becca and Ann are helping some of the businesses there, institute our business ethic. We had dinner with the King and he asked for our help. You know the Elliotts, we had to do what we could."

"Who's behind you?" A question shouted from the crowd.

"I apologize. Ladies please come forward. Friends, this is Sarah Elliott. Sarah was with us on our vacation to help with the children. After our accident and it looked like we would be there for a very long time, she agreed to become one of us. Next. This is Annie Elliott, same story, now she is one of us. Next. Mary Elliott came with us on the vacation to keep track of our nutrition, the rest is the same story. Next. This is Sandra Elliott. She was a flight attendant on the plane we leased. The rest is the same story and this is Barbara Elliott, who was working with Sandra. Now these five women have accepted the Elliott lifestyle and we have filed the documents making them a part of the corporate union. We also have five new children and five on the way. Whew. Can you believe it, that's the most I've had to say at one time in almost three years."

The laughter and applause rolled on and on. Finally, the questions from the press started and were fielded by Jessie, Molly and Tom. Sam stepped back and put his arms around his Darlings.

When the questions wound down, one of the reporters flanked the family and got Sam's attention.

"Mr. Elliott. I'm Ken Hunt, from the Item. Would you permit a one on one interview, kind of exclusive. I'd like to make my name in the newspaper business."

"Sure. How about tomorrow morning around ten. Plan to stay for lunch. We've got tons of media and some real interesting adventures."

"Thank you sir. Ten A.M. sharp."

Sam went around and shook hands with the Generals and the Colonel and several of the aides, who were surprised to be recognized. The Mayor and City Manager gave their greeting and welcome. Sam thanked them, shook hands and then was up the steps to the bus. The welcome was taxing on Sam and his family after the long flight. The two year olds were getting fussy and the rest of the children were anxious to re-establish contact with their friends.

The ride home seems longer than Sam remembers, but then there is the gate before them. Gasps of awe come from Sandra and Barbara.

"Oh Sam. I heard that the home was big, but this is a mansion." Sandra says.

"I hope you all will like it. At first, I guess the bungalows will have to be your rooms until we can expand the house."

"That will be good for me Sam." Mary says.

"It shouldn't be for long."

The bus stops at the front door and they get down and head for the front door. Brenda, Sue and the grounds guys are on the porch to welcome them home and unload the bags.

"Sir, welcome home. Ladies, Sarah, Annie, Mary, welcome home." Brenda greets them and then to Sandra and Barbara, "Welcome home Mrs. Elliott and Mrs. Elliott." She hugs both of them and introduces herself. Sandra and Barb hug her back.

"Thank you . . . . Brenda."

"Yes, Brenda, thank you." Barb adds.

Sue gives and receives greetings from all and goes to the bus to help the grounds people unload the bags.

Sam tells the grounds manager, "Senor Lopez, thank you. The place looks beautiful and thanks to you and your staff for unloading the bags. It sure is nice to be home."

"Senor. It has been my pleasure to keep your home properly groomed. We did worry mucho for your safety and your family."

"Thank you. How are your wife and children. We thought of everyone while we were stranded. The island was beautiful though. We would joke that Mr. Lopez must be around here somewhere."

"Oh Senor, very funny. My wife and children are well. My oldest boy is graduating from high school this year and plans to go to college. Thank you, Senor Elliott, we would not have been able to think about college without your generosity."

"My pleasure Mr. Lopez."

Sam gets into the kitchen and Mary has already started something on the stove and in the oven.

"Hungry Mary?"

"Oh Sam, just habit, but yes, I am a little and Sandra and Barb also asked if they could get something. Jessie and Molly are showing them the house, pool, greenhouses and children's rooms. Aren't you hungry? You have to eat."

Sam hugs her and kisses her warmly.

"Thank you darling. Yeah. I think I'll burn a steak. Have you looked in the freezer?"

"Yes. Still pretty full. The automatic deliveries must have continued for at least the first year. What kind of steak?"

"I'll see if there's a T-bone. What you cooking for them?"

"Corn on the cob, peas, red potatoes and in the oven chicken breasts, and strips for the kids. I also put in a stew that was in the freezer. Brenda must have put the freezer on it's lowest setting and everything was really frozen."

"Sounds good. I may steal a few boiled potatoes and throw them in with the steak."

"You got it, honey." She says and kisses him on the cheek.

Food is ready and so are the tourists. They gather at the breakfast table to eat. The youngest children are wide eyed. Sam is so glad that Mike, Sybil, Elizabeth, Delia and Carly are taking the duty of watching out for them. Tom reports to Sam that the estate is going strong. The greenhouses are kind of empty and the chickens and other poultry are all gone. Brenda tells him that they didn't have anyone to keep the greenhouse, so they were cleared and the poultry were all put into the freezer.

"Good work son. I'm going to let you handle the estate a little, while I get with the local authorities and see about your graduation and get us back in the swim of things."

"Can do easy Dad. It sure is nice getting into my room again. Momma Sandra and Barb are rooming together, in the empty bungalow and Sarah and Annie are in one of the bunk rooms upstairs, Momma Mary is in the bungalow with Carly. Carly asked her to."

"Okay. I have to get with Mr. Hawkins and get him started on the expansion, soon."

Sam and Tom go in to eat. Everyone is around the table. Mary hands Sam a plate with the T-bone and some boiled potatoes that have been browned in the steak's juices.

He takes the plate and sits facing Sandra and Barbara, whose faces are bright with smiles and eyes glistening.

"Sam this house is wonderful. The pool, in the house and the gym, had to be your idea. I love it."

"Me to Sam. I know why they all love you, just as much as I do. You are always thinking about the comfort and happiness of your family." Barb adds.

"It's the basis of our philosophy. If you love, you will be loved. Besides that, it is the one thing that gives me the greatest pleasure. When the women and children I love are happy, I am happy."

Jessie and Molly rush to him and one on each side hug him tightly between them. It's awkward, but Sam loves it.

"Sandra, Barb. Sarah, Annie and Mary already know, but it is the truth and it doesn't limit it to his family. In fact, that is how the Elliott corporation treats everyone. You'll get the hang of it and soon, you will see how true the philosophy is." Jessie tells them.

"Okay kids cover your ears. We will introduce you to the shower tonight. Then you can see the love in action. There just wasn't the space or privacy on the island or since then, until now. I promise, it is an experience and I won't try to hog him all to myself." Molly says and kisses Sam.

"Thank you Molly, Jessie for the introduction . . . Ha! Ha! Talk like that will get you everything. Now I hope that tonight, you and Jessie will also make a shopping trip plan and introduce your new sisters to unrestricted shopping. Someone will also have to interview new nannies and nutritionist."

"Sam, not right away. I know a couple of people, but we can handle the children still." Sarah says.

"I love to cook. We can wait a while. Maybe keep the cooking to ourselves." Mary adds.

"Mary's right Sam. Besides, you and I love to cook and Becca to." Molly injects.

"Sam, me to. I'm not great, but I'd love to learn, and taking care of the children doesn't have to be an outside job." Sandra says.

"Great. I'll leave it in your capable hands. We also have some young people, who are very adept at child rearing and cooking."

"Yes Dad. Me, Elizabeth, Sybil and Delia will handle taking care of our youngest sisters and brothers. Good training." Carly affirms.

"Dad, you know that me, Peter, Michael, Ryan and Wyatt will handle anything around the house and the estate. It's in really good shape now and we can keep it that way. You and the Mommas relax and enjoy for a while." Tom offers.

"Thank you. What do I call you. Children seems like too young. You can't know how proud I am of all of you. On the island, your work was the major factor in our survival. This world is greater with you in it." Tom, Carly and the rest nodded and smiled their acceptance of his praise. "But to change the subject. My steak is getting cold."

Everyone grins and laughs, eyes shining with love for the man who makes it happen.

The rest of the day progresses as Sam has said. The ladies plan to go shopping tomorrow, while Sam is having his interview with Mr. Hunt and then shower and bed.

"I used to see everyone coming to your room, at night and fantasized what was happening. Now I'm here and a part of what I always considered the most wonderful people in the world." Annie says.

"And welcome my Darling. It looks like I'm gonna have to get the shower enlarged and the tub as well."

Soon, hot, soapy women are sharing the feel of hot, soapy, naked flesh pressing from all sides. The contact is sending sensory overloads and adrenalin rushes through each of them. The passion begins.

Sam wakes, as light filters through the window over the tub. He is covered in women and his heart is ready to burst with a tidal wave of love. They were all wonderful and he has to say it, at least to himself, I was just a sex toy last night. He was doubly amazed that he lasted through seven female orgasms. Oh my God. Rachael, where are those supplements, he thinks, but what a way to die.

Molly stirs first. She is lying on his right leg and her head is on his hip and his foot is the saddle for her vagina. She runs a hand up his left thigh and grasps, his graspable part. Sam gasps and feels the electricity shoot through him.

"Oh, Molly. I don't think I have it in me."

"Mumfph ood oo." She tries to say.

"Hey Molly, save some for me." Sandra says.

Their talk, wakes the rest and soon the play time starts again. If it doesn't kill me, I can live like this, Sam thinks.

Two hours later and they are out of the shower and dressing for the day. The ladies and the girls with the youngest are going shopping. New credit cards for Sandra and Barbara were waiting for them. All of the credit cards and debit cards were renewed for everyone and had been delivered before they returned. Mr. Wade really did earn the family's gratitude. He also had extra keys made and had the documents to add them to the corporation. Brenda has everything on the breakfast table when they came out.

"I didn't think you would want to do this last night. Mr. Wade says that he also put the new ladies and children on the health plan and the children on the education plan. He has set up the paperwork for new bank accounts and needs you to sign the papers, at the bank. I think that's it, Sir." Brenda reports.

The women leave at 8 o'clock and Sam gathers the boys and they make a run to the DMV.

"I almost forgot. You need your driver's licenses. Tom you probably need yours renewed."

"You're right. I forgot to. Matt and Ryan had their permits when we left. Peter will need his permit. Do you think they'll give us any trouble?" Tom asks.

"I guess we'll see."

They breeze through the DMV. When they entered, they were immediately recognized and after a multitude of greetings and welcome homes, from the staff and from the citizens, they had all of their licenses renewed, replaced and Peter got a license, without the test.

"Don't think that this means you get to drive without supervision. I'm going to teach you. Dad taught me and you'll get the same thing." Tom tells him.

They get back home and Tom says he's taking the boys out and around town, while Sam gives his interview. Sam sits in the family room, sipping on a Coke from his soft drink dispenser and tries on the TV. My God, has it been three years? He asks himself. The programming hasn't changed much. A couple of channels bring non-stop movies, in different genres. There is a classic on the Science Fiction channel, *Forbidden Planet*, with a lot of B movie actors. It's kind of campy, but entertaining. Sam is getting into it, when the gate buzzer sounds.

"Hello, Mr. Elliott. It's me, Ken Hunt. I'm here for the interview. I came a little early, because I didn't know how to get through the gate."

"Hi Ken. Just let me buzz you in." Sam says, pressing the remote. On the monitor, he sees a newer model mini van come through the gate. Sam goes to the front door and opens it, just as Hunt is reaching for the bell.

"Come in, come in, Mr. Hunt."

"Thank you Mr. Elliott, thank you for taking the interview." He says as he enters and shakes hands with Sam.

"Look here now, call me Sam. The Mr. Elliott thing takes up a lot of time. Let me get you something to drink and you can stay for lunch, right."

"Yes Sir . . . Sam. Thanks again. No alcohol, it's too early. Maybe some ice tea or a Coke . . . which ever you have . . . Thank you."

"Get calm Mr. Hunt . . . ."

"Oh no, uh, call me Ken. Please."

"Okay, Ken. Calm down. You are welcome here and I'm anxious to get our story out. You were the only one who was interested enough to ask for an interview. I trust that you will report our story accurately."

"Oh yes sir, Mr. E . . . Sam."

Sam guides him to the family room and seats him in an overstuffed chair with a table next to it and goes to the bar and gets Ken a tall glass of Coke. Sam gets one for himself and sits in an overstuffed chair to Ken's right.

Ken pulls out a tape recorder and a steno pad and pen. He starts the tape recorder and says, "Sam do you mind if I record along with my notes. It will help me keep it straight."

"Not at all. I also have some material, for you. My eldest son, Tom made a copy of our 30 plus months of pictures, writings and videos; well he made several copies. That's one copy on the table."

"Oh my goodness." Ken says as his eyes widen at the stack of CD's and DVD's on the table. "All of this is of the Island and your survival?"

"Our survival and the pirate attack and the births of five of my children. As soon as we realized that we survived the crash, cameras and recorders came on from all of the grown children and from the wives. Things that weren't visually recorded, we wrote, or spoke the event."

"Wow. Do you think I could see a little of it. I may not need to do an actual interview."

"Sure. Tom loaded up the whole thing on a memory file and put it on a feed to the TV. Sit back, put your feet up, relax and enjoy."

Sam selects the source for the input and presses start. Immediately the plane and beach were on the screen. The camera follows three boys going up the beach. They are digging a hole. Another camera is following some women pulling a piece of the wreckage with a body on it.

The images go on and on, from the building of the shelter to the two funerals, the campfires, the gardens, the dairy cows, the wrangled wild hogs, the chickens and scene after scene of a family that loves one another.

An hour into it and Sam sees Ken's eyes running with tears. He hands him a box of tissues. "Too intense Ken?"

"Not that. It's . . . it's beautiful. Would you mind if I work this up into something that would be like a documentary instead of just an article. I'll, I'll write the article, but this has to be seen."

"Why not. If you let me go over it before it becomes public. Just to make sure nothing is misunderstood."

"Of course. Without question. I bow to your final approval on all of it."

"What say we get some lunch. I think Mary and Molly made up some kind of meaty casserole, with pasta, tomato sauce and cheese. I told them it sounded like Beef a Roni."

"Sounds good. I like Beef a Roni."

They both laugh and go to sit at the breakfast table. Sam gets the casserole out of the warming oven and asks Ken to get plates and table ware from the cabinet in the breakfast nook.

The women come back at two o'clock. They buzzed him from the gate to meet them out front. Sam thinks, what is going on, and ambles out the front door and spots not one, but seven mini vans coming up the driveway.

Jessie gets out of a new Ford, Free Star, tricked out with all the luxury features.

"What do you think Sam? We were in the middle of shopping and I remembered that none of them had cars and ours were getting old. So, Molly and I got ours, Sandra, Sarah, Annie, Barb and Mary got theirs and I ordered three more for Ann, Becca and Rachael. Those three will be delivered tomorrow and they will pick up the old ones. We really got a good deal, Sam. The trade-ins were one and a half blue book. Seems they are already sold to people who wanted an Elliott family car and they were such low mileage. Mr. Mc Laughlin gave us a big discount for buying ten at a time."

"Good. I like it. Anyone hungry?"

"We had lunch at Ruby Tuesday. How did the interview go?" Jessie asks.

"Good. That fellow, Ken Hunt was really eager and fired up about the story and he thought it might become a documentary. I told him, at least get something in the paper, to slow the phone calls down." Sam tells the women, who are now bringing their shopping treasures in through the front door.

The interview was two weeks ago and Sam was getting antsy about how the story was received. Just as he was about to call Ken and see what was going on, the gate buzzer sounds. On the monitor was the mini van that Sam recognizes as Ken's and behind him is a black limo. Sam pushes the intercom for the gate.

"Hi Ken, I was just thinking about you. Who's with you?"

"Sam, my boss and the chairman from the TV station is with him. May we come in. I have the proofs for you, as promised."

"Let me just get to the buzzer." Sam says as he pushes the gate on his remote.

Sam meets the three, at the door and welcomes them in.

"Sam this is my boss, Mr. Tidwell and Mr. Arnold is the chairman of WLTX TV 19. Gentlemen, Mr. Sam Elliott."

Sam shakes hands with each of the men.

"Welcome to my humble home. If you'll follow me, we can get comfortable."

"It's is a pleasure meeting you in person finally. For years, I have been printing stories about you and your family." Mr. Tidwell says.

"We've had more than a few broadcasts as well. Your style is innovative and apparently just what the world needed." Mr. Arnold says.

Sam ushers them into the family room and gets them seated.

"It's kind of early, but would anyone care for a wine cooler or something. I also have sodas, ice tea and lemonade."

"Oh yes. Lemonade if it's no trouble." Tidwell says.

"I'd like a lemonade to. Thank you." Arnold says.

"Ken?"

"My usual Sam."

Sam gets the lemonades and two Cokes and stifles a grin when he sees the faces of the two executive types.

"So, to what, do I owe this visit? I think I paid my subscription."

Mr. Tidwell laughs.

"No, it's not about a subscription. Mr. Elliott . . ."

"Sorry Tidwell, call me Sam."

"Sam, I'm Allen. When Hunt, here brought his proofs of the story he was writing about your . . . interrupted travel, I was amazed. There are literally years of material there and I don't think any of it should be lost. I contacted Arnold, uh, Bill and we agree that, with your permission of course, we professionally write and produce your story as a documentary and present it as a mini series. Perhaps as many as 12 two hour segments. We would use most of the original sound bites and most of the video footage and fill with the static photos." Allen says.

"Yes. A remarkable story and one that the world should hear about. Since nearly every country is emulating your business practices and your family unions are springing up everywhere and successfully as well." Bill says.

Ken is sitting back and watching the excitement in the eyes of these two big shots. He also notices that Sam, who is probably bigger than both of them, sipping his Coke and nodding occasionally.

"Gentlemen. You have my blessing. Do you need another copy of the material? My son, Tom made a lot of copies, just in case."

"Thank you, Sam. We already made copies, just in case. It was the first thing I had done. I had a real fear that some of it would be lost somehow." Allen says.

"Bill?"

"Thanks Sam, I'll be working with Allen. I'll use his copies."

"Will I be seeing any written stuff in the papers? Something that will occupy the public and keep the phone calls down."

"Yes Sam. Mr. Tidwell has assigned me to write twelve segments to correspond to the documentary and we will be publishing them at the end of this month." Ken tells him.

"Sam, you are probably wondering about getting paid for your story . . ." Allen begins.

"Not even worried about it. We are too rich already. Any payments you think are fair, divide them up between the Police, Fire, Salvation Army and the local school district."

The two executives freeze as the words sink in.

"You don't want anything for yourself?" Bill is incredulous.

"Not a dime. Look guys, we have a fortune and my philosophy is just like the Bible, 'Cast your bread on the waters and it will come back ten fold.' It's worked so far."

The group wraps up their talks and Sam shows them to the door. The goodbyes are cordial and both executives promise to keep him in the loop on their progress. Ken lags behind and when the execs are in the limo, he turns to Sam. "What they didn't say, Sam, is that the project is well on it's way. The story boards have been written, the media has been organized and they got some big name actor, with a voice, to do the narratives. It should be advertised by the end of summer and premier this fall. Sam, I've seen some of the preliminaries and it is going to wow the socks off of everyone."

"So, uh Ken, you think it's a good idea?" Sam chuckles.

"Yeah Sam, I do. I guess I sounded a little star struck, but it really is good."

"You I trust. You keep me up to speed, in case they forget."

"I'll do that. Thank you for the opportunity."

"You are welcome my friend."

Hunt goes to his mini and turns and waves. Sam returns the wave and goes back inside. This is the second time he's had visitors and no one else is in the house. May be he was too liberal on the, go shopping, line he gave the women.

Sam arranged for his eldest children to test out of high school and they will sit for the SAT/ACT before the end of summer. Not that they will need them. College of Charleston, USC Columbia and Clemson have already offered scholarships to all six of his children. The children, Tom, Ryan and Carly, respectfully declined the money, but left open the avenue to each University. When Raina, Cathy and Mathew come back next week, everything is already set for them to pick a college.

Work on the expansion is nearing completion. Mr. Hawkins is a master at this work. He managed to fit four more rooms and baths without sacrificing window space. He shrunk two of the children rooms, since there wouldn't be double sets at a time and with the one unoccupied, of the original six women's rooms, there were five available rooms.

Besides the new bedrooms, a garage to hold all of the extra cars and the bus is added to the pool side of the house. Mr. Hawkins tells Sam that the rooms will be ready on Wednesday if they wanted to begin moving furniture in. The ladies have beaten him to it and announce that the delivery truck will be here early Wednesday morning. He added that the bricking would take an extra two weeks, but the insides and roof is ready.

"That was quite a feat Tommy. You nearly had to build a house in only four weeks."

"Sam, you know I love doing jobs for your family. I had crews begging me to be involved in the construction. I ended up using double crews in the framing and two teams of electricians and plumbers."

"Still, I am amazed. I included a substantial reward for getting the job done early. You'll see that everyone knows how much I appreciate their efforts?"

"Count on it Sam and let us know when you want another estate built." Tommy says with a broad grin and a chuckle.

The week will be eventful, but Sam is anxious to get everything back to normal. He tries not to show it, but he is constantly worrying about the three who stayed behind with his babies and the five who are carrying his children. The expansion, the furniture buying, the high school, college, and this story for the paper and documentary and on Monday the rest of his family will be here. Airport and news conferences and he suddenly feels very tired. Then the thought hits him that Sandra asked to talk to him in private after dinner and he begins to imagine all sorts of things. It does cut through some of the worry, but also adds a, 'what if' to his train of thought.

Time seems to go in slow motion, waiting to learn what Sandra wants to tell him. Dinner has all the family together around the table. They talk about Ann, Becca and Rachael coming home. Barbara and Sarah bubble about their bedrooms. Tom and Ryan talk about . . . their girl friends. It was a pleasant distraction.

After dinner, sitting in the family room, the kids upstairs with the video games, Sandra stands up and reaches her hand to Sam. Jessie and Molly smile, what Sam recognizes as, a knowing smile and his misgivings melt away. He takes her hand and as they walk toward the door, Sandra says, over her shoulder, "Thank you sisters. I promise not to use him up."

In Sam's bedroom, Sandra turns to him and hugs him tight and with both hands, holding his head, kisses him like a farewell kiss.

"Sam, I love you. I love you more than I ever thought a woman could love a man . . ." Sam tries to speak . . . . "No, I have to say all of it first. I loved Bill and I thought it was everything. I still have a place for him in my heart, but you occupy 98 percent of it. It's not just the sex. It's not the money. It's the constant feeling of being loved by you, not just a couple of times a week, or days, but all of the time. Even now, when you're perplexed and want to say something, I feel the love. So, I wanted to tell you how strongly I feel and yes, I want to make love with you. When I told my sisters, they agreed and I think that Barbara, Sarah, Annie and Mary have similar statements to make. Now, mister, I have you and I want to make love to you, like there's no tomorrow."

Sam was speechless. He didn't know how he could not love this woman. She had one of the same attractive features as Jessie, only more intense. Freckles and they were almost like the aliens in the movie, *Alien Nation* and real natural red hair, everywhere. Her skin was like Rachael's. So white that it was translucent to the point that the blue veins were visible just below the skin. All of this is running through his head and bringing his adrenalin coursing through his veins.

"Sam, did I say it wrong?"

Sam takes hold of her blouse around the collar and tears it off of her and buries his face in her breasts. His hands slide the bra straps off her shoulders and he deftly unhooks it and lets it fall to the floor.

The scent of her bare breasts is fuel for his passion and he hooks his thumbs in the waistband of her shorts and panties and slides them to the floor.

"Sandy. I love you more than my life. I love our child that you have given me and this one growing inside of you. If it were possible, I would make love to you until the end of time."

The two spend more than an hour reveling in one another. Their passion doesn't flag and they only stop from shear exhaustion.

"Oh Sam. That was wonderful. You are so full of surprises. I never knew a man could have multiple orgasms."

"It's a learned trait, when you have more than one woman to keep happy."

They both laughed and pressed their bodies together and kissed long and warmly.

That was how the rest of the night progressed and Sam's pent up stress was gone. He fell asleep, well after midnight and Molly seems to have won the all night position again.

Wednesday arrives and with the help of his grown sons, the rooms are arranged and Sam's new ladies move into them.

Sam is staying out of the way and watches with Mr. Hawkins.

"You did it. Twenty some years ago, my wife and I started watching builders. We'd sit for an hour here and an hour there watching the construction and then come back at the end of the day and see how the crews ended their days. It didn't take us long to put you on top of our list of preferred contractors, Tommy."

"I appreciate that Sam. Ever since we did your two houses, with pools and gyms, we've had continuous contracts for similar projects. You are a good man to know. People try to be like you, which is also good for me."

They shake hands and Tommy waves as he takes his leave.

While the ladies are settling into their rooms, Sam asks Tom to fire up the pit.

"Great idea Dad. A barbecue would be great."

The youngest are with Elizabeth, Delia and Sybil and the boys are getting the food for the barbecue. The mothers brought up their children right. Whoever was doing any cooking, the kids were right there learning the tricks. Now there are four boys and Carly planning today's festivities.

"What's going on and can I help?" Jessie asks.

"Kids are doing a barbecue to celebrate moving in day. They've got it handled. I'm going swimming. Where's Molly?"

"Molly is looking over the poultry houses. She misses the chicken and egg thing and the baking. Mind if I join you in the pool?"

"I was kind of hoping someone would join me. I missed water walks with pretty women around me."

The water was refreshing and Jessie and Sam played like love struck teenagers. It wasn't long before everyone was in the pool. Sarah, Sandra, Annie, Barb and Mary brought the two and a half year olds with them. The older kids were occupying themselves with the barbecue.

"What's going on with the kids, Sam?" Annie asks.

"They're building a barbecue to celebrate moving in day for you and the family. All of them are great cooks. These little monkeys will get to learn from them when they get a little bigger."

"Luke already wants to hang around Mike all of the time." Annie says.

"Yeah. William is kind of attached to Peter." Sandra offers.

"They couldn't have better role models." Sam tells them.

"Hey Sam, I'm starting to prune up. I'm gonna pull a chaise into the sun and cook myself a little." Jessie says.

"Yeah. I think I need a little sun to."

"We're gonna stay a while. I like this indoor pool stuff. Molly is going to work out with us in the gym and cook us in the sauna." Barb says.

"Okay. Let me know when you're going to the sauna, I could use a bake as well. It clears the pores." Sam tells them.

They do gather in the sauna for a half hour and Sam and the women shower together in the pool's shower room. Dry and dress in cool shorts and light tops, they gather at tables, under sun umbrellas, for Tom's and Carly's barbecue. The afternoon is pleasant and Tom's barbecued ribs are every bit as good as Sam's.

"Tom. Excellent! Carly. Good job. This is a real feast. Hey, this Monday, everyone will be back from Thailand. If you all are up to it, a refreshing dinner that evening and on Tuesday a blow out barbecue. You guys invite your friends and don't forget Matt, Cathy, Raina and all the rest, their friends. It will be a big surprise for them."

"Oh Dad, I'm definitely on for that. You think we could hire, like a DJ or something?" Tom asks.

"DJ, local bands, I'm leaving it to you young adults to set the whole thing up. Maximum fun."

Sam has to smile. Carly and Delia mob him with hugs. Tom, Ryan and Peter are grinning and talking among themselves.

"Sam, that is so great. Tommy, Ryan and Peter are already like grown men. I'm so proud." Molly says.

"Yes, Darling. You have to be one of the most enlightened Dads on the Planet." Jessie adds.

"Thank you my Darlings, but it really is the money that loosens up everything. I wish there was a way to live without money being the bottom line of existence. How much happier would life be, if everyone could live this kind of life and not have to worry about money."

As the rest of the week rolls along, Sam spots Tom with the pickup, loaded with patio tables and umbrellas. Peter is with him when they pull around the back of the pool house and unload at the gate.

"Hey guys. Wassup?"

"Oh, Hi Dad. Peter and I went to Lowe's and got another five tables and umbrellas. We figured it out and we were short a few, now that the family is bigger and friends will be here and we also needed some, for the band."

"Good thinking. I didn't even consider it. Thanks Tom, Peter."

Sam looks out the gate and sees Sandra, Sarah, Annie, Mary and Barbara, with the youngest children, playing on the putting green. The paper birch trees surrounding it, offers a nice shady place for Mom and child bonding. Sam wonders why he never thought of it. Tom is watching him and when their eyes meet, Tom smiles.

"Dad, I hope I'm just like you. I see how much you love all of us. It was really, cool, watching you watch the Moms and the young ones."

Sam smiles. "Tom, it's the only way to be. Love your family and guide them with that love." Sam pats his eldest son on the shoulder.

Monday morning arrives quietly. The family is in a very good mood. Yesterday at church, they received a warm welcome from the congregation. The pastor's sermon on, 'Casting your bread on the water,' seemed to fit. He also made mention of the addition of Sandra, Barbara and the children to the congregation and they would be baptized at next Sunday's service, when the whole Elliott family would be there.

The boys, Carly, Delia and Elizabeth planned a pig roast for Tuesday and for today, thick Angus burgers with sliced tomatoes and pickles, French fries, ketchup and milk shakes. They also had trays of sliced, roast beef, chicken, salami, bologna, turkey, German bologna, Swiss cheese, cheddar, provolone and all the fixings for salads.

"Nice choice people." Sam admires the spread.

"I know when I talked to Cathy and Raina, they said they wanted American food. Matt said sandwiches was the thing he missed and Richard and Brian want burgers and fries. We also set up pulled chicken for the salads, that we thought the Moms would like and we got enough to feed an Army." Carly says eagerly.

"Good thinking. I don't know about you guys. You put most people to shame with your clear thinking. Thank you Carly, Delia, Elizabeth. You make your Dad proud."

"Dad. Tomorrow, we're also going to put on some ribs, chicken, steaks and bake twenty five pounds of potatoes and sixty ears of corn. I even put an order in for 50 pieces of fried chicken at Church's, just in case."

"That's great Tom. You guys are doing a bang up job. Thank you. You're not telling me this because you don't think I'll approve. Are you?"

"Well. Yeah, I guess. I don't want to disappoint you."

"Son. You are the best thing that has ever happened to me. I remember the day you were born. My son and first born. We gave you my Dad's name. You have made me proud, every day since. I trust you with my life, with the lives of my wives, my other children. You can never disappoint me, no matter what. I trust you."

Tom smiles a man smile and hugs his father. "Thank you, Dad."

"Carry on Mac Duff!" Sam says, squeezing Tom on the shoulder.

Sam goes in the house, through the family room and hears talking in the kitchen. Sandra is on the house phone and Sarah, Jessie and Annie are standing near her.

"Yes, we'll be there. Two thirty this afternoon. At Shaw. Yes. Sarah, Jessie and Annie are here, oh and Sam just came in. Okay. Sam, it's Ann, she wants to talk to you. They'll be at Shaw at two thirty."

"Hello, Ann. Yes, I can hear you. Where are you? On Air Force One over Illinois. We've missed all of you to. Yes, I've missed that to. Okay. The kids have whipped up a welcome home for you. Yeah, don't tell Cathy, or Matt. No. There is a surprise for them as well. Okay. Love you. Tell them I love and miss them all. Bye."

"Did she say they were over Illinois?" Jessie asks.

"Yeah. That's like only two maybe three hours from here. Okay, I thought it was earlier. The morning sure is slipping away." Sam observes as he looks at his watch.

"Sam, why don't you take a nap. We'll get the house in order and have Carly and them set up the food. I'll wake you at about one thirty. Sisters, I think that maybe just Sam and maybe one of the boys. There will be twelve to bring home." Jessie suggests.

"I'm down for a nap. Yeah, maybe Ryan, I don't want to put everything on Tom. We'll take two vans. Good morning ladies." Sam says as he gives and receives kisses and touches on his way to bed.

"Sam. Sam honey."

"Jessie. What is it. Something wrong?"

"It's time Sam. One thirty."

"I guess I was really tired. It seemed like I just lay down and closed my eyes." Sam says putting his legs over the side of the bed and sitting up.

"You take too much on yourself." Jessie kisses his forehead and rubs his back. "You should take a break and enjoy yourself."

"I think I may have been enjoying myself too much. Your new sisters are younger and strong and you and Molly are insatiable vixens and I love it so much."

Jessie straddles his lap and leans forward, pushing him back and lip locks his lips. She slides her hips forward and back, creating a hot friction, that Sam feels flowing up his back.

She rocks back and pulls him up. "How do you feel now?"

"Wow. Great. What does that mean?"

"It means you're a sex addict. A little hot pussy and you're ready to go." Jessie laughs and gives him one more kiss before jumping up, pulling him with her. "Get freshened up. I'll get you a coffee. Want anything to eat?"

"Just you, my love." Sam smiles and grabs for her as she twists away.

When Sam comes out, Ryan is at the breakfast table with a plate of cookies and a glass of milk. Sam sits at the place where Jessie has placed a cup of coffee.

"You up for this Ryan? Gonna be a lot of people again."

"Yeah Dad. Thanks for letting me drive one of the vans. I know you trust me, but I kind of like to be able to stand out doing something."

"You know I depend on all of you young men. I give Tom a lot of responsibility. I think it's because we named him after my dad. I probably just gravitate that way. It doesn't mean I count on the rest of you less."

"I know. I understand. My friends talk about their families and their fathers. I don't ask, they just volunteer the information. Dad, you are head over heels better than all of my friends' dads."

"That's good of you to say, Ryan. I always wonder if I'm doing the right thing, sometimes."

Jessie and Molly come to the breakfast table with cups and another plate of cookies.

"May we join you gentlemen?" Molly says.

"Our pleasure, Ma'am." Ryan says. Sam grins.

"More cookies guys. Scotch short bread and sugar cookies." Jessie says, putting the plate in the middle of the two.

Sam takes a Scotch shortbread and eats it and sips his coffee. He thinks that this is what family should be. He and Ryan have a few more cookies and are ready to head to the base to pick up the returning Mommas and Sam's children.

They are recognized at the gate and passed on to the flight line. The guards at the flight line, point out places for them to park and when they get out, a golf cart is there to carry Sam and Ryan to the canopied seats next to the parking ramp.

The generals are there, as is the base commander. Colonel Parker is surprised that Sam remembers his name. The crowd reacts to Sam's and Ryan's arrival. Sam recognizes several people and goes to shake hands and greet them. He thanks them for coming and that the family loves the people here. A Captain, Aide to the General, asks Sam to join the General.

"Well Mr. Elliott. This is a rare experience for us. Air Force One landing here twice in the same year." The Air Force General says. Sam doesn't remember his name and he doesn't wear a name tag.

"Yes General, I think you will be getting one more visit. I had a call from the White House Secretary. He said the President has a visit scheduled for next week, to meet and welcome us back personally."

"The President? I haven't heard anything." Both generals look perplexed.

"I'm sure that the notification is on it's way by . . . ." Before Sam finishes the sounds of an approaching heavy jet cuts across his hearing.

"I think they are arriving." Colonel Parker says.

Sam is excited and puts his arm over Ryan's shoulder.

"They're home son. The whole family together again. It sure is a relief for me."

"Yeah Dad. Together for a few more months, then six of us are off to college."

"I know. I dread it, but I also know that it's the way it's supposed to be."

The plane is taxiing to the parking ramp, where Sam, Ryan and the crowd is waiting. It feels like hours before the door opens and the steps are rolled up to the opening.

It is only moments before Cathy and Raina are at the top of the steps, followed by Ann, Becca, Mathew and then the younger children. Brian, Alex and Richard are holding the hands of Jamie, Carrie and Edward, then Rachael. Sam's heart finally begins to relax. They're home, safe and all of them are smiling.

They are all waving to the crowd, who go wild with cheers and shouts of, welcome home, we love you. Sam's eyes can't hold back his tears of joy. Ryan is applauding along with the crowd and smiles at his Dad.

Ann steps up to the microphone, Becca and Rachael flank her. Sam is aching to hold them, but this is their moment. Ann begins with greeting and thanking everyone for their love and support.

"It may be of interest to the citizens of Sumter, that no less than twenty-five towns in Thailand are modeling their government, educational system, police, fire and social services after you. Sumter is the model town for a very great number of people, on the other side of the world. I bring you their greetings and their heartfelt thanks."

The crowd is loud with cheers and whoops and howls. It continues for some minutes, then when it quiets again, Ann continues.

"I bring to you, America, from the King of Thailand. Thank you. Thank you for providing the atmosphere that sparked the emergence of this change in business ethics and this change in social living.

I was permitted to sit with the King and his secretary and we talked for hours. This king is noted as an enlightened monarch and he has asked the Parliament to enact laws to change the countries business organizations and the role that government plays in the people's lives.

I am carrying a dispatch case, filled with documents for our President, from the King of Thailand with offers of assistance and requests for trained people to go and live in Thailand and work and teach this American business ethic."

At the words of work for Americans, the crowd begin to cheer and the sound rises to deafening. While the crowd cheers, the Generals come forward and talk to Ann and the two with her. The women step down from the platform and come toward Sam. The children are coming behind them. Sam hugs and kisses each of them and extra hugs for the three youngest. Carrie is tearful when Sam hugs her.

"Baby girl. I really missed you. Poppa loves you honey and your sisters and brothers missed you. They're waiting at home for us."

"Poppa, we can't be apart ever again. I just missed everyone."

Ann came over and hugs Sam again and holds Carrie's hand. The crowd has quieted some and the General steps to the microphone.

"Ladies and Gentlemen. We've got to let these people go home. They have been apart too long. Can we give them a round of applause as they head for their transportation home."

The crowd's applause grows and continues, while the family load onto golf carts and are taken to Sam and Ryan's vans. A dozen Airmen come to the vans with the luggage and fill the back of both and cover the tops of each van. Someone produced rope and tied the bags down and Sam thanked the young men and they were off for home.

The women and the young children riding with Sam broke into tears as he drove up the last 100 yards to the house. He hears Carrie in the back seat with Ann, say, "We're home Momma. We're home."

It almost breaks Sam's heart. His poor baby was a real home body and missed her family, so much.

Jessie, Molly and the rest pour out of the house and as the two vans are spilling their cargo of loved ones, hugs and kisses and more hugs happen over and over. Tom and Ryan, greet Matt, Cathy, and Raina, then they all begin to carry luggage into the house.

Inside the house, Carly announces that there is food for anyone who is hungry, then accepts and gives hugs and kisses to the returning family.

Sandra, Sarah, Annie, Barb and Mary have gathered in the family room to wait for the three to come in with the children. There are long tables along one wall with drinks and plates of sandwiches, hamburgers, fries and condiments.

The family room is beginning to look too small. Thirty-four and all family. Sam thinks about how it can be expanded, then remembers that some will be leaving and some will not be in this room all the time.

"I don't know why I keep trying to make more work for myself."

"Did you say something Sam?" Sarah asks.

"Oh, I didn't think I said it out loud. I was just thinking about the room seeming small and how to make it bigger, then abandoned the thought and wondered why I try to make more work for myself. I didn't know I said it."

"You're right. You do take on too much." Sarah says.

The room starts to fill up. Sam takes a seat in the elbow of the sectional. Tom and the older kids, grab plates and fill them with food and disappear out to the patio, where Tom and Carly have set up tables with drinks.

Ann, Becca and Rachael drape themselves as close to Sam as they can. Molly, Annie and Mary bring them plates of food and big tumblers of iced tea, Southern style. Their thank you comes with glistening eyes.

"You were good at the base, Ann. You sounded really diplomatic. The President will be here on Thursday or Friday. The Secret Service will give us a heads up the day before. The general didn't believe it, when I told him. God, you three, I missed you. We can't do this again. It will have to be either all or none."

"Sam we missed you to. Every day was like a hundred days." Becca says, snuggling up tighter.

"Yeah Sam. Don't let us do that again. Even with the boys with me, it just wasn't the same. I missed my sisters to. Twenty years ago, you could have asked me if I would love anyone so much and I would have said, no. Now, I love so many people, so strongly that I cry when I don't see them." Rachael says.

"And Sam, I like the additions. Tell us about them." Ann asks.

"Four new, Momma bedrooms and when Mr. Hawkins started laying out the lines for it, he suggested the expanded garage. The brick work will be finished later this week. We have five more cars and probably more, shortly. Carly, Cathy, Raina and Matthew have to get licenses. Brian, Alex and Richard will need their permits. Oh and the three have offers from Clemson, USC and College of Charleston. We already turned down the money, but asked that they keep the offers open until everyone was back home."

"That's wonderful. The district let them graduate?"

"Yeah. They just go in and write a paper about their last three years and collect their diploma. The superintendent offered to set up SAT's, but they really don't need them, with the advance offers from the colleges."

Sam basks in the glowing faces of his loves. He really missed his Asian dolls and his nurse. Sandra, Sarah, Annie, Barbara and Mary join Sam and the returnees, with Jessie and Molly.

"I'm so happy you are all home safe. I missed our time together as sisters. I know Sam missed all of you." Sandra says.

"Ann, it was really good to get home. Annie and I were a little awkward, at first. Jessie and Molly set us straight. Mary is having a time. She jumped right in to cooking, until Sam talked with her. Now, we all cook and even the children, who are responsible for this evenings welcome home foods." Sarah says.

"It is really good to be home, sisters. I missed all of you so much. We really haven't done a lot of girl shopping. That whirlwind in Sydney, isn't anything like we do here." Rachael offers.

"I've heard. Jessie and Molly took us shopping our first week back. We bought cars and paid cash. That is really an unbelievable experience. I've never had that kind of feeling." Barbara exclaims.

The banter goes on for an hour or two and loving words are exchanged between the women and between the women and their man. Sam thinks that it will take several of these gatherings to soothe everyone's tensions.

"Sam, girls, I am down for a soak in the hot tub and maybe a hot shower after, some champagne and lots and lots of cuddling." Becca says, fluttering her eyelids.

The rest laugh and voice their agreement.

"Sam. Are you down for some hot females?" Becca adds, throwing her leg over his lap.

"I'm always down for acres of female flesh and hot pus . . . ." Sam starts.

Becca cuts him off with her lips on his, slides off his lap and pulls him up. They all move to the master bedroom. Shedding clothes as they pass through the door and are nearly completely naked when they reach the hot tub.

Sam and the ladies revel in one another for an hour in the hot tub and forty minutes in the shower, then dry and bed. The ladies have agreed, among themselves, that the returnees get to love him first.

The night doesn't end until after midnight, with Becca staying with Sam.

"I'm happy I get to stay with you. Remember when I told you that I could always feel your love?" Sam nods. "Well, do you know how terrible it is to not have that feeling for weeks and weeks. I missed you so much."

"Oh my Darling, I missed you so much. I know that with so many more, I am going to be spread thin, but I will always look forward to our time together."

Becca spoons into Sam and pulls his arm across her breasts and wiggles her bootie into his belly. Sam surprises her with an old subject that pops up.

"Again Sam?"

Sam kisses the back of her neck and whispers, "Sleep Darling, I'd love to, but I am worn out."

Becca sighs and snuggles down. Soon they are asleep.

Sam doesn't wake until almost eight o'clock. When he opens his eyes, Becca has turned to face him and he falls in love with her face all over again. He reaches out and strokes her shoulder and arm and over her waist and hip.

She moves and moans. Her eyes open and she smiles.

"Good morning my lover."

"Good morning my delicious China doll."

"Mmmm! I feel really good. Can we take a shower. I really like it, when we are all soapy and hugging."

"Yes, my Darling. I love it to. Ready?"

They take a nice long shower and make love again.

They dress and join the family at breakfast.

"Good morning ladies, where are the kids?"

"They piled into a couple of vans and are having breakfast at IHOP. Tom's and Carly's idea." Molly says, with a little pride.

"Great. What's on for today my loves?"

"We thought that we'd do a girl's shopping day. You don't mind, do you?" Ann asks.

"Not at all. Remember to be back by five and I think Tom has a plan for us. I offered to help cook, but he said he had it. Don't want to disappoint his plan, huh?"

"Don't worry Sam, I'll make sure we get back in time. I'm driving and I'm taking the 15 passenger van." Jessie says.

Sam nods his agreement, "Just remember, you have five mothers to be, with you. God, just saying it makes my heart swell with love."

"I'll take care of them Sam." Jessie says.

Sam spends the next two hours sipping coffee and watching TV. Around 11:30 AM, Tom returns with the kids.

"Hi Dad, what ya doin'?" Tom asks, as he comes into the family room with Mathew, Ryan, Brian, Peter, Richard and the younger, young adults.

"Just hanging out, watching TV, while the Moms are away. I told them to be back by five, so they don't miss the dinner you're gonna make."

Tom smiled, knowing that Dad didn't give away the surprise.

"The girls are taking care of the young ones and we're going to put together a light lunch. I thought, pizza, hot pockets, chicken nuggets and beef patty melts, then some sliced tomato, cucumbers and broccoli bites and a cheese dip."

"Sounds good. I thing I could do a beef patty with tomato, maybe two."

"You got it Dad."

"Hey Matt. What say you collect Carly, Cathy, Raina, Liz, Brian, Alex, Richard and Delia about two and we'll go to DMV and get your licenses."

"Great Dad! I'll get 'em together. Two o'clock, got it." Matt says.

Tom catches Sam's eye and winks.

Sam's cell phone rings while at the DMV. It's four o'clock and the ID says it's Jessie.

"Hello Jess. What's up?"

"We're getting ready to head back to Sumter. Should be there about 4:55, or 5 o'clock."

"Good. I've got Matt and the rest at the DMV for their licenses and permits. I hope we're done about the same time. See you at home. Love you."

They get their licenses without any problems. The DMV people give them the same treatment as the boys got when Sam brought the last group through. The sixteen year olds had to take the written test.

The new licensees vie for the drive home and Carly wins Sam's keys. She knows that they have to take their time and not arrive much before five.

Matt chides her for wrong turns that she makes getting to the home stretch.

"Oh Carly. You turned the wrong way."

"Silly me. You're right."

She finally is approaching the gate to the home and coming the other way is a familiar vehicle.

"Look guys. The Moms are back from shopping."

The 15 passenger van and the van with the new drivers go through the gate at the same time. Sam sees the surprise on the faces of his group, when they see the cars parked to the right of the house. Valets are standing at the front door when they pull up.

Carly hands the keys to the valet and tells him it's a family vehicle and should be parked in the long garage.

"Yes Ma'am. I did recognize ya'll.

The children stream past Sam and the ladies gather with their purchases and go up the steps to the house.

Ann stays back with Sam and walks with him.

"What's going on Sam?" She asks.

"Welcome home for all of you. Tom and Carly put it together with Ryan and Delia, Peter and Elizabeth. They have a band and their friends and ribs, steaks, the works."

The sounds of excited teenagers and the heavy beat of drums reaches them as they come in the front door.

"I guess it started." Sam says as he helps Ann with her packages to her room.

Sam leaves her at the room and goes to freshen up in his bathroom. He is amazed, when he comes out on the patio, to see so many people. The decorations are great and the food is set out on long tables near the upper patio. Tom already has the awning pulled over the entire patio and the blowers from the pool reversed and blowing cool air onto the patio.

Sam sit's at a table near the pool door and pours an iced tea from a pitcher on the table. Several of the teenagers spot Sam and wave. He knows most of them, some he probably knows but, since they have grown up, he doesn't recognize any more. He sees Tom with two young women. When Tom sees Sam, he comes over with them.

"Dad, this is April and this is May, Day. They're two close friends and I just found out that they are going to College of Charleston this Fall. I guess my college choice is decided."

"Pleased to see you again, Mr. Elliott." April says.

"Yes sir. Me to. Always good to see the father of a really great guy." May says.

Sam sees a slight blush on his grown son.

"I'm pleased to see you, April, May. I can see that I taught my son well. You are both very charming, grown into . . . can I say cuties?"

Both of them have the breeding to blush at his compliment. To Sam this is a good sign.

There is laughter, talking and sudden gasps of surprise as the women come through the doors onto the upper patio.

"Hey, it's a party." Becca exclaims.

"Who's responsible for this? Come on get a kiss." Rachael says.

"Hi Tom. Thank you. It's great." Ann calls out.

They descend the steps and spread out among the tables near Sam. Jessie and Molly go for plates of food to bring to the tables. Sandra gets a pitcher of Cola and a bucket of ice from one of the long tables and brings it to the gathered women.

"Where're Sarah and Annie?" Sam asks.

"They volunteered to stay with the five youngsters until they go to sleep. They have them in the game room, upstairs. It's sound proof." Molly says.

"I'm taking them some chicken nuggets and salad for the kids and some ribs for Sarah and Annie." Jessie says.

Everyone seems to be enjoying the evening. The band is surprisingly good. The teenagers' friends are dancing with and in deep conversation with Sam's young adults. The women, one by one, drag Sam out to dance, until he can barely stand.

"Oh my God ladies. I just need a pillow. I'm sleeping right here."

The fun goes on until nearly eleven o'clock, when some of the youngsters begin to come over and offer their thanks and good byes. Finally at 11:30, Tom releases the band and it's only the six grown children, the sixteen year olds and a few of their friends left. They sit at tables with soft drinks and a few are gnawing on ribs and chicken bones.

The women have drifted away to bed. Soon, it's only Molly and Sam.

"I'm glad the babies went to sleep early. I didn't want Sarah and Annie to miss it all." Molly says.

"Yeah. I bet they'd like to start looking for help soon. So, Molly what's up for tonight? Looks like I get to sleep tonight."

"Not if you don't want to. I'll stay, Sam. I never get tired of being close to you."

"Me to, Baby Girl. I almost feel like a teenager when I'm with you."

Sam waves to Tom, to let him know that he is calling it a night. Molly follows Sam to the master bedroom. They undress, hug and kiss a lot, but fall to sleep, almost immediately.

Sam gets the call from the White House on Thursday. The President will be at Shaw Air Force Base in the morning, at 9:30 and requests a private meeting with Sam and his ladies.

"We'll be there. Make sure the base commander and those generals know about it. The Air Force General was particularly upset that he didn't know anything about the President's impending visit."

"We'll make sure he knows. I believe that the President wants to talk to him after he talks with your family. Something about another star."

"Thanks. I'm sure the general will be happy about that."

Sam tells the women about the call and also lets Tom and Carly know.

Friday morning is unrushed. The only thing that wasn't quite right, is the breakfast room. Sam knows it has to be bigger, as well as the dining room. Breakfast is good. Jessie, Molly, and Mary produced a big, country meal of biscuits, sausage, ham, scrambled eggs, pancakes, grits, and gravy for the biscuits. Boxes of dry cereal, milk and orange juice are also there.

Sam has coffee and makes a sausage biscuit for himself. His mind is running over all the things that the President might talk about. It gets noticed.

"Sam. Sam. What's the matter. You looked like you were somewhere else?" Ann asks, concern in her voice.

"Oh. Nothing. Just thinking about what the President wants to talk about that he has to come here. I hope we didn't do something that got some international attention."

"I doubt it. He probably just wants a photo op, receiving the diplomatic pouch from Ann." Rachael says.

"That's probably it. It's getting close to re-election time." Becca adds.

"Yeah. That's probably it. He wants a picture with ten, gorgeous women around him, smiling . . . ." Sam chuckles.

Tom comes in the breakfast room with his cell phone out.

"Dad. The President's secretary is on the phone and wants to know if the six of us oldest can come with you? I told him I'd ask."

"Peter, Elizabeth, Brian, Delia and the rest okay with taking care of the young and youngest?"

"Yeah. I already asked them."

"Okay. Are ya'll ready?"

"Yes sir."

Tom acknowledges the secretary and tells him they will be there.

It's 8:30, as they load two vans and head for Shaw. They pass the gate and receive salutes from the guards. It's not bad being well known.

They are directed to a hanger on the flight line, where Colonel Parker is waiting. Sam doesn't see the generals.

Colonel Parker greets them when they get out. "Welcome back Sam, ladies, gentlemen. There are tables and seating inside. We got the air cooled down. Air Force One is sixty miles out. You can wait for him inside. Good to see you again, Sam."

"Thank you Orin. Good to be here. I didn't see the generals. I took special care to let the secretary know that they wanted to be kept in the loop."

"Oh, yes, they were. The president is meeting with them after his meeting with you and your family."

The Colonel nods to the men at the door, who open the double doors wide for the family to enter.

The first thing Sam sees is two rows of folding chairs, ten feet from the long oak conference table, surrounded with thickly padded executive chairs. There are pitchers of iced water and glasses down the middle of the table.

They sit around the table, at place cards, that someone has placed at each chair. The hanger is quiet and only the distant sound of the air handler cuts the silence. The family are seated only for ten or fifteen minutes, when the double doors open again and the presidential entourage enters. Sam and all stand.

"Please, Elliott family, sit, sit. Don't stand for me. I stand for you."

He reaches Sam and shakes hands. He then goes to each member of the family and shakes their hand before taking his seat across from Sam, Ann, Becca, Rachael, Jessie, and Molly. The President then turns to his aide.

"Please clear the rest of the room. I want complete privacy. Only my secretary, may remain."

"Yes Mr. President."

When the last person has departed and the double doors are closed, he continues.

The President talks and exchanges ideas with the Elliott family, for more than an hour. When the talks are over, he sends his secretary to let everyone back in.

His entourage returns, along with a dozen news people and TV cameras. When everyone is in position, the family gathers in a semi circle, with Sam, Ann, Cathy, Molly, Tom, Becca, Raina, Jessie, Ryan, Sandra, Barbara, Annie, Sarah and Mary in the front.

The President, Secretary and other dignitaries, with cameras flashing behind them, approach the family and with flourish, bestows medals on each of the seventeen family members.

He stands in the middle of them and has pictures taken. Then with just Sam and the original five women, then with just the new members and finally with the young people.

The news people throw questions at them.

"What did you talk about?" "Why did the President need to talk with you?" "What did you do to earn the medals?"

The President turns to the press and makes ambiguous president like statements and then bids the Elliotts farewell.

The family walk to their vans for the ride home. Sam and the women are nearly overwhelmed by the enormity of the things the president said. They don't talk much on the way home, but they are bursting with the pride that came with those words from the leader of the country.

Epilogue

The next three days are the longest that any of them could remember. Monday morning's Item newspaper, had the first of twelve articles about the family, written by Ken Hart.

They have dinner early tonight and are gathered in the family room to watch TV. The thunder storm is just passing by when the news comes on.

The news broadcast across the country, the unanimous vote of the congress of the United States to legalize Polygamy, in the form of Incorporated families. Twenty years to reach this point and it's like a weight lifted.

His family has gathered in front of the television to witness the vote on C-Span. The Senator from South Carolina stands and prefaces his Yea vote with a reading of the names of their corporate union and a recounting of the deeds and accomplishments that have been achieved by the family.

He ends his statement with a quote from Sam, "Love gets you love and respect gets you respect. Thanks be to God."

the End of the Beginning

Thank you!

My heartfelt thanks to many people. First, my wife for not stomping me when I didn't make dinner, because I was working on one or another of my stories. Thanks to Michelle, a teacher at the University of South Carolina, USC, who gave me so much constructive criticism and Sandy, a published writer, who worked with Michelle at the writer's workshop and inspired me to continue. Thank you Leah, at USC for her evaluation of my works, for the surprise on her face when a story had a twist and to Kendall, a published writer, who said that we could do it, because we were way ahead when we started to write. My young lady friends, students, when I was a Cosmetology instructor, who provided inspiration for my characterizations. Finally, thank you to Sumter for the color that is in my life.

Bio

Thomas Strange, was born in Neustadt, Germany and grew up in Germany, Wisconsin, Michigan and New York. He graduated from Waverly High, New York and received higher education in classes at San Jose`, California, Universities of Michigan, South Carolina and Central Carolina Technical College in Sumter. A veteran of the sixties and seventies Asian games and life partner of Somkuan 'Kim' Strange. Tom and his wife live in Sumter, South Carolina.